Praise for Simon Kurt Unsworth's

THE DEVIL'S
DETECTIVE

"A clever spin on the traditional police procedural. . . . We've seen other novels set in Hell, but we haven't seen a Hell quite like this."
—*Booklist*

"Dark and luminous, compelling and insidious, *The Devil's Detective* is a novel that transcends genre."   —Michael Marshall Smith, bestselling author of *The Intruders* and *The Straw Men*

"Hell as the setting for a noir investigation turns out to be as fun as it sounds in *The Devil's Detective*. Inventive and pacy, Simon Kurt Unsworth has created a world—underworld?—distinctly his own."
—Andrew Pyper, author of *The Demonologist* and *The Damned*

"Inventive and intriguing—Unsworth turns a journey through Hell into a heavenly read."   —Alison Littlewood, author of *A Cold Season*

"A layered, fascinating first novel that will put readers firmly in mind of Clive Barker as they indulge in the gorgeous detail of Hell and all of its squalid denizens. *The Devil's Detective* is an ambitious yet accomplished piece of work that will leave the reader not only wanting more Thomas Fool but hoping against hope that the reality of Hell isn't anywhere near as bad as the version in Unsworth's imagination."   —*This Is Horror*

SIMON KURT UNSWORTH
THE DEVIL'S DETECTIVE

Simon Kurt Unsworth was born in Manchester and lives in a farmhouse in Cumbria, in the United Kingdom. He is the author of many short stories, including the collection *Quiet Houses*. *The Devil's Detective* is his first novel.

simonkurtunsworth.co.uk

THE DEVIL'S
DETECTIVE

THE DEVIL'S
DETECTIVE

◄❯ A NOVEL ◄❯

SIMON KURT UNSWORTH

ANCHOR BOOKS
A DIVISION OF PENGUIN RANDOM HOUSE LLC
NEW YORK

FIRST ANCHOR BOOKS EDITION, FEBRUARY 2016

The Library of Congress has cataloged the Doubleday edition as follows:
Unsworth, Simon Kurt.
The devil's detective : a novel / Simon Kurt Unsworth.—First edition
pages   cm
1. Private investigators—Fiction.   I. Title.
PR6121.N795D48 2015   823'.92—dc23   2014012828

Anchor Books Trade Paperback ISBN: 978-0-8041-7292-9
eBook ISBN: 978-0-385-53935-7

Book design by Michael Collica

www.anchorbooks.com

Printed in the United States of America
10 9 8 7 6 5 4 3 2

To Rosie, the owner of my heart now and forever, who gave this novel its title and who holds my hand as we walk through the world and makes every day a thing of joy and wonder.

To Ben, my boy of boys, just because I love him.

To Mily, stepdaughter the elder, my diving partner and all-round cool girl.

To Lottie, stepdaughter the younger, who lives in Lottie La-La-Land and who sometimes lets us visit her there.

The four of you are the corners of my universe, the dizzying light above me and the great spaces to the side of me and steadying floor below me, and this book is yours if you want it, with all my love.

THE DEVIL'S
DETECTIVE

PART ONE
INFORMATION

PROLOGUE

From his vantage point, here up high, the lights were scattered out below Fool in an uneven swathe. They lay in tangled clusters, forming a map of the city and its outlying geographies; most were gathered around the Houska, pale firefly glimmers emerging from its bars and clubs and brothels. The smaller rashes were farther out, the estates where the heavier industries worked through the night, the walled glints of Crow Heights, the various ghettos and fiefdoms, flotsam circling that central brightness. The tiniest and palest shimmer of lights, farthest out from the center of the city, was Eve's Harbor, where most of the working humans lived. As he watched, new lights came into being and others vanished, shifting the bellies of the clusters but never their overall shape. It was like watching the respiration of some enormous creature, he thought, as life and death pulsed through each area. Beyond them all the Flame Garden glowed, dirty and guttering, the color of burning, diseased wood.

To Fool's back, the vast stone wall that separated the city from what was outside was cold, its chill breath wafting around his shoulders and head. At the edge of his hearing, he could just make out the wails of the things that drifted and spun on its far side, lost and hoarse. He turned, shivering, and pulled his coat tighter, hitching the weapon on his hip so that it didn't dig into him.

The cold coming off the stone smelled clean and wet, the only place Fool knew that did. At times like this, when the air shifted and brought with it heat from the Flame Garden, he was able to stand facing the stone so that his front was cold and his rear warm, and it was like being in two places at once. Escort duty was boring, but at least it brought him out here, where Hell became nothing but an array of light and dark that he could choose to turn his back on, if only for a few hours.

Fool turned again; if he stood still too long his feet began to ache. The ground on the Mount was hard and rough, and sharp edges dug through the soles of his boots and into his feet like teeth. Time was, a constant stream of sinners had walked this road and back, barefoot and bloody, but those days were long gone. He stepped a few yards back along the path, but went no farther. Partly it was duty; he had no idea when the delegates were expected and couldn't risk not being there for their arrival, but also it was caution. Out here at the edges, even a few feet from the wall, things lived that were wild even by the city's troubled standards. The gate itself and the area around it were safe, but away from the pale blue light that came from the tunnel, the shadows had claws and appetites.

Even now, Fool was being watched.

It was not simple instinct that told him this; twice, patches in the darkness had thickened, shifted, moved around him as he waited, and once a voice had called out "Man" in an elongated whisper that sounded as though the speaker's mouth was too full to form the sound correctly. Too full of what, Fool didn't like to think about. He turned again, thinking humorlessly, *Little spinning Fool,* and saw something moving in the tunnel.

How long the tunnel was, or what was at its end, Fool did not know. He was forbidden to enter, as was everyone except the delegates and the successful Sorrowful (who by that point were no longer the Sorrowful, Fool supposed, but more likely the *Gleeful* or the *Joyous*). It was long, though, he knew that, its illuminated length stretching as far as he could make out into the rock in a wide, arched corridor. There were no lamps in it that he could see, but it was bathed in light nonetheless, a cold gleam that seemed to come from the walls themselves and that cast no shadows. He went to the entrance, knowing that it would be some time yet before the delegates arrived but also knowing that this was the point of it, this was the Duty. He had to be there, honor guard and escort, from the moment they emerged from the tunnel, standing as an obedient servant, faithful as a dog. *Little dog,* he thought, *little Fool dog.* Looking up, he watched the clouds. Even at night they glowed, the gleaming whiteblue of promise and hope. They were never still, the clouds, scudding and swirling, occasionally breaking to allow him glimpses of the other city beyond them.

The shapes in the tunnel approached slowly, coalescing from the light as they came toward him. He watched them emerge, forming, imagining that cold blue light making itself into perfect, flawless, hard flesh, and flexed his toes in his thin boots. He was cold, the air settling into the folds of his clothes, puckering his skin and raising hairs across it. Fool waited, and watched, and made out details.

Four of them, as ever, one in front carving the air like the prow of a boat, and the others behind. One of the following, the one at the rear, was framed by arced patches of brightness that reached high above its head, moving, flexing wide to fill the tunnel. He sighed; they were almost here, their skin shining, bright and flawless. He had time for one last look up at the clouds, breaking again to reveal the city beyond and its white walls and myriad windows, showing the pillared glories of Heaven.

At the edges of his vision, lower than Heaven, he saw the frayed and dirty light of Hell, and then the angels reached the end of the tunnel and were with him.

The first looked older than Fool, its skin lined with perfect wrinkles that folded up into themselves as it smiled at him and said, "Hello. You are our escort, I take it? I am Adam." Adam was shorter than Fool and bearded, and his eyes were a startling, brilliant blue, like the air around the spires of distant Heaven. As he emerged from the tunnel's mouth, he opened his arms widely as though to hug Fool and his black robe swung around him in a way that reminded Fool of flowing water. His skin was so pale it was almost translucent, unmarked by the traceries of veins or the fleck of hair or pore. Fool stepped aside, looking down; looking at Adam was like trying to stare at a candle flame without blinking, but even the ground glinted as though reflecting Adam's light. It made his eyes ache.

"Welcome to Hell, sir," he said, feeling foolish. No matter how often he carried out escort duty, he never got used to the feelings of clumsiness and gracelessness that being next to these creatures raised in him. They were so beautiful, so graceful, a note of elegance in Hell's lumpen flesh, and he never knew how to act, despite his official status, or what to say.

Were these things even male? Was "sir" correct, or was there some other form of address he should know? He felt clumsy and uncoordinated in front of the angel, stolid and slow and heavy.

"Welcome?" asked Adam lightly. "No. There is no welcome here, I would hope, but only the opposite, the knowledge of pain and suffering and the distant chance of redemption."

"Perhaps it means to insult us," said a second voice, and one of the figures behind Adam stepped forward, came out from the blue and into the darkness, bringing with it a light that didn't so much gleam as *dazzle*, as though it were lit from within by an inferno. Glancing up, Fool could make out little through the light, except that it was naked and that great arcs hung behind it in the air, shifting and flexing. *Wings*, thought Fool, looking back down to where the dirt was awash with reflected light. *Angel's wings.*

"Welcoming the Lord's emissaries to Hell hardly seems appropriate, does it? It should be prostrate before us, begging our mercy and deliverance, praying that we allow God's mercy to burn it away to nothing, but instead it stands and extends welcome as if we were common visitors. No wonder it remains damned."

"Hush, Balthazar," said Adam softly. "He means no offense."

Balthazar, noted Fool. The arm and guard to Adam's brain and command; the other two would be mere archive and scribe, and would not be introduced. He sometimes wondered if they even had names, if they were not things defined solely by their roles and without personality.

"Perhaps it does not understand respect, or who it is and who we are," said Balthazar. His glow had faded, dropping and thickening so that now it was almost red, and Fool risked looking at him. He was taller than Adam and younger (*No*, he told himself, *not younger but* appearing *younger. They have no age except that which they choose to show, wasn't that what Elderflower had said once?*), and now there was something in his hand, held up, wavering in front of Fool. He thought at first that it was a sword, aflame, but it was not; it was simply a column of fire that danced and writhed around itself and threw its furnace gleam across his face.

"Balthazar," said Adam, his voice still soft. "Do not find battles where none exist, my friend. He is Hell's chosen representative and meant no offense, I am sure. Did you?"

"No," said Fool, looking into Balthazar's beardless, handsome face. The angel was smiling, revealing teeth like polished marble. The fire wavered in front of Fool's eyes for a moment longer and then was gone, not lowered but disappeared. Balthazar clasped one hand in the other in front of his flat stomach and stepped back, his wings flapping slowly in the air above him, alabaster-white and silent. He nodded, although whether to himself, to Adam, or to Fool, Fool couldn't be sure.

Fool turned and began to walk back down the path, glancing over his shoulder to make sure the angels were following. Adam was close to him, smiling, and his head bobbed slightly when he saw Fool looking at him. Balthazar came after and then the other two. They were smaller, their shoulders folded forward and their heads down so that their faces were invisible. Balthazar still held his wings aloft, angled forward so that they looked like scythe blades now, sickles against Hell's nighttime sky. As they walked, Adam's and Balthazar's light pressed the darkness back from the path, revealing thin, twisting plants and scrubby earth and something that capered just beyond the edge of Fool's vision. It followed them all the way down to the carriage, making slopping noises and lip-smacking sounds and, once, calling, "Man! Man and friends! Nice friends" in that too-full voice, stretching the last word out as though it were tasting it, sucking something sweet. At the sound of it, Adam cast his gaze into the darkness and said, "Be quiet, creature."

"Brave man, brave friends," said the creature.

"Be silent," said Adam, his voice not changing, "and bite your tongue." He glowed briefly, the blue flash revealing something large in the scrub that wheeled around and darted away, and they heard nothing more from it.

"Is this how we are to travel? Is this what they send for Heaven's delegation?" asked Balthazar when they reached the bottom of the slope. They were standing by the carriage, Balthazar in front of the rear door, blocking it, and Adam watching him. Fool was standing between the two angels, the scribe and archive at his side, faces still downcast. Balthazar was beginning to glow again, the light rippling out from his skin like sweat, his arms opened wide and his wings shivering as they slowly expanded, stretched out behind him.

"Balthazar," said Adam. Fool stayed silent, knowing that there was nothing he could do. The carriage was small and had seats for only four in the rear, meaning that the angels would be cramped for the duration of the journey, but this was what the Bureaucracy had given him. There were bigger vehicles, but not many, and none that he could drive. Most of the inhabitants of Hell walked or used the massive trains that shunted slowly back and forth between the farms and the industries, jumping on and off whenever they could. Fool and his colleagues, Hell's two other Information Men, were usually among them.

"We should fly," said Balthazar, stepping away from the carriage and beating his wings downward fiercely, sending billows of dust and grit into the air around Fool. One of the nameless ones, looking at Balthazar, began to unfurl its wings, and Fool watched, fascinated, as they unfolded from its back and stretched out. They were smaller than Balthazar's, less grand, reminding Fool more of the scrawny things that he had seen on the birds in Hell's flocks, flocks preyed on by the larger flying things that sometimes filled the sullen sky. Delicate feathers bristled at the wings' edges, and then Adam made a gesture with his hand and the scribe, or archive, immediately folded its wings back in. Pressed close against its back, they became almost invisible, fading and vanishing into its robe.

Balthazar looked angrily at Adam and beat his wings again, creating a savage gust of air that rocked Fool back on his heels and made the carriage shake. Adam watched patiently as Balthazar tried again, furiously hooking his wings around his body in brutal downthrusts. Another, much smaller, pair of wings unfurled from around the angel's feet, and these, too, began to beat furiously. Fool closed his eyes as the grit rose into them and as Balthazar's light flared, fiery and intense.

"Balthazar," said Adam, "this is Hell, the place of no freedoms. You cannot fly here, my friend, because flight is a joy and no true joy is allowed. Only the chalkis and their ilk can take to the air, Balthazar, because they take no pleasure in it; you know this. It was explained to you before our arrival. We are here by invitation, yes, but we have to obey the rules like everyone and everything here. Be calm, my friend."

The beating, shifting air settled and Fool opened his eyes again. Balthazar was staring at Fool, his face curling and distorting into something that was impossible to look at, something beyond human or demon, beyond beauty. Something terrible, a thing not of rage but of absolute belief in itself, of justice without question. He took a step toward Fool, one arm rising and the shimmering tongue of fire coruscated in the air, stretching out from his hand, and then Adam spoke again, saying only, "Balthazar."

The angel whirled away and wordlessly lashed his wings out, banging both into the carriage. The vehicle bounced violently, lifting and then settling back onto its wheels with a metallic groan and a splintering of glass. There were new dents in its doors, and one of the windows wore a starred crack.

"I apologize for my companion," said Adam, walking over to Balthazar, who was finally pulling his wings down, gathering them against his back and wrapping the smaller pair around his ankles, where they melted into his skin. The fire vanished again, leaving behind it an after-image of red embers, the memory of burning imprinted on the air. He did not turn as Adam came close to him, and did not flinch as a feather was pulled from one wing. Adam turned, bringing the feather to Fool and holding it out.

"Balthazar is, perhaps, overwhelmed to be here for the first time in the territory of the Great Enemy, and he forgets himself. Or rather, he remembers himself too much, remembers his role in the Above and forgets that an angel of Michael in Hell cannot act as he would in Heaven. He will learn, though, because whether he likes it or not, he and I and the rest of our delegation are your guests and must act accordingly," he said, holding out the feather farther so that it danced, like the flame before it, in Fool's face.

"A symbol of our regret. Please, take it as a sign of your forgiveness," Adam said.

Even detached from the wing, from its host, the feather glimmered with some internal glow. Flakes of light drifted away from the shaft, spun lazily, and then fell and landed on Adam's outstretched hand. Fool reached out, then hesitated. It was an angel's feather, and although he could feel no heat coming from it, he had the impression that it would burn him if he touched it, that its wonder was a raging, pure thing that would be too much for his Hell-born flesh to cope with.

"Please," repeated Adam. His smile widened, and in his face Fool saw a kindness that would accept no denial, a compassion that had no end. The thought of standing against it was more terrifying than the thought of taking the feather, even if its touch caused his flesh to burst into flame. Helpless, he reached out and grasped it.

It still shone, even after Adam let it go, but it did not burn; Fool looked at it wonderingly, waving it gently in front of his face. It left trails in the air, little constellations of light like the birthing of distant stars, and he couldn't help but smile. It was almost weightless, despite its size, and felt soft against his fingers. *To have these as a part of you,* he thought, *to know that these things* are *you, must be the most glorious sensation imaginable.* He waved the feather again, his eyes following the arc of glittering sparkles that it left behind. He felt he could look at it forever, be lost in its twinkling distances. *Little mesmerized Fool,* he thought, and then Adam said, "It is beautiful, is it not? Keep it, and may it bring you Heaven's truth. And now, please, we must go. There is work to be done. We have Elevations to decide upon."

Carrying a feather from an angel's wing, Fool took the four angels into Hell.

1

The day began with Gordie, who knocked on Fool's door and entered the room without waiting. He bustled over to Fool, waving a blue-ribboned canister in front of him like a torch that had lost its light as Fool pulled himself up onto an elbow, rubbing one hand across eyes that were thick with sleep. He was pleased to see that in Gordie's other hand was a mug, steam curling out from it and bringing with it the smell of weak, thin coffee. Gordie set the mug down on the table by Fool's bed and said, "One came through. It's blue. I've never seen a blue before."

Fool picked up the mug and sipped, glad of the heat of the coffee on his tongue even if the taste was buried beneath its scald. He twisted, careful not to spill his drink, and looked up at the high, small window, trying to work out from the light coming in around the grimy linen blind what time of day it was. Beams of gray, sickly illumination crawled across the wall at low angles, throwing shadows from right to left, meaning it was still morning. Escort duty hadn't finished until . . . when? Sometime between the bars starting to close and the factories starting to open, he thought. He had returned in darkness, that he remembered, although his eyes had populated the nighttime shadows with after-images of light, shifting and dancing at the corners of his vision. If it was still morning, he had had only a few hours' sleep. He groaned and sipped more of his coffee.

"It's blue," said Gordie again, helpfully, holding out the canister, its tangle of blue ribbon hanging down in loops. "It's a blue, it's just arrived. I saw it was a blue; we never get them, so I thought I'd better bring it to you. I wouldn't have woken you otherwise, you know. It might be a Fallen." As he spoke, Gordie was doing the thing he thought Information Men should do, darting his eyes around the room and looking for things. For *clues,* although what they might be, Fool had no idea. His room was tiny, as all theirs were, and usually contained little other than his bed, a table, a small set of open-faced drawers, a rail for his smock shirts and trousers, and a tiny bookcase that held no books except for his *Information Man's Guide to the Rules and Offices of Hell.*

Today, however, it also contained the feather.

Gordie saw it as Fool sat up fully and took the canister from his colleague's hand. The younger man's mouth fell open and his hands dropped to his sides and Fool smiled despite himself, despite the early morning and the lack of sleep, because Gordie looked, for the shortest moment, like a child, a thing of innocence and joy. There was awe on his face, and his skin looked clean and smooth, youthful, his eyes opening wide.

The feather was lying on the top shelf of the bookcase, alongside the *Guide* and Fool's gun, and it was beautiful. Curved, the shaft and barbs gleaming, it was perhaps a foot long and whiter than bone and it shivered lightly as Gordie walked toward it and reached out.

"Where . . . ?" he started, and then stopped loosely. "Where . . . ," he started again and then, again, stopped. Fool didn't reply. He looked at the feather and his eyes watered mildly, as though the brightness of the previous day had returned to the room for a moment.

"It was a gift," said Fool, "from one of the angels." Even saying it made him feel foolish, *little silly Fool,* because in Hell no one received gifts.

"Can I?" asked Gordie and Fool nodded. His colleague lifted the feather, gasped slightly, and turned to Fool.

"It's beautiful, like Summer," he said and then started, glancing down at the feather with a look on his face that Fool thought was almost suspicion.

"Yes," Fool replied. What else was there to say? Gordie was still holding the feather and suddenly, sharply, he wanted him to put it down, to let it alone, so that he could pick it back up himself. He took another sip of his coffee and nodded at the tube.

"A blue?"

"A blue!" said Gordie, the excitement coming back to his voice. He placed the feather back on the bookcase and twisted the cap off the tube, emptying out the roll of paper from within.

"Let's see what we've got," said Fool. "Let's see what Hell wants to show us today."

The body bobbed facedown in the water about six feet out from the shore, snagged on a clump of branches and leaves. It spun as it bobbed, caught in eddies that sent the water at the lake's edge into choppy arrhythmia. Despite the dark oiliness of Solomon Water, it was obvious that the naked corpse was human; its skin was pale and torn, hanging in loose ribbons that exposed the darker meat of muscles and flesh.

"I saw it on my way to work," the man by Fool was saying. "I mean, I saw the flash as I passed the lake, but I didn't see the body until a few minutes later."

"The flash?" asked Fool.

"There was a blue flash, I was up on the road and I saw a flash from down here, but I couldn't see what it was because of the trees. It was a blue flash, and then lots of blue light went up into the sky. I came down here to see what it was."

"Do you normally check out the things you see on your way to work?" asked Fool.

"If there's a chance that it might be a Fallen," replied the man. "It was a blue flash, I've told you. I thought it might have been a Fallen and I could claim it as mine. But it was only a body."

Ah yes, thought Fool. *This is only a body, so it's not important, just a dead human, but it could have been a Fallen.* Finding a Fallen was rumored to be a way of guaranteeing an Elevation, of escaping Hell's grip. "You must have been disappointed," said Fool. The man, whose name Fool had already lost but which would be in Gordie's notebook, tensed, hearing Fool's irritation.

"Look, I'm sorry he's dead, but people die all the time, every day, don't they? We're never safe, are we? It's not unusual, is it? And I've missed work waiting for you, and I'll lose food for missing a day. At least I waited."

"True," said Fool, unable to disagree with anything the man had said. There were murders every day and every night in Hell, too many to count, more than they could ever hope to investigate. Most went unreported except for the details in the canisters that fell from the pneumatic pipes, wrapped in red ribbon or thread, which Fool normally read and then marked with a "DNI" stamp for *Did Not Investigate* before putting them back into a canister and firing them up the pipe, sending them on to Elderflower. The only reason he was here now was that the Bureaucracy had registered the blue flash and had also wondered about the possibility of it being a Fallen. The canister had been blue ribbon–wrapped, and they had standing orders to investigate any of those that came through as a priority; it was in his *Guide*. Blue canisters arrived irregularly, and in all Fool's time in Hell, over five years now, there had never been a Fallen and he suspected there never would be. The rebel angels were already here, and the only ones left in Heaven were surely the followers and the trusted now, the arms of fury like Balthazar and of mercy like Adam; none of them would fall.

"We need the body," said Fool to Gordie, turning away from the man at his side, focus shifting, "before the things in there take him." Already, the body had jerked several times, and Fool suspected it was being eaten from below. Solomon Water was vast and full, its inky depths home to things that Fool hoped never to see. Not long ago, one had come ashore; it had eaten hundreds before being driven back into the water by a crowd of demons and humans in one of the rare moments when the two groups had worked together, brandishing flame and hurling rocks against it. This close to shore, and with only one body, it was unlikely that anything bigger than scavengers would approach, but there was always a chance. It was a chance that Fool did not want to take.

Gordie went to the water's edge and stepped gingerly in, the liquid lapping over his shoes as he moved out from the shore. As Fool waited, he turned back to the man. "Did you see anything when you got here?" he asked. He knew Gordie had already asked this, but the man might remember something new, describe it differently, or reveal something extra.

"No, just the body," the man replied. What was his name? "There were clothes near the water, but that was it." The clothes were in a bag by Fool's feet; he would look them over later. They were torn and bloody, that much he had seen already, and smeared with mud. Just up the slope, in among the trees, he had found a patch of churned and damaged ground, the earth freshly torn. Blood was puddled in the newly created hollows and had started to coagulate into a thick, brittle mess. Four teeth had been scattered around the saturated ground like frozen tears; Fool had picked them up and placed them in his pocket, wrapped in a handkerchief. One still had a piece of gum attached to it, dangling pinkly from the root, bloody and wormlike.

A crowd had gathered farther up the slope, perhaps ten or fifteen people massed beyond the trees and standing in loose clumps. They had also come in case it was a Fallen, he suspected, had seen the blue flash but hadn't been as close as the nameless man, or had heard about it afterward and come anyway. They looked lost, aimlessly staring down the slope, their features impossible to make out at this distance. They were all human, though, that Fool could tell; there were no demons among them, although if the crowd remained long enough those others would come, attracted by the crumpling hope and the disappointment and the smell of sweat and despair. They would come to feed.

"Sir," said Gordie from behind Fool. He had the body at the edge of the water but was struggling to pull it onto the land, and Fool went to help him, taking a grip on the corpse's legs and lifting as Gordie clambered onto the lakeside and dragged it by the shoulders. Fool didn't like the way the flesh felt, cold and clammy and loose, shifting under his fingers, and he was glad to be able to drop it on the ground once Gordie had made his way out from the water. It landed bonelessly on its back, and Fool winced at the state of it.

"Oh fuck," the man breathed from behind Fool. Fool had forgotten he was there, and now he went to the man (*West*, he thought, suddenly remembering the man's name, *West*), ushering him back and pointing at the others near the trees. West had gone pale, paler than before, and was gulping helplessly, staring at the battered body.

"Please, go up there and wait for me," Fool said.

"Who could have done that?" asked West, and then doubled over and was sick, vomiting explosively onto the ground by Fool's feet. The smell of it was sharp and sour, the vomit itself watery and gray. West hadn't eaten much recently; no one had.

"I don't know," said Fool, but suspected he did.

The dead person was, had been, male. There were bite marks around the base of the flaccid penis, scabbed and angry red gashes that covered the scrotum and the lower belly; more lined the stomach and chest. One nipple was gone, the breast topped by an open wound. There were one or two smaller, circular marks on the dead man's skin, and he thought that these were probably the marks from Solomon's inhabitants, small questing bites from the things at the bottom of the water's food chain taken before the larger creatures came to feed. The other bites, Fool recognized. They came from demons, were marked by a puckering of the flesh around the wound where the skin had scorched from the demon's heat. There were crescent marks across the dead man's face and neck from where his attacker had punched and hit him, these marks fresher, still not budded into full bruises. One cheek was torn open and flapping, revealing a lacerated gum and bloody holes for the missing teeth that currently sat in Fool's pocket. He crouched, peering at the ruined face.

The water had already started to bloat and wrinkle the corpse's skin, the eyelids pulling away from the eyeballs slightly. More of the small circular bites were dotted around the eyes, almost lost in the angry marks from the beating. The sclera of the left eye was blood-filled and the eye itself turned out, as though the force of the blows had snapped it from its moorings. Tears that were tinged with blood wept from the eyes in slow trickles.

"Do we take him to the Garden?" asked Gordie.

"No," said Fool. Something about the body bothered him. It wasn't the violence inflicted upon it, exactly; he saw similarly damaged bodies most days. No, it was the eyes, he thought; not their bloodiness or the fact that one had been so savagely abused that it had turned away from its companion, but the expression they contained. They were helpless, the helplessness of someone who saw his own death, or something worse, approaching and could do nothing about it. "I want Morgan to see him. I want him questioned."

"Questioned? Why?"

Fool's hand went to the feather that was safely tucked into his inner pocket, the feel of it reassuring him for some reason. "Because I want to know who did this to him," he said, and he did not add *and catch them and punish them* because he knew that, hope for it though he might, it was unlikely to happen. This was Hell, and sins here went often un-noticed and almost always unpunished. The best he could hope for was knowledge, something to put in a report to Elderflower so that he could pass it on to his masters, for *information*. He put his hand in his pocket, not the one containing the teeth or the feather, and fingered his badge of office, feeling the indentations that formed the words "Information Man," and grinned humorlessly. "I want to know," he said again.

"I'll arrange transport," said Gordie.

"No," said a new voice, "he is mine."

Trouble, little Fool, Fool had time to think, and then something hit him and sent him sprawling into the mud beside the body.

2

It was a demon, a tall, scrawny thing without a skin. Fool slithered away, trying to put space between it and him so that he could draw his gun, but it stepped with him, keeping close. The exposed flesh of its face and hands glistened wetly, a rich and startling red. Its skinlessness, Fool saw, was entire, and the musculature that crossed its head and chest flexed as it came toward him. Its fingers ended in curved and yellowing claws, smeared blisters of white-boned knuckles emerging from the rawness behind them, the strips of muscle that formed its lips drawing back from teeth the size and shape of river-rolled stones.

"It comes from the lake," the demon said, gesturing at the body. The words were distorted, warped into new shapes by its lack of lips, and it spat flecks of blood as it tried to form the sounds. "It is mine."

"No," said Fool, still trying to back away from the thing but prevented from going any farther by the body, "he belongs to Hell, to the Bureaucracy. As representative of the Bureaucracy, he is mine." Fool's head throbbed where the demon had hit him and he could feel something warm trickling around his ear. He managed to get a hand to his weapon but the demon dropped suddenly, its knees digging into the mud on either side of Fool, leaning forward so that it trapped Fool's arm across his stomach. Its leering face came close to Fool's, the smell of it rich and dense and sour. Dribbles fell from its mouth, from its weeping skin, dotting across Fool's face.

"It is mine," it said again. "Things in the lake are mine."

Fool tried to twist his gun free but his arm was pinned. The demon felt his movements and reached down, gripping Fool's wrist with a hand that was fevered and greasy, as though it wasn't just blood that flowed through its veins (*assuming it has veins,* he thought randomly), but blood and oil. His wrist slipped in the thing's grip as he tried to writhe away, but the hold did not loosen enough to free him. Behind the demon, just visible over its shoulder, Gordie appeared, his gun held out and trembling. Fool shook his head slightly, and the demon saw it.

It was fast despite its spindle limbs, whirling and slashing out at Gordie in a scuttle of spattering droplets and broomstick arms. Gordie, staggered by the thing's thrust, went back down the slope and overbalanced, falling into the water. The demon shrieked, wheeled back, moving on all fours like some terrible insect, scuttling past Fool until it was perched over the body. Fool rolled over, trying to move and rise at the same time and achieving neither successfully. His skin burned where the thing's blood had spattered down on him and where it had grasped him, and he wanted to wipe it, to scald himself clean, but instead he tugged his gun from its holster and pointed it at the demon, shouting, "No!"

It gave him a contemptuous look and then its face flexed as its jaws glided open on hinges that moved sideways. It turned, lowering itself down over the dead man, its mouth yawning wide, the glistening flesh stretching back and clamping around the dead man's head. Fool pressed the barrel of the gun to the back of the demon's skull, not liking the way its flesh slithered away from the muzzle, and said, as firmly as his pain and fear and adrenaline would allow him, "Stop that." To his astonishment, the demon jerked back from the body, knocking into Fool and banging his arm up. His finger tightened automatically and he loosed a shot, the bullet passing over the demon and entering Solomon Water with a sizzle.

"Empty," said the demon in its warping, breathy voice. "Empty. What did he do? What? What?" It was looking at Fool, creeping back from him and shaking its head without taking its eyes from his face.

"Empty," the demon repeated, its clawed hands gouging at the earth as it slithered back. Fool pointed his gun at the retreating figure, a pointless gesture; his weapon would not reload for several more seconds yet. He had asked Elderflower whether the delay could be lessened and had been told that a request would be put in. That had been almost a year ago.

The demon spat, or at least tried to. A mass of bloody phlegm dripped over its teeth as it made a sound like the pneumatic pipes when they sucked away a canister, and then it turned and ran, following the curve of the lakeshore. Fool watched it until it was a distant blur and then, finally, nothing. For a moment he did not move, and then he let his gun drop and slumped to the damp earth, waiting for the shakes of old, unspent adrenaline to make their way through him.

A hand fell on Fool's shoulder, startling him, and he twisted, thinking that the thing had come back or that it had companions, but it was only Gordie.

"Are you okay?" he asked.

"I think so," Fool replied. He raised his head, feeling something that had to be blood roll down the side of his face. He lifted a hand to it, finding a short tear just below his hairline, another wound that would scar to a keloid ridge and add to the story of his time here, a story written across his skin in the language of Hell.

Gordie and Fool watched as the corpse was wrapped in heavy sheets that had once been white but were now a weary gray. Mud from Solomon Water's shore smeared the material as the handlers rolled the body over and black water spilled from the dead man's ruined mouth. The two attendants, their uniforms the same gray as the sheets, lifted the body and waited for it to drain before carrying it up the slope, threading through the trees and finally disappearing from sight. Fool rubbed at the bandage they had also taped to his head; it itched.

"Are you sure you won't go back to the office? Get some rest?" said Gordie, looking worriedly at Fool.

"No," said Fool, nodding in the direction of the departing corpse. "I'll follow it to the House for the Questioning." The two men began to move up the slope, following the attendants and their cargo. As they came close, Fool saw with surprise that there were people in the trees, that the man who had found the body was still there with some of the others who had formed the scrappy crowd. They were almost hiding, half lost in the shadows of the stunted trunks and twisting, bowed branches.

The man, the witness, came forward as they approached, hunched and scuttling.

"Yes, Mr. West?" said Gordie. *Even after all this,* thought Fool, *he knows, without having to think about it.*

"You scared off that demon. You scared it, you shot it, and it left you alone," said West, his voice not much more than a whisper. He sounded reverential, had a look in his eyes that Fool couldn't easily identify. Awe? Respect? Surely not. "I've never seen that before. None of us have." He gestured behind him, taking in the other figures.

"Well, no," said Fool. "It wasn't me, not really. It was—"

"It was. We all saw," said West. He stepped closer to Fool and reached out, taking Fool's hand. Fool saw his own hand in West's clean white one, saw that there was dried blood on his fingers and mud scurfed under the nails, and was suddenly ashamed. He tried to pull his hand back but West held tight, as though Fool were a lifeline and he were drowning. "You scared it," he said again, "and it ran. I just wanted to say thank you." And with that, he let go of Fool and darted back into the trees. Fool looked at Gordie, who shrugged.

"What was that thing, incidentally? Anything we know?"

"Not a named one," said Gordie after a moment's thought during which Fool could almost see him flicking through the vast store of knowledge he had in that unassuming head. "Just a minor demon, although what it said about things from the lake being his reminds me of something, but I can't think what. Perhaps I could go back and check?" There was hope in his voice, small and desperate. He hated Questionings, had vomited the first time he saw one and never really got over what Morgan and the other Questioners had to do, and tried every way he could think of short of asking to avoid them.

"That's probably sensible," said Fool. "And check if we've had any other deaths here, maybe that we didn't investigate. I'd hate to miss a pattern, if there is one."

"What about the blue flash?"

Fool had forgotten that, and it was his turn to think. Blue flashes were a sign of the Fallen, so it was said, but could anything else specific generate them or were they another of Hell's turbulent, maddening occurrences? "I don't know," he said finally. "Check that as well. The flashes never amount to anything, not that I remember, but my memory isn't always perfect. See if there's anything in the records about them."

"Should I speak to Elderflower? Ask him?"

"No, I'll do that when the Questioning is over." Fool rubbed at the bandage again, pressing at the wound through the rough material. The pain that flared briefly across his temple made him think of the battered features of the dead man, and he exhaled. Another corpse, another collection of injuries to note and collate, more questions, more unspooling lines of investigation that would probably lead nowhere. More fuel for the Flame Garden. Fool had little hope that they would solve this murder, just as they failed to solve most of the murders that came through to them, but he would try. *This is, after all, Hell,* he thought bitterly. *What else can I do? We have little hope, but we are doomed to try. Little trying Fool.*

Solomon Water, once a bowl of flame in which sinners burned but now still and black, watched him, impassive and silent.

3

Fool, mostly, liked his job but never admitted it out loud or even to himself except in his most private hours. Admitting any kind of pleasure would be to raise his head above the parapet, to invite the notice of Hell and its closest attentions. Better to keep low, to keep hidden, and to keep any pleasure a secret, buttoned-down thing. Like everyone, he had been born to his role, assigned it once his newly fished flesh had stopped shivering, and he thought in his darkest hours that in his work, he might be one of the few humans in Hell who had some sense of purpose. Despite this, though, he did not like Questionings.

When he arrived at the Questioning House, Fool found Hand and Tidyman in the building's large foyer. They were arguing over the body, which was still wrapped in the gray tarpaulin but had been placed on a gurney that was too short for it; it sagged over one end, dribbles of muddy water pooling beneath it.

"He's mine," Tidyman was saying as Fool entered, "I'm on the rota next."

"You can't have him," said Hand. "I've a new idea about how we might question this type of flesh and I need him to experiment on." The men ignored Fool, which suited him well enough; he disliked them both. Hand was fussy, endlessly tinkering with the techniques of the Questioning without ever apparently improving the result, and the less said about the incompetent Tidyman the better. The argument went back and forth for several more minutes, Tidyman querulous and Hand insistent, before Fool finally interrupted.

"Is Morgan available?"

The two men turned to look at him, and for a moment neither spoke.

Then Tidyman said, "It is not Morgan's turn. He is not on the rota until after both myself and Mr. Hand."

"Nonetheless, I'd like him if he's available."

"He's not," said Hand, turning back to Tidyman, dismissing Fool. Tidyman, however, carried on looking at Fool as though studying some particularly interesting dead meat.

"Why Morgan?" Tidyman asked.

"Because he's quick," said Fool, unable to tell them the truth, that Morgan was the only one he trusted, and seeking an excuse, "and I need answers fast. The Bureaucracy has demanded answers." Besides, he liked Morgan, and he respected his handling of the flesh of the dead. Compared with the two men in front of him, Morgan *was* quick, as well as far more professional. There were only three Questioners in Hell, one House for all the abused and torn meat that Hell created.

"You cannot demand," said Hand, turning back, speaking as though he were swatting at an insect with his voice.

Fool sighed, seeing himself reflected in the gleaming surface of the House's marble walls, rich with veins that crawled across the image of his face. He was pale and dark-eyed and his hair was shaved close, revealing the contours of his skull and its palimpsest of scars, older than some people in Hell but younger than others. He had been born from Limbo into his flesh in a place where age meant little and how people looked was mostly lost under layers of grime and pain, fished from the ocean outside to wear his skin and act out his role without choice. He was an Information Man, one of only three in Hell, and he ached and he was tired of things being put in his way.

"Then I ask, not demand, that you'd please get him. Now."

"There's no need," said a third voice; Morgan, coming down the stairs from his rooms above. "If you'd like me to speak to this poor thing, I will. Tidyman, I know this is out of rota order, but we can rearrange things. Hand, you can have the next one. Agreed?"

Fool had never worked out whether there was an official hierarchy within the House, but the unofficial one seemed to be that Morgan was first among equals. Tidyman certainly deferred to him without question, and Hand also fell back after a tense moment in which his mouth opened and closed and his brow furrowed, but he ultimately said nothing. Morgan smiled and took hold of the gurney's handle, starting to wheel it about. "Let us see," he said, "what he has to say."

Morgan moved into the House, leaving the atrium and passing under a sign that simply read FLESH before going along a short corridor that was clean and sterile and lined on either side with closed doors. Fool followed, remaining silent as Morgan opened the last door and pushed the body inside. Glancing back along the corridor, Fool saw a trail of filthy water, as though the dead man had left himself a path to follow so that he could escape the House. Given what was about to happen, Fool wouldn't have blamed him.

"He's a Genevieve," said Morgan once he had the body unwrapped in the Questioning room. "There's damage, old damage, to the inner cheeks of the buttocks and scarring around the anus. I'll bet when we roll him over, I'll find injuries on and around the penis." Fool, remembering the bites, nodded in agreement.

The body was lying facedown on Morgan's table, and Morgan was pointing as he walked around it. "There are old marks on the shoulders as well from where they hold on as they fuck." "They" were demons; the dead man had been a prostitute whose clients had been demons. Fool had no idea why prostitutes were called Genevieves, but it was the term everyone used for them and had as long as he remembered. It might make identifying the corpse easier, knowing that, but it also confirmed what he had already been expecting: that this case was going to take him down into the Houska.

"Will you help me turn him?"

Without waiting for a response, Morgan took hold of the dead man's shoulders and lifted. Fool took his legs and, clumsily, they rolled the body over. More water spilled from its mouth, leaving new black trails down its chin. The water pooled under its head as though its shadow were escaping, coagulating. "My word, he took a beating, didn't he?" said Morgan. Fool didn't reply.

Leaning over the corpse, Morgan gently pressed on its chin, opening its mouth. After a few seconds, he said, "There's terrible damage in here. Apart from the teeth and cheek, the tongue's been torn partly away. He won't talk easily, I don't think. Still, I can try."

Fool watched as Morgan bustled around the room, gathering pieces of equipment and chemicals. Some of them he recognized—scalpels, needles and thread, a vial of something that looked like cloudy urine—but most Fool had no idea about. Each Questioning was different, was unique to the corpse, and Morgan rarely chose to explain himself. Now he dripped a tiny bead of the discolored water into the corpse's mouth and then closed the jaw, pressing the lips together with his fingers. The dead man's throat bulged as though he were swallowing a bolus of something solid, and then settled back. Morgan let go of the lips and said, "Can you tell us what happened?"

The room was silent.

Morgan repeated himself, listened to the silence again, and then leaned over, looking into the mouth. "Interesting," he said quietly. "I wonder."

"Wonder what?" asked Fool.

Morgan didn't reply. Instead, he asked the question a third time, this time pressing hard under the corpse's ribs and forcing air and strings of discolored, foul-smelling water up out of its mouth. It bubbled out past the teeth and lips with a sound like shit slipping into water. There were no recognizable words in the sound.

"Wonder what?" asked Fool again, seeing the look of confusion on Morgan's face.

"I'm not sure. Even with the damage to the tongue and the jaws, we should be getting some kind of response, whether it's understandable or not, but there's nothing. It's unusual, but not insurmountable; we'll just have to try something different."

Taking a piece of equipment that looked like a flattened spoon, Morgan placed it under the dead man's undamaged eye and then, with a swift, sharp movement, prized the eyeball free. It came out with a sound like a nauseous swallow and lay, quivering, on the spoon as Morgan severed the optic nerve. He took another bead of water from the vial, letting it drip down in the top of the eyeball, and then placed it on top of a glass pane held horizontal in a metal frame. Above the pane was a lamp, which he lit, moving the lens so that the light angled downward, shining through the eye and onto the desk below. Morgan moved the lens several times, then shifted the eye around on the pane before stepping away and saying, "No. Nothing."

"No images?" Sometimes the dead held images of the last thing they had seen in their eyes, frozen into the jelly, able to be seen when projected by the lamp.

"No, not even something that makes no sense, which I might expect. Just light." Morgan sounded intrigued now, his voice distracted, distant. He didn't look at Fool as he spoke. Removing the eye, he placed it on a sheet of heavy, absorbent paper and slit along its length, letting the thick mass of its insides spill out. When it had soaked into the paper, he held the sheet up in front of the light. The damp areas glistened.

"Recognize anything there?" he asked Fool.

"No."

"Me neither. This is very unusual. Someone really didn't want this poor fellow talking, did they?"

"How could they stop him?" asked Fool. In all the previous Questionings he had attended, no corpse had ever been completely silent. Many were garrulous in death, the words coming from their mouths in long, breathless streams, their eyes full of images or descriptions or names.

"I'm not sure. There are ways, one in particular. I'll check in a moment. First, though, there are other things I'd like to try."

None of them worked; the dead man's hands refused to write, he would not smile or frown in response to even the most elementary yes-or-no questions, and his fingers would not tap out answers. Finally, Morgan took a small bottle of clear water and held it gingerly in front of him, removing the stopper and dripping a small trickle of water onto the corpse's forehead. It rolled down its temple before dripping off and spotting onto the table under him, where it steamed. Then he took a small white disk from a drawer and smeared it with something that smelled, to Fool, like excrement. This Morgan inserted up the corpse's rectum before standing back and asking, again, a question. The dead man did not move and the question remained unanswered.

"It's like his whole mind has been taken away," said Morgan eventually. "There are no answers because he hasn't anything left with which to comprehend the questions. It's not his brain, as that's essentially unmarked, undamaged, but it's what drives the brain that's missing."

"Drives the brain?"

"Yes. Tell me about how he was found. What do you know?"

Fool told Morgan everything that West had told him, and then about the nameless demon by Solomon Water.

"Ah," said Morgan slowly after Fool had finished. "I understand. I thought perhaps I did, but I wasn't sure. It's a very rare thing, what's been done to this man. I've certainly never seen it before, only read about it in some of the older books. Well, if we can't ask the intellect, then we must ask the body."

"What's been done to him? Rare how?" asked Fool, but Morgan again ignored him. Instead, he clamped poles to the table by the dead man's shoulders and hips, each pole topped by a short chain at the end of which hung a small hook. Then he quickly slashed a cross into the flesh of his chest and belly, the two lines crossing each other just below the base of the sternum.

"This is an older method of Questioning. It's very basic, and very crude, but it may work and the answers it gives are usually accurate. You have four questions, Fool. Keep them simple and use them wisely."

Fool thought for a minute. The man was likely a Genevieve, Morgan had said, so his first query was simply "Were you killed by a client?"

Morgan took one of the flaps of quartered flesh and pulled it, stretching it away from the corpse and up to the hook, pushing it onto its sharp tip. The chain wobbled and tautened before settling to stillness, the hook punching through the skin easily. The flesh twisted but didn't tear, remained held up away from the body.

"Yes," said Morgan simply. "Or at least, he believed his murderer to be a client. Next question."

"Was it a regular client?"

This time, the flesh tore away from the hook as soon as Morgan let it go. "No," he said. "Next question."

Fool thought again, trying to ignore the headache that was building under his bandage like water gathering in a balloon. The dead man was killed by a new client, likely a demon given his usual client group. He tried to work out what the flesh could tell him. No names, certainly. Yes-or-no answers, essentially, but what was the most useful thing to know? *Think, little confused Fool, think!*

"Did you meet him in the Houska?"

The third quarter of flesh, and again, it tore from the hook as soon as Morgan let it go. "No."

One more, one more, but how to make it count? Fool was still considering when Morgan spoke. "If you're struggling with a question, might I be permitted to ask the last one?" Fool nodded; he had nothing else useful to ask anyway.

"Do you think that separating your soul and your flesh was deliberate?" Morgan asked the body, and this time when he attached the flesh to the hook, it stayed, the chain clinking quietly as the muscle and skin pulled down against it. Morgan nodded, as though the answer confirmed something that he already knew, and said to Fool, "I think that's all we'll get. I'll get him ready for the Garden and then we'll talk."

"His soul is missing," said Morgan, handing Fool a hot drink. Coffee, good and strong, not like the brew at the station. "It's entirely gone. There aren't even remnants of it left, nothing in the corners of him or clinging on deep inside. Gone. If there was anything there, he would have reacted to the water or wafer."

"Water or wafer?" repeated Fool, feeling far from home, lost on unexpected streets.

"The water I put on his forehead was holy, and the thing I inserted into his rectum was wafer befouled with shit; the extremes of Heaven and Hell. He didn't react to either of them, and anything with a soul would. Especially in this place." Morgan gestured with a sweep of his arm, taking in not just the Questioning House but everything beyond it, Hell and the Limbo that surrounded it.

"It's not just the violence that will have split soul and flesh," he continued. "Violence alone can't achieve it. It was deliberate—it would have to be. There was *intent* there, Fool; the likelihood is that a demon fed on the soul after it released it. I know that they all do to some degree or another, eating whatever fear and pain they can generate, but this poor bastard's soul seems to have been consumed completely. The blue flash that your witness saw was the actual splitting, the separation of soul from body. It takes some great energy, some great *desire,* to achieve it,

Fool, and violence is only the tool used to break the soul's moorings so it can be torn free. Very few demons can do it, which might help narrow your search. The minor thing by the lake wouldn't have the strength or the desire; it would probably have just fed on any scraps it could get its teeth into, the bad dreams and worse memories. Something that can devour a whole soul, no matter how shriveled that soul is, is unusual, almost unheard of, Fool."

"Is that why the demon by the lake was so horrified? Because there was nothing left for it?"

"I'd think so. All that dead flesh, empty and tasteless. Plus, it means that there's something moving around capable of eating whole souls, and I'd imagine it was frightened. Even demons have souls, Fool, and can become prey to those things further up the hierarchy."

Fool thought about the thing that had come from Solomon Water those months back, about the dark and slurring voice he had heard out by the wall, and nodded. He thought about the place Hell had been, about the flames and the burning, about the vast things that had stalked its terrible plains, and groaned to himself.

"So we're looking for something old and powerful, powerful enough to eat entire souls?"

"No," said Morgan, looking at Fool over the top of his mug. "I'm pleased to say that we're not. *You* are."

4

"Who are they?"

Fool did not speak. The ballroom of Assemblies House, the administrative heart of the Bureaucracy, was huge, and Balthazar's voice echoed into its arched heights. The angel's tone was one of polite, amused incomprehension, as though he were asking an insect he was sure couldn't reply to a question whose answer he wasn't bothered about. It was something to fill the anticipatory silence before the discussions began, and Fool's presence here was one merely of tradition, not because he had any real part to play in the trading or decision-making. *Little pointless Fool,* he said to himself, thinking about demons so powerful they could eat souls.

"Who are they?" Balthazar asked again, his voice harder. Fool looked out of the window at the crowd that had gathered in the square in front of the building. They were packed tightly, humans and some demons, simply standing and staring. Fool wondered whether they could see him looking out at them, but he doubted it. The windows of Assemblies House were filthy; to look out through their smeared panes was to look out at a Hell made distant and indistinct by the layers of grime.

"They're the Sorrowful," he said eventually. "They know what's being discussed here."

"And they come here why?"

How could he answer? Fool wondered. That they came in the hope that they could somehow influence the outcome of the discussions, that it was easier to come and wait where they could at least see the building, that it was impossible to work or wait elsewhere when the hope of being picked, of being *Elevated,* hung in the air? And even if it was a vain hope, it didn't matter because all the inhabitants of Hell had was hope, tiny and shriveled and stunted. "They come to wait," he said finally. "They come because there is a chance of Elevation, that this time it will be theirs."

"Of course," said Balthazar, clapping his hands and sounding delighted, "and they hope for Heaven's glory and graciousness to be bestowed upon them."

"I suppose so," replied Fool, but doubted it. It wasn't Heaven's grace they were hoping for—that, Elevation offered them—but the far more appealing prospect of simply escaping Hell itself, of escaping the fear and drudgery and the hunger and the violence.

"And you," said Balthazar, "would you rather be out there with them? Be one of the Sorrowful, hoping that we choose you?"

"No," said Fool. "Elevation is random, I know that. Standing there and hoping will achieve nothing. They'll all go home cold and tired later. Colder and more tired. But do I hope that I'm picked? Yes." There. It was out, and he was irritated, not by his admission, because it was almost certainly true of every human and most of the demons in Hell, but because he had made it to Balthazar.

"Really? And why are you here in Hell? Do you deserve Elevation? Have you atoned, do you think?"

Fool couldn't answer. He had no idea why he was resident in Hell, none of them did, and he had no idea how to atone for sins he had no memory of. Besides, he knew atonement had little or nothing to do with Elevation; what was decided in this room between the Bureaucracy of Heaven and the Bureaucracy of Hell was decided not because of the goodness of action or thought by the inhabitants of Hell, but according to rules that the two Bureaucracies alone understood.

"Well?" said Balthazar, and his voice was quiet and dangerous. He stepped close to Fool, forcing him to lower his eyes against the painful gleam of the angel's naked flesh. "I expect an answer, Fool. Do you not know, Information Man? Have you no information on this subject? Perhaps we should put you out there with them, until you find your tongue and your answers?"

"You have no right to do that, Balthazar, and I'd thank you to step away from Thomas."

It was Elderflower. The bureaucrat was tiny, only slightly over four feet tall, and he was thin, his skinniness emphasized by the black coat he habitually wore, its hem brushing the floor as he walked. He bustled across the room, his tangled hair bobbing as he moved, and inserted himself between Fool and Balthazar.

"It might be good for you to remember your place, Balthazar," he continued, and somehow, despite being so small, he managed to loom over the angel, to block Fool's view of that glorious flesh for a moment. Fool had never quite known whether Elderflower was human or demon or something else entirely; most of the time he appeared to be a man, tiny and delicate, but at other times he was something more, something alien and unknowable. "You are new here, but I know you and I know *of* you. You are one of Michael's creatures, yes? Equipped with savage weapons and a will to use them? But there is no war for you to fight, not now, and I'll thank you to keep your furies at bay and retain a civil tongue in that beautiful head of yours.

"Ah, but I see you are disappointed in the home of the Great Enemy, yes? You expected, perhaps, the lakes of fire, the bodies torn asunder on racks, the flesh of sinners consumed by tooth and maw as they repent their sins? Where are the burning sinners, you wonder? Where are the serried ranks of abused flesh, row and row as far as the eye can see? That is no longer Hell, little angel, and hasn't been for an age or more, for several ages. Hell evolves, Balthazar, mirroring the worlds about it; the sanctity and terrors of the flesh replaced by something far, far worse."

Balthazar, his skin beginning to glow, gestured toward the crowd and said, "Where is the punishment? Where is atonement? They stand as though waiting for news or instruction, as though this were an everyday occurrence, and this one tells me he has no knowledge of the sin that brings him here!" The angel's light was fiery now, its ripples filling the room, causing the shadows at its edge to dance. "How is this Hell? How is this just?"

"Balthazar, where do they live?" Adam, his voice cool. "What life do they have?"

"Hell is a place of fire," said Balthazar obstinately, sounding like the petulant drunks Fool sometimes encountered. "They should be burning, screaming in the torment."

"Adam, your companions have grown naive since your last visit," said

Elderflower. "You should educate them better before bringing them here."

Fool wondered whether Balthazar would produce his flame again, coax it from nowhere, and for a moment it seemed he might; his hand danced downward, his fingers twitching, and Fool's own hand started toward his gun. The air thickened, tensions curling like mists around them.

"They have no safety," said Elderflower quietly, almost thoughtfully, "none. Look at them. Their lives are short, brutal, and brutish, mostly ending in violence and starvation. They arrive as flesh from the seas outside, shriven not of their sin but only of their knowledge of it, knowing they are being punished for something without knowing *why*. They try to do good in the hope that it helps, living each day in the expectation of death or worse, watching as it happens to those around them. They see demons acting without consequence, see Elevations happen without apparent reason, and they suffer. Not the burning agonies of bodies chained to rocks or flesh afire or torn to pieces, no; something worse.

"They suffer the terrors of the approaching unknown, of ending without redemption or logic, and know that they are powerless. But this is Hell, and there has to be worse than mere violence; the Sorrowful have something worse than no hope—they have *some* hope. Only a sliver, to be sure; only enough to make the terrors so much worse. Perhaps today is the day that the demon leaves them alone, perhaps this is the day that Fool or one of his officers prevents the crime, brings something to justice. Perhaps today is the day of Elevation for them rather than for some other apparently undeserving ones. *Surely this is my time,* they say inside themselves where only they can hear, and then when it is not, they are left to carry on and their only hope is that tomorrow it might change, that tomorrow might be different. This is Hell, Balthazar, a place of savageries so vast and shifting that you cannot even conceive of their beginnings or endings, and only some of those are of the flesh. Souls burn here, little angel, but the flames are rarely seen.

"Now, can we start?"

Elderflower slipped out from between Fool and Balthazar and walked away. Fool watched as a look of confusion writhed across Balthazar's face, his skin darkening further, and even at a distance, Fool felt the heat coming off him. The angel stared after Elderflower and then shot a look at Fool, saw that he was still being observed, and made a visible effort to calm himself. The color drained from his cheeks, his skin returning to the smooth pink of clean marble. On the other side of the large room, Adam made a noise somewhere between a cough and a summoning, and Balthazar and Fool followed.

Adam and Elderflower sat facing each other, a low table between them. Balthazar positioned himself behind Adam, and although he kept his wings folded in, he flexed his broad chest and shoulders so that they shuffled, the feathers rattling and punctuating the start of the meeting. The scribe and the archive took places on either side of Adam but at a distance, bookends around a space waiting to be filled. Adam smiled at Elderflower and said, "We find ourselves here again, old friend."

"Yes," said Elderflower. Fool didn't recognize Adam from previous delegations, and assumed that his last visit had been before Fool's emergence from Limbo.

"We shall take five this time," said Adam.

"Ten," replied Elderflower immediately. "The spaces beyond the wall grow full."

"As you wish," said Adam. "Ten. Do you have candidates?"

Elderflower did not speak. Instead, he waved a scurrying thing out of the shadows at the edge of the room, which darted forward and handed him a single sheet of paper. Elderflower handed the paper to Adam, who passed it without appearing to read it to one of his silent companions. The angel began to read the names aloud as the other, the scribe, held out a large book; it appeared in its hands as though it had been removed from between two flaps of air. None of the names meant anything to Fool, just as they hadn't during previous Elevations. They were the anonymous of Hell, farm or factory workers, Genevieves, barmen. No one special.

On the seventh name, Adam spoke. "No," he said quietly.

Elderflower raised his eyebrows, but Adam merely smiled. Elderflower nodded, and then gestured at the shadows again. The scurrying thing darted out once more, carrying another piece of paper. Elderflower took it and passed it to Adam, who again handed it on to the archive, who in return gave Adam the first piece of paper. Adam handed it to the scurrying thing, which scuttled back to the shadows, its clawed hands already crumpling the sheet. After a short moment, the archive started reading again, its voice dusty.

After the ten names had been read out without comment from Adam and recorded, Adam spoke again. "We will take another five of your choice if you agree to receiving one of ours."

"No," said Elderflower. "We have to take from outside. The flesh clamors at our walls."

"Ten," said Adam, still smiling.

"Perhaps," said Elderflower. "We might require further concessions in addition to the extra Elevations."

"Such as?"

Elderflower started to talk about some of the other trades currently being discussed between Heaven and Hell, outlining changes to various treaties and deals. Adam replied in the negative to almost all of them, and soon he and Elderflower were deep in discussion, speaking something close to another language as they discussed how the deals could be made to work. Fool tuned them out, looking instead at the Sorrowful beyond the windows. They were gray under the layers of dirt on the glass, reduced to shapes rather than people. He knew that Elderflower and the representatives of Heaven could trade for hours now, coming to agreements on the numbers taken and received, on the individuals Elevated or Lowered (*never Fallen, though,* he thought briefly, *never Fallen*), on the grease that would move the wheels of the give-and-take. They would repeat it every day for the next six days, until after seven days of trade and countertrade the delegation would return, those chosen would be Elevated, and Hell would welcome new inhabitants from Outside or Above. Sometimes, Fool would be asked to contribute to the discussions, to say whether he knew or had opinions on individuals, numbers, types of person, but mostly his presence there was, he suspected, to even up the numbers. He was Elderflower's Balthazar.

In the square, the Sorrowful watched, silent and still.

The train stank of unwashed flesh and sweat and dirt but they used it anyway, not having time to walk. They found a space in the second carriage, managing to get one seat so that Summer could sit. It was touching, really, thought Fool, watching Gordie offer the seat to Summer and trying to pretend that it was merely a thing that he did as a colleague and not as a lover. Summer knew that Fool had guessed about their relationship, but it was clear that Gordie still thought Fool was in the dark about it. It was typical of the man's naïveté, thinking that Fool wouldn't see; they lived in tiny rooms in the building that also served as their offices. Fool heard them sometimes, in the night, heard the creak of the bed or the patter of their feet as they crept to each other's rooms. There were only the three of them, three Information Men for the whole of Hell, so working out who the creeping feet belonged to hadn't taxed his skills of deduction too much. Having a relationship with a fellow officer wasn't forbidden, but Summer and Gordie didn't want to reveal it for the same reason that Fool wouldn't talk about the fact that he liked his job; it paid to keep even the tiniest of happinesses secret.

"Have you got it with you?" Gordie asked suddenly. Fool didn't need to ask what he meant: the feather.

"Yes," he said. It was in his inside pocket, safe. He carried it with him everywhere now, unwilling to let it go far from him. He liked the way it felt when his fingers trailed over it or when it brushed against his skin through the thin material, and he tried to ignore the joy in case it marked him out in the eyes of the Bureaucracy.

"Can—" Gordie began, and Fool interrupted.

"No. Not here, not among people." *Can I see it again? Can Summer see it? Can I hold it again?* Fool could hear the queries as clearly as if Gordie had spoken them aloud.

"Oh," Gordie replied, obviously upset. Summer touched his hand, briefly, and Fool understood that she was telling him, *It's okay, he's right, I'll see it later.*

"It's from Balthazar, isn't it?" asked Gordie after a moment.

"Yes."

"He's a warrior, one of the angels that patrolled the borders of Heaven when Hell was different, when there was a war. He's one of Heaven's greatest weapons."

"Yes," said Fool again, thinking of the heat of him, the flame that climbed from his hands. He touched the feather again, just for a fragment of time, and felt its strength, its purity. Creatures of beauty that were weapons, blue flashes, dead bodies with no souls and eyes that pleaded from somewhere back in the past, from when they were alive and whole; it was too big, made no sense. The feather was cool against his fingertips, and he said, "We're here." The train had brought them to Hell's battered, sordid heart.

The Houska was quiet. The train disgorged, along with Fool and Gordie and Summer, most of its night staff, the Genevieves and Marys and barmen and musicians joining the thieves and beggars who already lined the streets. The demons would start arriving soon, when full night had fallen. When the Houska had started to generate its sour, rank heat.

Summer had spent the day drawing the dead man, healing him in her sketch as best she could so that his face was whole and unmarked and recognizable. She and Gordie had then made as many copies of the sketch as they could, sitting at the small table in the kitchen; Fool had arrived back from the Elevation meeting and stood in the doorway as they worked and had spent a moment watching them, at the way they touched at the shoulders and hips, before turning away. This thing they had was new, delicate, and he had not wanted to intrude on their privacy. Instead, he had retreated from the room and then returned more noisily, and by the time he reached it they were sitting on opposite sides of the table and not looking at each other as they traced and copied.

Both Gordie and Summer now held sheaves of paper, a hundred sketched versions of the man; young, eyes whole, lips untorn, flat and lifeless and dead. *Would anyone look at them?* Fool wondered. Anyone see the man's image and recognize him, tell them who he was? Probably not, despite the number of people who even now filled the Houska's streets. The crowds moved about them, stragglers from the factories that were the Houska's daytime employers climbing wearily onto the train, taking the stink of their unwashed skin and the chemicals they worked with into the miasma of cheap perfume and sweat within the carriages.

The Houska was the last place Fool wanted to come, especially after a day with Elderflower and Adam and Balthazar, but he had no choice; if he was to investigate the body from Solomon Water, it had to be now. The tubes that had gathered during the day were all ones he could legitimately ignore, stamp with his *DNI* mark, and send back to Elder-flower. They were a normal day's story for Hell, rapes and assaults and robberies that the victims probably hadn't even reported but that Hell knew about anyway. Each stamp bit at him, a mark of his uselessness, but today he was grateful for them; he could not shift that battered face from his memory. The man's four teeth were still wrapped in a hand-kerchief, in Fool's drawer, waiting for the chance to put them back with the body and take it to the Flame Garden. At present, the body itself was wrapped back in its dirty sheet and was in the office basement, which was cold enough to act as a morgue and which had few rats. How long before something came through with orders to investigate that he could not ignore, though? Not long, he knew. Not long enough.

"We'll try the parlors first, before they get busy," said Summer, and Fool nodded. They had arranged to meet later, to work the bars along the main street together for safety, but the parlors were slightly less dangerous and he hoped that the two of them would be okay. He didn't tell them to be careful as they walked off; there was little point. Neither was that long from being fished out of Limbo, but neither was stupid, and both had survived this far as Information Men. If anything, Summer was safer than Gordie, as she tended to back away from trouble, whereas he still thought that his office should mean something, should be respected, and tended to push back when challenged. There was no real advice or guidance he could give them, even if he wanted to, that he had not already passed on, and he could not go with them. There had been a message waiting for him at the office when he had returned earlier. He had been summoned; he had to visit the Man of Plants and Flowers.

The Man of Plants and Flowers lived in the center of the Houska in a building set back off one of the small side streets and that looked to be held together by the Man himself, by his growths. Its stonework was crumbling and most of the windows gaped, glassless and blind. Roots and vines squirmed out from between the bricks, displacing the mortar and covering the building's fascia. There was no door to the Man's home, only a doorway whose wooden frame was torn and splintered, although the damage was old. The wood was pulpy with damp, not from outside but from within; the house breathed, and each exhalation was moist.

Inside, the building seemed to be made from angles that buckled and twisted as Fool looked at them. It was partly the lack of light, but also that the walls and floor and ceiling were covered in roots and stems and leaves; plants and flowers grew everywhere. Some had small petals, some had leaves, and some had vast, open cups lined with thick hairs and rimmed with heavy, fibrous stems. "Most of me is safe," the Man had warned Fool during an earlier visit, "but parts of me are not. Don't approach the openmouthed ones, Fool, not ever." On another visit Fool had seen one of the cups suddenly lunge and close around a scuttling thing as it ran past, and the near-human scream that the thing made, choking off with a sizzle like burning hair, made him glad he had heeded the Man's advice. Sometimes the thick vines that covered the floor moved languidly, wriggling, coiling and uncoiling, as he passed; he tried not to tread on them. In some places, roots emerged from the plants and disappeared into the stone of the walls, and Fool thought that the stone itself looked desiccated around the roots, friable and brittle, as though he could crumble it with the least pressure.

The Man lived in the room farthest back from the door; the part of the Man that usually spoke to Fool did, anyway. Fool walked cautiously along the hallway, making sure that he didn't go near the open cups as he went. He didn't bother to call to the Man, who had known Fool intended to respond to the summons as soon as Fool had spoken the words aloud back in the office. It was what the Man did, was why Fool was here; the Man knew things. He stretched across great swathes of Hell, and he saw and he heard, and sometimes he told Fool things. The Man very rarely allowed Fool to visit, so his summoning must mean something. *Hopeful Fool,* Fool thought as he reached the doorway to the Man's room. Even before he stepped through, the Man was calling out, "Hello, my friend! The demon killer arrives!"

When Fool had first visited the Man of Plants and Flowers, he was still recognizably human, although even then his corpulent shape was being lost to the mass of growths. Before he took to his current existence, he must have been vastly fat; on that first visit, the rolling topography of his belly, with its pale and hairless stretched skin, had bulged out through the thin covering of leaves and stalks and mosses like the lips of some endlessly flapping mouth. The Man's arms had still had movement then; now they were thick cables of greenery, held out from his sides and clinging to the walls, motionless and cruciform. His voice had sounded human then, but now it did not.

"My home is a simple place, Fool, hardly a fitting venue for a slayer of demons," said the Man. The words sounded as though they were being formed by rubbing pieces of leather together, liquid and hoarse, and Fool wondered how long the Man would be able to carry on talking. Not long, probably, and after that, would he communicate by rasping his leaves together? Or would one of those cups start to flap, forming words without breath or tongue? He was almost completely lost now, Fool saw, entirely buried beneath a riot of plants and flowers that filled the entire back half of the room. *The Man of Plants and Flowers,* he thought. It was what the Man had introduced himself to Fool as, was what he had been then and what he was now, more so than ever, and then what the Man had said filtered through Fool's brain and he was brought up short.

"Demon killer?" he asked. "What?"

"Haven't you heard?" asked the Man, laughter bubbling under his words like things being torn from mud. "You killed a demon at Solomon Water yesterday."

"I didn't," said Fool, "I—" and then he stopped. Killed a demon?

"Of course you did," said the Man. "The humans are talking about it. They bring me the news, Fool, all my human friends, who need favors from me or want information in return for information. I hear them, Fool! You were seen, my old friend, and if only I had grown that far I would surely have seen it for myself. You tussled over the sad remains of a poor, dead human, fighting to give him the dignity in death that he lacked in life, and killed the demon that challenged you. It's everywhere, this tale of Fool the demon killer."

"But I didn't," said Fool again, suddenly feeling the world yaw beneath his feet. Demon killer? It made no sense, it wasn't even close to what had happened, and he had no idea how the other demons might react, or the Bureaucracy, if they thought he had killed one of their own. The Man's flesh whispered around him, drifts of light and dark fragmenting in the air as he moved, the noise of him soft and sly. *I didn't,* thought Fool, and he felt suddenly hot and cold and tiny and lost and yet somehow terribly, awfully *visible.*

Was this it? Was this where Hell noticed him?

"Of course you didn't," said the Man, still slipping about him. "I'd imagine that you didn't even scare that minor thing, did you? And how is your head, beaten Fool?"

"Sore," said Fool truthfully. The pain was melting now, losing its fresh sharpness and becoming the dull bloom of bruised flesh.

"But even that, Fool, even that is something to the watching crowds. You were injured, and yet still you stood your ground against the little nameless thing. A human standing against a demon? Unheard of! Not and surviving anyway, Fool, you know that; this is Hell, and no human ever challenges a demon, but you did. Demons are Hell's original inhabitants, and they hate us for our very existence and for invading their domain, and they kill that which stands against them and that which they feel like killing. But not you, Fool. You stood against them, *killed* one of them, and yet you live.

"Whether it's true or not doesn't matter, of course, because those humans saw what they have waited for a long time to see, a human challenge a demon and win. Who cares about the truth when they have a story like that, Fool, eh? And stories, like me, they grow, don't they? You, above all, should know that."

It was true, Fool knew. On the rare occasions that he and the others managed to investigate one of the crimes whose details were contained in the canisters, every witness, every person, gave them different information. The greater the time that elapsed between the crime and the investigation, the more disparate the stories became, fed by the fear and the uncertainty that everyone in Hell felt, each version gathering weight, increasing in size, until finding the truth at its core became almost impossible. The job of the Information Men, he often thought, was not so much to gather information as to sift through it, trying to find the common threads among all the differences.

The mass in the corner of the room shook slightly, the fronds rustling, and although Fool could see no face within it, he had the impression that the Man was peering at him intently. Around him, the stems and cables of greenery twisted, as though there were a breeze in the room, the leaves and flowers and fringed open cups turning toward him.

"Give, Fool," said the Man, and the cup nearest Fool's head seemed to open even wider, the raw purple of its interior gleaming wetly. "I hear strange tales about the body, about what was done to it."

"The man's soul was gone," said Fool. "Completely consumed."

The Man made a noise like a sigh, and the room itself trembled around Fool as he absorbed the information. Fool waited until the trembling had subsided, watching as the last vestiges of it made their way along the branches and shimmered out of the petals and leaves that filled the room, and then asked, "What can do that? Have you heard of anything?"

"It would have to be big, and old," said the Man. "I haven't heard of anything, haven't felt anything like that. Hell was full of them once, but not for a long time. I suppose it may only just have raised itself, or have been asleep for these last years. There's a delegation from Heaven down at the moment." It wasn't a question, so Fool didn't reply.

"Sometimes, delegations rattle the balances of Hell, and things emerge from the mud and the dirt because of them. This is a small place, Fool, inhabited mostly by humans who are little more than a moving feast and the demons who live off their nightmares and pain and misery but whose appetites are weak. There's little real evil left. Most of it has retreated, lives in the darkness at Hell's heart, and rarely emerges. There's savagery there, Fool, savagery that makes the everyday cruelties you see look like mere love bites."

Fool listened in silence, thinking of the people he saw every day, their eyes always wary, the heads down, and wondered about how much worse a greater evil could be. How much more fear could people feel? How much more terror and pain could they carry? As if to punctuate his thoughts, one of the Man's mouths lunged and grasped an unseen creature, clenched around it with a crunch of splintering bones and a wet spray of blood.

"I'll listen for it, Fool," said the Man a moment later. "If there is something, it shouldn't be hard to find, should it? It'll wear its horrors like a suit of clothes, don't you think, and nothing it goes near will remain untouched, human or demon or plant."

The Man's bulk shifted again, this time away from Fool. The tangle of him, of the things that sprouted from his flesh and grew away from him, filled the space from floor to ceiling. In the corner of his eye, Fool saw a flying thing alight on the edge of one of the cups. It bent, sniffing cautiously at the fleshy palms within. The Man made a sound, almost inaudible, wet with desire, his attention now completely off Fool. Fool turned to leave, not wanting to see or hear what would come next, but he was too late; another wet, ragged crunch came to him as he reached the doorway, accompanied by the Man's own gasp of delight. As Fool stepped back into the dim corridor, the Man, once a human but now something that Fool did not have a word for, called, "Come back soon, Fool, and I'll tell what there is to be told."

There was a dead man in the road.

His head was missing and blood still spilled slowly from the ragged stump of neck, spreading in a clotting pool around him. Two small demons, little bigger than the missing head, were perched on his back, picking at his flesh; a third was lying in the gutter, covered in blood and rubbing at its swollen, stubby genitalia. Fool went toward the dead man, shooing away the demons. They hopped back from the corpse, glaring at Fool, not retreating far. His feet on the bloodstained dust, Fool knelt, and as he did so the one masturbating ejaculated, making a hooting, whistling sound. The other two darted over and began licking at it but neither, Fool saw, ever moved its attention from the dead body for more than a moment, even as they sucked at the strings of yellow semen that rolled across their companion's belly.

The headless man was barefoot and wearing thin trousers; his top half, what remained of it, was bare. There was dirt, old and black, ground into the man's skin; a factory worker, then. There were scratches across his back, some shallow (from the little demons' claws, Fool supposed) and several deeper, more aggressive wounds. The soles of the man's feet were scored and raw, and his left heel had a piece of glass impaled into it. A trail of bloody footprints led to the fallen figure, winding raggedly back across a few feet of cracked pavement to a cluster of buildings, bars, and closed factories. These were the straggler bars, out on the edge of the

Houska, violent in a grimy, small way, dressed in less glitter and with fewer attractions than the larger establishments closer in to the center.

As Fool looked along the trail of footprints, someone appeared from between the buildings, saw the body and Fool crouched over it, and stopped. It was a human. The three little demons chattered to each other and one, taking advantage of Fool's shifted attention, darted toward the body and tried to snatch another piece of flesh from the sundered neck. Fool saw it coming and hit out with the back of his hand, sending it skittering back. Its body was hot, the heat sending a flash of pain across his knuckles, and the demon snarled at him, baring tiny, blood-streaked teeth.

Fool looked at the three warily; they probably couldn't hurt him— they were too small and had fed too well on fresh flesh and old fear to be a serious threat—but still. He drew his gun and pointed it at the snarling one, gesturing with the barrel. It snarled again, and the one in the gutter made another whistling sound; the third, finding no more ejaculate on its companion's belly to suck up, started to lick the blood from its companion's face. Fool glanced over at the figure by the buildings. Whoever he was, he had started to jitter, hopping from foot to foot, and Fool suddenly understood that he wanted to tell him something, *needed* to tell him, but not where he could be seen or heard, that he was frightened of the telling and that the fear was growing and he was preparing to run. Fool had to get to him now.

When he looked back, the first demon had returned to the neck, was harrying at the flesh with tiny, pincered claws. Even as Fool cried out angrily and hit at it with his gun, the demon popped a tiny piece of dripping skin into its mouth and started to chew. As it tasted the things caught in the skin, released by the rapid movement of its tiny jaws, a triumphant look came over its face. Fool made one last effort, poking at it with his gun, but the thing merely snarled again, baring teeth that had pieces of torn human between them, and batted at the end of Fool's gun barrel, trying to knock it away. If there was danger, it was from this one, not the other two; it was the leader of the little pack, stupid as dirt, trying to face down Fool. *Silly thing*, he thought briefly and remembered the crunch of things being eaten by the Man, and pulled the trigger.

The gun boomed, the sound rolling across the expanses of road and then bouncing back in a flat plosive, and the demon vanished in spray of orange. This close, the bullet tore through its belly, the vacuum of its passing reducing to steaming vapor what intestines it did not drag out and spatter in a wide fan across the road. The other two demons screeched, darting away, pleasures forgotten as shadows leaped, startled, away from the corpse and then snapped back into it.

In the flash of angry light from the gun's blast, the figure between the buildings was revealed as a young man, his face wide and moonlike as he watched the little demon disintegrate. He looked at Fool, his expression one of terror, terror and something else that Fool couldn't identify, and then he turned and ran.

Fool gave chase without much hope of catching the man; he was younger than Fool and looked like a factory worker, thin and cordlike. Not healthy, maybe, but healthier than Fool, who did little physical exercise, who had noticed his muscles becoming less taut in these past months.

The man darted back between the rows of shuttered doorways, and Fool went after him, already feeling the stitch of lost breath punching into his side. Instead of escaping, however, the man slowed by the entrance to a small bar. In the pallid, streaked light falling through the glass door, the blood that lay across him in a spray stretching from his waist to his neck was clear. He looked back at Fool, then at the bar, and then he ran again, this time fast, and when he disappeared around a corner, Fool didn't bother to follow.

The man had slowed by the bar, looked at it. It was as clear a message as Fool could ever remember getting, information unbidden, unforced. He didn't know the bar, but then, he didn't know many of them that well. He sometimes went to one of the few Sorrowful bars, places where humans could drink without demons bothering them, but most of the places in the Houska were demon places where humans were mere staff or chattel. Some of the ones on the outskirts, like this one, nameless and small, were places where uneasy crossovers occurred, where the factory workers drank on their way home, mingling with demons starting their night's entertainments, and mostly the two groups left each other alone.

No one would talk to him, no one would welcome him there. *What was the point of entering?* he wondered.

The dead man's head had been torn from his neck.

Fool shook his gun, feeling the reassuring weight of the next bullet forming, another of Hell's random gifts; only Information Men had guns, and their ammunition was created from the air by the Bureaucracy according to a system only they understood. Fool thought about Hell, about nameless death, about a human brave enough to try to show him something even as he ran, and about bodies on streets. *How many have I investigated during my time here?* he wondered. *How many haven't I investigated?* It was impossible to remember. How many of those deaths had he given reason to, solved? That was easier to remember: perhaps fifteen or twenty, and for those few, how many had he brought to justice? Even easier: none. Whether it was the predation by a demon powerful enough to tear a person's soul loose in a flash of blue light, or the savaging of a factory worker and a set of footprints that marked out the last walk they had taken, death was a constant here, and all of them, Fool included, were merely links in the chains it formed.

Fool didn't have the luxury of believing what he did was of any use; he had seen too many of Hell's leavings for that, and was honest enough to recognize that his own activities were rarely more than ineffectual scuttling around the edges. When he looked in the mirror, he saw someone tired, someone trying to find his way through Hell without creating waves but who wanted more, an indefinable, elusive *more*. He had been part of the crowd that drove the thing back into Solomon Water, yes, but that was different; there hadn't been a crime to solve. There had been no malicious intent there, merely a demon grown huge and bloated and hungry but still stupid, following its instincts. There had been nothing to consider, no clues; the thing had simply slaughtered its way from the water into Hell and had retreated only when the resistance to it became too much for it.

Solving crimes was the purpose of the Information Men, yet they almost never achieved it and even when they did, the facts they scraped free were lost, buried again in the labyrinthine mess of the Bureaucracy. *You do nothing, little purposeless Fool,* he thought bitterly, and then remembered the soulless flesh by the lake's edge, the shit-stained wafer being pressed into its anus, the missing head and demons that ate their fill and masturbated afterward. He remembered the feather that nestled in his pocket glowing with an internal light as clean as anything he had known, and thought, *No.*

Clasping his gun and trying to ignore the lope of his heart, Fool entered the bar.

5

It was holding the head.

The demon was sitting at a table in the bar's gloomy depths holding the head, using it like it was something it had bought over the bar's counter, chewing at the dripping neck and smacking its lips like this was a particularly pleasant drink, and Fool walked up and shot it without pause and without thought.

The head bounced from the demon's hands and rolled, disappearing into the shadows as the other demons and humans scattered, shrieking. Even as his gun began to grow slowly heavier, the new bullet forming, Fool was approaching the splayed, injured thing on the floor, and it backed away from him, blood like liquid dirt spilling from the ragged hole in its belly.

The air stank of gunpowder and of the demon's insides. One of the other demons, descended from the same ancient father as the injured one by the looks of it, started toward Fool when he pivoted toward it, pointing his gun. It hesitated, its lips drawn back from a mouth that was little other than a dark hole in which unseen things writhed, and then darted away, circling wide around Fool and making for the door.

"Why?" asked Fool.

He knelt down next to the demon to be heard. He wished he could remember all the little details and add names to things; Gordie would see the suggestion of feathers around its shoulders, of fur around its legs, would see the skin that peeled and the dull and cherry and angry light that came from within, and simply know what it was, what its name was and history was, what it could and could not do. Fool couldn't do that, had no idea about this thing that he just shot. It looked up at him, a tongue like a string of purple threads spilling from its mouth, and hissed, "I was hungry. It was food."

The gun was heavy again, heavy enough. Fool raised it and pulled the trigger and the demon's head exploded in a hammersplash of bone and flesh and fountaining liquid that was thicker than blood and clung together like wet rags even as it spattered back across the wooden floor and forward across his hands and shirt. Something shrieked; Fool didn't know whether it was him or another of the bar's inhabitants.

Is this what it feels like? Fool asked himself as he walked down the road. *Is this how it feels to have the fire burning in you? Is this what Balthazar feels like? Adam? Elderflower? Those little nameless demons, feeding on scraps that they find in the street or floating in Solomon Water?*

Fool was at the upper edge of the Houska, at the point where the bars began to grow larger and brighter and the streets busier. Gordie and Summer would be waiting for him somewhere down there, in among the tangles of people and demons and the things that scurried and walked and ran, all of them pushed up close and sweating and stinking and shouting and rutting, and how could they stand it? It was all around them, all the time, all this chaos and noise, pressing in on them. *How were they so numb to it?* he wondered. How could they not see it? Hear it? *Feel* it? He looked down, saw that he still had his gun in his hand, and put it back in his holster. His hands felt clumsy and nerveless and it took him three tries to drop the barrel of the weapon into the holster's leather throat and another two to cross the strap over the top of the gun and tie it. His hands were spotted with dried and flaking blood that was dark, itching against his skin, and he looked at it wonderingly before turning and bending and vomiting into the gutter.

Vomiting made Fool feel more alert, as though it had ripped through a caul that he hadn't known was draped across his face. Kicking some of the road's dust across the thin gruel of his puke, he carried on walking down into the Houska, thinking hard. What had he just done? What trouble had he caused, for himself and for Gordie and Summer, for the rest of Hell's human inhabitants? He looked down as he walked, seeing more clearly the dark spatters of blood that had soaked into his trousers. He rubbed at them, scrubbing the blood away as best he could. He should be bothered, he thought, that he couldn't remove it completely before getting into the center of the Houska, about what it signified and about who or what would see it, about who or what might already have seen it, but found that he wasn't. There seemed to be little space in his head for any sort of concern, only a kind of narrow, firing attentiveness that made his memories hard-edged with clarity. He felt warm inside, burning.

Alive.

There were few lusts in evidence on the pavements at this hour, only the tidal movement of living and unliving things heading for bars and brothels, to fuck or be fucked, to drink or be drunk, the tides thickening as he came closer to the center. Most of the humans ignored him as he walked, but some of the demons looked at Fool curiously, seeing the blood on him or perhaps smelling it; one came in close, blocking his path and sniffing at him, darting a tongue out to taste the air close to his face, but Fool merely waved an irritated hand at it and stepped around it. It released him, confusion evident on features that didn't seem to quite fit around the warped and horned skull, although whether from the smell or from Fool's refusal to show the normal human reactions of fear and passivity and deference, Fool did not stop to find out. The internal, burning attentiveness stretched to more than memories, he realized; he seemed better able to read things, to know that the demon was only intrigued rather than aggressive and that the humans around him were studiously avoiding seeing the blood, avoiding being seen as seeing it.

Into the Houska proper now, its rhythms bucking around him, watching for Gordie and Summer, aware of the smell of death upon him, aware of the glittering swords of revenge and punishment that must be hovering above him. *Foolish Fool,* he thought, but still couldn't stop the sense of exhilaration from racing through him. He had pulled the trigger not for defense, nor even for revenge, but for something else, something harder to define. He wanted to—what? *To balance things,* he thought, *to balance scales that are almost never weighted against the demons in Hell.* The humans had cheered, he suddenly remembered, as the demon's head had spattered out across the floor and dribbled away through the cracks between the rough boards. Cheered, despite the fact that they might be seen, and one had clapped.

What had he done?

Even forty-eight hours after it had been taken from Balthazar's wing, the feather still held light. Fool wondered whether it would ever truly fade; he hoped not. In his room, naked, Fool held it and let its gleam play across his skin. His feet ached from the traipse around the bars with Gordie and Summer, and his skin felt raw where he had scrubbed the blood from it in the shower after their return. Under the slow crawl of warm water, Fool had cleaned himself as best he could, using a rough cloth to make sure his skin was free of both demon and human blood. Gordie and Summer had accepted his "It's nothing" comment without further question, but in Summer's eyes at least, Fool had seen the recognition that it was far from nothing.

They had searched until they had only a few of Summer's sketches left, and gotten nowhere. When they could get the bars' staff or customers to look at the paper, they received only blank looks in return; mostly, they were ignored. Fool, uncomfortably aware of how he looked and smelled, stayed behind Gordie and Summer, but it didn't work and by the time they went back toward the train, most of the demons around them were staring openly at him. None of them approached him, though, and for that he allowed himself to feel grateful.

Returning to the office on the train, they sat in silence. The feeling of clarity, of confidence, had left Fool, dissipating on their trek around the bars and brothels, and he felt slow and exhausted. When Gordie spoke he missed it at first. "Pardon," he said, looking at his colleague's lined, weary face.

"No one knows him," Gordie had said, looking dolefully at Summer's sketch.

"Of course they do," said Summer, putting a gentle hand on Gordie's arm without, thought Fool, realizing she had done so. "They just won't tell us anything. They never talk to us." Fool, thinking about cheers and applause and a man who stopped outside a bar, said nothing.

Later, with the cool, calming light from the feather playing across his skin, Fool tried to stitch together the pieces of his day into something coherent but found he couldn't recall much of it except in a way that was both fragmentary and uneven. There seemed to be messages for him, things of significance, in everything that he had seen or heard, but he couldn't fit them together to form a coherent whole.

There was a knock at his door. He put the feather on the shelf and stared at it for a moment. His gun was on the shelf as well, and it made him uneasy to see two things next to each other. He didn't like the way the gun glinted, oily and metallic, in the feather's glow and he moved it, putting it on a lower shelf. The knock came on his door again, more urgent. Pulling on a pair of clean trousers, Fool went to the door and opened it to find Gordie outside. He, like Fool, was only partly dressed and looked exhausted, and in his hand was a tube. Tied around the metal canister was a torn and dirty white ribbon.

6

It told him that it was called Rhakshasas and was the head of the arch-deacons of Hell, and it was dressed in entrails.

The demon was sitting behind a long table, peering at Fool as though he were a new bug, fascinating but ultimately unimportant. Which, Fool supposed, he was. *Little nothing Fool*, he thought, and then Rhakshasas leaned forward. As he did so, the loops of gut tightened around him, sliding about his chest and shoulders like snakes. "You shot one of the guards of Hell," it said, and its voice was like air rising through decaying mud, emerging in wafts of stink and heat. Beside it, the other arch-deacons leaned forward; one, whose hands burned with blue, dancing flames, hissed.

The archdeacons were the judges of Hell, the face of the Bureaucracy, and Fool's white ribbon was a summoning. He had initially considered running rather than attending at the time stated on the scroll within the canister, but where would he run to? How long would it have been before they caught him, the demons or the humans? Not long, he knew; so here he was, called to the court of Hell to face the closest thing it had to an inquisition.

"You killed one of the guards of Hell," said Rhakshasas again. A gray curl of gut loosed itself from his shoulder and uncoiled languidly, droop-ing to the table. After a second, it tightened, drawing itself back into the demon's chest, and Fool suddenly had the idea that the intestines weren't a part of Rhakshasas but were something independent of him, something alive in their own right that chose to live on the demon. "You shot it."

"Yes," said Fool. There was no point in denying it; the corpse of the demon he had shot was lying on the floor between Fool and the table. It had already started to blacken and dry out, its skin flaking around it, drifting to the floor in ashy clumps. The mess of its head and the hole in its belly stared at Fool; he tried not to look back at it, keeping his eyes on Rhakshasas.

"A human, killing a demon, one of the owners of Hell," said Rhakshasas, his voice low. The flaming one hissed again, its mouth opening to reveal a tongue that curled about itself and that also burned. "Why, I wonder?"

"Because he killed a human," said Fool, unable to help himself, remembering the way the demon had spoken about the dead man. "Because he had committed a crime."

"No," said Rhakshasas, "little human, you misunderstand. I wonder, why have we allowed you to live untouched since this transgression? Why are you still breathing, Information Man Fool? Have you wondered this?"

"Yes."

"And what conclusions have you reached?"

"None," said Fool. He wished Elderflower were here; the little man always seemed to be able to talk to the archdeacons, his masters in the Bureaucracy, without becoming tongue-tied or nervous, whereas Fool could not.

"We are interested, Information Man Fool; interested in watching to see how far you will go."

The thing on fire hissed a third time, flame spattering from its mouth and sizzling against the table's surface. One of the other demons on the panel, something wrapped in shadows that billowed like black oilcloth, made a noise like two rocks being ground together.

"Ah, yes," said Rhakshasas, leaning back in his chair, the entrails around him loosening. "Information Man Fool, we have a job for you. A task, if you will, to carry out in recompense for your sins." The archdeacons laughed at this, their voices loud and harsh.

"A task?"

"A task," agreed Rhakshasas. "You are, we know, acquainted with a human currently in the process of becoming something new. We wish you to investigate him for us."

"I don't—" said Fool, and then stopped because he did; of course he did. The Man.

"Yes, you do," said Rhakshasas. "He is a concern to us. We have been Hell's administrators for a vast number of years, have seen all its various faces and appetites, and yet he is something new; or at least, something unremembered. We wish to understand him, and you have been suggested as a way of achieving this without attracting undue attention to the fact of our interest. If he proves to be nothing, then no matter."

"What do you want me to look for?" asked Fool, his fists clenching. "How can I investigate the Man without being discovered? He, *it*, has eyes and ears all over Hell."

"Precisely," said Rhakshasas. "He is not yet everywhere, but he might be. He may already be so powerful that he thinks to challenge for the leadership of Hell. Find out what he is, Information Man Fool. Find out, and tell us."

"Yes." What else could he say? *Little ordered Fool,* he thought bitterly.

"And consider, Fool: if he is already what we think that he may become, in investigating him you might find your murderer, the one who is powerful enough to eat souls. Go, Information Man. You have your orders."

"Yes," Fool repeated, and went.

The question was, where to start? How was he supposed to do this thing that he been tasked with? Fool had been fished from Limbo a little more than six years ago and given this role, but apart from the *Information Man's Guide to the Rules and Offices of Hell* he had never been trained or given guidance. When he had first started, there had been nine Information Men, but three had died later that first year and had not been replaced, three more had died the second year, one of whom had been replaced by new flesh, and then another three had died, two of whom had been replaced. Fool had ended up as the senior Information Man not because of any skill but simply through a process of winnowing. There was a line in the *Guide* he remembered, that the Information Man should "root through Hell in search of Hell's truth and justice . . . ," and it made him think of something questing through dirt and earth, forcing its way forward in a focused, driven quest. Try as he might, he couldn't see himself in that way; he had crawled through dirt, yes, but it had been a helpless, prone slither, an attempt to escape from a demon that had attacked him and his colleagues during an investigation a few years ago.

Blind rooting, questing, that was the activity of the Man. It was odd, thought Fool, that he had been told to investigate the Man, yet the Man was a better Information Man than Fool would ever be; he had parts of himself across huge tracts of Hell now, had eyes and ears wherever there were crops and dark places and earth to root in. There was no one else who knew as much about Hell, or its denizens, as the Man did.

No one? *True,* Fool thought, *but there is someone who knows a lot; there's Gordie.*

On the train back from his meeting with Rhakshasas, Fool did something he had never done before, not really; he tried to plan. As he saw it, he had two things to do; find the stealer of souls and prevent it from carrying out any more attacks, and find out something about the Man to feed to the Bureaucracy, to Rhakshasas, to keep them happy. If the Man was as powerful as Rhakshasas seemed to think he might be, or might be becoming, though, if he was involved in the killing of the Genevieve by Solomon Water, investigating him would be dangerous. Fool remembered again that wet, leathery crunch as the Man's mouth closed around one of the tiny chalkis, crushing its flesh to a mangled pulp with little apparent effort, and shuddered. He would have to be careful and not let the Man know what he was doing if possible. As for the dead man, he had had no real idea.

The offices were dark. Fool, as they all did, entered silently so as not to disturb anyone who might be sleeping. They worked separately or together, depending on the job and the amount or canisters, and each had learned early to consider the other two in their actions. Without lighting a lantern, Fool made his way to Gordie's room, stepping over each board that squeaked without really thinking about it, and then knocked at the younger man's door. There was no reply, so Fool opened it quietly but found the room beyond empty. Gordie had been called out, he assumed.

There was a groan from behind him.

Fool's reaction was so fast that, afterward, he was surprised at himself. He whirled, head filled with images of spindly demons with no skin, drawing his gun. The hallway was still dark, still empty, and then another groan came from behind one of the doors and he saw one of his friends injured or dying, bleeding, and he kicked at the door and crashed into the room beyond with his weapon held out.

Gordie was on top of Summer, in her bed, and as Fool burst in he groaned a third time. He was thrusting, his back arched up, and he was covered in sweat. Fool stumbled to a halt in the middle of the room, his gun pointing helplessly about. Summer, her arms wrapped around Gordie's back and her legs pulled up, pressing into him as he thrust, made a noise that was partway between a shriek and a groan. Fool mumbled a wordless apology and backed out, and as he did so, Summer looked at him over her lover's shoulders and her eyes were wide and scared.

Fool waited in the kitchen for them, drinking more weak coffee, staring at his reflected face dancing on the surface of the liquid. When Gordie and Summer came in, neither met his eye and both kept their heads down, making themselves drinks in silence. Finally, as though they were on trial, both sat on the opposite side of the table and faced him. "Please don't say anything," said Summer.

"Who would I tell? And why?" asked Fool, but he knew what Summer was really asking: *Don't think about it, don't draw attention to us, don't don't don't.*

"We didn't mean to," said Gordie, not looking up from his cup on the table.

"Yes we did," snapped Summer, startling both men. "I won't be ashamed of this, Gordie. I won't tell anyone, but that's not because I'm ashamed, you mustn't ever think I am." She reached across the table and took his hand, squeezing it. After a second, he squeezed back and raised his face slowly to look at Fool.

"None of my business," said Fool. "There's nothing in the *Guide* about Information Men having relationships one way or another." This was true; he'd checked while the two of them had dressed and while he was waiting for the water to come to the boil to make the coffee.

"As far as I'm concerned, you do what you want."

"Thank you," said Gordie. Summer smiled at him, and it made her face lift and appear suddenly younger. Fool reached out and placed his own hand over their linked two. He had no idea what the feelings they had for each other might actually *feel* like, had never felt anything even remotely similar, but he knew about what they were sensing, had heard about it. Their hands were warm under his own, and he realized with a sudden start that this was the first time during his life in Hell that he had touched another human being by choice; their skin moved under his own, hot and soft and as alien and as wonderful as the feather itself.

"Do what you want," he said, "only, be careful. I've brought attention to us, to me and, by association, to you. Be careful, and be cautious, and love each other. Now, Gordie, what do you know about the Man of Plants and Flowers?"

"No one knows who the Man is," said Gordie later, "but there are rumors."

What time was it? wondered Fool. He wasn't sure; after leaving Summer and Gordie, he had gone to his room and fallen asleep, and dreamed of nothing that he could remember. The feather, lying in its place on his near-empty shelf, cast its light about the room, sending glimmers into its dusty corners, bathing Fool's skin in its cooling, calm touch. Rising later, he had dressed and placed the feather in his pocket and returned to the kitchen, where Gordie was waiting.

"He's supposed to have been human, once," continued Gordie.

"Yes," said Fool, remembering when he had first met the Man. How long ago had that been? Three years? Four? Tracking time in Hell was hard, unless you made an effort; each day was like the one before and the ones that came after, blurring into a long string of similarity and fear.

"The other theory is that he's never been human, that he only appeared that way," said Gordie. "He's actually a demon, an odd one even by Hell's standards. He's able to merge with the plants, any plants, and he eats other demons. The chalkis mostly, the smaller flying things, or some of the scuttling ones. There are supposed to be parts of Hell where you can't escape from the Man, and parts where he's not reached yet, but no one really knows where each part is, or whether it's even true at all. He knows things and says it's from the extending parts of himself seeing things, hearing them, but maybe it's knowledge gained from eating things and absorbing what they know. He helps humans, but only for a price: information, news, gossip, sometimes getting them to carry out jobs for him, but the jobs never make any sense. Place a rock on a particular street, draw a pattern in chalk on a particular house, carry a dead plant to the river and throw it in.

"There's a story about the Man, that a group of demons got tired of him because they thought he was a human that dared to eat even little demons, that helping humans was unacceptable, so they went to kill him. None of them were ever seen again, and the Bureaucracy did nothing. He's supposed to know everything. I have no idea whether it's a true story or not."

"How did you find all this out?" asked Fool.

"I asked, while you were asleep," said Gordie. "Most humans will talk, if you catch them when they're tired, or if I'm not asking as an Information Man. I just ask, that's all, and they tell me what they know."

"Do you believe any of the rumors?" asked Fool, thinking, *Just ask, that's all.*

"Not really," said Gordie. "I mean, yes, he's unique in Hell as far as I can tell, but he's not odder than anything else here, is he? He's a human, I think, or was once; demons tend to avoid damaging each other except under extreme circumstances."

"Yes," said Fool again. It fitted with what he'd seen, that demons considered themselves to be Hell's real inhabitants and the humans interlopers. Besides, why would they need to attack each other? There were always humans to take their lusts and anger and desires out upon, and more waiting outside the walls if the damage on any one body grew too much and the human died.

"What's more interesting is how demons react to the Man, or to the mention of him. I mean, it's hard to talk to demons, but as an Information Man you can sometimes get them to answer you, but never about the Man. It's like they're scared of him, because they don't understand him. They almost pretend he doesn't exist."

"Is he dangerous?"

"Everything in Hell is dangerous; you told me that on my first day with you," said Gordie, smiling. "But the Man, specifically? Well, he eats some of the demonkind and scares the rest. He's huge, no one knows how big or where he is or isn't, and that makes him powerful. So, yes, he's dangerous, mostly because no one really understands him."

"He's growing," said Fool. "Getting stronger. More dangerous."

"Yes," said Gordie and then stopped as a canister dropped out of the tube in the corner of the room. It clattered to the floor and rolled toward them, ending up resting against Gordie's foot. Even in the murky lamplight, the blue ribbon wrapped around its exterior was easy to make out.

7

The house glowered. Its boards were darkened with old flames and in places they had burned or broken completely away, revealing glimpses of a shadowed interior. It had windows but they were boarded as well, the wood crudely nailed across the frames in a crosshatch of splintered and sooty planks. The doorway held no door, was empty, openmouthed and sucking, drawing in the light and letting out something worse; the house was blind but not mute, and it screamed at them.

"It's an Orphanage," said Gordie, unnecessarily. Even if Fool hadn't known, the tiny corpses in the grounds around the house would have given it away. There were only a few, charred shapes lying on earth that was scorched and blackened. One of them still burned, brief orange flames licking around its skull and dancing across its back. A trail led from the doorway to the burning child, still visible, shallow furrows cut through the dust by limbs that were tiny and weak. Flesh gleamed where the flames drew back the skin in curled, blackening skeins. And the house, or whatever was inside it, screamed.

"Perhaps you should enter?" someone asked.

"Perhaps you should," snapped Fool without looking around. He had never been inside an Orphanage, had no urge to enter one now; the burning child outside the house was bad enough, and whatever was inside would almost certainly be worse.

"No, no, I think that would be your job, Thomas," said the same person, and this time Fool recognized the voice: Elderflower's.

He had approached silently, was standing behind the three of them and smiling. It was impossible to tell whether his smile was one of amusement, irritation, or boredom; it was an expression as distant as the clouds above them, and as hard to read. Fool nodded, hoping to look contrite, but Elderflower waved the nod away and said, "I come with two messages, Thomas, important enough to be brought in person rather than wait for you to pick them up via the tubes.

"The first is that Rhakshasas is pleased to be able to grant your request, Thomas."

"What request?"

"Your weapon, Thomas, your weapon. All your weapons, in fact. Their ammunition will form far more quickly once spent. You are the only people in Hell to be allowed the use of weaponry, Thomas, besides that which occurs naturally or that which can be converted from other purposes."

Naturally? thought Fool, and then realized: *The teeth and claws and rocks and poisonous fangs. Natural.*

"It is felt that," continued Elderflower, "given the current circumstances, you should be allowed more efficient guns. The Bureaucracy has agreed that their Information Men require equipment that supports them in their roles as protectors and investigators. The archdeacons pass on their regards and hope that this pleases you."

"They do? They have?" said Fool, confused. They protected people? Investigated? Well, in theory, yes, but in practice? No. Only now they were, he realized, in some small and ill-formed way, searching for some kind of truth about dead humans, and the origins and plans of the Man. "Thank you. Or them."

"Indeed," replied Elderflower. He waited, looking at Fool, his gaze intense. Under his scrutiny, Fool felt again that Elderflower was something he did not understand, was impossible to read. Human or demon, his place in Hell was unclear to Fool. At times he portrayed himself as little more than a glorified clerk, and yet at others he spoke as though he had some minor level of power and influence within the Bureaucracy. He ran the Information Offices, or at least was the link between it and the Bureaucracy, and all his and Gordie's and Summer's reports and findings went to him, and all their tubes were delivered by him or by the administrators who worked for him. Fool thought again of the thing in the Assemblies House retrieving papers from Adam, its clawed hands scrunching the unwanted sheets up, and wondered what else those hands might do if Elderflower ordered it.

"Really, Thomas, you disappoint me," said Elderflower eventually, still smiling. "You have had such an interesting day, have proved yourself so unexpectedly dogged in your pursuit of the truth, and yet you do not ask the most obvious question."

Fool's head felt thick, muzzy. If there were questions, they weren't obvious to him; there was simply the knowledge of a blue ribbon, of a murder committed in the house behind him, a house that even now shrieked in something that might be pain or might be horror or might be fury or might be all three. What did Elderflower want?

"Why has the request been granted? Why now, and not before?" asked Summer, rescuing Fool. She had, Fool saw, removed her own gun from its holster and was staring at it, as though looking for changes to its metal solidity to indicate its new functioning.

"Precisely!" said Elderflower, clapping his tiny hands together. They were perfect, Fool noticed, the fingers delicate and the nails that topped them smoothly arched and clean. The sound of his clapping was loud, cutting through the wails from the house and through Fool's muzziness.

"And the answer is?"

"You have been *noticed*, Thomas. Two demons dead in such a short space of time! No human has done that for a long time, and certainly not with such determination. The little one means nothing, but the one in the bar, it has a parentage in Hell's hierarchies, and siblings who even now are wondering who Thomas Fool is, and why the humans are talking about him in tones of awe and respect. Oh, don't look so worried, any of you," Elderflower said, looking at their faces. *Frightened Fool*, thought Fool, *silly, idiotic Fool. Noticed Fool. How could I have been so stupid as to think that I might have gotten away with it? Walked away from Rhakshasas and the others without a mark, gotten away scot-free?*

"You have done nothing wrong, Thomas. Quite the opposite; whether you know it or not, you acted within the rules, and besides, you are interesting, have amused those who judge these things. The archdeacons find you interesting, Thomas. You are a bright spark in the boredom of Hell's days, and their eyes are upon you. There are many eyes upon you, not just those of the archdeacons of Hell.

"Besides," Elderflower said, "they need you equipped for the mission they have given you."

Fool said nothing, thinking that being *interesting* might be even more terrifying than being merely *noticed*, and feeling an odd, dangerous anger sweep over him. He was interesting because he had done what? Killed demons? Things, human and inhuman, died every day in Hell, every hour, and nothing seemed interested in them or what had killed them. Elderflower talked about obedience, but what choice did he have, really? They were here because blue ribbon tubes were compulsory to investigate, and if he or Gordie or Summer did not? How *interesting* would they be then? And who made the decision about whether a death warranted a blue ribbon? He did not know.

"What's the second thing?" he asked.

"Good, Thomas, that's better. Your presence is required tomorrow."

"My presence? At an Elevations meeting?"

"No, earlier. The delegation wishes to see the Flame Garden and then the wall and what lies beyond, and Balthazar has requested that you be their guide. They are our guests so Rhakshasas has, of course, willingly agreed."

For a moment, Fool was speechless. The words were there, in his mouth, on the tip of his tongue and the front edges of his teeth, and his lips twitched to let them out but he would not. A tour guide? A fucking *tour guide*? For Balthazar and Adam and the scribe and archive, Heaven's beauteous inhabitants, come down but not Fallen, not them, come instead to decide and Elevate and now wanting to sightsee? A reward, perhaps, for their hard work? "No, I can't," he said finally. "I have jobs to do, things to find out."

"Fool," said Elderflower, the smile weeping from his face. "Their wishes were clear. They have specifically asked for you, and we will comply because we are all servants of those who sit above us. Your colleagues can keep your investigation's fires burning as you carry out these other duties. You may not like them, but be aware: you *will* carry them out to the best of your ability, you will be courteous and answer the delegation's questions as best you can, and you will take them anywhere they wish to go and show them whatever they wish to see. Is that clear?"

"Yes," said Fool, not trusting himself to say anything else.

"Good. Now, there is a body awaiting your attentions, I believe." Elderflower turned and began to walk away, his feet making delicate taps on the surface of the roadway. Where he was going, Fool wasn't sure; the Orphanage was in the hinterland between the area most of the humans lived in and the farmlands beyond, and they had traveled here on the train and by walking the last mile. Somehow, he couldn't imagine Elderflower on a train, even one that would be, out here at least, nearly empty. He grew angrier as he watched the small figure move away; he moved like a man with no cares, almost bouncing as he walked, a man who has done his job and can leave safe in the knowledge that what happens next is for someone else to deal with.

"Elderflower," Fool called, knowing he shouldn't speak but letting the burn inside him power the words. "You send us the tube, and it tells us that there's a body here, that there's been another blue flash. Were there witnesses?"

Elderflower turned but didn't come back toward them. "No," he said, another unquantifiable look on his face.

"Then how did you know? About the murder, and the flash?"

"Because this is Hell, Thomas. This is Hell, and this is a place where things are known without understanding the knowing."

"Then you know who did this, what we'll find inside?"

"No, but Hell itself knows, Thomas."

"Then why should we investigate? If Hell already knows?"

"Because this is Hell, Thomas—have you understood nothing? We all do what it requires of us, no matter how pointless or trivial those things appear to be. We are, all of us, at the whim of forces and desires and urgencies far greater, far wider, than we can ever hope to recognize or understand. Hell knows what you will find in there, but it will not pass on that knowledge, because you need to find it for yourselves. That, too, is important, although I cannot tell why because I am told as little as you. I simply know that it is important, critical, that it be found. Rhakshasas and the other archdeacons instruct me, and I instruct you. Does that answer your questions? I can see by your face that it does not.

Then let me try again, Thomas, and I will keep it simple to aid in your understanding.

"This is Hell, and there is only the illusion of choice here. If you are told to go, then you go and you hope that you arrive at your destination without injury. You are valued, Thomas, important in your own way, although it may not feel that way to you; you have a destiny, Thomas, as we all do. We are placed in positions designated us by architects that we may never know, in structures we only see the barest fragments of. These are the mechanics of Hell, Thomas. Be happy with this and do your job."

"Yes," said Fool, thinking, *No*. He turned his back on Elderflower and in the shrieks echoing out of the Orphanage he heard the savage reflections of his own anger and impotence.

"No," said Summer.

"It's an order, Summer. Both of you, stay here. I don't know what's inside, and neither do you. There's no point in risking us all."

"No," said Summer again.

"Besides, we do," said Gordie. "They are only children."

"There are no children in Hell," said Fool, "and you shouldn't believe the rumors that there are. The things in there aren't children, they're the young of the succubae and the incubi." That wasn't quite true, he knew. There were three or four of these Orphanages scattered across Hell, places where human women came to give birth after being impregnated by incubi. The incubi took the sperm gathered from men by succubae and used it to make the women pregnant, and the resultant children were part demon and part human, and wholly monstrous. The human part of them, Elderflower had once told Fool, weakened them and made them unable to control the burning inside that came from their demonic parentage, and their flesh warped and burned almost from the moment they were born. Most died in the Orphanages; those who lived long enough to emerge tended to become predators out by the wall, where the light was lowest and the living most brutal. In Hell's past, they might have been given jobs as torturers or harriers, those things that stalked around the lakes of fire or that operated the vast, black wheels of torture; now they became part of the fabric of Hell's nightmares.

"We're coming," said Summer. "This is for all of us to do. We're all Information Men."

"We know what's in there," said Gordie again. "You know I do, better than you probably."

Summer's tone was firm, Gordie's merely conversational, and Fool didn't argue. Whatever protection he may have offered them once was gone now, he suddenly understood, shredded by the interest being shown in him. They were his colleagues, the closest things to friends he had in Hell except, perhaps, he realized with a sad little jolt, Elderflower or the Man, things he wasn't even sure were human.

They came to the doorway and the shrieks and cries were almost unbearable, not just loud but agonized and piercing. Fool, who had heard screams of most timbres during his years in Hell, had heard nothing like them before; the Orphanages were not a place he had ever had call to visit previously. The cries were continuous, tremulous, and they tugged at him even as they made his flesh crawl. Gordie felt it as well, it was obvious; he was frowning, his forehead low above his eyes, as though he were in pain, but it was Summer whom Fool was most worried about. She was already sweating, and the look on her face was as alien as anything Fool had seen on Elderflower's features. There was longing there, as though she were attracted to this tumultuous noise, wanting to open her arms to it, as well as a determination not to let it catch her. *It has barbs, this sound,* Fool thought, *ones that are already sinking deep into Summer.*

The house, or something in it, shrieked again and Summer moaned slightly, closing her eyes. Gordie put a hand on her shoulder but she shook it off sharply. As though Gordie's tiny gesture of sympathy had galvanized her, she opened her eyes and said, "Are we going?"

As they walked swiftly to the door Gordie said, "I've thought of something else, about the Man. Something I heard once."

"Later," said Fool. The Man was a problem for later, and whatever Gordie had remembered could wait.

"It's a strange thing, about how he grows. About what he eats," said Gordie.

"Tell me after we've done this," said Fool. They were at the doorway now, surrounded by wafts of heat and the smell of burning hair. The three stopped, and then, looking at each other briefly, they all stepped forward.

In the house's darkness, something glowed momentarily, the light showing them a long hallway studded with doorways on either side, and then it dimmed again. Fool moved inside, looking around as Gordie and Summer followed. As his eyes adjusted to the lower light, he saw that the nearest opening was only a step away. Through it he saw a grimy room with tangled piles of sheets and old mattresses scattered across the floor. Most of the mattresses were stained, dark blooms covering their surfaces as though shadows had become liquid and then dried. The smell of burning hair and meat and sweat crept around them, and still the shrieks came from all about them and from somewhere ahead of them, deep in the Orphanage's terrible womb.

Apart from the mattresses and sheets, the first room was empty. The room opposite it contained more mattresses and sheets along with piles of discarded towels, brittle with age and dried fluids. Sickly moss, ashy in the half-light, had furred the floor around the piles, and Fool thought that he saw the moss pulse slightly as though drawing in breath when he came close to it. Gordie started to shift the mattresses, lifting and then letting them drop, and for a moment Fool wondered why before realizing he was looking for clues. The *Guide* stressed things like "finding the information contained at the scene of the crime" and "the reading of the environment," and Gordie had taken it all to heart. Fool had tried to tell him that the book was old, ancient, making reference to rules and ideas of policing that Fool had never even heard of, but Gordie had simply replied, "But it must matter, or they wouldn't have given us them, surely?" How could you argue with that? And even if you could, why would you? Was this desperate optimism any worse than the helpless rage Fool himself had felt standing in the street over the headless corpse? He supposed not. *Poor fool,* he thought, not sure whether he meant Gordie or himself, and then something shrieked and scuttled in though the doorway.

It was aflame, low to the floor and casting off thick smoke and flickering light in oily wreaths as it went. It darted past them, crashing into the mattress that Gordie was holding, knocking it from his grip and disappearing under it as it fell. Gordie staggered, unbalanced by the collision, and Summer cried out his name. The air filled with the stench of burning meat and material as flames licked out from the underside of the mattress, more black smoke pouring out with the smell, making the air acrid and sharp. Whatever was under the mattress, it thrashed against the weight, shrieking again, the sound shuddering the hanging smoke and echoing around the room. There was an answering shriek from somewhere else in the house and the mattress shifted, bucked up, and released a drift of jittering sparks before falling back to cover the thing.

"It's a child," Summer cried, crouching. More flames capered across the mattress's surface, stopping and sizzling at the edges of the old stains. Summer tried to lift it, but the flames caught at her fingers and she dropped it. "Gordie, please," she called as the thing screeched again. Fool heard pain and longing in the cry, and anger and something more, unknowable and fragile. Gordie went to Summer, throwing a helpless look at Fool, and pushed at the mattress with her, throwing it back from the burning creature that was turning in frenzied circles under it.

"It's a child," Summer said again, but it wasn't.

It had some human flesh, that was true, but the thing on the floor was mostly demon. As well as the two human legs and arms, there were four more legs sprouting from its sides, insectile and black. Things that might have been wings had erupted from its back, but they looked wretched and stubby. Charred black lumps that might have been the remains of feathers emerged from the wings, and flesh hung from them in tatters. When it turned to them, its eyes were huge and black, taking up half of its face, and its mouth was a torn circle from which spittle and fire fell in equal measure.

And it burned.

The flames came from its mouth and from its ears, bled from around its eyes and from its anus, spilling down its legs and to the floor, where they spread in a viscous circle. It saw Summer and opened its mouth even wider, crying out through the fires, raising itself onto its human knees, and holding out its arms. It was tiny, Fool saw, only two feet long at the most, and its belly was rounded and pudgy, bouncing as it moved. It was almost completely covered by the fire now, the whole of it emerging and vanishing behind flickering blue and orange flames and the smoke that they threw off. The insectile legs hadn't grown naturally but had punched their way out of the flesh of its sides, leaving weeping, crusted scabs at their exit points. Claws were extending at the end of the legs, snapping, and tiny human hands were opening wide.

Movement behind Fool, catching at the corner of his eye. He turned to find that more of the children had arrived in the doorway, all different but somehow similar, tiny and pink and charred and warping and burning. One clambered up the doorframe, its hooked hands digging into the wood and plaster and leaving scorch marks behind. How many of them were in the hallway? Fool couldn't tell. He drew his gun, turning back to the one in the room. As he turned it scuttled forward, darting at Summer. Gordie shouted something unintelligible and fired his weapon, and a chunk of floor exploded in front of the child, sending splintered wood leaping into the air and making the thing veer sideways. It circled them so that it was between them and the door, regarding them warily, the flames dripping from its mouth and onto its chest. The ones behind it continued gathering in the doorway, the hall now lit by the unsteady, rippling illumination of their burning.

"Where's the fucking body?" asked Fool.

"Somewhere close to the door," answered Gordie without looking around. "In one of the front rooms, the tube said." He shook his gun. "It's already full, I can fire again," he said.

"Good, you might have to," said Fool. "How did the killer get in here and get out again? How many of these things are there?"

It was impossible to see the floor of the hallway now, so thick were the shifting, darting bodies. The base of the doorframe had started to smolder, gray smoke rising to join the oily black expulsions from the creatures, old burns sparking back to life in orange, glowing patches. Mouths opened, claws clicked and extended, wings broken and fully flexed. Fool raised his gun and saw Gordie do the same.

"They're demons," said Fool. "They're newborn but they aren't stupid. If they understand we can hurt them more than they hurt already, they'll let us past."

"How?" asked Gordie.

"No," said Summer, her voice low, understanding. Fool fired.

Three in one day, he thought as the nearest thing broke apart into a splash of flesh and a bright burst of flame that collapsed in on itself almost as quickly as it had expanded. *Very noticeable Fool,* and then Gordie fired and Summer screamed.

It was a worse noise than anything the demons were making, a rising howl that seemed to tear at her throat as it emerged. She pushed past Fool and Gordie but already the things had scattered, leaving the hallway empty apart from the smoke of their passing and the remains of the one Fool had killed. As the three of them emerged, the one that Gordie had shot was trying to crawl away, its broken legs twisted behind it. Even as it bled, more flames burst to life in among the exposed and torn meat of its belly. Fool stepped forward and raised his gun, but Summer pushed past him again and shot it, sobbing as she did so. "They're children," she managed to say, and then she fell to her knees in the growing pool of blood and intestines that it had left behind.

"Summer," Gordie said, "you have to keep moving. They'll come back." She raised her face to him and nodded, tears trickling across her cheeks and dripping from her chin.

"Just children," she said again, holding her arms out to Gordie. He helped her up and they hugged, unself-consciously. He whispered something in her ear and she nodded, tilting her face back and kissing him on the mouth.

"I'm sorry," Fool heard Gordie say and then the screaming started again, not Summer but the orphans, their voices twisted and brittle and furious. Already, the uneven glow had started to gather beyond the hallway's farthest doors as they massed.

The body was in the next room. It was splayed on the mattress in the corner, lying on its back, naked and exposed. It was covered in bites, small and shallow, that made Fool think of the marks left by the tinier inhabitants of Solomon Water; the orphans had been at the corpse, but they had not done much damage. The skin around the bites was reddened and raw, but the worst of the damage was around the face and genitals. Its penis was torn away at the root, the pubic hair now soaked with blood from the wrenched and ripped skin, the flaccid tube lying draped over the left thigh. Larger tears, these more destructive, were scattered around the belly and across its chest, exposing muscle under ruptured skin.

His face was gone.

"Find something to wrap it in and let's go," said Fool. Strips of skin peeled back from the skull and had been left to hang like hanks of unbrushed hair at the side of the head. One eye was a ruined mess but the other peered at Fool with a wide, owlish glare. What had done this? What demon tore off the faces of the things it fed upon, bit and ripped at them? And did so in the Orphanage, where the offspring of demons and humans might amass and attack at any second? Was it so desperate to loosen the soul from the flesh to eat it that it would treat the man like this, would tear him to a mangled, shredded mass? Just what were they hunting?

"Fool, help, please," said Gordie miserably. He was trying to lift a sheet from a pile on the other side of the room and the gray moss was rippling across its surface, pulsating, slithering toward his hands. He shook the sheet but the moss clung tight, moving like a pool of slow-flowing oil. Fool went to Gordie and gripped the other side of the sheet and they shook it as hard as they could, but still the moss clung.

"Don't call Summer," whispered Gordie as they shook. "This moss, I think it's feeding on what's left after they're born, and I don't know if . . ." He trailed off as they whipped the sheet again. Most of the moss dropped off, hitting the floor with a damp sound and immediately starting to ooze down between the floorboards. One last flick removed the remnants from the material, along with a drift of flakes from older stains whose surfaces cracked in spiderweb patterns.

The two of them rolled the body in the sheet as quickly as they could. Fool was acutely aware of the increasing ferocity of the screams filling the room, and the undercurrent notes of scurrying and chittering. The orphans were coming back, closing in on the room. Already, wisps of black smoke were coiling around the doorway, lit from within by a pulsing heartbeat of flame. He fired another shot out into the hallway, blowing a hole in the plasterboard opposite the doorway and creating a cloud of hanging white dust. Something darted past, shifting the dust, making it swirl.

"Where's Summer?" said Gordie.

"I don't know," said Fool, dragging the body toward the door. The weight pulled against him and his grip on the sheet slipped. "Help me, Gordie. Quickly."

"Where's she gone?" said Gordie and grabbed the sheet. The two of them hauled the wrapped corpse to the door. In the leaping, sinuous light, moving shadows danced across the floor and up the walls, filling the hallway. The screams' volume was a physical thing that beat at Fool's ears. He made out little and could not see the entrance to the Orphanage, so thick was the gathering smoke, but he could feel the violence, the predatory stances, the impending attack.

Summer was standing in the middle of the hallway.

8

She was wreathed in tendrils of smoke, her gun hanging loosely at her side, and she was speaking. "Please," Summer said, "I know you hurt, but a part of you is human. We only want to help this man, to find out what happened to him. Won't you tell us, please? You must have seen. And if you can't, please can you let us pass? Please?"

Amazingly, the orphans stopped moving for a moment. Fool sensed rather than saw them regarding Summer with blank-eyed malice. "Summer," he called quietly, dropping the sheet and taking a step into the hallway.

"Summer," shouted Gordie, his voice wavering, "come here. Run!"

Summer ignored them, crouching and holding her hand out to the nearest orphan, a ragged thing with a human face melting into a body that appeared to consist of a black, pulsating carapace covered in count-less limbs and a bristling, whipping tail. It retreated from her hand, hissing and shrieking, spitting fire to the floor, where it sputtered and went out. Summer held out her gun and let the orphan see it before dropping it to the floor. "You're human, just a baby," she said, "and I know you hurt, and you're angry, but hurting us won't help." Behind Fool, Gordie moaned, a low wail that sang under the cries of the orphans. And then a movement shivered around the hallway like a whirlwind collapsing in on itself and the orphans surged toward Summer.

She got off one shot, scooping up her weapon and aiming at the thing that, moments before, she had been holding her hand out to. Fool saw it spin back into the crowd, the flame of its death spraying wide above its companions. Summer threw herself backward, but she was too slow and the closest orphans leaped upon her.

Flames snaked across the thin material of her uniform as Summer screamed. Something on a thread that was burning dropped down on her from the ceiling, long legs opening to clamp around her head, and she screamed again, the cry muffled by the orphan that even now was wrapping silver threads about her. As Gordie started toward her, the threads began to blacken, their outer layer drying and crackling, flaking away, and by the time he reached her, the first flames had appeared along their cabled length. He tore at the strands, crying out as the flames snatched at his fingers, Summer screaming and pushing up at the orphan on her head as more crawled up her body. Fool fired, shooting the nearest scuttling creature, and joined Gordie in pulling the creatures from Summer. He pulled his cuff down over his hand to protect it from the twisting skeins of flames, knocking orphans to the floor and kicking at them. Most were light and hadn't gripped onto Summer strongly, but there were so many that their tide was inexorable and began to swamp them.

Gordie fired and an orphan clambering up Summer's legs exploded, the violent burst sending shards of sickly light into all corners of the hallway. He pulled the trigger again but the gun clicked emptily. Bending, he dragged Summer's gun from the mass of darkness of flesh and flame on the floor, pulling the trigger as he did so; it did not fire, and would not for anyone other than Summer. She was still tearing at the limbs of the thing that had wrapped itself around her head, untangling her hair from its grasping legs. Gordie pushed her gun into her hand and then guided the barrel up, calling, "Fire!" when it was pushed up against the body. There was another flash and a crown of flesh leaped up and danced in the air above them for a moment and then fell, spattering, to the floor.

Gordie began to drag Summer toward the Orphanage's entrance, kicking and punching at the orphans as they came close. Fool followed, dragging the corpse in its filthy shroud behind him, batting at the creatures when they approached him or his burden. Flames had caught around the edges of the torn plasterboard of the walls and were winking in and out of life. *The Orphanage must have some resistance to the flames, or the flames were not strong,* Fool thought as he moved. Summer's hair had not ignited despite the burning threads and the orphan that had been upon her head, and the wooden floors showed only superficial damage, vast black blooms almost hidden under the writhing mass of orphans.

Gordie fired again, as did Fool, their bullets carving paths through the things ahead of them, opening up a space that they moved into. Summer, sobbing, fired and then staggered as one of the orphans jumped at her and landed on her shoulder. She went to one knee and Gordie pulled at her as she knocked at the thing. They both fell, coming to rest in an ungainly heap against the wall, and the orphans swarmed again.

This time, they went for Gordie rather than Summer. Summer righted herself and started pulling at them, tearing them from him, but every one she pulled away was replaced by another, black eyes gleaming, limbs clenching and grasping, burning. Fool pushed at Summer, driving her ahead of him, pulling at the corpse. Reaching for Gordie, he kicked at the things clustering over him, but they were thicker than ever, more of them falling from above, leaping onto the writhing pile and trying to find a purchase, the man below lost to sight. Flames, bright and strong, curled from somewhere within the struggling mass and Gordie screamed. The orphans momentarily backed away from these flames before darting back in, and Fool had the oddest flash of insight: these were human flames, not demonic ones. Despite the apparent weakness of the orphans' burning, Gordie had caught alight.

"Take this," Fool shouted, pushing the knot of sheet in his hand at Summer, forcing her to grasp it and carry on with the corpse, and then turned back to Gordie. Most of the orphans were ignoring Fool, sensing Gordie's weakness, and they did little more than nip at him as he pulled them away, simply circling back to the fallen man from wherever Fool threw them. The flames, the human flames, were growing fiercer and Gordie was screaming louder. Somehow, he managed to raise himself to his hands and knees and started to crawl. Demons dangled from him, locked tight, their jaws clamped on his clothes and their clawed arms and legs grappling him. Here and there, tiny human arms and legs kicked and waved. Something with a face that looked human but that was glowing red from within hissed at Fool as he tried to knock it loose.

Fool swept an arm across Gordie's back, knocking off everything that clung to him except the rapidly growing flames. They had taken hold of his uniform, the material already charring, the flames releasing the scent of burning flesh and hair and the sound of bubbling fat, and the demons shrieked, and still they darted in and bit at Gordie, tiny mouths drooling fire, lips moving, eyes glittering. Gordie raised his face to Fool, his own mouth moving, screaming, as the fires from clothes leaped across his skin, singed it from pink to a swelling red mass. His stubbled hair sparked as it burned free from his scalp, tiny fireflies of light leaping from his head and disappearing into the roiling smoke above him. Fool tried to flap the flames out, but they had too strong a hold and merely swayed out of reach of his hand and then leaned back in, sucking eagerly at Gordie's clothes and skin.

Gordie took another stumbling lurch forward, still screaming, and raised a burning hand to Fool. Fool reached out but Gordie knocked his hand away. "Go," he said through a mouthful of flame, "go. Look after Summer." Fool took a step back as Gordie collapsed in a swirl of sparks and leaping fire and the orphans swarmed in again.

Behind Fool, Summer screamed, her voice joining the swelling chorus as the Orphanage's inhabitants began to feed.

Summer was in her room, but she was not asleep; Fool could hear her weeping.

The body Fool and Summer had dragged from the house was in the cellar, transported by two unsmiling, silent men who had used the sheet from the Orphanage rather than use their own. Gordie's corpse was still in the Orphanage and would remain there, despite Summer's exhortations to Fool to return for him. It wasn't cowardice that made him refuse to return; rather, he didn't think that, between the demons and the fire, anything of Gordie would be left. His body would be picked clean of flesh, the orphans stealing every scrap of him to eat whatever emotions they could find. Fool had a terrible vision of them, replete, still shrieking as the demonic part of them degraded the human part but somehow, for the first time in their lives, satisfied. *Would Gordie's love for Summer make them feel better?* he wondered. Were they full of stolen memories of the good times that Gordie and Summer had managed to find with each other? He hoped so, and hated them for it.

Returning to the office, Fool had found a tube from Elderflower, the contents of which had been a single sheet of parchment. In its center were the words *I am to inform you that a replacement will be provided,* and reading them had filled him with that helpless, directionless rage again. Summer had simply started crying again when she read the message and had gone to her room.

The area behind their building was walled. It was flagged, an old courtyard from when Hell had been a different place and the building had a different use. There was a mosaic set into the ground at its center, the design swallowed by earth and age and decay. The stone slabs were choked with weeds and dirt, tendrils of growth pushing up around them, lifting them and making the space an uneven buckle of edges and dips. Worn and shapeless statues lined its walls, their sightless eyes staring into the center of the space as though waiting, silent and patient and solid. Fool went out there now, still holding the scroll and leaning against the wall between two of the statues, staring up into the sky at the clouds. Even they were beautiful, he thought, graceful and distant and uncaring. He watched as they moved and shifted, catching occasional glimpses of Heaven, of its towers and spires and windows.

Gordie was gone.

He hadn't even known him that well, not really, but he had liked the man, liked him especially for his memory and for his eagerness to do his job and for how he and Summer had been together. How long that eagerness would have lasted he would never now know because, of course, Gordie was gone and he would be replaced at Hell's convenience. He and Summer were the Information Men now, and their job went on because the violence and murder went on. Somewhere, a demon was eating souls, somewhere humans were being beheaded in the streets, somewhere demons were using the flesh of humans for their pleasure, and just for a moment, Fool allowed himself to forget about it and to look at Heaven and to dream of a life where his clothes didn't smell of the scorched flesh and burned hair of his friend.

"Fool," someone said, although they stretched the word out so that it sounded more like a weary exhalation than his name. He dropped his gaze from the city above him, trying to persuade himself that the blurring of vision was a result of staring at its brightness rather than tears gathering in his eyes, and looked around. He could see no one, but the sound came again, stretched long and thin and rasping oddly.

Fool pulled his gun free, holding it out before him. Something in the overgrowth rustled and the voice called out again, this time a greeting that was soft and sibilant. "Hello, Fool."

Fool didn't reply. He didn't like the way the voice sounded, dark and rough, and he was acutely aware of the attention Elderflower had told him he was generating. How many more demons had he killed in the Orphanage? Two? Three? Was this when those dues were called in?

"Fool," said the voice again, the rustling in the plants growing more vigorous. The voice was stronger, and in a moment of clarity, Fool knew who it was; not someone in the bushes, but the bushes themselves. The Man was calling him.

"Yes?" he said.

"Come to me, Fool. I have news."

"News?"

"Of bodies and soulless things, Fool, bodies and soulless things. Tomorrow, Fool."

"Fine," said Fool, slumping back against the wall and holstering his gun. Waves of tiredness, kept at bay by activity and fear, surged over him and he wanted to sleep. "After serving the delegation and attending the Elevation meeting. I'll come then."

"Yes. And Fool?"

"Yes?"

"Bring the feather."

9

The Flame Garden swallowed the body with little fuss. Around its blackening form, for a moment, the fires leaped more wildly and then faded back down, glaring orange. No blue flames appeared, but Fool hadn't expected them to; the blue flames that danced around the bodies they fed into the Garden were the souls of the dead being released and returning to Limbo to wait before being called to fill more flesh, and this body had no soul to burn.

"And what happens now?" asked Balthazar.

"Nothing," said Fool. "It burns."

They were standing on an observation platform that jutted out from one of the thick stone walls that snaked their way through the Garden. Even this far above the flames, Fool found the heat uncomfortable and he was sweating heavily. Adam and Balthazar were both dry, their skin unmarked by perspiration or by the ash that drifted down from the skies and settled on everything else. They had been here for only a few minutes and already Fool was covered; he knew from experience that there was no point in brushing it off until he left the Garden, as more would simply fall in its place. Below them, in the flames, dark shapes moved, clumsy figures searching for the treasure the Garden irregularly gave up.

"Purification," said Balthazar, leaning out from the edge of the platform to look down into the flames. His toes curled as he leaned, clenching into the stone with a noise like the grinding of metal against granite. He kept his body straight, pivoting out at a seemingly impossible angle. "This is what Hell should be, of course, what He intended. These are the fires that give you release, are they not? Where the damned can achieve absolution?"

Fool didn't reply. He had no desire to contradict Balthazar, but the angel was wrong; the Flame Garden offered no release, no absolution, at least not in the sense that Balthazar meant. The souls were burned free of their fleshy shackles, yes, but only to disappear beyond the wall and float in Limbo until they were called and found their way into some new body. The only absolution, the only release, was Elevation. In a funny way, he suddenly realized, the soul that had occupied the body they had just dropped into the flames was freer than most; it had already been released, although to what he wasn't sure. Perhaps the blue flash that West had seen meant the soul, or some part of it, had escaped being eaten by whatever demon had attacked it. It was a nice thought.

As he thought about that first body at Solomon Water, Fool remembered the nameless one that had attacked him and Gordie. What had it said? It nagged at him, made him think that there was more there he should have done, but he couldn't work out what. He would ask Gordie later, when he returned to the office; the younger man would remember and they could work it out from there.

Ah, but no. Gordie was dead.

"What are they doing?" asked Balthazar, pointing at the shapes that crawled through the flames.

"Things appear in the Garden, and sometimes they have enough solidity to be useful," said Fool. "Furniture, tools, other things. The workers collect what they can and bring it to the shores." As they watched, one of the shapes started back to where the flames began to fade and the earth rose from them in scorched patches. Fool could not identify what the figure was carrying, but it was large and ungainly. Between that and the suit the human wore to move among the flames, the worker looked less like a human and more like some warped and distorted demon.

"Where do the things come from?" asked Balthazar, turning toward Fool but still leaning out at that impossible angle.

"I don't know," replied Fool. "The things simply appear. The demons that manage the Garden may know. I could find a supervisor for you to ask, if you like?"

"I think not," said Balthazar, dismissively. "There is no guarantee of truth from a demon." Again, Fool resisted speaking, pointing out Balthazar's error. Demons rarely lied; they had little need to.

"Perhaps the things that appear are the remains of things burned in the worlds around Heaven and Hell," said Adam quietly, "the ghosts of things lost to the flame of house fires and arson and bombs and accidents? Finding their way here through destruction and pain? It is a sobering thought, is it not? That even the simplest things in Hell are born of pain and loss and fear? We should go on, we have more to Elevate today, and I am keen to see more of Hell before we attend to that pleasant task."

They made their way back to the transport that the Bureaucracy had provided them with that morning, the same small and dented thing that Fool had been given on that first day of escort duty. Balthazar had seen that it was the same and bristled, but he had climbed in silently, and he did so again now. His wings scraped against the doorframe as he folded himself into the seat, which Fool suspected was a deliberate act, a point being made. Adam, as ever, slipped in silently, a small and patient smile never leaving his face. The scribe and archive climbed in after him, ever quiet, ever obedient.

The farmlands started not far beyond the Flame Garden. The number of buildings they passed fell, replaced by vast fields covered in thin, stunted crops. The plants were a sickly green color, and the earth below them a dark gray. Dust hung in the still air, shifting as they passed. Here and there, people worked the fields, lines of humans picking the crops or weeding while demons, singly or in pairs, looked on disinterestedly. As they drove, Adam asked infrequent questions and Balthazar muttered to himself like a chattering kettle.

"Stop," said Adam suddenly. "Stop. Stop now."

Fool pulled the transport over to the side of the road, a cracked track that threaded its way between two fields. One of the fields was full of the crop, a grass that would eventually be turned into the food that every human in Hell ate. The other was fallow, a gray expanse stretching away from them and covered in a writhing heat haze.

"Who are they?" asked Adam, getting out of the vehicle and standing by the collapsing wooden fence that surrounded the field. "What are they doing?" He was looking at a line of naked humans crouched in the cropless field, crawling slowly across it. Fool joined Adam, as did Balthazar. As they watched, one of the humans defecated, the semiliquid excrement spattering down his legs and into the dirt. He turned, churning the shit into the earth with his fingers, digging it down and then covering it with the dusty topsoil. Before he turned back, he lifted a handful of the dirt and fed himself with it, chewing and swallowing with a look of determination on his face. Then he turned back and joined the others making their way slowly across the fields. As they watched, another one of the line shit and turned, carrying out the same ritual.

"I ask again, Fool: who are they and what are they doing?" said Adam, and for the first time, his voice contained something other than patience and compassion. He sounded disgusted, horrified, his nose wrinkling as though the smell of the effluvia had reached him. Maybe it had, although Fool could smell nothing.

"They're fertilizing the ground," said Fool. "They're Aruhlians. They are born to the task, as we all are in Hell, given our roles when we are brought in from outside. They eat the dust and earth and drink rainwater and use what they produce from themselves as food for the ground. All Hell's farms are kept alive by them. They hope to achieve absolution by eating enough of Hell's dirt." Fool knew about the Aruhlians because he had been called to them not long after his own birth, after several of their number had vanished. The investigation hadn't taken long; Fool had followed a set of churned and broken tracks and eventually found the missing workers; they had been dead, buried in one of the fields like the shit whose remains stained their companions' fingers.

Up close, the Aruhlians *stank*, a lurid stench that had an almost physical presence forming a ring around them. Their skin had been almost as gray as the earth they ate, he remembered, and had sagged from them like old sacking. They had clustered together, nestling into each other for safety as one of them had asked, "Why us? We make no trouble. Why should something wish to hurt us?" Their chief, if that's what he was, had looked at Fool with troubled eyes, tears tracking down the dirt on his face. His eyes were yellow around pupils of a watery, bloodshot blue.

Something, Fool had noted, not *someone.* They already suspected what he knew, that their compatriots had been murdered by a demon, probably one of the farm overseers, bored and hungry. *Why you,* he wanted to say, *why you? Why not? Because you have hope, perhaps. Even amid this terrible life you have hope, hope that if you eat enough dust and shit, you will be Elevated, and to demons it must taste as sweet as your flesh is foul,* but he didn't. Instead, he arranged for the bodies to be removed to the Garden and left the Aruhlians to mourn and to continue eating dirt, chewing their way, they hoped, to salvation. He had not investigated, and he sent a tube to Elderflower stamped NO FOLLOW-UP and had not thought about them since.

"Christ's love," said Adam softly. "You see, Balthazar, how Hell's very earth is seeded by misery and foulness?"

"It's Hell," Balthazar said. "How else should it be?" He unfurled his wings and beat them lazily. In the distance, one or two of the Aruhlians had seen them and had stopped, were looking in their direction. Fool wondered whether they were the group he had spoken to those years earlier, whether any of them had survived on their diet of dirt and roots and rain. He supposed not.

With a noise that sounded weary with pity, Adam returned to the transport and, after a moment, Fool followed.

The sea swelled, a wave rolling forward to crash into the wall and then falling back, the surface undulating just below the upper edge of the thick stone barrier, and the faces in it twisted and roiled, mouths opening and closing silently. Fool had never been sure whether those faces meant the souls in Limbo were in pain, or whether it was simply the way souls were when they were cleaved from flesh, constantly moving and searching and wanting. *This is Hell,* he thought as he looked down from the wall, *they're in pain. Of course they're in pain.*

"My Christ," said Adam almost inaudibly.

"They suffer," said Balthazar. "The souls of sinners. Good."

"Why are you so cruel? You're an angel, aren't you?" asked Fool, unable to help himself and stunned at his words. *What's happening to me?* he wondered. *What's happening to me, that I'm being like this? Little brave, stupid Fool.*

Balthazar, surprisingly, gave Fool's question a moment's thought and then replied in a calm voice. "Am I cruel?"

"Yes," said Fool, entertaining a sudden image of Balthazar's flame curling around him and slicing him in two.

"Perhaps so," said Balthazar. "I am angelic flesh, Information Man Fool, created for the purposes of flame and strength. In Heaven, my job is to patrol the walls, to be a soldier in the armies of light and good. I am created not for showing grand mercies, nor much compassion, but for the muscular brutalities of goodness."

"There are so many," said Adam, still almost inaudible. "I had not realized." Another wave rose from the ocean, the water's shifting surface a splintered and bucking mosaic of faces that shrieked without sound. It was impossible to tell whether the faces were male or female, young or old, and their edges blurred into each other in places, making larger images with myriad eyes and countless mouths, all open and wretched.

"How are they given flesh?" asked Balthazar. "Brought in from Limbo to suffering?"

"They are fished," said Fool, pointing along the top of the wall. Farther along it, on a ledge sticking out over the water's surface, was a crouched figure, hunched down over its haunches and with long arms dangling in front of it. It was peering intently into the waters of Limbo, watching the flow and eddy of the ocean at its feet.

"What is it?"

"I don't know. A demon, I presume. Even among demons, these are supposed to be the eldest. They inhabited Hell first, so it's said, and never talk to anyone, human or demon. For most demons we're food, or slaves, or sport, or all three, but these never acknowledge our existence except once, at the beginning."

As they watched, the thing on the ledge reached into the water; its hands were huge and webbed. It swirled them around in the water and then withdrew them. Water dripped from the long, curved claws and something gray and sodden hung in its grasp. The thing sniffed at it, let out a long, black tongue to lick at it, and then gently placed it back into the water. After another moment, it withdrew a second dripping thing that it sniffed and tasted; this one, it placed at the side of itself on the ground.

The gray thing trembled and then began to inflate. It bulged, fluttering and swelling, gaining color so that it lost its gray pallor and became a pale pink. Tendrils unfurled from it, rolling across the ground and then filling, forming into arms and legs, as the air above it filled with dust motes and shadows that swirled and descended into the growing flesh. A sound like the dragging of blades across metal and glass shrieked about them, setting Fool's teeth on edge. Adam and Balthazar watched, not reacting, as the soul accreted flesh about itself, bulging and rippling into a semblance of life. As it grew, the demon crouched next to it, also watching.

Finally, the soul formed a complete human about itself, a young man who gasped and rolled over onto his front, spewing water from his lungs. The demon watched him, impassive.

The demon finally rose, lifting the man to his feet.

"What will happen to him?" asked Adam.

"He'll become a Genevieve or a laborer," said Fool. "The younger ones usually do. I was older, less beautiful, so I was created as an Information Man. He'll know where he is but not why, know he is punished but not the reason."

"And this is how it always is?"

"Sometimes they come from deeper," said Fool and pointed out at the fragile surface of the sea. Far out, a tiny coracle floated, another of the demons crouched in it. This one had a net clenched in its hands that it was trailing through the water, occasionally twitching it.

"How do they know which ones to bring, and how many to bring?"

"I don't know," said Fool, thinking about the canisters that fell from the tubes. "Hell has ways of communicating. Rhakshasas and the other archdeacons, the elders in the Bureaucracy, they make the decisions and we are informed about what they decide."

"We? You are a human, Fool, yet you equate yourself with the demons of Hell?" Adam was smiling as he spoke. *Do I?* thought Fool. *Do I? I don't know, I'm just me, little Fool, little Fool in Hell.*

Back on the wall, the demon began to lead the young man away, pushing him none too gently along the path atop the wall back toward one of the warehouses where he would be clothed and given his new life. "Where am I?" the man asked as he walked.

"Hell," replied the demon. "You are in Hell."

As Fool and the angels turned to go, they heard the man start to sob.

10

The Sorrowful were different today.

At first, Fool couldn't decide what it was about them that had changed, but then he realized: they were moving. Not all of them, certainly, but enough to give the watching masses a motion like the movement of the ocean beyond the wall, creating human eddies in front of Assemblies House.

Behind him, the process of Elevation was in full flow, the back-and-forth between Elderflower and Adam a background noise that he had learned to ignore. If he was needed, he would be called, but until then he waited and as he waited, he watched.

Through the dirt on the windows it was impossible to make out individuals in the crowd of the Sorrowful, but he saw how they shifted. They pushed, had an urgency to them that was not normal. Although he couldn't read them, and they were never raised for long, one or two people in the crowd had brought along painted signs on the end of poles. Perhaps most unusually, he could hear the crowd's voice whereas normally it was silent; its communication was a low rumble, not speech exactly but the thing that happened before speech, the sound of a throat being cleared, of something attracting attention before announcing or requesting.

Before demanding.

What was happening here? The Sorrowful were helpless, desperate, not this moving, volatile thing. Volatile? Yes, he realized, they were volatile in a way they hadn't been before, restless and tense. He could *see* it, see the change in them; these weren't the crowds of Hell he was used to. Even as he watched, someone threw something; whatever it was looped through the air before falling short of the building, landing in one of the abandoned courtyards that stood, railed off, in the space between it and the crowd. The missile was a chunk of masonry, its edges jagged. More signs were fluttering about the crowd's heads now, dotted across the mass like speckles. Fool rubbed at the dirt on the window, trying to clear a space, but it helped little; the words on the signs remained little more than shifting blurs. Another lump of something rose from the crowd, arced over their heads, and fell inelegantly to the ground near its earlier companion. The crowd surged around the place it had emerged from, the surge's ripples flowing out to the edges before dissipating. The volume was rising, a chant forming from the mass, growing higher in pitch.

Another missile came from the crowd, this one thrown from closer and with more force, hitting the wall of the building somewhere to the left of the window Fool was peering through. Another, and although he didn't see it connect, Fool heard the sharp crack of breaking glass. Someone cheered and, as though some secret symbol had finally been recognized and a code broken, the Sorrowful found their voice.

He still had the shouts ringing in his ears when he arrived at the Man's house.

Fool didn't enter immediately. Instead, he walked around the property and looked at it, *really* looked, for the first time. It was large and rambling, and its foundations and the lower parts of its walls were lost behind thick tangles of plants and bushes. Although there were none of the mouths that Fool had become used to seeing within the house, he saw an awful lot of chalkis' skeletons caught in the foliage, strands and leaves and branches twisted around the tiny bones, emerging from eye sockets and disappearing into fleshless mouths. Blooms grew on some of the plants, large red buds that stank of something like burned and rotted flesh. Was that how he attracted the chalkis outside? By a smell that made them think of torn flesh bleeding emotions and memories?

The rear of the house opened onto what had probably been a walled garden at some point in the past but was now little more than a thick, furious wasteland filled with more of the Man. He had grown bigger here, stunted trees emerging from the hectic greenery, bent and dark.

Through the remains of the gate, rusted bars bent to odd angles by the pressure of the growth from within, Fool watched as the Man moved in a constant undulation, the sound of him like paper constantly being drawn across paper. There were shapes in the tangles of the Man, larger ones; whiteness showed as the Man moved, bones long since stripped clean glimmering into view and then disappearing again.

Were they the skeletons of humans? Fool wondered. Or of larger chalkis, the ones that were as large as men or larger? Or were they the skeletons of something else entirely?

Was the Man eating demons? Was that what Gordie had intended to tell him, just before they entered the Orphanage?

"Fool," said a voice that was not, truly, a voice, "what are you doing?"

"Nothing," said Fool, almost truthfully. "Thinking."

"Indeed? Well, I would prefer you come inside and speak, Fool. I have need of entertainment. Oh, and Fool?"

"Yes?"

"Did you bring it?"

Inside the Man's home, it was dark, the shadows bristling and shifting about Fool as he entered. Things rolled and slipped under his feet as he went to the far room, the skin of them rough and warm through the thin soles of the boots. Once, something gasped in the blackness above Fool's head, the gasp accompanied by a sound like dry twigs snapping and a tiny, sickly flash of blue. The Man, ever hungry, ever eating.

Once Fool was in the room, the Man stretched his ever-growing limbs around him, the fronds and branches covering all the walls now. The doorway to the room, to Fool's back, was the only space left empty, an open mouth spitting him into the Man's foliage and flesh. He stepped toward the mass in the corner, where he assumed the Man to be, where the human skin and bone of him had been in those first visits, and finally replied, a low "Yes." He took the feather from his inner pocket, marveling even now at the way its light filled the room, and held it out.

One of the Man's mouths rose up before Fool like a snake, the furred head split wide and with the purpled flesh of its maw showing. Curled thorns along its edges looked like teeth, and although the mouth had no eyes above it, Fool was suddenly convinced it was looking closely at him, that it was licking lips that it did not have with a tongue that did not exist. "Give, Fool," said the Man, the words elongating as though he were breathing as much as speaking, the sound coming from all around the room. Fool hesitated, knowing he had little choice but reluctant nonetheless.

"Give," said the Man again, the word stretching out even further, and Fool placed the feather into the open mouth. It snapped shut, trembling, locking the glow into itself, and then whipped back into the Man's mass.

There was a stillness in the room, and then the Man's bulk began to shake, shivering vibrations dancing along the stems that surrounded Fool and setting the room about him into a palsy that continued for several minutes. As the Man pulsed around Fool, he made a noise like bubbling water that Fool realized, after a moment, was laughter. The movement alarmed the creatures that clung to the room's ceiling, setting them fluttering, dropping away from perches on water-slicked cornices and in the holes in the plaster to dart through the air above him.

The feather's glow was traveling along the Man, traveling *through* the Man; Fool tracked it by watching the pale gleam as it moved around the room, sometimes close to the Man's surface and at others almost disappearing, visible only as a fragmentary glimmer or as a set of leaping, shifting shadows.

"Fool, it's magnificent!" said the Man eventually. "Truly magnificent! In all my time here, in all the places I have grown into, and in all the things I have consumed, I have never held anything so magnificent. And to think, this is a thing of mass and weight and touch! Sometimes, just sometimes, I can see the attraction of the meat and flesh, of remaining tightly bound in a single shape, if this is the way in which that binding can be. Although, of course, this isn't really from a thing of mass, of bound flesh, is it? This is something else, something above and beyond, the gristle and bone and skin of an angel that is neither truly gristle nor bone nor truly skin, but something more, a thing of Heaven's lightness and Heaven's grace. Fool, do you understand what you have been given here? Understand its power?"

"No," said Fool, "but I know it's beautiful."

"It is, it is," said the Man, "but it is so much more, Fool, so much greater than mere beauty. It is a tool, Fool, so powerful that I do not like the idea of giving this back to you, of you possessing this when I do not.

I am considering killing you so that I may own it, Fool. You entertain me, it's true, but you also investigate me, peering around my home and setting your quisling to ask questions about me so that you can tell Hell all about me, and I worry, Fool, I worry that you are becoming a nuisance."

Mouths rose up around Fool, opening, purpled inner surfaces and thorn teeth rustling like dry leather. They swayed as they rose, hypnotic, sinuous, their stems curling back and forth, writhing around each other. Fool dropped a hand to his gun but one of the mouths was quicker, darting forward and tearing the weapon from Fool's leg and sending it spinning across the room. It clattered against the far wall and he went to follow it, but the stems came together and stopped him, fatter limbs threading through the barrier so that he could not tear his way through. He stepped back, hoping to find the doorway without turning, but bumped into another moving wall of fronds and jagged, hard edges and knew he was surrounded.

Vines, or something like them, began to curl around Fool's feet, humping up over his shoes and catching at the edges of his trousers, tearing the thin cloth as they twisted about him. More of the vines wove themselves around his arms, pulling them out from his body, tugged at his legs, and then lifted him, spreading him out and holding him above the floor. The flying creatures began to screech, chittering to themselves and to the Man and Fool, swooping around him as the Man's many limbs dug into his skin and more of the mouths rose up, trembling and snapping.

"No," said the Man after another long moment during which the mouths came closer and the vines drew tauter. "No, not now. Despite your inquisitiveness, you are too interesting, Fool, what's *happening* is too interesting to interrupt it now, and you are such a part of it that if I took you away it might all stop. Besides, you may prove useful yet." The mouths dropped away, closing and drooping so that they looked like seed pods again, their stems coiling in loose whorls on the floor, and the vines unthreaded themselves from around his arms and legs, springing away so that he fell to the floor. It smelled of dirt and wetness and old, dead blood.

From somewhere in the Man's bulk a pale glow reappeared, fractured and torn by his writhing branches, growing brighter as the feather was brought out and held toward Fool. It was clenched in a mouth, unmarked, its barb sticking out from between two thorns. Fool reached out and took it, pulling so that it slipped out from the closed mouth with a low, silken sound. As the Man released the feather, the room around Fool shivered again, violently at first, before calming. Fool had the idea that it was a shiver of release, as though the Man had shuddered his way down from orgasm into relaxation.

A moment later, a languid stem rose in front of Fool with his gun twisted within it. Fool took the gun and slipped it back in the holster, finding that the Man had torn the straps when it ripped the weapon away and that he could no longer secure it. The stem retreated slowly back into the Man's mass, which settled all around the room into comfortable, watchful stillness.

"Fascinating, don't you think, Fool?" said the Man. Fool didn't know what to say, so he stayed silent. "Why do you think, Fool, that I told you I was considering killing you? That I know you've been asking questions about me?"

"I don't know. To toy with me? Because I don't matter?" Fool's heart was still beating too fast, his skin clammy with sweat and sick with unused adrenaline. *Little helpless Fool, little vulnerable Fool,* he thought briefly.

"Ah, Fool, but you do matter! I told you because I could do no other," said the Man. "The feather is a tool, I told you that; it is the angelic matter, and it compels the holder to be truthful. It is the stuff of God's closest, Fool, of God's trusted servants and mightiest weapons, and it is created of God's truth and beauty and honor and love. It allows only the truth because it is, itself, absolutely true."

"I don't understand," said Fool. He understood so little, not Hell nor Heaven, certainly not demons nor angels nor people. *Perhaps the only thing I understand is violence,* he thought, *murder and rape and beatings. Headless corpses and flesh with no soul left within it and babies that burn. Perhaps that's all I'm allowed to understand.*

"What is there to understand, Fool?" said the Man, interrupting Fool's thoughts. "What is there to comprehend? This is Hell, and you have been given a piece of Heaven. Treasure it, Fool, for you may not have it long; it has no place here in Hell."

"Then why give it back to me at all?"

"Because it amuses me to leave it with you," said the Man, "to know that it is out there somewhere out of my ownership, exposed to Hell and Hell exposed to it. It is a spark of order in Hell's chaos, Fool, and chaos and order do not mix well. They make infernos, Fool, great conflagrations that can burn entire worlds to the ground. I shall enjoy seeing this play out, I think, enjoy watching you dance to tunes you cannot possibly comprehend played by beings you cannot see, lighting flames around you as you go."

"And you do?" said Fool, angry and weary and thinking of Gordie, burning. "You understand? You comprehend, do you? You can see everything? So tell me what's going on, tell me where to look for this demon."

"You're growing brave, Fool, and that's part of the joy of this situation, and the Bureaucracy is growing nervous and that's joyful, too! Who would have thought Fool the Information Man could kill demons, would dare to speak to me like that? Would be charged with investigating me? Would venture into an Orphanage, would emerge dragging the corpse of one of Hell's slain? Oh, Fool, this is fascination itself, and watching it unfold is an endless delight! I could tell you some of this, Fool, but less than you might think or hope. No, this is for you to sort, Fool, to solve!

"And Fool? Be careful. I have chosen not to kill you, but I can change my mind. My reach is long, Fool, from the great trees that line the Flame Garden to the moss that creeps up the walls where the humans live. My vision may not yet take in all of Hell—there are some places that are not yet available to me—but most places are reachable. *You* are reachable, Fool, you are takeable, don't forget that.

"But still, the feather deserves something, does it not? And I brought you here with the promise of news, yes? Very well. First, a suggestion that you have no doubt considered but that I will make anyway: look to the Heights, Fool, to Crow Heights. It is where Hell's grandest and oldest live, cloistered together, hidden from Hell's tawdry delights. Ask yourself, Fool, where would something ancient and violent live? In among the ancient and violent, where it might stay hidden or ignored. Surely this is where the thing you seek must hide itself, in the sight of things that would consider it normal? And a last thing, Fool, a last piece of information for you to take: yesterday, Fool, yesterday there were miseries in one of the boardinghouses out beyond the Houska's edges, where the Genevieves live. Someone has vanished, Fool, a beautiful someone with young flesh. Purchasable flesh. Beatable flesh, Fool, maybe the beaten flesh that you are investigating and that refuses to talk to you despite Morgan's most tender ministrations."

"A boardinghouse? Which one?"

"The one with the demons lining its roof, Fool. Now, I have told you what I know and I shall tell you what more I can, when I can, but I expect payment for my wisdom, Fool. I expect amusement, not orders or anger, Fool; remember that. Investigate away, Fool, investigate! Find me a demon that I have not seen before, a murderer of humans and a devourer of souls. Tell me where it is that I might introduce myself. Tell me what the Bureaucracy thinks, what Rhakshasas asks about me, and tell them what you want about me, tell them all of it so that they might fear me more, that the knowledge of me and all I am and might become can sew threads of disquiet about them. I am growing, Fool, every day, and they have reason to fear me and I would have them know it. Tell all, Fool, and catch your demon."

It sounded so simple, so compact, put like that. Merely find it and catch it, this demon newly emerged or newly woken and capable of doing such violence to human flesh. Fool closed his eyes for a moment, seeing in the darkness body after torn body, human and demon alike. "Aren't you worried? Scared? You were human once, and this thing could discover you helping me, could find you, find your soul. Kill you."

The Man shook around Fool again, this time with amusement. He was laughing, Fool realized, laughing at Fool's question. Laughing at Fool. "No, Fool, my soul is a splintered, spreading thing, hidden in the tiny and invisible, in the plants. I am the drab greenery, Fool, and I am spread too wide to be worried about any demon. Parts of me die every day, Fool, torn up or eaten or crushed flat, yet I live on unharmed, and the heart of me is protected. I have weapons and defenses, Fool, more than you or that flesh-draped lickspittle Rhakshasas will ever know. Now, Fool, we are done. I have to eat, and you have to entertain me. Go, Fool, and be amusing."

Amusing Fool, little entertaining Fool, thought Fool and turned to go. The Man pulled himself apart, revealing the doorway. Above Fool, darting back and forth in the humid air, the flying creatures swooped toward the doorway, flashing around his head. One of them came too close and its wing brushed his face, its touch surprisingly soft and smooth, the smell of it powdery and dry. It chirped, high-pitched and shrill, as it went past him, its wings beating, moving the air across his scalp in a warm, anxious breath.

As Fool stepped out of the room there was a crunch as one of the Man's mouths caught a flying thing, and a long, moist sigh from the Man.

11

It was night when he heard it; someone was crying.

Fool wasn't in bed, hadn't even made it back to his room. Rather, he was in the little kitchen waiting for the water sputtering from the tap to run clear rather than brown so that he could have a large drink. He had spent the time after his visit to the Man walking the streets of the Houska, simply looking. People and demons moved around him in thick, oily streams, the air dense with the smells of candle smoke and sweat, simmering with anticipation and fear. As he had left the Man, another human had been entering the Man's home, furtive and scurrying. *What secret had he been carrying?* Fool wondered. What knowledge had he been seeking, and what price would he pay? He imagined the Man's limbs stretching out through most of Hell, secrets and rumors and knowledge pulsing along the veins of him like sap, allowed to flower in some places and curdled to nothing in others, a network of information and exchange. And him, Fool, where was he in it all? A tiny morsel drifting along the Man's pathways, or something outside, an irritation to be tolerated until Rhakshasas's demands on him made the Man choose to remove him? *Little moving Fool,* Fool thought, seeing himself as a tiny thing being buffeted along streams not of his making, and made his way to the train. There was nothing more he could learn here.

Summer was the only other person in the offices. Fool went to her room, but even from outside he realized that the crying was not coming from there. He turned, going instead to the doorway of Gordie's room. The door was shut and he knocked upon it, gently at first and then harder when he received no answer. When he still heard nothing from beyond the door except crying, he opened it slowly, other hand dropping to his gun; it was rare, but not unheard of, for ghosts or demons pretending to be ghosts to take up residency in the rooms of the recently dead and use whatever grief and upset they could generate to feed.

The door opened onto a room without light. Fool stepped back from the doorway and peered into the gloom, trying to make out something, *anything*, that would tell him what was in there. "Summer?" he asked, but still there was no reply but tears. A patch of the darkness shifted, something glinting as it moved, and then was gone. A long, low moan came from the darkness, feral and raw, and then a long, rough scratching. His hand tensed on the butt of the gun and then loosened, then tightened again, indecisive; there was little point in drawing it if it was a ghost, bullets would do nothing to it and would be no defense. If it was a demon, though, come to avenge the death of the thing in the bar, or simply to punish Fool for allowing himself to be noticed, for being a human who had the temerity to be something other than a victim, then he might have a moment in which he could defend himself. He stepped back from the doorway and said, trying to keep the catch and shake from his voice, "Show yourself."

More scratching, another moan, and then a voice said, "I can't remember his face."

It was Summer's, almost. Her voice was thick, slurred, and wet. Fool stepped into the room, lighting the lamp and letting its sallow glow curl around the corners of the space. Summer was sitting against the rear wall, knees drawn up to her belly, a pad on her knee. Her face was reddened and puffy, slick with tears and mucus, hair disheveled. She was running her hand back and forth across the paper, sketching furiously. As Fool watched, unsure of what to do, she tore the paper from the pad and crumpled it, casting it aside where it joined others scattered about her.

"His face," said Summer, "I can't remember his face. What did he look like? What did my Gordie look like?"

Fool sat beside Summer against the wall. She had already started sketching on the blank paper, pencil lining in a face that might have been Gordie but might equally have been a stranger on the street or one of the bodies they sent to the Garden. After a moment, he reached out and gently put his hand over Summer's, stopping her drawing. She looked at him, more tears flowing, and said, "Please."

"He looked like Gordie. He looked like this room," said Fool, gesturing about him. Unlike his own austere chamber, Gordie's was cluttered and cramped. The walls were covered in pieces of paper, each piece thick with notes and ideas and morsels of information, all in Gordie's tidy, efficient hand. Phrases and words leaped out at Fool like sparks jumping up from fires: *The Ronwe can speak, The Man builds, an island? Cattle? Food?* All Gordie's thoughts and knowledge and ideas laid out before them. Some of the pieces of paper were connected by pieces of string or cord, links between his suspicions or facts, links between this demon and that murder, this place and that rumor.

"This is Gordie," Fool said. "All this, all these things that he knew and learned and wanted to know, these things are him. He gathered so much together, knew so much more than I do. That was Gordie. I don't know who the Ronwe are, do you? Or the island? What island? We don't know, but Gordie did. This is Gordie, this is what he was and this is what he did. This is how to remember him."

Summer took a deep, ragged breath and looked around the room. "Yes," she said eventually. She began to sketch again, and this time the face that appeared under her pencil was Gordie, the real Gordie, the man who had been Fool's treasure trove of information and Summer's lover for these past months. Fool, watching, felt a sudden clenched ache inside himself, knowing that no one would ever sketch him in the passionate, desperate way Summer was sketching Gordie, and closed his eyes so he could not see.

In the darkness of his mind, Fool wondered. Gordie had died in the Orphanage, burned and savaged, and he could not help but wonder, was it a punishment for the things on the walls, for the things that Gordie had learned and tried to learn and known that he was not supposed to know?

Had Fool killed Gordie by asking him to know about Hell?

With a torn sigh, Summer stopped sketching and collapsed against Fool, weeping again. Fool put his arms around her and pulled her into a hug, the first time he had ever done so, and they sat for a long time in the absence of Gordie.

12

NAME OF DECEASED: Unknown

RESIDENCE OF DECEASED: Unknown—probable resident of a boarding-house, see IDENTIFYING MARKS below

LOCATION OF DECEASED: Western Pipe Orphanage

DESCRIPTION OF DECEASED: Male, early twenties, blond hair. Average height. Average levels of undernourishment. Evidence of vitamin deficiency.

IDENTIFYING MARKS: None, although there are scars evident to the buttocks, legs, and shoulders consistent with victim having been a Genevieve.

INJURIES/CAUSE OF DEATH: Severe trauma to body and head; flesh has been torn from skull and one eye punctured. Penis has been removed—likely torn free rather than cut or bitten. Evidence of smaller wounds from postmortem predation, and of older wounds to the buttocks and thighs. Burns to skin. Cause of death: take your pick. Major organ trauma and blood loss are the technical reasons, but each of his injuries alone could well have killed him.

ADDITIONAL INFORMATION: Fool, this one wouldn't talk much either. He's had his soul removed—there's nothing left in him at all. He's definitely another Genevieve, although he's not been doing it as long as the first victim. The damage to the buttocks and thighs isn't as well established and there's less older, healed trauma. He's looked after himself, as far as it went, despite a lack of good food. I eventually had to ask questions of his flesh using the four chains, like last time. He told me it was a client but again not one met in the Houska, and also that he didn't have any suspicions about the client. Whatever hired him didn't look violent or disturbing, at any rate. The four chains are limited and can generate only yes-or-no responses, of course—although if you have enough bodies from the same event you can sometimes ask the questions of them in sequence and get fuller information. Still, it's enough for me to be confident this is the same murderer of the man recovered at Solomon Water.

The violence here is, if anything, worse than that first one, more sustained and wide-ranging. Tearing a penis off at its roots takes not just strength but will, determination, and isn't something that can be done that easily— muscle and tendon is stronger than you'd imagine. I think the scalp was peeled back by hand as well—there's damage to the flesh and bone of the skull that might correspond to fingers or claws. He was alive when all this was done to him, incidentally, and he must have been screaming and fighting. There's damage to his fingernails as though he was scratching against something, but there's no residue under the nails, which makes sense if the attacker is demonic—they're rarely soft enough to be harmed by human hands. This is something terrible doing these things, Fool, something very powerful indeed, and I'd imagine old and not keen on being investigated. Be careful.

Fool read Morgan's report, what there was of it, on the train out to the flatlands beyond the Houska. It was typed on paper that was thin and gray, the ink smearing as he held it, and it told him nothing that he hadn't expected. The report had been waiting for him when he awoke, cramped and cold and still sitting against the wall in Gordie's room after only a couple of hours' sleep. He had been alone when he awoke, surrounded by Gordie's memories and thoughts, and he had ached when he stood. Fool had crumpled the flimsy sheet into his pocket without looking at it and gone to rouse Summer, wanting to move, to focus, to keep investigating.

Summer was gone.

It wasn't that she had vanished, but that the things that had made her Summer had seemingly disappeared; her body was there, she moved around, but when she spoke, her voice was flat and uninflected and she neither questioned nor made suggestions when Fool told her about the Man's information and that he might have given them a way to identify one of the dead Genevieves. Her eyes, rimmed with scarlet puffiness, looked downward most of the time, coming up only once, when Fool mentioned Gordie. She made no reference to the previous night. It was as though the losing of his face and finding it again had made his death more real for her, and that in dying Gordie had taken with him the part of Summer that she had let him have, the part that made her something other than mere animated flesh. *Perhaps he did,* thought Fool. He had never given even the smallest part of himself to someone else and had no idea what it might feel like, what it might be like if they went away and took that gifted part with them. He had no idea what to say to her, so he said nothing. After he read the report, he handed it to her. She read it and handed it back silently.

The train was nearly empty. It was early in the afternoon, and most people either slept or were at their Bureaucracy-appointed tasks. In the distance, the smokestacks belched their greasy breath into the sky; the noise of the factories reached them through the open window of the train like the rumble of approaching thunder.

They moved slowly through the Houska. It seemed smaller during the day, its walls and streets more claustrophobic without the glamour of darkness and the lights that breathed from each doorway when the heats of sex and drink and violence rose each night. Some of the bars were open but they appeared quiet. There were few demons visible.

The train rolled on, its rhythm lolling Fool into an uneasy doze. How long since he had slept well? A month? A year? Never? He felt as though he was always lagging behind, always one or two or three steps behind where he ought to be, missing things, too tired to see straight or clearly. Rests were always taken between other things, squeezed in like this, wedged in between this meeting or that body, and even when he made it to his bed, the time available to him was too little. He thought again of the two dead men, of flesh torn beyond recognition, of another soul set loose, of Gordie aflame, and of Summer, and he thought that there were different types of death and that they were all as terrible as each other.

Gordie had once told Fool that Hell had been a place of rigid hierarchies somewhere back in its history, that each area corresponded to the punishments meted out for a particular sort of sin, and that explained why it still had distinct geographies. The Houska, where the rakes and addicts had been punished, was now for nightlife, for the bars and prostitution. Crow Heights' walled solidity had always been for the residences of the ancient and powerful, the humans living cramped together in Eve's Harbor (which was nowhere near water and which the demons called Cattletown and which had once been the place of rack and confinement), the demons in the sprawling expanses of North and South Hope (actually one huge, curving area surrounding most of the Houska and abutting Eve's Harbor, and which the humans called simply Pipe). Intertwined with these inhabited areas were Hell's other spaces: the Bureaucracy, which described both the area itself and the function attended to in the offices and halls that it consisted of; the industrial estates that sat permanently under vast clouds of spewing gray and black smoke; the Flame Garden where the dead went; and the farmlands. Each area had its functions and its inhabitants, and there was little mixing between them except in the Houska and in places that were sometimes called the Sisters. The boardinghouses were in one of the Sisters, a blurred edge between the Houska and North Hope filled with numerous squat buildings constructed of old, black wood.

Fool had never been to the boardinghouses before, had never needed to. He hadn't even known where they were until that day, when he had had to look them up in a thin book called *The Places of Hell: An Information*. Until a day ago, he would simply have asked Gordie, who seemed to know things like that, to have it all in his head or on his walls.

As they climbed down from the train, the boardinghouses all looked the same; long rows of one- or two-story buildings with no windows, made of heavy wooden planks with doorways carved roughly into the front walls, but as they approached, Fool saw that there were differences. One or two had porches, long walkways in the front of the building with railings and chairs scattered about them, and others had extra doorways or small huts leaning against their front or side walls. Unlike the Houska, there were signs of life here; humans walked down the streets and demons watched them proprietorially from doorways as they walked. Some of the boardinghouses had names scratched into the wood above their entrances; most simply had numbers.

"What are they?" Summer asked, the first words she had spoken since they had left their rooms, and the first without prompting since that morning.

"The demons keep their Genevieves here, the ones that they put to work in the Houska," replied Fool. "Protecting their investment. They offer them a degree of safety, they get to live among their own kind, and they travel in and out of the Houska together in packs at the beginning and end of their shifts. They have food, a place to sleep, the illusion of freedom, but they're prisoners."

"You sound angry," said Summer.

"No," said Fool, and then realized he was lying. He *was* angry, not because the place existed exactly, but because it had failed; the Genevieves were supposed to be safe here, to be able to find some kind of peace between their times offering themselves to demons, and yet two of their number had been taken and killed.

"What did the Man mean, the boardinghouse with demons on the roof?" asked Summer. Her voice was still flat, but at least she was asking something, was engaging. Coming back? No, maybe not that, not yet, but it was something.

"I don't know," said Fool. He looked at the roofs around them. Most were sloped, covered in shingling that was cracked and warping. Although he couldn't see any at that moment, there was evidence that Hell's birds, the chalkis, used the edges of the roofs for perches; smears of green and gray shit ran down the walls and pooled in thick, sludgy piles on the roofs' faces. Some of it was fresh and Fool smelled its tang as they walked; some was older, dried and disintegrating into powdery wisps as the breeze teased at it. As he and Summer walked, the humans avoided looking at them. Demons, on the other hand, peered at them with undisguised interest.

One of them, a short thing with skin the color of burned copper and with wings hanging from its back that were broken and torn, emerged from a doorway and leaned over the porch rail, calling, "Little man! Little girl!"

Fool stopped, looking at the demon, deferential but trying not to show fear. The demon took something from a pouch hanging at its belt, a rolled tube of paper, and put it in its mouth. With its other clawed hand, it lit a match and ignited the end of the tube, drawing a breath in through the burning paper. Smoking was a rarity in Hell, partly because the leaf was hard to find but mostly because demons often didn't have lips flexible enough to hold the tube without chewing or damaging it. It was a habit brought from the worlds outside, Fool had been told, although who had told him, he didn't know. Gordie, maybe, or Elderflower in one of his more expansive moments. The demon sucked again at the tube, and as he did so its eyes glowed as red as the embers of burning paper. It let the smoke out from its mouth in a stream, sending a darting tongue into the thick clouds as though to get a last taste before it dissipated in Hell's heavy air.

"You're in the wrong place, little man, little girl," said the demon conversationally. There was no aggression in its voice, not yet.

"No," said Fool. "We're where we need to be. We're looking for somewhere."

The demon looked around itself, its gestures exaggerated. "Everywhere is somewhere," it said, "but this is not the somewhere you need to be. Turn about, little man, and take the little girl with you and go."

"No," said Fool, surprising himself with the steadiness of his voice. "I am one of Hell's Information Men and I am here to gather information." He looked about, oddly hoping that he might see plants, that the Man might be watching and be amused, but there was nothing but dust and the boardinghouses.

Everything stopped. A group of men, boys really, crossing the dusty street behind Fool and Summer turned to look at them. From the corner of his eye, Fool saw more men stop and peer at him, faces appearing in doorways and from around buildings. *Noticed for one thing, noticed for all things,* he thought, and then the demon was flexing itself, swelling, the burning leaf and paper falling to the decking by its feet, forgotten. It exhaled, smoke that was not from the cigarette pouring from its mouth, darkening and wreathing around its head, its eyes glowing red, its claws digging into the wooden rail and tearing splinters from it.

It felt like they were paused, hovering, for a moment, everything motionless around them. The demon glared at Fool and Summer, the men stared at them, the houses glowered through doorways in which the shadows were thick and heavy. Fool's instinct was to retreat, to tip his head in apology and hope that it would be enough, but he didn't. That anger still burned in him, its flames as sullen as the glow in the demon's eyes. "Tell me, demon: where is the house with demons on its roof?" he said, keeping his voice even, thinking, *Little Fool going a step too far, little overreaching Fool.*

"He'll kill you," said a voice from behind the demon. It started, jumping slightly and looking around and then whirling back to stare at Fool. The glow in its eyes had faded and it was trembling, and the smoke pouring from its mouth was uneven for a moment.

"Is it him?" the demon said, and it moaned, low and uneven.

He's scared! Fool realized, and the realization astonished him. *He's scared of* me*!*

"Better tell him," said the voice again, and a man stepped out of the house behind the demon. The man was older, fat and scarred and hard looking.

"He might shoot you otherwise," the man continued, "and then where would we be, without our owner?" The demon looked at the man, and the glow came back into its eyes, furious and hot. The fat man, perhaps realizing he had gone too far, stepped back, mumbling something that might have been an apology or a more general susurrus of fealty and obedience.

"I won't shoot you," said Fool. "Why would I?"

"You shoot demons," said the demon, surly, turning back to Fool. "You've shot hundreds. Why should I be any different?"

"I haven't shot hundreds," said Fool. Hundreds? Where had that come from?

"You kill demons when they don't tell you what you want. You've been seen," said the demon. "You're a human but you kill demons. It shouldn't be allowed."

Allowed? thought Fool. *I'm not allowed, I don't do it!*

Only, that wasn't true, was it? He hadn't done it hundreds of times, true, but he *had* done it. Experimentally, he let his hand fall to the butt of his gun; the demon flinched. It pulled itself another tube of rolled paper from its pouch and lit it. Its hand shook slightly as it held the flame.

"You kill demons?" said someone on the street behind Fool. When he turned, he found that a large number of young men had gathered to his rear. There were no women; they lived in another Sister, he remembered, and the places they were sent to and the demons they serviced were different from the men's.

"No," he replied.

"Yes he does," said Summer, her voice still flat but loud, rolling across the street. "He slaughters them when they don't obey him."

"What do you want from me?" the demon asked, and its voice was wheedling, unhappy. It had shrunk again, appeared thinner, its skin a dirty bronze, the glow in its eyes guttering. It was only a minor one, Fool realized, puffing itself up to be bigger than it was, and now it was punctured, back to small again. It probably didn't even have a name, only a species, like the chalkis, things without individual identities. Unimportant to Hell, important only to the things and people they could control and brutalize.

"Tell me about the house with the demons on its roof. Where is it?"

For a second the demon was quiet, and then it spat on the ground at Fool's feet. Its spittle bubbled and steamed, a cheap trick intended to frighten. "At Sister's end," he said, pointing to the end of the long street. "The biggest house."

As Fool started walking, Summer by his side, he was aware that they were being followed, not by demons but by humans, by men who came out of the boardinghouses and joined a swelling crowd trailing behind them. They didn't talk, these men, and their feet were a soft shuffle in the dirt. When Fool glanced back, he saw that most were barefoot or had cloth wrapped around their feet; their clothes, however, were gaudy, glittered with brightly colored rags and polished stones or pieces of rubbed metal or glass, things to make them attractive, to catch the eye of potential clients. They looked clean, some still with wet hair or skin, but they kept their eyes down and walked hunched over, shrinking into themselves.

"Why are they following us?" he asked.

"Because you kill demons," said Summer. "Maybe they're hoping to see you do it."

"I don't," said Fool, helplessly.

"You do," said Summer. "You killed two the other day. You killed orphans. Not enough orphans. Not enough." Fool didn't reply; what could he say? Behind them, the crowd followed.

The largest house in the Sister was three stories tall, although it was no grander than the others. Like them, it had roughly constructed walls of thick planking with holes hewn out for the doorways and windows on the higher floors. Fool saw the thick tangles of bush growing around the boardinghouse and thought of the Man. He smiled, having to stop himself from nodding or gesturing at the plants.

The roof of the building was sloped, coming downward from the rear, and at its front edge were several smaller demons.

They were short, crouching and staring at him and Summer and the crowd behind them. Their eyes glittered, segmented and dark. They were the color of dead and rotting leaves, mottled in shades of brown and black and gray, and their outlines were hard to make out against the layered planks of the roof until they moved.

"This is the house of the Bar-Igura," one called down. "What is it you want? You do not belong here."

"I want information," replied Fool, "about one of the Genevieves who lived here."

"We have no information," said one of the things, although whether it was the same one Fool couldn't tell. "Best to leave, Information Man."

"We came for information," repeated Fool.

"Perhaps you mishear, little Information Man," said the demon and then its head exploded.

It was Summer. Her gun was out, the barrel dribbling smoke as the demon's corpse rolled off the edge of the roof and fell to the ground with a damp thud. The noise of the shot rumbled away, echoing down the street in a flat plosive and then, for a moment, there was silence. Fool stared at Summer, but she was looking at the roof and ignored him. She jerked her hand as the next bullet formed in her gun and then she swung the weapon to point at the next demon along.

"He is not a little man and I am not a little girl," she said loudly. "We are not little, none of us." The demons on the roof began to screech, and then there was bedlam.

The crowd behind them began to cheer, muted but clear, as people and demons poured out of the buildings around them. One of the things on the roof dropped, landing with a heavy crash on the porch in front of the house, raising clouds of dust around it. Even as it landed it was skittering forward, low and quick, leaping down from the porch toward them. More of the things were dropping from the roof, loosing howls and screams as they came. The crowd behind them screamed as well, shouts mingling with the cheers as it surged forward, flowing around Summer and Fool, buffeting them. The demons and humans met, two waves crashing against each other, snarling and slashing and kicking.

The demons were stronger, more violent, but the humans had the weight of numbers and soon there were tumbling, writhing clusters around, masses pinioning the demons, hauling them back, attacking them. *What's happening here,* thought Fool, *what?* Over his shoulder, he saw demons emerging from the other boardinghouses, wings and claws and teeth and limbs unfurling, moving toward the struggling mess of humans and demons. *They'll slaughter them,* Fool thought. *They'll slaughter us!*

The first of the new demons reached them as Fool pulled his gun free from its holster and fired upward. The blast was loud, louder than the noises around him, another plosive shock of noise that crashed over everything around him, dragging silence in its wake. Humans and demons stopped, startled into stillness by the noise.

"Stop!" Fool shouted into the silence, moving as swiftly as he could to the porch. The reassuring weight of a new bullet was in the gun as he reached it, turning so that he faced the crowd. "We just want information. Give it to us and we'll go."

Summer stepped out of the crowd; she had a fresh bruise forming across her cheek and her hair was disheveled, but the hand holding her gun was steady, pointing at the demons that remained on the roof. Fool's own gun had pointed itself, apparently unbidden, at the nearest demon and the humans holding it down. "Let it up," he said.

He wasn't sure at first whether the humans would do as he said, but they eventually did. Already whatever rage had driven them was evaporating, he saw, and the realization of what they had done was coming upon them. Their eyes wouldn't rise from the ground and they were backing away, hunching their shoulders back and trying to bury their faces into the crowd's anonymity. The demons, hissing and spitting, started to move after the men, but Fool raised his gun and fired again, another burst of flame and smoke and metal tearing into the sky, and said, "No."

There was another of those pauses during which Fool felt his world teetering. The demons glanced looks off each other, calculating, the humans backing away, trying to undo the notice they had brought upon themselves, and there were Fool and Summer, pivots around which everything seemed to move. Then, with a sensation like the slipping of some great weight, things untangled slightly. Claws retracted, the demons pulling themselves back a little.

"Let them in. Give them what they need." A voice from above, from another of the little demons on the roof. Fool looked up at it; it was peering down at him and Summer with a strange expression in its baleful eyes. Hate? Fear? No, something else, something Fool had never seen before in a demon's eyes.

Uncertainty. The situation was unclear to it, and it didn't know what to do. It wasn't in charge, and it didn't like it. Things were shifting, new events occurring, events beyond its control, beyond all their control, and Fool and Summer and everyone else appeared to be caught up in them and had little choice but to move along with them and try not to get caught in the currents as they eddied and swirled. Nodding at the demon, Fool stepped across the porch and, with Summer at his side, entered the building.

Inside the boardinghouse, it smelled. It wasn't a single scent so much as a mess of different odors, of fresh sweat and old sweat and cheap soap and burned hair and meat and food and piss and shit and other, less easily identifiable, things. The hallway past the entrance was narrow and cramped and without much light, the walls uneven and rough, hemming them in. Fool walked slowly along, listening to the sounds of the house around them. There were footsteps from somewhere ahead and above them, quiet voices, something being dragged slowly.

"What is it you want to know?" asked someone. A shadow moved at the end of the hallway, huge and indistinct, and Fool's hand tightened around his gun. The shadow came toward them, collapsing in on itself, solidifying into a grossly fat human form. "Carter," he said, holding out a hand that felt, when Fool reached out and shook it, like the cold and damp flesh of the body they had pulled from the river. The man stepped back to where the hallway opened out into a larger room, into the light, and Fool saw that he was very pale, almost white, and that his skin was greasy with moisture. "Carter," the man said again, as if that explained everything.

"Who are you? What do you do here?" asked Fool.

"I run the house," Carter replied. "For the Bar-Igura. I make sure the boys are clean and smart and ready for their work. I bed them down when they come back and turn them out in good time for the next work. I stitch them if they need it."

"You're paid for this?" asked Summer. "For preparing the flesh of other men for sale to demons?"

"Given board," said Carter. "I do my job, I keep quiet, and I stay out of the way. I'm safe, the Bar-Igura keep me safe. I work for them. The flesh gets prepared for sale anyway, so best I do it. Best I get the benefits."

Fool could feel Summer trembling beside him, felt his own muscles tense. Carter wasn't unusual, of course; they all worked for the demons in one sense or another, he and Summer included, but this was a job Fool had never considered. The man took his own kind and prepared them for possession by the demonkind that frequented the Houska, prepared them for penetration and burning and abuse. Fool wondered whether he sold them himself or left that to the demons, whether he had ever been sold or bought. *Questions,* he thought, *I have questions. I'm investigating.*

"You know all the boys? Who stay here?"

"My job to know."

"You know if they all come back? After the night, I mean? When they finish work?"

"My job to know," repeated Carter.

"Do all the boys go to the Houska?"

"All boys leave the house, the Bar-Igura tell them where to go. Places in the Houska, yes, sometimes other places."

"Other places? Are there private sales? Outside the Houska?"

"Ask the Bar-Igura," said Carter, glancing up to the ceiling. *The demons on the roof,* Fool thought. Gordie would have known, of course, would have recognized them and their name from all the books he read between shifts, would have known about them before they got here. He'd have known about Carter, or people like Carter, wouldn't have been surprised by him or disgusted by him. Was there a Carter in every boardinghouse? In every boardinghouse in each of the Sisters? Hundreds of them? Thousands? How had Fool not known? What else didn't he know? How much?

"There's a boy missing," said Summer, not a question but a statement of fact.

"Always boys missing," said Carter. "They don't come back after the night, too tired and too used up. Every day, new ones and lost ones."

"No," said Fool, remembering the Man's information. "This is something unusual, a different thing."

"What is usual? Boys vanish, boys come back. Usual," said Carter and then, before Fool could stop her, Summer stepped forward and slapped him. The slap sounded heavy, and it was only when Carter dropped to his knees with blood pouring from a ragged tear in his forehead that Fool realized she had not slapped him but hit him with the butt of her gun. She knelt beside the man, jamming the barrel of her weapon into the side of his head and twisting it so that his skin bunched around its muzzle.

"There is a missing boy," she said, and she was crying as she spoke, "missing this week, not just after being in the Houska but in some other way. He might look like this." She dropped one of the few remaining sketches of the first victim onto the floor in front of Carter and used her gun to force his head toward it.

"Information Men are the only people in Hell to carry guns, you piece of shit. I've never shot a human with my gun, but I will if you don't tell us what we need to know. Look at him, you fat turd," she said. "Look! Who is he?" Blood from Carter's head spattered down onto the paper, mingling with the tears that fell from Summer's eyes to form a pale pink wash across the sheet.

"Summer," said Fool.

"No!" she said, her tears falling harder. "He knows! He knows, and he'll tell us."

"Summer, he belongs to them!" Fool said. "If you damage him, they will take payment from you. From us. I'm not sure what's happening here, but whatever protection we have, it's fragile. Summer, please." In his mind, he saw Rhakshasas, his entrails tightening and loosening in anticipation.

Slowly, Summer rose from her knees. Tears were flowing freely down her face and she was making a low keening, not quite a howl, not quite words. "Keep her away from me," said Carter, his voice thick and slurred.

"Tell us," said Fool, and then, as inspiration struck, "or I shall investigate the rest of the house by myself and leave you with her to talk."

"No, please," said Carter, "Diamond. It's Diamond. He came back and then went out. Bad boy, I told him, stay to sleep and get ready but he said no and went."

"When?"

"Two nights ago? Three? I cannot remember. So much always the same it is hard to remember, yes?"

"Did he have a room?"

At this, Carter raised his head. A flap of skin curled redly down from his scalp and his eyes were white within the blood running down his face. "He shared, had space in room three. They all share."

"Show us."

"There are boys sleeping in it."

"Show us," said Summer. She was no longer crying. "Show us Diamond's space."

Room three didn't have a door, only a curtain hanging down from a piece of rope strung out along the top of the doorway. From beyond the curtain Fool heard snoring, flatulence, someone crying softly. When Carter pulled back the curtain, a ragged sheet threadbare with age, Fool didn't at first understand what he was seeing. The room appeared full of distorted shadows, blotches that twisted weirdly around, not the sleeping figures he had expected.

"Wake!" shouted Carter, his voice still slurred. He reached into the room and pulled at something and the shapes collapsed in rapid succession. Wires, Fool realized; they had been sleeping standing up, leaning against wires crisscrossing the room at chest height. Carter had released the wire and now the sleepers were awake, sprawled across the floor, swearing and groaning and struggling to stand. "Is it time? Please, no, please," someone called.

"Visitor!" shouted Carter and then said to Fool, "Diamond's space on other side of room. Shelf with clothes. Help yourself."

It wasn't much, Fool found; two shirts, both brightly colored but fading, and a spare pair of pants. As he looked, the room's inhabitants gathered around him.

"That's Diamond's," said one of them. Another, looking at Summer, said, "Who are you?" There was no aggression in the voice, only a tired curiosity.

"I'm—" began Fool but someone interrupted him.

"It's Thomas Fool," they said. "He's the human the demons are scared of."

"No, that's not true," said Fool.

"They are," said the same voice. Another called agreement and then everyone was talking at once, calling and asking and demanding.

"Please," Fool called, and then shouted, "Please, let me speak.

"I'm Thomas Fool, yes, but I'm not special, demons aren't frightened of me. I'm just trying to find out what happened to Diamond and another man, another boy like you. They were killed, killed horribly, and I need to know if you can help. Why did Diamond leave the house the other day, the day before he died? Where did he go? Do any of you know?"

There was an uncomfortable silence. Eventually someone said, "Why are you bothered?"

Because his soul was torn out of his flesh, because I'm learning to investigate, because I want to know. Because my friend died trying to find out. Because I'm a Fool, a little searching Fool, and the Man of Plants and Flowers wants entertaining and Hell wants me to provide answers for questions I don't really know how to ask. Because. Because. Aloud, he said, "Because it's my job. It's our job," indicating Summer, "and we're trying to do it as best we can."

"Did you shoot a demon?" A different voice.

"Yes, but that's not why you should talk to me."

"Did you kill it?"

"Does it matter?"

"Did you kill it?"

"Yes."

"More than one?"

"Yes."

Another silence, this one more speculative. Fool could feel their interest in him, feel their need for him, or for something he meant to them, these boys. He wanted to point to Summer and say, *She did it, too, she killed one of the things on your roof,* but didn't.

"He was meeting a client," said someone in the room, another new voice. "He said they'd spoken to him as he waited for a train."

"Did he say who?"

"No. He said it wasn't a usual client."

"He said it wasn't a normal client," someone else said, clarifying. "That it was someone new."

"He didn't tell you anything else?"

"No. We don't talk." The interest in him was waning; Fool could feel it slipping away. Some of the boys had started to move toward the shelves, pulling shirts and pants off them and starting to dress. Killing demons was something to hear about; a dead Genevieve wasn't. Their dismissal hurt, and they told him nothing else.

Later, during their journey back, Fool slumped in his seat on the train and thought. What had he learned? Really? That the first body had been a person called Diamond, that he had been, what? Solicited? Yes, solicited after finishing in the Houska, not in the Houska itself but away from it, in the darkness before the ride back to his boardinghouse. Could they assume the second victim had been gathered the same way? That Diamond was killed and his soul released before being dumped in Solomon Water like so much garbage, the demon then moving on to the second victim, that it made contact with them, lured them to one of Hell's lonely places, and then took them without witness or obstacle? He supposed so; without anything to tell him otherwise, he would have to assume yes and move forward with that assumption. So, a demon prowling the edges of the Houska, unseen unless it made itself known, picking Genevieves, taking them away, and then tearing their souls from the flesh? Yes, yes, that made sense, it had a logic that Fool thought was sound. And if that was the logic of it, then could they step ahead of it, predict it? Yes, again yes, they could try to be where the demon was before it got there, could try to prevent it happening again. But how? There were no other Information Men to help, and the space around the Houska was huge, and how would he and Summer know where to go, to wait? *There's so much I should have asked,* he thought as he fell asleep to the rattle of the train's heavy wheels. *Where did Diamond catch the train? Where in the Houska did he work? Where was he that night? Where was he when the demon took him? Where?*

A new blue ribbon was waiting for them when they got back to the office.

13

Another of Hell's houses, this one huge and abandoned.

Most of its facade had warped, slowly losing its battle against Hell's heat and storms. Wood, stained black by exposure to the sun, had buckled away, revealing sticky shadows and struts beneath like bent and rotting ribs. Here and there, planking had come loose and was swinging, banging against its neighbors as though the building were holding down its fingers and tapping out its own slowing rhythms. There were larger holes in the roof, beams crossing the spaces. Chalkis, littler ones, had nested in some of the gaps, and their shit was the building's only decoration, streaks of white and green and brown slathered down the tiles and gathered into solid lumps in the guttering.

"What is it?"

"I don't know," replied Fool, not looking around. "A farm ranch, maybe, abandoned when the land died." Around them the low, wiry bushes that dotted the scrubland bobbed in the breeze. Behind Fool, Adam made an interested noise. The note had been in the tube, along with the details of the death. *The delegation wishes to see an investigation. Pick them up and show them, Thomas.* He wanted to argue with Elderflower, to ask how he could show them an investigation when he didn't know how to do one himself, not really, when he was making it up as he went along. He hadn't, of course, had simply obeyed, and now here they were.

"It is inside?" asked Balthazar.

"*He* is inside," said Adam. "He is inside, Balthazar, or she. It is a human being's end we have come to see, not mere meat or goods."

"Yes," said Balthazar, but he did not sound contrite or convinced.

Rusting machinery lay in the house's front garden, collapsing slowly into the earth and threading with weeds and dirt like the skeletons of long-dead beasts. Fool led the delegation along the path to the building's doorway. The door was closed, sticking when he pulled on it, and opened only after several hard yanks.

"Where?" asked Balthazar, stepping past Fool and into the house.

"I don't know," said Fool. "The information wasn't that detailed. We search." Fool walked past Balthazar, and Summer followed.

Inside, the house was in as poor shape as the outside suggested. Its walls bowed into the rooms and the floors were patchworks of holes and rotted wood. Fool went gingerly along the hallway, his shadow moving ahead of him, testing the floor with his advancing foot before settling his weight anywhere. Summer stayed close behind him as, farther back, the angels watched. The glow sweating from them, unnoticeable in Hell's sunlight, pulsed a pale bluewhite in the gloomy space, making Fool's shadow waver. The building was silent apart from the noises Fool and Summer made as they moved into its interior.

There were rooms and other corridors off the hallway to either side, near empty and filthy. In one a pile of old oilcloths was crumpled into the corner, covered in dust, and in another was the remains of a fire, a blackened circle scarred into the wooden boards and the smell of old smoke thick in the air. Fool went past them and carried on to the passage's end. It opened out into a large kitchen that smelled of burned food and mold and soured meat. A table stood in its middle, furred with dust and grease, and an old metal cooker thick with rust and soot was pushed up against the far wall. The shells of cupboards lined the walls, their doors and shelves long gone, their wooden bones warping into slow curves. The floor was bare wood, its carpet of dust and grime undisturbed.

On the other side of the kitchen another doorway yawned, and beyond it stairs led down. At their bottom something rippled and glittered in the angels' light as it came around Fool and fell into the space. Fool reached for the wall, found the cord that he knew would be there, and tugged on it. Sparks of light jumped in the cellar below them, gone as briefly as they arrived. He tugged again, and this time the sparks staggered to a sulphurous, greasy light as the gas lamps caught aflame.

Behind Fool, Adam clapped his hands delightedly and said, "Such ingenuity, even in Hell!"

"I'm surprised they work," said Fool, "given how long this place looks to have been abandoned."

"Perhaps God is assisting," said Adam. Fool looked about him at the decay and said nothing.

The steps proved solid, thankfully, but the cellar was flooded, thick oily water swirling over the bottom risers and swallowing them. Crouched on the step closest to the water's surface, Summer and the angels to his back, Fool saw that the cellar ran under the entire length of the building. It was now a huge pool of gently undulating water whose surface danced with the orange and blue reflections of the lamplight. Most of the lamps lining the walls hadn't lit; some had rusted to flaking metal lumps, others were caked with dirt, their glass broken or missing. The air smelled of stagnant water and the sharp odor of gas.

The body was floating in the middle of the cellar.

At first, Fool didn't see it and then the way the water broke around it and over it gave it shape, made the humps into the curve of a back and the outstretched arms of a person drifting facedown. Fool stepped gingerly down another step, thinking of Solomon Water and the little things that lived in it, and hoped that none were here. The water lapped over his feet, cold, patches of oil on its surface breaking around his shoe, glimmering in rainbow constellations before fading. Another step, deeper into it now, the water coming to his knees, and then Balthazar stepped down next to him.

The water curled away from the angel, drawing back into two lips around him and pulling away to reveal a muddy floor that dried as Fool watched, its surface cracking and buckling into something solid. Balthazar stepped farther into the cellar and the water retreated farther, a pathway opening up between the bottom of the stairs and the body. As the separating water reached the corpse and peeled away from it, the body bobbed and then came to a gentle rest on the floor. The air filled with a crackling sound as the newly exposed mud dried to a crust.

"Does that help?" asked Balthazar.

"Yes," said Fool. "Thank you."

"Take it as my apology. They deserve dignity," said Balthazar, "something which I may have forgotten earlier."

"Yes," replied Fool, "he does."

"You know it to be a man?" asked Adam.

"No," said Fool, peering at the pale dead thing. "I assumed it was because the others were men. Boys, really."

"And you know this to be another link in that chain?"

"No," said Fool again. "I assumed it because of the blue ribbon."

"I see. And what do you do now?"

"I investigate," said Fool, and went to the body.

It was another young man, and being in the water had bloated him and bleached his flesh down to a ghostly white. It had also cleaned his wounds, which made them somehow worse, showing them in clinical dark reds and purples against the pale skin. He had bruises across his chest and shoulders, as well as tears into his muscle across his thighs and belly, and his face was a mass of grazes and cuts. There were indentations on the back of his head and when Fool placed his hand above them, he thought they might be where the demon's fingers had pressed so hard they had ruptured skin and fractured bone. Most of the man's teeth were cracked or broken, and several had dirt ground into their fronts; more grit and earth were lodged in the man's gums and crushed up into his nostrils. Bent above the corpse, Fool had a sudden image of the man being held down, battered, his face forced through the foul water and into the earthen floor, the mud flowing up his nose, granules scouring his teeth and driving themselves into his flesh, the back of his head bowing, cracking under the pressure with a noise like snapping twigs.

"His clothes are here," said Summer from behind Fool. Turning, he saw that she was pointing to the wall of water at her side in which he could just make out something colorful moving. Summer plunged a hand into the liquid and grasped the thing, pulling it out; it was a shirt made from different strips of material sewn clumsily together; the stitches were visible even from a distance, hanks of twine crossing and crisscrossing each other. It dripped in Summer's hand, making puddles on the newly dried floor. She drove her hand back into the water and this time came out with trousers, sodden black and torn almost in two.

"What happened?" asked Adam.

"They came here," said Fool, "and the human was murdered. He was beaten and probably drowned, his clothes were torn off, and then he was left here to float like something worthless and old." The rage was in him again, the *fury*, and he felt his hand drop to his weapon, but what would he shoot? He looked up, wondering if he might see some evidence of the soul's passing embossed into the ceiling above him, but there was nothing except a mess of dancing reflections and beams and dirt, just as chaotic and answerless as everything else around him.

"And you know this?" asked Adam.

"I'm guessing," said Fool. "I'm always guessing; it's all we can do. We guess and sometimes we're right and most times we're wrong and it never matters anyway."

"Nothing ever changes," said Summer, and the *drip-drip-drip* of the water falling from the shirt in her hand was like the beat of a tune that Fool couldn't hear.

"And what will you do now?" asked Adam, apparently not hearing or choosing to ignore the anger in Fool's voice.

Perhaps he hears it but doesn't care, thought Fool, *because he knows I have no choice but to answer him and serve him, little slave Fool that I am.* Out loud, he said, "Try to work out what happened. Try to find out who he was, where he was from."

"How?"

"We'll send the body for Questioning," said Fool, "and see if that turns anything up, although if it's like the others, I doubt it."

"And is it like the others?"

"Yes."

"And then?"

"I don't know," said Fool, but even as he said it, he realized that he did know. It wasn't conscious knowledge, not exactly, but something underneath, something turning and writhing, making itself known. There were safe assumptions here, safe enough at least to work with: that the dead man was a Genevieve, that he had been killed by something enormously powerful, that his soul was gone, that he had been taken not from the Houska but from somewhere outside it. On the journey home? And the anger in Fool, in his head, was forcing the assumptions into new shapes; they could ask the other Genevieves about the dead man, make sketches, could see if he had been seen. The Bar-Igura might know him, or one of the other boardinghouse operators. This man had a name, had as much of a life as anyone in Hell had, and Fool could make his death less pointless if only he could find it.

He had a killer, and Fool would find it as well, he hoped.

"Forgive my questions, but we have nothing like your investigation in Heaven," said Adam. "We have no need of it; there is no crime. I'm fascinated to see how you carry out your duties, what steps you take to apprehend the culprit."

"We'll ask questions," said Fool, ignoring the comment about apprehending the culprit. "We may uncover something useful. I'll look around, see if there are signs I can read. There's no way of knowing what we'll find. The Man may be able to help, although there are no plants down here that I can see, so I doubt it." There weren't even mosses or lichens on the walls, and nothing in the water except dirt and oil.

"The Man?"

"The Man of Plants and Flowers," said Fool. "He helps people, gives them information for a price. I don't know his real name. He likes to be entertained, so he helps me by telling me things that are useful, and I appear to amuse him by following his leads." Fool did a little, bitter parody of a dance, shaking his hands in front of him and shuffling his legs like a puppet, and then stopped, ashamed. He felt helpless, dull with fury, stupid and sightless and a step behind everything.

"What can you tell from the body?" asked Adam, coming closer to the dead flesh.

"Not much," said Fool. "He's young. He's dead."

"This Man will want more entertainment than that, will he not?" asked Balthazar. What little compassion had been in his voice before had gone and he sounded bored. He was gazing about the cellar, looking out over the sundered water, and his glow was the red of distant fires. "Are all investigations like this? This slow?"

"Yes," said Fool. "It's all slow, so slow we almost never catch the demons that do these things."

"And it is always demons?" asked Adam. "Never humans killing humans?"

"Always," said Fool. "It is always demons, never humans."

"I suppose if humans could kill humans, you'd slaughter each other just to escape Hell," said Balthazar.

"Yes," said Fool, the weight of his gun heavy against his thigh, and he turned again to the body. Above them, he heard the sound of the porters arriving.

The porters trudged up the road, carrying the body between them. It was wrapped in tarpaulin, sagging down; trails of liquid spilled from the wraps of material and left shadows on the dusty road. Fool watched as the men walked back toward the Houska, their shapes dwindling into the hazy light and losing definition as they went. When he could no longer see them except for the weakest of impressions, he turned back to the house to find everyone looking at him expectantly.

"What do you do now?" asked Adam. The scribe and archive, behind Adam, stood with their heads bowed, waiting. Balthazar was apart from them, still looking at Fool, standing in the tangled growth to the house's side. The chalkis had returned to the building's roof and from above them came their noise, chirrups and squeals and the occasional clatter as they moved and hopped across the beams and tiles. What did he do now? Fool had no idea.

No, he told himself, *I do* not *have no idea, that's how I used to be but now it's different, now I'm learning, I'm understanding this better. I have ideas.* He looked at the house and tried to remember—had the door been open when they arrived? No, it had been shut and they'd had to force it, pushing it back against the swelling planks of the hallway floor. Which meant what? *Think, Fool, think,* he urged himself, *so what?* It was important, but he couldn't work out why; why should it matter that the front door had been shut, that it clearly hadn't been opened for months or years, that it had protested its movement with a noise like a distant scream?

Because it meant that the man, and his murderer, had not gone into the house through the front door, and if not the front there must be another entry.

Fool left Adam and Summer and walked along the front of the house. Balthazar stepped out of his way as he reached the corner of the building and went around it. Here the foliage was thicker, more tangled, matted, and dark as the land fell away from the roadway. "Have you been here?" asked Fool, turning to Balthazar.

"You wish to ask me questions? Am I under investigation?" replied Balthazar, and his glow was rising again, red and rich and creeping from his flawless skin, his warrior soul calling itself to arms.

"No," said Fool as patiently as he could, "but there are trampled plants here, and I need to know if you trampled them. If not, it's probable that this is where the thing that killed the Genevieve waited."

The patch was a rough circle about five feet across, close to the side of the house. At night, something standing there would have been hard to see. Fool stood in the center of the patch, turning around slowly, ignoring the angels, ignoring Summer. He tried to see things from the demon's view: waiting for a lone Genevieve, stepping out from the shadows and plants, and snatching the young man from the street as he walked back toward his boardinghouse. He reached into his pocket and brushed his fingers against the feather, still thinking, still pushing his mind against the facts he had, trying to see them from new angles, to force them into new shapes.

Plants. The demon had been standing in the plants.

Plants.

The Man would have surely seen him and would be able to tell Fool what he looked like, where it had gone after! Suddenly Fool was elated; the Man would help him! He went swiftly along the side of the house, reaching its rear to find out that it looked out over more scrubland, the earth a sickly yellow and brown. The sound of the chalkis was louder here, angry squawks and screeches rising into the dusty air. A group of them was clustered a few feet away, scrambling over each other, the ground writhing and dark with them. Fool drew his gun and went toward them; they rose at his approach, flying in tight, angry circles around him, swooping in but never quite hitting him. Their shit spattered in long strings on the ground around him, its stench strong, making his eyes water.

Something hissed in the air over Fool, a streak of flame slicing past him, and the chalkis started screaming. Pieces of them began to fall as the flaming thing curled and sliced again, this time in the other direction. More pieces of chalkis dropped to the floor around Fool, smoking.

Fool's hand went to his gun and then Balthazar said, "They will not bother us again."

As Fool turned, the angel's flame vanished, his hands dropping back to his sides. Balthazar smiled, broadly, teeth showing. It was the first time he had shown any emotion other than anger or boredom, and Fool thought it awful, a flaming, exultant joyousness. The warrior angel had at last been able to kill something.

The chalkis had risen higher, though, were no longer swooping or crapping, although they were still screaming. The sounds were oddly human, almost-words falling from the sky as Fool inspected what Hell's birds had been so desperate to get to on the ground. It was a stain, overlaid now by the spiral patterns of the chalkis' excrement, stretching in a ragged circle and creeping several feet up the building's rear wall. It was dark, soaked into the earth and the wooden planking, but it was still obvious that it was blood. Fool had found where the dead man had been attacked.

Just beyond the stain was a set of steps cut into the ground and the remains of a pair of wooden doors. The doors had been torn from a doorway set into the wall that was partly below ground level, and the pale center of their broken planks was visible; these had only recently been damaged and had not had time to darken and rot. Fool went to the top of the stairs and saw that they continued down into a darkness that glinted.

"They go to the cellar," said Summer from beside him. He hadn't heard her approach, so engrossed was he in this new sense of investigation, of finding things.

"Yes," he said. "This is how they got in."

"Was the boy alive?" Adam this time, standing behind Summer, his robe drifting about him. Fool thought about the stain, about its size, and about the damage he had seen on the body, and said, "Possibly, but if so it must have been only just. I think he was beaten here and then the body was taken into the cellar and drowned."

"To hide the corpse?" Adam again.

"I don't know," replied Fool. Had the other corpses been hidden? The one in the Orphanage, possibly, but the first? No. He had been discarded like something unimportant, certainly, but not hidden, unless the demon was hoping that Solomon Water's inhabitants might eat it before it was discovered. No. No, that wasn't right, it didn't feel right, this was a demon without fear of capture that simply left the bodies where it wanted to.

"It does it to make it hard for us," said Summer. "In Solomon Water where we might meet other demons, in with the orphans who would attack us, and now in the cellar where we couldn't get to it easily. We wouldn't have found it so easily without Balthazar's help."

"You think this is about us?" asked Fool, surprised.

"The murders? No," said Summer. "But this? Where the bodies are? Yes."

Fool's head was almost spinning with the idea, with its enormity. Hell had noticed him, was watching him, Rhakshasas had given him a task to carry out, the Man was entertained by him and was using him to feed back his own growing power to the Bureaucracy, and now whatever ancient demon was doing this was thinking about them when it abandoned the bodies of the Genevieves it killed? Could that be right?

Could it?

"Why?" he asked, probing the idea in his mind.

"To stop us finding it?" said Summer.

"No, of course not. You're merely an amusement to it," said Balthazar, coming closer to them. "It likes the idea of making your job difficult, of making you clamber through water and mud and wherever else it chooses just to retrieve the bodies. It's a demon; it uses each of its actions against as many humans as it can. If this is not the Hell of fire and torture, as I must accept is the case, then it is the Hell of inconvenience and difficulty and fear and uncertainty, and it is merely contributing to that. These dead souls are part of its game."

"It is not a game," said Fool, thinking again of bodies drifting in water and left lying in mud and bleeding out, headless, on the Houska's streets. "They are not things to be used and then thrown away, they are humans."

"No. They were human, but no more," said Adam quietly. "The thing that made them human is gone and now they are mere sundered flesh."

14

The discussions were shorter that day because of the delegation's morning with Fool and because of the near riot that happened prior to the trading taking place, but while they went on they still seemed interminable.

Crowds of the Sorrowful had already gathered outside Assemblies House by the time Fool and the angels arrived, and they flocked against the transport, slowing it to almost nothing. Hands banged on the windows and faces pressed in pale moons against the glass mouthing *Take me* and *Please* and *It's my turn, my turn.* They were almost at the building's gates, which were swinging open, when the first missile hit the roof.

It impacted with a loud, violent crash and a dent pocked into the metal, dimpling down above Balthazar's head. For a moment, the crowd outside the car fell silent, and then they began to clamor again. This time there were notes of discordance, of anger, in the noise. Fool moved the transport forward, pushing it through the crowds; a sign, a piece of painted material on a wooden pole, swung out from the press of people and banged into the windshield. For a second the material covered the glass, the words *We Deserve Better* visible, and then it whirled away into the press of people. More bangs sounded against the roof, hands hammering down and other, harder, things. Something hit the rear window with a sharp crack and a splintered star leaped across its glass face.

As the transport passed between the gates, demons moved to shift the milling crowd back. More rocks and chunks of masonry fell into the courtyard around the transport as Fool and the angels alighted. Balthazar had his flame drawn again and was slicing at the air, each slice performing intricate patterns that connected with the missiles, sending them spinning to the sides with a metallic clattering noise. Sparks leaped like bloated fireflies each time flame and rock collided, pale and short-lived in the chaotic air. Adam, meanwhile, simply walked to the entrance to the building, head down, and the scribe and archive followed. Nothing falling from the sky hit him, seeming to veer away at the last moment to bounce harmlessly on the ground. A single stone hit the scribe in the side of the head as he scurried after Adam; he did not seem to notice and the angel did not look around.

Balthazar pushed Fool, none too gently, toward the door. The angel was glowing a fiery red, his skin like burnished bronze reflecting nearby pyres, and he was grinning broadly, his teeth showing. He was enjoying himself, his arm and flame now indistinguishable from each other, an incandescent blur tearing at the sky and keeping them safe. His eyes, Fool saw, were blood-red orbs without pupil or sclera. Despite his beauty, he was more terrifying than anything Fool had seen, and when the angel turned his gaze on him and said, "Move," Fool almost ran for the door.

By the time Adam and Elderflower were seated around the table, attendants waiting patiently behind them, demons were moving among the crowd and stopping the stone-throwing. Fool watched through the grimy windows, only barely listening to the discussions beginning behind him, as the mass of humanity outside the building shifted and roiled. Signs appeared and disappeared, emerging and then dropping as a demon approached, its passage visible as an odd wake that reminded Fool of the movement of the swimming things in Solomon Water that could be seen only as a disturbance on the water's surface. Some of them had a slogan he was getting used to, *We Deserve Better*, but others had ones he hadn't seen before: *Help Us* and *Take Us Up*. One that he didn't see clearly had a single word printed upon it, and for a moment he was convinced it had said simply *Fool* before dismissing it as a stupid notion.

"They are restive," said Balthazar. He had faded back to his usual, paler skin tone and his eyes were almost human again.

"You sound impressed," said Fool.

"Impressed? Yes. They are no longer acting like cattle but are acting like humans, fighting against evil as God intended them to." Behind them, the litany of names being accepted and refused was soft in Fool's ears, like water spilling into thick dust.

"What do you do next in your investigation?" asked Balthazar. For the first time, his tone was almost pleasant, as though Fool were, if not an equal, then at least some more interesting kind of inferior.

"I go to see the Man," said Fool, "to see if he reaches as far as the building we were at today. He may have seen something."

"And if he has, he will tell you?"

"I don't know. He may, if he finds it amusing or I have something to trade. I'll take your feather; he may bargain with me for it."

"And this is how your investigations usually work?"

"No," said Fool. "Usually no one cares about the dead."

"Even you?"

"Even me," said Fool, ashamed at the truth. "There are so many of them, so much violence and misery, so many crimes that we can't solve them all, so we end up solving none of them. *I* end up solving none of them."

"And this one? It's different?"

"This one? Yes. I mean no, it's no different, not really, but I'm different. I'll solve it."

"Why?"

"Because if not me," said Fool, "who else?"

"We're finished," said Elderflower loudly from behind them. He had not asked Fool a single question during this discussion. As Fool turned to go, Balthazar grinned at him, showing his teeth again, and said, "Why, Fool, you should beware. You are becoming Hell's hero."

"No," said Fool.

"Oh yes," said Balthazar. "I come from Heaven, Fool, and Heaven is full of heroes. I have learned to recognize them."

Heroic Fool, thought Fool as Balthazar went to Adam, *little heroic stupid Fool.*

PART TWO
TRAILS

15

After the delegation had finished their discussions Fool updated Elder-flower, which took a long time. The small man asked a large number of questions, picking over every aspect of the investigation and of what the delegation had done and said. Fool was jittery, wanting to be gone, aware that the day was crumpling into night and that his office would already be full of canisters that would need stamping with *DNI* and sending back to wherever they had come from before he could visit the Man and update him, *amuse* him, with the information about Diamond and ask if he had heard anything more. He was exhausted, and wondered when he had last slept in his bed. He had dozed on the train, he remembered, and before that in Gordie's room, but in his bed? Yesterday? Two days ago?

Elderflower eventually let Fool go, saying, "You seem eager to move, Thomas. Being noticed has given you energy."

"I have something to do," replied Fool, "in relation to the murders, the blue ribbons, I mean. I have an idea, a . . ." He realized that he didn't know how to describe what he was trying to do, had never really done it before. He had a single piece of information, less than that, really, more a hope of information, and it had laid a path out before him.

"I'm following a trail," he said eventually. "There are signs being left, like pieces of a puzzle, a guess, each one a few steps farther on than the last, and it might lead somewhere. I don't know."

"You're doing well, Thomas," said Elderflower. "You are being watched with interest. Rhakshasas passes his compliments, and instructs me to tell you he awaits your report with interest. The archdeacons meet later, and they require your attendance. This is a new thing for Hell, this thing that you are doing. You should be proud."

"Yes," said Fool noncommittally. The path, the trail, was all he cared about now, about where it would take him. He was being led, was following something's lead, and he was eager to see where he ended up.

"Go, Thomas, go," said Elderflower. "Be an Information Man."

The Man's house looked even more rotten somehow, damper and more warped. Fool walked along the path to the doorway, opening blackly before him, and heard the chittering things inside squawk his approach.

He had returned to his office after leaving Elderflower and collected the report from the last body's Questioning. It was briefer than the report Morgan had done on the body from the Orphanage, simply reading:

Similar, although the wounds were cleaner. The murderer used their bare hands, there were no claw marks or slices, and it told me nothing but a hint that the poor child was killed by a client, but not one that he had met before. The soul is gone.

It was what Fool had expected, yet he was still a little disappointed that Morgan had found nothing for him, no new things that could open up more paths. No more leads.

He had left Summer sorting through the canisters. There was a pile of them, and more had fallen out of the tube's spitting maw while he read the report, more descriptions of battery and rape and theft and a hundred other things that would never be addressed. It was as he left the office, the feather thrust in its usual place deep inside his pocket, that Summer called out, "Fool, this one's different!"

She was holding a thin sheet out to him, its ends curling back on themselves from being inside the canister. He took it from her and glanced at it, then read it more carefully. For the first time in his duty as an Information Men in Hell, a tube's contents were not about demons abusing humans, but the other way around; a group of humans had set upon one of Hell's smaller demons, itself little more than a slave of the Houska, and beaten it to death. It had been found in an alleyway on the Houska's outskirts at the beginning of evening, twisted and bloody and almost unrecognizable, according to the brief report.

"Was the ribbon blue?" Fool asked.

"No," said Summer, "red like all the others."

"Then it gets treated like all the others," said Fool and very carefully, very slowly, stamped it *DNI* and placed it back in its canister; the canister he placed into the pipe in the corner of the room, and they watched as, with a pneumatic whoosh, it was sucked away. Fool found that he was smiling; so was Summer.

The streets were quiet; it was still early enough that the evening hadn't flowered fully yet, the petals of fear and aggression and subservience still curled closed around themselves. Knots of humans were dotted here and there, some moving to or from the train routes, others heading to the Houska's bars and clubs. Outside one bar, a larger group of humans, filthy from working in one of Hell's factories, were drinking. As Fool passed, they saw him and, for some reason, cheered.

The Man of Plants and Flowers' house was lit from within, a pale glow shimmering in most of the windows and through the gaping doorway. Fool had never come to the Man's house uninvited before, and although he expected that the Man knew he was coming, he was still wary. Fool, despite having the feather and being entertaining to the Man, didn't overestimate his value; he was a small thing that had achieved the dubious honor of being noticed by the Man and others in Hell's hierarchies, nothing more. He made sure that his holster was only loosely strapped closed and that the feather was deep in a pocket, and went in.

The glow was stronger inside, wavering bright to dim and to bright again like a phosphorescent heartbeat. "Hello?" called Fool, treading cautiously over the corded vines that straggled across the floor. They were writhing slightly, clenching and shuddering, and he made sure that he didn't step on them. The Man's mouths opened and closed rhythmically, dipping and swaying and jerking. One closed around Fool's trouser cuff but immediately opened and let it go, leaving a powdery green streak where it had been. Flying things swooped in the air about him, chittering, as he went along the hallway and to the entrance of the room where the Man was most present.

The glow was brightest here, pulsing lazily along the Man's outstretched limbs from the central mass of him nestled in the corner. Everything in the room was shaking, shuddering, so that the air was filled with rustling and the noise of fronds rubbing against fronds. Something within the mass moved, shifting around, and then spasmed.

The Man's tendrils writhed violently for a second, several of them jerking away from the walls and waving in the air before falling to the floor. Leaves all along the Man's many limbs curled into clenched balls and then seemed to relax. One final pulse of light danced about the room and the Man sighed, long and slow.

Fool waited; he might come to the house without an invitation, but entering the room without the Man's permission was a step beyond where he was prepared to go. He wasn't sure what he had just seen, and had no idea what mood the Man might be in. Was that the Man expanding somehow? Growing into a new place? Or had, somewhere, a part of him been burned or trampled? Fool suddenly wondered about the farmland, about the scrubby crops that grew there, and whether they were also a part of the Man. Did he feel himself harvested and resown, the roots churned into the dry earth as the stems were reaped? Or was that one of the areas he had told Fool he had little access to? There was grass at the edges of the Flame Garden, Fool suddenly remembered; were they the Man, or was the heat too great, was the burning at the grassland's edge too much to bear? Fool supposed he'd never know, caught a sense in that moment of just how far from human the Man had traveled, how sheerly *other* he had become, and wondered how to communicate any of this to the archdeacons, to Rhakshasas. Even demons were understandable, quantifiable, had a logic across the species despite the individual differences, the variations in size and shape and look and history, but the Man had become something unique in all of Hell.

"Fool?" said the Man, and his voice was low.

"I'm here," said Fool.

"Come in," said the Man, still quiet. His voice sounded different, breathy and hoarse. Fool entered the room, again stepping over the parts of the Man that lay strewn around the floor. Most were motionless, although one or two were moving slightly, in tiny jerks and contractions. As Fool made his way to the center of the room, the Man's various branches and leaves that wound their way all around the room began to move more, lifting themselves from the floor. The Man's mouths opened and when he spoke next, his voice was stronger.

"Well, Fool. Am I to be entertained?"

"No," said Fool, uncomfortably, "questioned."

There was a pause, during which the Man's limbs continued to move, stretching and then curling. It reminded Fool, absurdly, of the movement he made when he awoke sometimes, stretching his arms out and then wrapping them back in.

"Well, Fool?" said the Man eventually.

"The building where the latest body was found," said Fool. He didn't explain which of Hell's many bodies he was talking about, assuming that the Man would know, would have been tracking him all day.

"Yes?"

"You can see it? You're around it, I mean?"

"Yes."

"What did you see that night? Did you see the thing that killed the Genevieve?"

"Yes," said the Man, still moving around Fool. Flying things were swooping and chirping above Fool's head, landing on the Man and taking off again. One alighted on the edge of an open mouth, its wings brushing against the barbs that lined the mouth's lips. A moment later, it took off, unmolested.

"What was it?"

"Something terrible, Fool," said the Man. "Something shrouded in darkness and old, something that lives at the heart of Hell. It was too terrible to look at fully, Fool, clothed in flame and blood, and it took that boy from the street and tore him to pieces."

"Is that it?" said Fool, frustrated. "You didn't see anything else, something that might help me find it? Catch it?" *Little optimistic Fool,* he thought. *Little foolish optimistic Fool.*

"You intend to catch it?"

"Yes," said Fool. "I'll catch whatever's doing these killings and . . . and . . ." He tailed off. And what? Tell Elderflower and hope that he did something? Tell Rhakshasas and the other demons of the court and hope that they acted? Write it into a canister and send it up the pneumatic pipe in his office to wherever it was they went, to be read by whoever it was that read them?

"Have faith, Fool," said the Man. "Keep the feather close and keep pushing on. You are engaged in a noble cause, trying to find the murderer of those poor dead children. You will, I am sure, prevail."

"How, when I have nothing to go on, no trails to follow?"

"It was an old thing, Fool," said the Man. "Where do the old things live, here in Hell? Perhaps you could start there."

"They live in the walled section," said Fool, thinking, *Yes. Yes, he said that before, to look to the highest point. They live on the hill looking down upon us, the elders and the things that no longer wish to be seen. They live in Crow Heights.*

16

"Elderflower is wrong," said Rhakshasas. Around him, the other arch-deacons nodded and sounded assent.

"You should not be proud," continued Rhakshasas. "There is no pride in what you do. You are a grub, wriggling through Hell's shit, blind and lost."

"Yes," said Fool, thinking, *No*.

"You are a worm, set to quest where we send you. Set to investigate the Man. Tell us what you have found." Rhakshasas leaned forward over the table, the intestines tautening around him. A noise like the buzz-ing of flies filled the air, metallic and hot. One of the other archdea-cons gleamed blackly, its mouth open and its tongue emerging in a long, writhing wave. The air above it was hazy and seemed full of things that Fool could not quite see, swooping and darting.

"He is strong, and his soul is spread throughout the parts of himself," Fool said. "Destroying the parts of him doesn't destroy all of him. I think it's a deliberate thing he's done, somehow."

"Yes," said one of the other demons, something nominally female with strings of what looked like excrement, dried and crumbling, for hair. "It's an old magic he's found. He has a body, though. Flesh. Dreams. He is not invulnerable."

"I don't know," said Fool, thinking about the skeletons he had seen in the tangles of foliage to the rear of the property, about the way the Man moved and his speed, about the way his pale skin had gradually been lost to view in the room so that now there was only the mass of greenery in one corner, pressed back against the house's wall. "I mean, yes, I think there's still some flesh, that his center is still in the house. He must have a heart, I suppose, but he's protected to the front and back."

"Does he dream?"

Who had asked that? Fool couldn't tell; it was simply another voice from the table in front of him, all the archdeacons leaning forward now, clothed in flesh and dung and mud and fire and smoke, all peering at him. Dreams, they always wanted dreams and fear; it was the demons' food, chewed out of the flesh like marrow sucked from bones. Did the Man dream? Fool remembered the way the Man had shivered as he withdrew the angel's feather from one of his mouths. Had that been an orgasm? Was that a dream as well, a dream made flesh for one brief moment? "Yes," he said, after a moment, "I think he does. He dreams of Hell burning, changing. Of chaos. Of pleasure."

"Does he?" asked Rhakshasas, and the entrails around him tightened and pulsed, angry.

"Pleasure," said another of the archdeacons. "It thinks it is allowed pleasure? It dares to dream of pleasure? It cannot be allowed. It cannot."

It, Fool noticed, not *he*. The Man was so far past what the archdeacons understood now that he wasn't even human enough to have a gender. There was a rumbling from the room, from all around him now, as the rulers of Hell considered the Man. One of them began to froth at the mouth, spitting liquid out that hissed and sizzled where it landed, before collapsing from the table and thrashing arms and legs that were little more than tentacles around and making a noise like a badly warping kettle boiling dry. The others ignored it, focusing on Fool. Their attention had weight, burned his skin in prickles as though he'd thrust his hand into a nest of faintly poisonous plants or slightly acidic water.

"And the murders, Fool? What of the murders?"

"They happen," said Fool. "The dead have their souls eaten."

Fool's statement cut through the noise. The archdeacons must have known, he thought; they must, as they wrote the parchments that Elderflower sent him and they were who Elderflower reported to, and he wondered why it bothered them to hear it before realizing; they were the only things with anything like enough power to consume a whole soul in all of Hell, yet they were not responsible for these deaths. *They're worried,* thought Fool suddenly. *They're worried because they're unsure. And I know they're worried because I'm getting better at seeing through the surface and glimpsing the things beneath.*

"Find us more, Fool," said Rhakshasas. "You are proving a more useful worm than we anticipated, and we are pleased. We may have rewards for you if you carry on performing so well, burrowing so sweetly. Find us more about the Man, about these murders."

Fool thought of the bones again, of the mouths that rose up and opened and closed, about the Man's voice and the way he writhed and grew and ate, about bodies with their souls ripped from them, and said nothing. What could he say? He was Hell's Information Man, one of only two, and he had a trail to follow. Turning, he left the archdeacons as they turned toward each other and began to talk, their conversation sounding like a coarsened version of the trading delegation meetings he had attended, and left them to their work.

It was late, too late to keep investigating; the streets were unsafe. Even on his short walk between Assemblies House and the Information Offices, Fool could sense the danger. Of course, danger was a constant in Hell, always there, always hovering, but at night it became more distinct. At night, all but the heaviest of industries stopped working and the workers were free to come to the Houska. Some, those who had something to trade, would come and drink; others would simply hang around, hoping to steal or beg or borrow drinks. Some demons would buy drinks for humans in exchange for minor bites and brutalities before finding a Genevieve to use more harshly; others would simply take what they wanted by fist or claw or tooth. Even here, in the relatively quiet streets of the Bureaucracy, things held themselves in the shadows, shapes that beetled in patches of darkness and followed, waiting to see if a chance presented itself. Fool walked with one hand on the butt of his gun and hoped that he would not have to draw it.

The offices were quiet. Summer had gone to bed but was not asleep; he could hear her through the door, crying. For a minute he stood by her room, fist raised to knock, wondering whether he could comfort her somehow. He caught a glimpse of himself in the small mirror that hung in the hallway, its glass warped and dark, his battered and lined face a mess of bruises and scratches, his hair short and partially stubbled where the orphans' flames had touched him, and thought, *What comfort can I give?* He let his hand fall and turned away, retreating to the main office.

Despite having cleared them earlier in the day, there was already a pile of new canisters on the floor below the tube. Fool, sighing, sat at his desk and started to open them, stamp them, and return them. After a few, however, he stopped and stared at the battered metal containers. Each one was a crime, each one a flat record of pain and fear and loss, sent by Rhakshasas and the other archdeacons, a never-ending tide that Fool could neither stem nor prevent. He thought of his face in the mirror, older than Gordie's, and wondered how much longer he might last. Another day? A month? A year?

Leaving the canisters, he went to his room, stripped, and lay on his bed. Sleep came quickly and he did not dream.

17

Crow Heights was Hell's oldest habitation, so the rumors had it, a huge walled enclave in which the oldest, most powerful demons resided. It was, besides the wall between Hell and the oceans of Limbo outside it and the Mount, on which the tunnel to Heaven sat, the highest point of Hell's topography. Fool had never been farther than its gates.

Rumors; there were always rumors, passed like currency from person to person, always bad so that atrocity layered upon atrocity until the truths, if any existed, were lost. Black transports crawled Hell's streets, it was said, picking up stragglers, bringing them to the Heights; demons drove the transports, minor ones, and once they delivered the humans, those people were never seen again. The Heights' inhabitants had retreated there when Hell had drained its lakes of sulphur and doused most of its fires, disgusted with the changing approaches to the punishment of the Sorrowful, and no one and nothing, besides the black transports carrying the humans intended as food for those oldest and most powerful of Hell's demons, ever entered or left the Heights. The buildings at the center of the Heights were permanently afire, flames boiling inside blackened walls; Satan himself lived permanently in the flames, never leaving, burning and watching and grinning all the while.

Of course, most of these rumors were nonsense, Fool knew. The delegations from Heaven sometimes stayed in the Heights, in vast decaying buildings not far from its main gate, and both food and documents were delivered here and waste removed by large gray transports driven by humans with demon escorts. Fool had accompanied Elderflower here several times, and although he had never been allowed to enter the place itself, he had seen through the gateway when the wooden barriers, black with age and filth, were opened. In those short moments, the Heights were revealed to him as a series of muddied streets disappearing between buildings constructed of damp and crumbling stone. Curls of mist rose from the mud, filling the streets with wraiths. With the exception of Elderflower and members of the delegation, he had never seen anything besides the mist move inside Crow Heights.

Before approaching the gates, Fool walked some distance around the Heights' perimeter. It was early, still dark, and he had brought a lantern with him. Its flickering light showed him things he had looked at before but never truly seen. From a distance, the wall that encircled the Heights looked huge and solid, but closer to it Fool saw signs of slow decay. Plants burrowed through the mortar and wrapped themselves around the rusting metal spikes that topped the brickwork like a rotten crown. Moss, green and gray, furred most of the great blocks, and those that were still uncovered seemed to sweat moisture like anxious flesh.

In at least two places, Fool found that the wall had collapsed, leaving jumbled stone on the ground and gaps through which he could see more of the Heights' silent streets. These were also rutted and muddy, and the buildings that hemmed them old and collapsing and black. Mist curled across the ground and up to the buildings in long, probing fingers. Nothing else moved.

The problem was, Fool didn't know what he was looking for. Some grand demon, wandering the Heights' streets and picking flesh from between its teeth? Dressed in flame, the Man had said, and black. Surely there were hundreds of demons like that, older ones at least; they rarely came into view but he knew they existed, even as he knew that Hell had once been a place that clothed itself in fire. Some of Hell's rare older human inhabitants claimed to have memories of those times, when terrible things with horns and claws and eyes that were segmented and black moved among the humans and Solomon Water burned and all was repetition and pain, but it had not been that way for years. Elders were thought to be grotesque, but in a world of grotesqueries, how could he tell the difference? One of the archdeacons had been surrounded by flame, he remembered.

How could he know anything?

Most of the demons Fool came into contact with were small, spiteful, and violent and claimed ancient bloodlines but were not elders themselves. They lived together, carrying out the tasks assigned to them and dreaming, so Fool had been told, of being allowed to rise up to the human worlds beyond, of being summoned to serve in the places that came before Hell. They dreamed of slipping among humans, terrifying them and gorging themselves on their bad dreams, of living enough millennia to become something ancient and powerful, just as the humans dreamed of escaping Hell's reach, of being Elevated. Everything dreamed of somewhere else, everyone dreamed of something different.

There was nothing here, nothing he could see anyway. What did the Man expect him to find? Even if he saw some flame-wrapped elder, he would have no idea whether it was the elder he was looking for; standing outside the Heights was like standing on Solomon Water's shore and peering into its black water and hoping to understand what was in there. He would have to enter or forever be ignorant, and he was not allowed into the Heights and never would be.

Only, he wasn't sure that was true. Elderflower had once used a word, *jurisdiction,* saying that the Information Officers had *jurisdiction* over the whole of Hell. Fool hadn't paid attention at the time, merely filing the comment away in his head and trusting that Gordie would understand it and be able to explain it if that was ever needed. Didn't jurisdiction mean he could go anywhere?

Did it?

He took a step onto one of the scattered blocks. It moved slightly under his weight and his foot slipped on the damp surface before steadying. Another step and he was up on its top, balancing, holding his lantern out ahead of him. A third step, and he was on another block. *Am I doing this,* he wondered, *really?*

No.

No, not because I think I should not, but because if I go in, I will not do it like a thief, creeping in through a hole in the wall. If I go in, I will go in through the gates, because I have the right, because I am one of Hell's Information Officers and I have jurisdiction.

Standing on the blocks gave Fool elevation, allowed him to see a little more. The Heights' streets rolled away in wide, straight lines, and as far as Fool could make out, its buildings were uniformly shabby and deserted. In the distance, some of the structures were larger, darker, shadows against the slowly lightening sky. Swinging his lantern, Fool gazed back along the rutted road toward the main entrance. A light flickered briefly ahead of him and then went out; somewhere, a guttural howl rose and fell away again. Crow Heights was no worse than any other part of Hell that Fool had seen. In some ways, he thought, it was better; quieter, certainly. Stepping down from the blocks, he returned to the track around the walls and went back to the main entrance.

Fool hammered on Crow Heights' gate with the butt of his gun three times. The hammering left pale crescents etched into the rotting wood and sent dull echoes thudding into the air. For a few seconds nothing happened and then a hatch opened in one of the gates, clanging back to reveal a patch of pale shadow. It was above head height, a square a foot long on a side, seven feet or so from the ground. In the light from Fool's lantern, the patch shifted and swayed; he had the impression of eyes at its center, staring at him, although whether human or demon he could not tell.

"Tradesmen around the side," said a voice.

"I'm not a tradesman," said Fool.

"Then fuck off," said the voice and the hatch started to swing shut.

Startled, Fool stuck the barrel of his gun up into the space so that it couldn't shut and said, "I need to come in."

"Fuck off," said the voice again. The hatch banged against the gun but Fool didn't withdraw it.

"I have questions," said Fool.

"And the only answer available here is 'fuck off,' " said the voice, and Fool felt that fire again, the one that had sparked in him after shooting the demon in the bar. He tilted the barrel, pointing it downward inside the hole, and said, "Open the gate."

Something inside the gate laughed, disbelieving, and Fool let the fire blossom inside him and pulled the trigger.

The sound of the weapon's discharge was muffled by the thick wood of the gates, the flash filling the hatchway and scaring away the shadows. Fool's hand jerked up from the recoil, the barrel banging into the top edge of the hatch, and then he leaped back from the gates. He expected something to happen, but nothing did. He retreated another few feet, holding his gun up, and waited as the reassuring weight of the new bullet formed.

"Open the gates or I fire again," shouted Fool, and he was surprised to find he meant it, was almost looking forward to it. There was a heavy thump behind the gates and then a sound of something wet sliding, and they began to swing open.

Whatever fury Fool had expected to emerge form the gateway, eyes blazing and smoke pouring from its mouth, didn't come. Instead, he faced a small demon, its face almost human. It was dressed in a too-large tunic covered in torn brocade, the stitching trailing threads and with a smoking hole low in one flapping lapel, and beside it was a large box; it saw Fool notice the box and tried to move in front of it. There were footprints on top of the box.

"What do you want?" asked the demon, and Fool recognized its tone of voice. It was one he'd heard humans use, heard them use all the time, had used himself; brittle, trying to project confidence when you were scared, unsure of yourself, putting up a front.

"To come in," said Fool.

"No one comes in," said the demon, tugging at the hem of its jacket. What Fool had taken for thicker cords of frayed material was part of the demon, he realized, dangling extremities of fur and skin and scale twisting slowly around each other.

"I am an Information Man of Hell, and I am coming in," said Fool and walked past the demon into Crow Heights.

It screamed.

Fool had never heard anything so loud; it was a volume that had mass, weight, edges, was more than mere noise, and it slammed into his ears and sent him to his knees. He managed to look back over his shoulder, twisting his neck painfully around. The demon had its mouth open, its neck extended, its tongue stuck out and waggling back and forth so that the sound trilled. The dangling pieces of itself had tightened and lifted and Fool saw that each had a tiny mouth at its end, and that each mouth was contributing to the cacophony. *Did you think it wouldn't have weapons?* he thought as the sound tore at him, and it seemed to be Gordie's voice he heard. *Did you think it wouldn't be able to protect itself? Little overconfident Fool!* His teeth gritted of their own accord and his hand opened. His gun fell to the ground as he raised his hands to his ears to try to block the sound. It didn't help.

Keeping his eyes open became painful, as though dust was blowing in his face. He managed to blink away tears, eyelids flickering, and saw movement from the buildings ahead of him. Shapes slipped from the doorways, stooping as they emerged and then straightening, long ripples of darkness and redness that came across the earth toward him. They blurred, the sound vibrating his head, his eyes losing their focus, but he managed to make out flame and claws and horns. Something roared, audible even over the terrible scream. Fool's bowels clenched, his stomach muscles tightening. He reached down, fumbled for his gun, and found it. It was thick with mud, slippery in his hand, but he raised it anyway. He couldn't see, couldn't hear, couldn't smell anything except dirt and flame and the stench of rotting flesh.

Crow Heights' inhabitants were coming.

18

"What is this?"

The scream stopped suddenly, a new voice cutting through it. Something took hold of Fool's shoulder and hauled him upward. He came upright, managing to get his legs under him and feeling the earth beneath his feet but then carrying on rising, finding himself lifted into the air. He tried to focus but his eyes were still loose in their sockets, feeling slack. He spun, blinked as his focus caught, and then was lost again before something large passed across his vision. It was holding him with a single long tentacle and it appeared and disappeared in his view, and he turned.

"An intruder," said the little demon from the door. The sides of Fool's face felt wet and he wondered whether his ears were bleeding but decided it was probably just tears and mud; now that the screaming had ended, the pain had also gone.

"Intruder?" said the second voice. Fool felt himself jerked farther up, the thing around his shoulder tightening. Something else slipped about his waist and another curled around his wrist. It dug in sharply and his hand opened, letting the gun fall for the second time. He had a brief view of it spiraling down, away from him, and then he was face-to-face with the demon holding him.

It looked like one of the smaller inhabitants of Solomon's Water made large, a huge mass with no obvious limbs except for tentacles and something that might have been a set of wings but could equally easily have been fins. Its eyes were black and watery, the size of dinner plates, and its mouth was thick-lipped and full of needle teeth.

"Intruder," said the thing as though tasting the word for the first time, and Fool knew that the only thing keeping him alive was that he had intrigued it, that it was wondering about him. The feeling wouldn't last long, he didn't think. He had to act now.

"My name is Thomas Fool," he said, "and I'm an Information Man. I work for Hell. I have questions for you, for anyone here who can give me answers."

He was briefly weightless, falling, and then shock leaped through Fool's body; the thing had dropped him and only the mud, thick and slimy and accommodating, had prevented him from being injured. He lay on his back staring at the morning sky, seeing the gray clouds wheel above him, shot through with streaks of whiteness from the distant gleam of Heaven, and then he rolled, scrabbling for the gun. After a frantic moment he found it and pulled; it came free from the mud with a sucking noise. Around him the demons were gathering.

They did not attack, but simply formed a tight semicircle about him. The entrance to Crow Heights, now also his exit, was behind him and he tried to slither crabwise toward it. He had gone only a few feet when his back banged against something solid—the little demon's box.

"So this is him."

The voice came from somewhere in the crowd. Light flickered beside him and Fool saw his lantern lying on its side in the mud, one of its glass panes broken but astonishingly still alight. The illumination it gave was uneven and dirty, producing as much smoke as light, but he grabbed at its handle, fearful of attack. Still none came. He lifted the lantern and the gun, sitting up to try to regain his balance. His stomach muscles protested, tautening painfully. He tasted mud, smelled it, felt dirt against his teeth. Spat.

"It is," said another voice from in the crowd.

"Fool," said a third.

"It is," the second voice repeated, and even through the high-pitched whine of pain and fear in his ears, Fool recognized it. Something was moving through the demons, pushing past bodies that were myriad colors, furred and scaled, smooth and adorned with twisted outgrowths of hardened skin.

"The killer of demons," said yet another voice, this one threatening. "The protector of humans. And he comes to ask us questions."

"It is," again, and then the figure was out from the mass and moving across the narrow expanse of muddied road toward Fool. None of the demons moved; if anything, they shuffled back, clustering together more tightly.

"Hello, Fool," said Rhakshasas and held out a clawed hand. Ropes of gut twisted around the demon's arm, shapes within the gut moving and pulsing. Fool, too startled to move, thought at first that the archdeacon was offering assistance in rising, and then he saw different. Rhakshasas was holding out a tube, and even in the guttering orange light from his lantern, Fool saw that the ribbon wrapped around it was blue.

"You are out of place, Fool," said Rhakshasas and dropped the canister in the mud by Fool's feet.

"This is the killer of demons and it must die," said something from behind Rhakshasas, and the demon that had held him up lurched closer. Its mouth worked as it spoke, teeth clashing and saliva spilling over blubber lips and spattering to the ground. A rumble of agreement swilled around Rhakshasas and Fool, and he had the sense of claws unsheathing, of lips pulling back from teeth, of spines and horns stretching and lowering, of something like a huge spider, new legs emerging from its body and then retracting, rising up.

Of things preparing.

Fool blinked again, his vision still shifting in and out of focus, and thrust his gun around, jerking it left and right and trying to aim at the entire pack of demons at once. His hand shook, the barrel of the gun yawing to and fro as he moved it, mud dripping from it. The trigger was gritty under his finger, and slippery. He would get off maybe one shot before they tore him to pieces, he thought; no more than that.

"No," said Rhakshasas, standing and turning. Suddenly he seemed much larger, the entrails around him swelling and standing out like wings. Against the sky, he looked like some angel gone to corruption and rot, dripping with holes and stinking of shit and blood. He was nothing like the archdeacon behind the table giving Fool his instructions, wary and confused by the Man, but was now wild and terrifying. Claws curled out of a hand that had elongated and twisted, and his legs were gnarled and thick below the living cloak of ropey guts. When he breathed, clouds of dark smoke fell from his mouth. Another cheap trick, or was Rhakshasas himself a thing of flame when he was roused? Fool didn't know.

After a moment, the gathering crowd shifted back, creating a gap through which Fool could see buildings and streets and space and, perhaps, escape. Keeping his gun and lantern up, he used the box behind him to push himself to his feet. His clothes were filthy with Crow Heights' earth, black and clinging and soaking through the thin cloth to kiss his cold skin. The thing that had lifted him snarled and Fool simply nodded at it; what else could he do?

"There has been another slaughter overnight, Fool," said Rhakshasas, turning back, his caul of guts drooping and twining back around his body. He held out the canister again, its blue ribbon dangling. "It seemed opportune to hand it to you in person rather than instruct Elderflower in its delivery."

"Thank you," said Fool, taking the canister.

"The archdeacons continue to watch you with interest, Fool. You fascinate us. What did Elderflower report to us that you said? That you described this as a trail, that you follow its route step-by-step? Fascinating! Go, investigate, bring me the Man, Fool, find your killer. Follow your trail and we shall follow you, we shall watch you. We will be ever there, Fool, ever at your back. Remember that, our little fascinating Fool."

Fascinating Fool, he thought as he backed toward the entrance, gun still aloft. *Little fascinating Fool, watched by all of Hell.*

Summer was already there. She was standing on the edge of the pit looking down into it, and as Fool came close he saw tears on her face.

They were on the edge of a field out beyond the Houska, in the hinterland between the farmland and the inhabited areas. The journey had taken perhaps an hour, walking and using one of the battered trains, and in that time the air had darkened to a sullen gray, the daylight filtered by gathering, thickening clouds. The field was cast yellow with flickering from the Flame Garden, several miles away but still visible. The farm overseer, a demon covered in coarse brown hair with short, bowed legs and long arms that dragged through the dust, was setting up lanterns on poles along the edge of the pit. With each one it lit, the scene below Fool's feet became clearer.

The pit was filled with bodies, each torn and battered. Blood soaked into the earth of the pit's sides, thickening it, and Fool had the blackly humorous thought that the soil would be healthy and well fed in this part of the farm at least. The field stank, of soil that was fertilized with shit and of the Aruhlians' blood.

"How many?" asked Summer.

"Six," said Fool, holding up the message from inside the tube. It looked like more, so mangled were the bodies and so strewn the pieces. "They can't have put up a fight, not really." On the edge of the mass of broken flesh lay the torso of a male Aruhlian, his head turned to an unnatural angle, peering back over his shoulder at Fool. The skin of his face was painted with blood, his own or someone else's, and his mouth was open. He looked reproachful.

"Why were they here?" asked Summer, her tears falling harder now.

"Their home," said the demon, hammering the last pole into the earth. The lantern swung on it, making the bodies below them move in sinuous, shadowy undulations.

"It's a hole in the ground," said Summer. "A fucking hole! There isn't even a roof or walls." She began to cry in earnest now, long, hitching sobs, and Fool wondered whether she was crying for the dead Aruhlians or for the orphans or for Gordie or for herself. For all of them, maybe.

"Home," repeated the demon. Fool, remembering the Aruhlians he had met, with their yellowing skin and foul breath and stained teeth and their placid attitude, thought that it was probably their choice, another self-imposition in the hope of reducing their time in Hell. And now, here they were, dead. Their souls, he was prepared to bet, had been released from their flesh. Perhaps, after all, they'd finally got what they wanted.

"We're going to need more porters," Fool said, looking back into the pit.

They needed to sort through the bodies, so Fool had no choice but to climb down, stand ankle deep in earth that had become blood-soaked mud, and try to piece the flesh and bone together. Summer joined him, crying all the while as she picked up and sifted and rolled. Fool didn't think she realized she was crying, and then wondered whether he was as well. His face was wet, although with sweat or tears, he could not tell. As they worked, Summer spoke.

"I've been in Gordie's room, reading," she said, voice catching and hoarse. "He was making notes on the Man, about what he eats, about the blue flashes. People talked to him, told him things, I don't know why. They trusted him for some reason."

"Yes," said Fool, picking up another piece of body and putting it in the neat pile they were creating. Blood covered most of his lower body and arms, was thick in his nostrils. The smell of shit, sharper down here in the pit, mingled with the sour odor of the blood. Thin strings of excrement curled around his legs and feet as he went to and fro among the dead, trying to sort and catalog the pieces. The porters, lining the rim of the pit, refused to help, agreeing only to lift the body parts that were too heavy for Fool and Summer to hoist over the edge of the earth slope.

"He didn't know much about the Man, but he wrote that he might stretch over all of Hell and that he had done deals with many humans and even a few demons."

"Deals?"

"For information, protection, to sort out a problem. There's so much we never knew," Summer said, "so much we never even guessed at. The Man helps people, and then calls in favors later. Revenge, food, information, keeping things for people, he does it all, and not just for humans but for demons as well."

And that's why Rhakshasas really fears him, thought Fool. *Because he has his tendrils wrapped tight around demons as well as humans. How can they trust their demons, when the Man might own them because of some favor he's done them?* In his mind, he saw a demon approaching the Man, wanting some specific kind of flesh, and the Man sourcing it for him out of the Sisters, a trade in bodies and minds and knowledge. And for what end, ultimately? He didn't know. He would tell Rhakshasas and then let the archdeacons deal with it.

"What did he find out about the blue flashes?"

"There's never been one before, not like these," Summer replied, lifting a piece of unidentifiable flesh, dripping and torn, and placing it with the rest on the pit's edge. Tears rolled down her face, slow and steady and inexorable. "Best he could figure, the blue flash is the soul being released not to return to Limbo the way the Flame Garden does, but to go on to wherever souls go to out of Hell. It's almost the exact reverse of a Fallen, he thought; an Ascension."

Fool didn't reply, simply lifted another piece of a dead and torn human upward, as though offering it to the thickening clouds. They were almost done, finally, the pieces gathered and the mounds they made as neat as could be. After a moment, Summer spoke again.

"He tried to draw the feather, you know? He couldn't draw at all, but he made little sketches of it all on one piece of paper, lots of them, over and over."

"Really," said Fool, hand reflexively moving to his inner pocket and then realizing he wasn't wearing his jacket; it was folded onto the earth away from the blood. Even from here, he thought he could *feel* the feather, though, calming and smooth and gentle. "Did he write anything about it?"

"No, there were just pictures," she said. "Lots of badly drawn little pictures."

Another piece of body, leaving only fragments at their feet, and the stink of it in Fool's nostrils so that he thought he might never be free of it. Another piece, dripping, fragments of bone splintered through the flesh and digging at him like needles, and he lifted and the porters watched impassively and the sky above them turned and did not care.

"Why didn't they fight? Or run?" asked Summer.

"I don't know," said Fool. "Perhaps they tried but weren't strong enough or fast enough."

"Perhaps they accepted their deserved fate as sinners," said Balthazar from above them. Fool looked at the angel, who had appeared with-out sound. Adam was standing beside him. Elderflower was with them, and Fool thought that the two figures behind the angels were likely the scribe and archive, still faithfully following their masters around.

"No one deserves this," said Summer. "They lived in a furrow in a field and something's torn them apart. This is . . . ." She trailed off, as if she couldn't find the words large enough or bitter enough to describe it.

"Is this God's justice?" asked Fool, standing and gesturing about him at the stained earth. Most of the body parts were up on stretchers now, and only the last few pieces remained for them to sort, floating among the shit in the liquid mud. "Is this what God wants?" He reached down and lifted a long snake of something that might have been intestine from the bloodied ground. It slipped through his fingers and he felt small lumps inside it, the Aruhlian's food, he supposed, his or her last meal now forever trapped in the tube of gut. Balthazar did not reply but Adam said, "God's love is even here, although it may take forms that we cannot comprehend."

Fool looked about him, wondering where God was hiding. In the mud? In the earthen slope, where tangled roots jutted from the soil? In the shit and blood? It seemed impossible.

"What happens to them now?" asked Adam when Fool and Summer finally climbed out from the pit, clambering up the sides by sinking their feet and hands into the moist soil and using the roots for stability.

"They go to be questioned," said Fool, "assuming Morgan can get anything from bodies in this state." He thought about the roots and said, "And then I have to visit the Man, to see if he can tell me any more about what he saw, or whether there was anything here of him."

"They will be questioned? Have more indignities piled upon them?"

"They may have seen something and be able to tell us. This is the same murderer, according to the tube, but it's different. These aren't Genevieves, and there was more than one. This is frenzied, out of control, and it may have missed something."

"Missed something?"

"Some piece of soul, still in there. Morgan may find it, may be able to speak to it."

"How?"

"There are artisans even in Hell, Adam," said Elderflower, the first time he had spoken since arriving with the angels. "Morgan and his colleagues have ways of speaking to the souls and the flesh of the dead."

"Perhaps I can help," said Adam and walked over to the pieces of folded tarpaulin laid out on the ground with their damaged contents. The porters moved away, their gaze dropping. One raised his hand to shield his eyes from Adam's gleam; Fool realized that he no longer saw the light unless it changed or increased, that he had gotten used to looking at both Adam and Balthazar. *What did that say about him?* he wondered. That he was changing, or becoming hardened? He didn't know.

Adam unfolded the corner of one of the tarpaulins, wrapping it back to reveal the corpse of a woman. She was still dressed in a loose jacket and smock, stained with mud and blood. Her head was twisted around and tilted, her broken neck bones bulging under her skin. Adam knelt and placed one hand on the dead woman's head. His dark robes trailed in the mud, his light increasing, and then he rose and said, "No. There is nothing left."

"Nothing?"

"No. This poor thing and all her companions are gone; this is all that remains. Mere flesh."

"Still," said Fool, "I should like Morgan to at least view them. He may have some skills learned from Hell that may be useful."

"No. They should suffer no further indignities," said Balthazar, stepping forward. He raised one hand and he *gleamed,* as bright as Heaven, brighter, the light rushing through red and becoming an inferno of white and glaring, forcing Fool to turn away. He heard one of the porters moan, and then the light was gone, leaving ghosts of itself crawling in his vision. When he turned back, greasy smoke, gray in the evening light, billowed from under the sheets of tarpaulin. Fool watched as the woman's head, at the center of a wash of whiteness, began to smile. No, not smiling, it was her flesh shriveling as though being burned without actually burning, the hair tangling up and vanishing, her lips pulling back, her eyelids sparking to nothing, her eyes boiling and then evaporating. Her skin peeled back to reveal the muscle and then bone beneath, and then they, too, were aflame, crumbling down to dust, and then she was gone. The other tarpaulins bulged and rose as harsh blue light and palls of smoke poured out from under them and then mud around Fool's feet bubbled briefly as the blood steamed and evaporated. The stench of something scalded filled the air and he heard someone vomit.

"They were the property of Hell," said Elderflower when the burning had stopped.

"Yes," said Balthazar, "and I gave them release."

"Which is not your responsibility."

"No," said Adam, "and he will be spoken to about this act. Heaven will take ten more souls to compensate Hell for its loss."

"Fifteen."

"Agreed."

"Acceptable," said Elderflower. "Shall we go? We are done here and should rest. There are more Elevations to discuss tomorrow."

19

"It wasn't there," said Fool. "It was somewhere else. It killed again, more this time. Where did it go? Where will it go next?"

The Man did not reply in words but his many limbs lifted and rustled around Fool, the mouthed things turning toward him and opening and closing aggressively. "You expect me to predict the future for you, little Fool, little man?" came the leathery voice eventually. "To tell you the what and where of things? No, Fool, you are my amusement, nothing more. I gave you the information I had, but what you do with it is your business."

"I went to the Heights," said Fool. He was angry again, the stench of the dead Aruhlians still thick in his nose despite the fact he had slept, washed, and changed his clothes since wading around in their remains. He had attended the morning's discussions in the Assemblies House ballroom, bored, listening to the trading. Souls going upward, extra slotted in for Balthazar's indiscretion, bartered and bought and sold. Looking through the grimy windows and the roiling, ever-moving crowd, he had kept his face still and raged inside. What was it, this demon that seemed to slip through Hell's streets unnoticed? That could slaughter apparently at will? Had nobody seen *anything*?

After the meeting, Fool met with Summer before going to the Man. She had spent the morning asking people, scattering messages printed on thin paper on the trains asking for help, had pinned more of her pictures of Diamond on walls all around the Houska, but had received no responses other than dismissal.

"It's strange," she told Fool. "Normally, I think that people do know but they won't say, but now I think they genuinely don't know. The demons left me alone and let me talk to people; people weren't aggressive with me. The opposite, really; it felt like they wanted to help but just couldn't. Even Gordie would have struggled, I think."

So, no one had seen anything, no one knew anything; even the dead remained silent, their lips torn apart but sealed. He knew as little now as he did when he and Gordie had found the first corpse.

No, that wasn't quite true. He knew that it was a demon so old and powerful that even other demons were likely to fear it, that it had no interest in fucking but only the violence it could inflict, that it tore the souls of the dead loose and consumed them in its frenzy. *There's more,* thought Fool, *more I know, more I have learned. I know it takes only those who are alone, which must mean it can be seen but simply doesn't want to be. Why? Because it must have some fear of being recognized, or caught, which means it can* be *caught. Genevieves are the perfect victims because they have so many demons in their lives, spend so long alone with them, that one demon must blend into another after a while.*

And it was getting more confident. The Aruhlians, alone in their pit, couldn't be seen from outside the field, but there were six of them and it had attacked anyway, sure that they couldn't escape or harm it. It must be huge, powerful. Someone had to know something.

Which left the Man, and his information.

"I'm glad I entertain you," said Fool, "but I need more help."

"A fair exchange, Fool," said the Man. "Tell me about the Heights and I will tell you what more I know."

"The Heights? There's nothing to tell. I saw nothing."

"Nothing?"

"I went inside but I had no chance to ask anything—not that they'd talk to me anyway. Only Rhakshasas being there allowed me safe exit."

"Really? They would kill you?"

"Without a second thought. They're demons, the oldest and most powerful in Hell, and I'm simply a human. Now, tell me." He was giving orders to the Man, he realized. *Little foolish Fool,* he thought, glancing at the Man's many mouths ranked next to him and behind him and above him, lining the branches that the Man had become. Many of the mouths looked hungry, their edges and thorns browning, not their usual lustrous green.

"It's a terrible thing," said the Man, "carrying out terrible acts. Those in the pit had little chance against it. It filled the sky with blackness and fire and tore them apart before they could scream, Fool, as it did at the lakeshore with that poor man, and then it went back, went toward the Heights. Go back, Fool, go back to the Heights and wait for it. It will come, and you will know it when it does; wait for the most terrible thing of all and that will be what you're looking for, Fool. The most terrible thing of all."

Fool thought about the roots in the pit wall, about how the Man spread, and heard himself speak, the voice sounding as though it came from someone else, somewhere else.

"Is it a demon? You're sure?" What was that tone in his voice? Disbelief? Accusation? Fool wasn't sure.

The Man went into a shiver, the room bucking and whirling around Fool.

"Why would I lie?"

"Everyone lies," said Fool. "There's little truth here, didn't you once say that to me?"

"There is truth," said the Man. "Go back to the Heights, Fool, and find Hell's truth there."

Fool waited but the Man said nothing more. Finally, he reached into his pocket and removed the feather; it was with him all the time now, and he drew some odd sense of security from its presence in his jacket. Holding it aloft, its glow filling the room, he waited for the Man to respond, to offer more in exchange for a chance to hold the feather again, but he did not speak again. *Dismissed Fool, told to go back to Crow Heights, back to the center of Hell, and expected to do what he is told,* he thought, and turned to go.

And then turned back. "Why are you so desperate to get me to go back to the Heights? If this demon is as terrible as you say, you could tell me when it emerged and then I should be able to spot it easily. And how do you know what it did at the lakeshore?" he asked, moving back toward the Man. "You told me that you don't yet reach that far, that you hadn't seen it. What's going on?"

Fool waited for the Man to speak, but he did not.

Instead, he slumped.

The mass of him in the corner relaxed and folded down on itself, the limbs around the room dropping. His mouths fell, dangling down. From some a thin green slime trickled and the air filled with a smell of rottenness and mold. Fool had never seen the Man like this before, and as he looked more carefully, he saw other discordant notes in the room. The flying things were clustered in among the Man's branches, but there were more of them and they did not react to the movement of the mouths, seeming less skittish. Less scared. Puddles of the green slime were scattered across the floor around the room, some dried and some still fresh, and tangled vines lay in knots across the floor. It was the changes to the Man himself that were the most marked, though; he had shed leaves and they lay in the corners of the room and in thick piles at the base of the walls. He had little luster left in his remaining foliage, and his branches were dry, their bark beginning to peel.

Fool stepped toward the Man's main bulk, the place where his body had been when he first came here. "What's wrong?" he asked. The Man did not reply.

Fool, unsettled, sure now that something was wrong and had been wrong for a while but that he had not noticed, drew his gun. The flying things shifted and muttered around him.

"What's wrong?" He wished that he knew the Man's name, but he had always simply called him the Man of Plants and Flowers or the Man. With a little jolt, he realized that he only ever used the name of one other human in Hell, Summer, now that Gordie was gone. He knew the names of more angels and demons than men or women. It was Hell, he knew, made to keep people apart, people keeping themselves unnoticed where they could, and at that moment he hated it, not with his everyday hate, the hate everyone felt for it, but with something more, something that burned and burned and kept burning inside, that took the fires that were already in him and drew them ever onward. He hated, and he was angry, and the Man was silent.

For the first time, Fool reached out to touch the Man. He did so with the hand holding the feather, keeping it gripped with his bottom three fingers and stretching out with his index finger. The top of the feather brushed against the tightly whorled fronds that made up the Man's body, its bone gleam bright against the Man's darkness. This close, Fool saw that the tiny petals and leaves that formed the branches of the Man's chest and belly were curled and browning. He ran the feather up and down the Man, not knowing why but sensing it might be useful.

At the feather's touch, a long groan came from the Man. It wasn't words, exactly, more the sound of an exhalation being squeezed out from lungs and over vocal cords that were struggling to function. *Did the Man have lungs or vocal cords? A heart? How much humanity was left in him?* Fool wondered.

The Man groaned again as the feather ran up and down him. This time, Fool thought he recognized a word in there, "lies" stretched out and made into something elastic and uneven.

Another brush, another groaned "lies." Instinctively, Fool turned the feather around and thrust it, stem first, between the Man's branchlike ribs. It slid in easily, the most perfect dagger into desiccating flesh, and the Man groaned, much louder this time. "Lies, Fool," he said, "all lies."

"What are?"

"Me, Fool . . ." The Man's voice was ragged, distorted, trailing off at the end of the words. "Me."

The feather's light shone out from the Man, pulsing, throwing shadows across Fool. "I'm a lie, Fool."

"How are you a lie?" asked Fool, thinking he understood but not wanting to.

"I'm dead, Fool," the Man said.

Fool yanked the feather out of the Man as his bulk began to tilt forward. He jumped back, tripping over a strand of cabled, woody flesh stretched out across the floor behind him and falling heavily. He lost his grip on the feather and for a second it drifted up in the air above him, illuminating the scene with a vivid clarity.

The Man was coming loose from the corner, pitching forward in a slow, elegant arc. Pieces of him tore away from the walls around Fool with a noise like gunshots, filling the air with spores and dust. The flying things took off from the Man's limbs, adding their raucous squawking to the cacophony, setting off in wide, panicky loops, and banging into the walls. Coils of the Man sprawled across Fool as he struggled to rise, keeping hold of his gun and reaching for the feather. He managed to grasp it, and then the Man's bulk crashed into the floor, sending up more dust in spiraling motes that looked like misting breath in the pale light. A smell of blood and mulch came from the Man's fallen flesh as the room collapsed around Fool.

Branches came loose from the walls, vines snapping and flailing, hawsering through the air above Fool. Leaves swirled up in ragged, capering circles and then started down on musty zephyrs. Fragments of broken wood, chips of branch and twig and frond sprayed down on Fool, the Man's limbs collapsing over him, burying him. There was a noise of tearing wood, crackling and ripping, a tattoo of dull snaps accompanying it.

When the Man's limbs had finished falling, the room slowly settled back to an uneasy silence. Fool slithered out from under the Man and stood. The feather drifted down past him and he took it from the air, amazed at how even now it could fall with such grace and gentility. Smoothing it, he tucked it away into his jacket and turned, approaching what he now knew was the Man's corpse cautiously. He picked his way over the tangles of branches and leaves and mouths, his feet crushing parts of the Man, wondering just what had happened here.

The Man had come away from his usual place in the corner of the room, and the indented V of the walls behind him was dark and stained. Fragments of root and leaf still clung to the plaster, had grown into it, and there were two holes in the wall at the center of the space normally occupied by the Man. When Fool looked, he saw two holes in the center of the Man's now-exposed back. Here, his original flesh was still visible, pale pink and smooth with tendrils sprouting from it, burrowing out from the expanse of skin. The holes were ragged-edged and raw, their insides glittering russet with bloody, reflected light.

Fool had little choice but to clamber up the Man's flanks to reach the holes in the wall; through them, he saw the rear garden of the Man's home. A great swathe had been torn through the foliage, bushes and branches and trees ripped aside, and what hadn't been torn up now drooped loosely over. The hole in the brickwork was fresh, Fool thought; the naked faces of the wall had no moss and were the fresh pink of brick that had not been exposed to the elements. The torn swathe through the tangled undergrowth ended at the wall, just below the holes.

He turned to the holes in the Man himself. They were deep, about six inches across, and they looked ... what? Not clean or smooth, ragged, but certainly fresh; as though they were punched rather than sliced into him. Fool had a sudden, terrible thought, and put his gun back into its holster. Slowly, he reached into the holes, one hand in each, his arms descending up their elbows into the Man's back. The flesh was cold, clammy, filled with sharp edges that scraped against Fool's skin. He pushed deeper, pressing against the resistance, smelling an odor of rot and wet and mold, and then he could push no farther and he was inside the Man almost to his shoulders.

At the bottom of the holes, he felt carefully and wrapped his fingers around what felt like a set of thick strings and cables. Experimentally, he squeezed the cables (*not cables*, he thought, *tendons and muscles and strips of flesh, branches and stems and roots all bound together*) and then squeezed harder and then pulled.

Pieces of the Man moved.

It was only a small movement, a twitch on the other side of the room in some of his limbs. Fool pulled again, struggling against the stiffness of the things he held, and another part of the Man snapped taut, mouths jerking open. Fool relaxed his grip; the mouths collapsed back to the floor. He took his arms out of the holes, thinking, *Someone operated the Man like a puppet, manipulated those holes of flesh and voice to give me the wrong information, to send me down the wrong track.* They had torn into the Man from the back, taken hold of him and twisted and grasped and made the Man say what they wanted him to. *Little manipulated Fool,* thought Fool, and felt sorry for the Man. He hadn't really known or even liked him, had been scared of him, but he hadn't deserved to end up this way, little more than a tool, discarded once it was finished with.

It wanted me dead, he thought, *wanted the Heights' residents to kill me, but why? And why not kill me itself? Why do it this way? Because I'm too visible? Because there's a connection between me and it, or because I'm a threat, because it doesn't want me finding it, because I pose some kind of risk to it. But what? What can I do?*

From outside, Fool heard something crash and then the sound of screaming.

———

The air was full of smoke.

Down the street, flames leaped from the windows of one of the smaller bars, sending orange and red shades dancing across the buildings around it. The screaming was louder, coming not from one voice but many at once, containing the trebles of terror and the bass notes of anger and the roar of demons. Fool began to run, heading toward the fire and drawing his gun. A group of figures dashed across the road ahead of him, disappearing down a narrow alleyway; they were shouting as they ran. From somewhere farther away came the noise of breaking glass and more shouts and screams.

Fires were burning, their light lifting the sky above Fool, creating a ceiling of roiling colors and smoke. He passed several smaller conflagrations, barrels and piles of rubbish blazing against the fronts of bars. Demons milled around, stamping at the flames and sending sparks leaping into the streets. Humans ran amid the thickening smoke, some obviously Genevieves, others customers of the bars. One man was on fire, his sleeve and shoulder alight, and his companions were flapping at him as he yelped.

As Fool came closer to the Houska's center, the streets became busier and more chaotic. He passed a group of people throwing stones at bar windows and another launching missiles at any demon that came onto the street. Outside a bar called simply Flesh, a huge group of humans were barricading the main door as demons clamored on the other side of the barricade and, behind them, flames spread.

Hell was rioting.

Fool had heard the term, of course; it was one of the major crimes listed in his *Guide,* but he had never seen one before. No one had. Instead of scurrying about and keeping their heads down, humans were fighting demons, gangs surrounding the demonic beings and throwing rocks at them, hitting them with sticks and wood torn from window frames. Even as Fool tried to decide what to do, the volume was increasing, the shouts growing louder and more frenzied. All the fear, all the hate, was coming out in a ragged blast as men and women howled and fought back. Fool heard chants of "We deserve better" and more. It was one of the slogans he'd seen on the banners held by the crowd outside the

Elevation meetings, he remembered, and suddenly wondered whether this was not something random but something organized.

Fool was torn. As a human, he wanted demons to suffer, to get some kind of payback for all the times they had abused or dismissed him, but as one of Hell's Information Men, he knew that his jurisdiction was over everything and everyone; it had to be, or it wasn't jurisdiction at all. It was in his *Guide* that his role was to protect all Hell's inhabitants; in practice, that was usually impossible and he was reduced to simply clearing up their messes. Now it meant he should be protecting the demons from the human mobs.

There was a group in the Houska's main square, surrounding a demon; Fool recognized it as a server from one of the larger bars. It was one of the many, not grand or powerful or well connected, little different from the nameless scribe or archive, defined solely by what it did and nothing else. Fool had seen it and its ilk carry out innumerable small, thoughtless cruelties, just as he had seen all demons do the same. Now it was on all fours and the crowd was battering at it, rocks clenched in fists descending hard and fast, glass shards wrapped in material or stuck in wooden shards slicing at it. Its flesh, dense demon matter, was resisting the assault, but it would not do so for long; already, tears were opening in its sides and across the crown of its scaly head, and the tip of its tail had been severed and was twitching, forgotten, in the mud. People spat at the demon, stamped on it, shouted abuse at it. A kick slammed into one of its glowing yellow eyes, extinguishing the light of it like a snuffed candle in a spray of pale fluid, and Fool's mind was made up. He raised his gun and fired into the air.

Although the riot continued in the distance, the people in the square fell silent as the gunshot echoed around them. Fool pushed through them, taking advantage of their surprise, and said, "Enough."

"It's a demon," said someone from in the crowd.

"Yes," said Fool, "and that's enough."

The demon rose up behind Fool; he felt rather than saw the movement, managed to move sideways as the creature flung itself forward and cannoned into the nearest member of the mob. For a second nothing happened and then everybody moved at once. The demon and the human in its grasp rolled, knocking people aside as they went. Others flocked toward them but didn't dare hit out in case they struck the man. The demon's jaws were clamped around the man's face, its head bulging and expanding as it sucked the nightmares from the man. Its teeth tore into the man's cheeks, sending blood spatters into the air as they rolled. Fool followed them, shouting, feeling the weight of the bullet drop into the gun in his hand and then grabbing at the demon. Its flesh was slippery and hot, slithering through his grasp as he called "Stop," but it carried on chewing, more flesh tearing from the man's cheek and exposing teeth that were brown and uneven and blood-slicked. Fool, helpless, jammed his gun against the base of the demon's neck, angled the barrel so that it was pointing away from the man, and pulled the trigger.

The bullet tore through into the demon's neck and exited from the far side in a huge fan of milky blood. It howled, thrown sideways, letting go its grip of the man. The crowd immediately set about it again, and this time, already weakened, it had little chance against the rocks and wood and glass. Blood, still spurting from the hole in its neck, pooled on the earth beneath it and then soaked away, trodden in and churned by the feet of the mob.

When the little demon was dead, the crowd surrounded Fool and he was pummeled by fists and slaps, not of violence but of congratulation, and then they were gone, streaming away to find something else to attack. Fool stood over the corpse of the demon and felt suddenly weary, wearier than usual. What good had he done here? He looked over at the man's body, his face torn, shreds of flesh dangling to the dirty ground.

Around him, the air was staining orange with flame, smoke agitating in thicker and thicker skeins over his head. Sparks skittered and danced as ash drifted like black snow. The flames smelled, not the fresh fires of the Flame Garden but sullied and sharp, full of boiling alcohol and shriveling hair and charred cloth.

Hell burned.

It couldn't last. As Fool watched, a phalanx of older demons appeared at the edge of the square, jogging and shambling in a loose formation, peeling off in twos and threes down side streets and into bars. Soon the screams filling the air were human and the running was in terror. Fool, suddenly exhausted, sat on the ground by the demon's body. The rioter lay dead at his feet, his face set into a blood-slicked skeletal grin.

The now-straggling column of demons arrived at the center of the square, and from out of its center came Elderflower. Somehow, Fool wasn't surprised. He took his gun from its holster and grasped it by its barrel. The metal was still warm. When Elderflower reached him, he held it out without looking up.

"What are you doing, Thomas? I don't want that."

Now Fool raised his eyes. Even sitting, his head wasn't that far below Elderflower's; lit from behind by the flames that now raged across the Houska, his hair curling across his head in corkscrew twists, the smaller man's features were hidden in shadows. Screams echoed across the street and around the square and smoke spewed into the air from broken windows and from holes in roofs. Embers swirled about them, sparking and glimmering. *Perhaps this is how Hell used to be,* Fool thought, *hot and loud and full of death and pain.*

Fool held the gun out again and said, "I killed a demon. You're here for me."

"No, Thomas, no, you are not in trouble for killing that little thing," said Elderflower. "Quite the opposite, in fact. Hell is pleased with you. Rhakshasas and the other archdeacons are pleased! The Man is no longer an issue, and you make further and further progress in finding our mysterious killer." Elderflower reached into a large bag that was hanging over his shoulder and pulled something from it that he draped over Fool's outstretched arm. When Fool held it up, he found it was a dark jacket with large pockets and braiding around the shoulders. It had large brass buttons that glowed in the firelight. Elderflower pulled something else out of his bag, a pair of dark trousers, and handed them to Fool as well.

"This is a mark of Hell's gratitude, Thomas."

"Gratitude?"

"You protected a demon, Thomas."

"No, I killed it."

"Your fellow men saw you kill it, yes, but before you killed it you saved it. Hell sees these things, Thomas, and it does not forget. You are intriguing, Thomas. You are attempting things that have not been done in Hell before, and there is a keen excitement in seeing where your new activities take you. You investigated the Man and you investigate a murderer, and your investigation stirred up the murderer so that it used the Man against you and, in doing so, rid Hell of something that was becoming troublesome. This riot is a reaction to that, to the Man's death and to something else, something you are doing. You are *creating* something, Fool, and creation is not usual in Hell. These new clothes, your uniform, is a mark of your new status. Or rather, it is a reflection of the fact that Rhakshasas and the archdeacons, and through them the Bureaucracy itself, are recognizing a status you have always had but that has never been properly acknowledged previously."

Fool didn't know what to say. He looked at the jacket and trousers, at the shiny buttons, feeling the heavy, rough cloth with his fingers and then rubbing the thin material of his current jacket. He looked at Elderflower again; something seemed called for, so he said, "Thank you."

Something crashed into the ground on the other side of the square, spraying glass and metal shards across the ground. Shouts came from above them; when he looked up, Fool saw a man running along the edge of the roof of one of the buildings that wasn't on fire. He was scattering paper as he ran, and the white sheets drifted down through the smoky air toward them.

Elderflower reached up and caught one of the falling sheets as it drifted down past him. He held it up and looked at it, turning it around and around. The paper was thin, and in the shifting, dirty light, Fool made out the shape of words and some kind of image.

"Well," said Elderflower, handing the sheet to Fool, "you are noticed by more than even I realized, Thomas."

The sheet was cut badly, the sides uneven, and the writing on it was thick and blocky.

We can fight the demons
We deserve better
The Man is dead but this man stands up for us

Underneath the words was a crude drawing, and it took Fool several seconds to realize that it was meant to be him.

20

Fool then spent the strangest few minutes with Elderflower that he had spent in all his time in Hell. The bureaucrat began to list trouble spots, detailing what was happening and who was involved; which bars were on fire or had been damaged; the places groups of humans were currently congregating and what they were doing; which demons were injured and which were rampaging through the streets.

It wasn't simply in the Houska, either; a group of Genevieves had attacked their masters in one of the boardinghouses and had then tried to burn the building down, and on one of the farms a field of workers (*not Aruhlians,* Fool thought abstractly) had turned on their overseer. Several of them had died in the ensuing violence when the overseer's companions had come to its aid, and the rest were even now, Elderflower said, huddled in an outbuilding with the doors barred, hoping for rescue but expecting death. Things burned and were being torn down, people hid and ran and rampaged.

Fool listened to Elderflower with the riot swelling all around them, but it was as though the conversation were happening in a bubble, with him and Elderflower on the inside and the rest of Hell outside. The noise of the violence, of the screams, of the damage and the fires and the roars and the shouts and the running feet and clawed toes striking the ground came as though from a great distance. Nothing came near them in the square; no humans ran into it, no demons tore through it. Even the smoke hovered above them but did not descend to the ground, forming a ceiling over them.

Eventually, Elderflower finished and said, "So, Thomas, what are your recommendations?"

"Recommendations?"

"What should we do, Thomas, to douse the fires, to bring these situations under control?"

Fool was lost. Summer had arrived sometime during Elderflower's speech, he realized, and was standing behind him. She was dressed in a new uniform much like his own; it hung baggily on her slight frame, and if he hadn't known her, it would have been impossible to tell whether she was female or male. He made a confused face at her, but when she made to step to his side Elderflower hissed at her. For a second, the small man's face twisted out of shape, his mouth stretching as his lips pursed into the sibilant noise, and only when Summer stopped moving did it fall back to normal.

"I don't know," said Fool eventually. "What can we do?"

"How do you want to deploy your troops?" asked Elderflower.

"What troops?"

"Your troops, Thomas, the willing soldiers come to help restore Hell to its former state," said Elderflower, gesturing behind him at the uneven column of demons. "The demons that want order, Thomas, that dream of times when they were Hell's rightful rulers and when humans were simple slaves, things to torture with flame and oil and rock and whip. They will even serve under a human, for a time, to achieve their aim of bringing Hell back to order, Thomas. They are yours to use as you wish."

"Troops?" repeated Fool, and looked down at the uniform that was now draped over his knees. What was this? What was going on here? He felt like Hell's earth was dropping away from under him, leaving him in free fall, dizzy with something that might have been exhilaration or might have been terror. The paper sheets were still falling, some dropping and then lifting again as they drifted into the heated updrafts, sent off in spirals to disappear over the rooftops. There was no sign of the man who had thrown them down.

"Someone needs to go and stop the overseers killing the farmhands," he said eventually. "They're the farthest away, so someone needs to go now."

"Who?" asked Elderflower.

"I don't know," said Fool, and then, "those two," pointing at the first two demons in the line. They immediately left, moving quickly back up the line and disappearing into the swirling smoke.

"And?" said Elderflower.

I don't know how to do this, thought Fool and then felt Summer's hand touch his shoulder gently. He looked down at the dead demon and the dead man, saw his toes scuff into the drying bloodstains, thought of Gordie and notes and string tying things together, and made a decision.

"The fires need putting out," he said, "or everything will burn flat. It'll spread." Fool quickly went through the rest of the incidents Elderflower had listed and sent demons to sort them out; stop the fighting, release the humans, put the fires out, restore order, prevent the death, prevent the destruction, instruction after instruction, and after each one the demons he pointed at left without question. *I'm a human, giving orders to demons,* he thought. *And they're obeying!*

When all the demons were gone, Elderflower nodded at Fool, spun on one delicate foot, and also left. Fool's last sight of him was as a tiny figure being swallowed by the swirling black clouds, his corkscrew hair jutting from his head in twists that reached above him into the shadow.

"What was that?" asked Summer, finally coming and standing next to him.

"I don't know," said Fool. Soot gritted and crunched under his feet and the smell of fires felt painted into his nostrils. He looked up; the man with the leaflets had reappeared on the roof, and although he was too far away to see, Fool was suddenly convinced that he was looking straight down into the square and had seen everything that had happened in these last few minutes. As Fool stared at him, the man thrust a fist into the air and shouted something that the heat took and whirled away, and then a violent blue flash rippled across the sky, turning the man and the building he was standing on into an angular and depthless black shadow.

It didn't register at first, was just a blue flash, another part of the Houska burning, and then comprehension came; it had been a flash, a *blue* flash, lifting into the sky. It couldn't be, could it? So close, just streets away? No.

Yes.

Without thinking about it, Fool dropped his new uniform and rose, starting to run toward where the flash had originated. Moments later, Summer joined him, her longer and younger legs easily keeping pace with him. As they dodged a pile of burning wood and started down an alleyway between a bar and a Genevieve parlor, another flash tore apart the night ahead of them, this one, if anything, even brighter. It left afterimages glazed across Fool's eyes and he stumbled, his shoulder striking the rough brickwork wall. There was a third glaring flash, filling the passage with dancing blue illumination into which Fool and Summer ran.

The alleyway opened out into a filthy space, a wide yard that stretched across the rear of several of the Houska's businesses. Piles of rubbish rotted up against each other, the stench of them thick and sewerish, and mud that felt loose and watery moved under Fool's feet. Old furniture lay in broken pieces between the piles, chairs without seats and benches with splintered legs and tables with tops that were broken and scarred and torn. This was the part of the Houska, abandoned and fragmented, that few people saw; Fool and Summer and Gordie had taken bodies from places like this most weeks.

They went cautiously along the yard, staying close to the rear wall, skirting the rubbish when they needed to and both holding their guns ahead of them. On the far side of the yard, more building rears faced them, hidden behind a long wooden fence that was itself partly obscured by the piled refuse. "Was—" Summer began, and then something pale leaped from between two of the piles ahead of them.

It rose through the air and slammed into the wall in front of them, unpeeling and slithering down the brickwork with a sound like tearing paper. Summer screamed, firing, and the flash of her weapon sent warm orange light lurching in elongated fingers around them. Mud and liquid sprayed up from the ground where the bullet struck and it whined as it ricocheted away, leaving a tiny twist of steam behind it.

It was a body.

It didn't have as many injuries as the earlier victims, but the ones it had sustained were, if anything, worse. It was a man, not a Genevieve Fool didn't think but a customer, some factory worker dressed in oily clothes with dirt pressed in dark moons under his fingernails and into the skin around his nose and mouth in the shape of one of the cheap masks they were given to wear when working. His throat was missing, the flesh gone back as far as his spine and the edges of the wound ragged and furrowed. His upper body had been twisted completely around so that his legs bent back from his belly instead of forward and there were tears in his shirt near his shoulders. Under the tears, the flesh was punctured as though by huge claws, opened down to bone that was startlingly white against the red muscle around it. All this Fool took in during a brief glance, marveling at how much he was seeing, how far his eyes had opened, even as he was moving past the body toward the gap between the rubbish piles from which it had emerged.

There was a crash from somewhere deeper in the yard, a gate swinging open and then rebounding shut and Fool was running again, chasing the sound, chasing the demon that had made it, that had left so many people dead. Rubbish spattered and clung to him as he ran, water splashing up his pants and slithering in over the top of his boots to take his feet in its cold grip, and then he was at the gate.

It was one of several set into the fence, wooden and old and battered, its paint peeling. Fool pulled it open, ducking back from it in case the demon was waiting for him. It wasn't, the opening revealing nothing more than another alleyway, short and empty and open at the other end. Fool ran down it, Summer still at his heels, emerging from it to find himself in one of the demon quarters.

The Houska, Fool knew, was much smaller than it appeared in memory; it acted like a drain at the center of a hole, pulling everything, including people's attention and fear, toward it, but in reality it was only a long spinal street and several shorter tendril streets and alleys, all lined with brothels and bars, places where demons ate their way through the fears and losses and horrors of the humans they bought. Much like the Genevieves had the boardinghouses and the working humans had sections of Hell they considered theirs, demons lived together in cluttered groupings called quarters even though there were, to Fool's incomplete knowledge, at least five of them making up the whole area of demon habitation called the Pipe. Fool had never been in one before, and stepping into one now gave him pause; he was farther out than he had ever been, past reason and sense and safety, but he wasn't yet lost to himself and his sense of self-preservation. This was a demon quarter, this was the Pipe, and he and Summer had to tread carefully.

Within seconds, being in the Pipe began to disturb Fool. The architecture of the buildings was wrong, somehow. In front of him, the short, squat houses appeared normal, but as he and Summer went slowly farther into the area, walking down the center of the road, the ones that drifted to the corner of Fool's eyes seemed to bend into unusual shapes, as though they had been fit together wrong by whoever built them or were warping as they fell behind him, were twisting to watch their passage. Most of the windows were boarded over, the wood buckled and black; from behind at least one set of windows water trickled in thick rivulets, staining the walls in a pattern that looked like constantly drying and moistening tears.

"Where did it go?" whispered Summer. Fool didn't reply but gestured with his gun, sending Summer to the far side of the street while he went to the near side. He tried each door he came to, but none opened. Summer shook her head when he looked over at her, rattling at one of the doors to show him what she meant.

Some of the doors were actually gates, and Fool stood on tiptoe to peer over one of them. Behind it was a narrow strip between the buildings, almost too thin to even be called an alleyway. Similar narrow passages stretched away behind the other gates, most of which were empty, although in one Fool saw a pile of something that might have been bones, smeared with mud and showing signs of having been gnawed.

Nothing moved, nothing made a noise, but Fool sensed that he and Summer were being watched, peered at from countless places behind the wood and the doors and on the rooftops. It was colder here, and Fool's breath misted on each exhalation, damp clouds of vapor trailing him as he moved along. He caught glimpses of movement from behind the boarded windows, dark patches shifting as he went past. Something whispered, a long sound, drawn out and venomous. Movement skittered behind the doors, the sound of things without toes attempting to move quietly as they weighed up the new arrivals.

The road wasn't well used. In places thick banks of mud and detritus had formed, heavy ridges that had packed down over time and that gave little as Fool stepped on them. There was one ahead of him now, perhaps two feet high and rippling across the ground in front of him. He stepped on it, keeping his eyes on the doorways near him, glancing over at Summer, who was still on the other side of the road but was maybe ten feet ahead of him. She looked back as he stood on the mound and he saw terror flitter across her face. He tried to jump away but he didn't react quickly enough to avoid the thing that rose up from the ground under his feet.

He was thrown back, had a brief image of something covered in mud and ordure emerging from the earth where it had buried itself, something that unfurled huge arms and that came toward him with its eyes glinting and its teeth bared. He managed to fire his gun, the flash dazzling him, and then something crashed into him, spinning him violently sideways.

Fool's spin ended against the wall, the impact rattling through him, the shock of it making him drop his gun. He was half down, face against wall when the demon struck him again, driving him sideways and fully over, his face scraping along the brickwork as his legs gave out from under him. He felt his skin tear, felt pain like the sting of insects dart across what was left of his cheek, and then his shoulder was into the mud and his head bounced against his gun. The demon leaped onto him, its feet pressing him farther down, forcing his face into the earth. He tried to breathe, took in a mouthful of foul-tasting dirt and choked, spitting, feeling the grit work across his teeth and grate over his gums. He took another breath, felt fragments hit the back of his throat, and retched, but he had nowhere to retch to, his mouth filling rapidly with bile and exhaled air and dirt and he was choking, couldn't breathe, and then there was a booming sound and the weight lifted off him.

Fool rolled, dragging his face out of mud that seemed reluctant to let him go and spitting out a mass of saliva and vomit and filth. Coughing, he hauled himself over, drawing in a great lungful of wretched air, his throat raw and painful, and then vomited again. His eyes ached, his face burned, a thin gruel of puke spattering across the backs of his hands. Using the wall, he managed to pull himself to a sitting position, wheezing. His eyes were unfocused, and in the blur something pale and dark in uneven patches scrabbled away from him. Fool blinked, clearing earth from his eyes, and saw Summer approaching, gun held in front of her. She fired again and a shriek filled the air. The demon leaped past Fool, darting back down the road toward the Houska, slamming into one of the gates. The wood broke under the assault, tearing loose from the wall, and then the thing was gone; Summer fired once more, and then she was through the gate after it.

Fool managed to get to his feet. His cheek felt inflamed, and when he put his hand to it, it came away wet with blood. He blinked again, rubbed at his eyes, and his vision resolved itself. He coughed again, spitting. The gobbet that he expelled from his mouth was brown and semisolid. He reached down for his gun, steadying himself as a wave of dizziness swept through him, and then went after Summer and the demon.

The gate was situated between two of the buildings that wept water from behind their wooden-bound windows, and beyond it was another alley, the narrow strip sloping down into a pool of dark brown liquid. Fool had heard of this, of demons that lived in water above the ground, filling the buildings of their residence with the fluids they needed. As it spilled out, the water flooded around the buildings; here, it had gathered at the rear. The surface of the water was choppy, ripples banging into the walls and then moving back toward each other and tangling. Darts of light rode the ripples, fracturing and re-forming. There was no sign of Summer.

Fool stepped into the water, feeling ahead with his toes. The ground felt soft, pulpy, and he wondered what he was treading on. He felt sick, a swelling nausea that made his jaws clench and sent his stomach flipping and roiling. His vision was beginning to blur again, separating into two images and then coming back into one. He clenched his eyes shut, tried to concentrate, and as he opened them there was a bright flash.

It wasn't blue but the bright, bleached yellow of a muzzle flash, and on its heels there was a dull boom. The air jerked about him and he stumbled, falling to one knee; the water came up to his chest, smelled stagnant, made his nausea worse and he vomited a third time, unable to help himself. What came out was thin and mostly liquid, bitter on his tongue, but he felt better after and managed to stand again. He wondered about calling for Summer but didn't have the strength.

The alley came to a T-junction in a few more feet. Fool went left, following instincts he hadn't realized he had, reading a handprint on the wall and the way the surface of the water broke and merged to know that this was the way they had come. The water was deepening the farther he went, was now up to his waist. He wished he had a lantern or light with him; the buildings loomed about him now and the flooded alley contained little light. Something brushed against his legs and then moved away, and he hoped it was floating garbage rather than any living thing. Which demons lived like this? He tried to remember but couldn't; Gordie would've known, of course, but Gordie was dead.

It was a dead end. Fool came to a brick wall where the buildings joined. Just above the waterline was a window and next to it was a missing chunk of brickwork, the crater clean and, when he put his finger against it, warm. *Summer's shot,* he thought. The window was open, and he pulled himself up onto the lower edge of it and then slowly climbed in through the opening. He ached, and it took several minutes to manage it.

The space beyond was dark and as he dropped into it, Fool had the impression of size and emptiness; it felt like a warehouse or a barn. The air was cold and the sound of his movements came back to him in repeating, descending patterns of echoes. He could see little, the damp light from outside falling only a few feet through the window. Fool listened but heard nothing from Summer or the thing they pursued. He couldn't see where to go and wished he had some light before remembering, finally, that he did.

Fool took the feather from his pocket and held it up above his head. Although it wasn't bright, its gleam seemed to spread throughout the space around him and gave shape to the shadows. It showed him a wide expanse of emptiness, the floors wooden and dusty. Here and there, square pillars of brick rose from floor to ceiling. A single set of footsteps, dark and wet, led away across the room, each slightly more faded than the last as Summer's feet had dried. Fool followed them.

The tracks threaded their way around the pillars, sometimes widely spaced, sometimes closer together. *She was running and slowing, getting her bearings, maybe listening,* thought Fool, and then, *Little show-off Fool.* It was a distraction from his fear, he realized, to think like this. Each step he took was a step after a demon whose violence was enough to loose souls from flesh and twist bodies into new, warped shapes; he had no reason to think he could stand up to it or defeat it, but he was following anyway. *Why,* he wondered, *why am I doing this? Because of the dead?*

Because of all the Genevieves, sleeping on wires? Because of justice? No, no, none of those things.

Because of jurisdiction. Because if I don't, who will?

There was another gunshot, roaring in the near silence, and then a second later a scream, Summer screaming, the noise choking off suddenly in the middle, leaving things unsaid. Fool began to run, heading for where he thought the scream had come from. Summer's ghostly footsteps had faded to nothing, leaving little more than indentations in the dust every few feet that went toward the space's far wall. Light came from ahead of him, paler than the feather's glow, almost lost in it, wavering. He sped up, feeling the breath tear in his throat, feeling his body resist the effort, the damp cloth of his trousers pulling against his skin, his face throbbing, his belly clenching and flopping. The feather shook as he ran, its light shuddering back and forth. Fool came around one of the pillars, still following the marks in the dust and hoping that Summer would make another noise so that he could pinpoint her, that he would hear what sounds she might make over the rasp of his own breathing.

A shadow rose up ahead of Fool, arms outstretched, held up on innumerable spindle limbs like some huge spider waiting for him, emerging from its web toward him. His feet went from under him, somehow moving ahead of his upper body, and he crashed to the floor.

His first thought was that he needed to escape, and his second, following hard on its tail, was that the building was descending somehow, was dropping back into water. The floor was covered in liquid, thick and curdling, coating Fool as he rolled and scrambled. It slicked across his face and got into his mouth, was salty and bitter, and he spat, expecting the demon to pounce on him at any moment. His gun slithered in his grip and he tried to reassert his authority over it but it shifted, his finger slipping from the trigger and fumbling to find it again. He fell against one of the pillars, used it to brace himself, turning and holding the gun out, the feather up.

The thing hadn't moved.

It was making a noise; Fool risked looking up at it and saw liquid spitting and sizzling from it, tiny wisps of steam rising. Shadows pooled under it, stretched out toward him. No, not shadows, something else. It covered the floor and he saw its color, a dark rust, and it was blood, blood swathed across everything, so much blood, and the thing above it wasn't a demon but was Summer.

She had been strung up between two of the pillars, her arms held taut in the grip of her torn uniform jacket, wrapped around the stone columns in two strands. Her head was down, her hair hanging in front of her face, and her belly had been ripped open and her intestines torn free and left to hang down in great loops, swaying slightly. Her trousers had also been torn and tied to the pillars, used to drag her legs apart and hold them open. Her flesh was white where it was visible, the rich and glittering red of spilled blood everywhere else. Tiny blue threads of lights played up and down her, bubbling out of her and then sinking back. *Her soul,* Fool thought, and then he caught a glimpse of something pale at his side and something crunched, hard, into the side of his head.

The blow sent Fool crashing back down into Summer's blood and slithering across the floor and it hurt, lashing spikes of pain across his head, and he was angry, raging, helpless. He tried to rise but the messages were warping somewhere between his brain and body, fracturing, so that he stood not upright but sideways, his legs refusing to do what he wanted them to, and he tilted and then fell again. There was blood in his eyes, and pain, and it was like drowning, the world thickening around him, losing definition, Summer's body suspended and decaying into a thing without edges and he could see the pale thing coming toward him and knew that this was it and he was done with it all, done with the helplessness and the fear and the agonies and uncertainties and his choices were being removed, each step of the demon's approach narrowing the strip of his life by another fragment until nothing remained. His gun was gone, drifting out somewhere in the tide of Summer's blood, lost to him, but he still had the feather clenched in his hand and he lifted it, marveling at the way it threw out its light, and despite everything Fool managed to smile as he waited for whatever came next.

21

"You're a very lucky man," said a voice. It was a soft voice but it still crashed in Fool's head, echoing like the rolling of rocks down a canyon. He tried to sit but bands of pain tightened across him. Muscles in his lower back went into spasm, yanking him back to what he now realized was a soft mattress under him, bending him around as a dazzling wall of pain reached out through him and took tight hold. He heard himself moan and the voice said, "Don't try to move, not yet."

While the pain receded, not vanishing but at least falling back to a place of threat rather than attack, Fool obeyed the voice and remained still. Someone moved around the foot of the bed and came to his side, took hold of his wrist. Experimentally, Fool moved his head; his cheek throbbed and his teeth ached, his whole jaw ached, but he could at least move. His vision was hazy, though; there were lanterns hanging from the ceiling of wherever he was, turned low, but their light and their shape were indistinct. He lifted his arm but the owner of the voice, a white hovering, restrained him and said, "A bit at a time. You've taken a serious beating and you'll hurt."

The voice moved farther up the bed, and Fool saw that it came from a young man. He was dressed in a dirty white coat over Hell's usual thin gray smock shirt and trousers, and there were crescent moons of dead flesh under his eyes, stained black with tiredness. He was in focus, and with a sudden perspective shift, Fool saw that there was muslin hanging over his bed, draped in billowing waves to the floor, blurring everything beyond the bed. The man saw Fool looking and said, "To give you some privacy."

"Where am I?" Fool tried to ask, but his voice came out as a battered croak, unrecognizable even to himself. The man put a hand behind Fool's head, ignoring Fool's flinch, and very gently lifted him up. With his other hand he brought a glass of water to Fool's mouth and said, "Sip. Slowly."

Fool sipped. The water was cold, cutting through dust he didn't know his throat contained. He took another mouthful, washing it around his teeth and feeling its chill bite against the molars on the left side. He probed the area with a tongue and found most of the teeth loose.

"Where am I?" he asked again, pleased to hear that his voice sounded more normal.

"In the Iomante Hospital," said the man. "I'm Drow."

"What happened? Why am I here?" said Fool, looking down at himself. He was clean and naked, had bandages wrapped around his chest. Under the sheet that came up the bed to his waist he could feel that his nudity was complete. "Where are my clothes?"

"You were brought here," said Drow. "Your clothes we burned."

"But—" began Fool, but Drow interrupted him.

"There's no need to worry, the little man brought another set of clothes for you."

"Little man?" asked Fool and then realized whom Drow meant. "Elderflower?"

"I don't know. Two demons brought you in, which is usual for this place. I thought you were a little old for a Genevieve, but I've seen older. The little man, Elderflower did you say? Elderflower turned up not long after carrying a pile of clothes for you and a gun. He told me that you're Fool, the Information Man."

"Yes," said Fool and then remembered Summer. "Did anyone else come in with me?"

"No."

It was a vain hope, he had known before asking. Summer had been torn apart, brutalized; there was no way she could have survived. First Gordie and now Summer, taken from him and each other, ripped loose from Hell in moments of fire and blood. *Perhaps they're the luckier ones,* he thought, *because they're out of it and I'm still here.* To Drow, he said, "The Iomante Hospital? What is this place?"

In answer, Drow lowered Fool back to bed, this time propping two thin pillows behind him so that he remained slightly elevated and could see better. He pulled aside the muslin, hooking it to a rusty curl of metal hammered to the wall. "The Iomante," he said, sweeping his hand out to take in the room beyond Fool. "We treat Genevieves and Marys."

It was a long space with a high, vaulted ceiling, the walls light brown wood panels lined with beds. Some had muslin hanging down around them, shielding their occupants, but others were open, and in each that Fool could see was a young man. Some were awake, their eyes open and staring up. Two were sitting up, talking to each other; others were asleep or unconscious or worse, their faces pale in the lamplight. "Demons can be rough with their toys and break them," said Drow. "They bring them here sometimes, in the hope that we can fix them so that they can play again."

The man in the bed nearest Fool was swaddled in bandages, bloodied white strips wrapping around his chest and up to his neck. His face was marked with scratches, scabbed and red. Past him, one of the Genevieves was peering at Fool. One of his eyes was bloodshot, entirely red around a pupil that was huge and black, the skin around the eye a rainbow signature of bruises and scrapes. His neck was ringed in more bruises in which Fool could see the marks of thick, clawed fingers. He wanted to speak but didn't, unsure of what to say to the man. Instead, he turned back to Drow.

"They're all men," he said.

"Boys, really," said Drow. "All the Genevieves are. Women have separate wards in the Iomante, to stop the arguments."

"Arguments?"

"The Genevieves and the Marys. They don't get on, fight each other about who the demons prefer. We try to keep them apart, otherwise no one gets any rest."

Marys, the female equivalent of Genevieves, and they were all treated here and yet he hadn't realized that the Iomante existed. *How many other things had he missed in his journeys around Hell?* he wondered. How many other brutalities, how many other places like this? How many people had crept under his notice? But then, wasn't that the point of Hell? To avoid the notice of anything, to keep hidden and hope that nothing took an interest in you? To be nothing, less than nothing, in a place where being something was a dangerous thing? Fool sighed, wincing at the pain it caused in his chest.

"You've got some serious bruising," said Drow, becoming businesslike. "And probably a fractured rib or two. Your face has extensive superficial damage. What happened?"

"Thomas was attacked," said Elderflower from the side of the bed, "in the execution of his duties. Hello, Thomas. How are you feeling?"

"I don't know," said Fool honestly. "I hurt when I move. I hurt about everything."

"Yes," said Elderflower. "It was a savage attack."

"How did I get here? I assume you were responsible?"

"Of course. After your excellent deployment of the troops, the situation in the Houska and the surrounding areas was quickly brought under control. Rhakshasas gave me permission to deploy two of the troops who had completed their allotted task to find you. They followed your trail to the water demons' home and found you."

"Was it still there?" *It*, the thing he still didn't have a name for, the thing that had killed Summer and the Genevieves and the Aruhlians and, indirectly, Gordie.

"It fled when it heard the troops arriving," said Elderflower. "It likes the shadows and its privacy. Still, Thomas, there will be other times, I'm sure. You were so close."

"Yes," said Fool. *Little close Fool, just not close enough.*

Elderflower held something out to Fool. It was a tube, wrapped not in blue or red ribbons but green. "The first Elevation," he said. "It takes place tomorrow and your presence is required."

"Yes," said Fool, taking the tube. The movement of souls, the raising of the lucky few. It meant the delegation was nearly finished, that there were only a few more days of their presence. "Where is Summer?"

"Dead," said Elderflower. "Ah, but you mean her body? Sent to the Garden, Thomas, along with all the flesh of Hell."

"No," said Fool urgently, leaning up, ignoring the pain in his belly and chest and arms and legs and head and heart. "No, I need her sent to Morgan. She needs Questioning. Now."

"Really? If you insist, Thomas. I shall send one of your troops to the Garden to retrieve her before she goes to the flames. Do you have any other orders?"

"No," said Fool and then, "Yes. The body in the Houska needs to be questioned as well, and I want Morgan to do both, not Tidyman or Hand."

"As you wish," said Elderflower. "I shall see to it. Now I shall leave you to rest. Let me leave you with something to read, though, before I go." Elderflower took a sheaf of papers from his pocket and passed them to Fool. The top one he had seen before, the leaflet that had been thrown from the roof in the Houska yesterday, and the other papers were of similar size. The second one had another crude picture of him on it, and the phrase *This man kills demons* below it; the next one a different though equally rough picture of him and the phrases *He fights for us* and *Fight with him*. The others were similar, variations on the same theme. Looking at them, reading them, Fool felt a new pain grow in him; or rather, an old pain made large and fresh.

"I don't want this," he said to Elderflower. "I didn't ask them. I'm not responsible."

"The Bureaucracy knows," said Elderflower. "Trust that it knows, Thomas, because you are still alive to protest your innocence. You did Hell a service yesterday evening, but it appears that Hell's human inhabitants are also grateful for it. These have been appearing all over Hell, Thomas. You are becoming noticed not simply by those at the top but by those at the bottom as well. You are in the middle, Thomas, and Hell is pivoting around you. These are fascinating times, are they not?"

"I suppose," said Fool, still uneasy. He let the papers fall to the floor, trying to show Elderflower his disinterest.

"I should go," said Elderflower. "Unless there's anything else?"

"Yes," said Fool after a pause during which he tried to think, to concentrate. "I don't understand."

"Understand what?"

"Any of it. Nothing's making sense. Like here, this place, the Iomante Hospital. Why?"

"Why what, Thomas?"

"Why is it here? It heals these few Genevieves and Marys but not them all; why not just let them die, replace them from Limbo?"

"Thomas, you've become good at observing these past few days; perhaps you should practice your listening skills as well. Adam has already told you. Hell is not a place of no hope, Thomas, but a place where tiny amounts of hope are allowed to flourish. Most Genevieves live short, brutal lives, even by Hell's standards, get beaten to death or savaged by the passions of their clients, but one or two or ten are brought here and made well. They go back and they tell their friends, if they have any, their fellow Genevieves, about this place, and suddenly there is just the tiniest fragment of hope in a hundred hearts that if they are injured, they might also be saved. This place is the same as the Elevations.

"There is no real charity or goodness, of course. Allowing this place to exist is, for the demonkind, a mere business decision. The Bureaucracy's reason for allowing it to exist, though, is much more complicated. Look at Drow. A good man? Yes. Will he ever be Elevated? No."

"Why?"

"Think of the answer yourself, Thomas. Think about what you've learned and answer your own question for me."

"Because," said Fool after a second's thought, "that would show people that Elevation was something to earn, would give them not just hope but *goals*. The hope of Elevation has to remain something random, impossible to see properly, given not to those who earn it but to those with no discernible right to it. Resentment, fear, loathing, and a tiny, flickering light of hope always just out of reach, *that* is Hell, yes?"

"Of course. The Iomante, the Elevations, those occasional people who seem to achieve some kind of happiness here like your two dead colleagues, these are the things that Hell allows to flourish in tiny, stunted bursts, to make it immeasurably worse for everyone else."

"Yes," said Fool. Elderflower had known about Gordie and Summer, despite their creeping and their care. Had he expected otherwise? No. He had hoped it, and at that moment he knew he had hoped to find something similar and he hated Elderflower for exposing that hope to his understanding. He lay back on his bed, looking up at the muslin above him.

"Hell isn't meant to be easy, or nice, Thomas," said Elderflower, surprisingly gently. "It's Hell, it's meant to be a punishment. We are all of us meant to suffer. We dance to tunes played by those above us, even me, and we hope the dance pleases our masters."

"Yes," said Fool again and closed his eyes.

"Tomorrow, Thomas," said Elderflower, still gentle. "In your uniform. The Elevations begin tomorrow."

He hadn't intended to, but Fool must have fallen asleep, because he was woken later by the distant sounds of movement. Doors opened and closed, voices called to each other; somewhere, someone shouted loudly. Fool levered himself up onto his elbow, wincing at the darts of pain that traveled across his shoulders and back.

"It's just the new shift," said one of the Genevieves, seeing him look around. "Don't worry, they'll quiet down soon. Drow and the others go home and some new ones come. They aren't as nice as Drow, and they don't know shit about how to make us better, but they'll help you get to the toilet if you need it and they bring drinks around sometimes. You're him, aren't you? The one who kills demons?"

"Yes," said Fool, uncomfortably aware of the flyers scattered under his bed and a pressure in his bladder. He sat, very slowly, swinging his legs around and letting them drop over the edge of the bed. He looked down his naked body, seeing the new damage written across his skin. The sickle curves of his hip bones were dark with bruises, and a long graze stretched down his left leg; his right was mottled with scratches and bruised and swollen around the knee. Moving it hurt.

"Swing your legs back and forward," said the same Genevieve. "You'll be stiff, you need to loosen your muscles."

"Thank you," said Fool, doing as he was told. It ached, but moving did loosen the pain's grip. "Have you been here long?"

"A few days. I'm nearly ready to get out and go back," said the young man. "I'm Parry. You're Fool?"

"I am," said Fool, and then the screaming started.

At first, Fool thought it was simply another of the Iomante's occupants; there had been screams at irregular intervals during the hours he had been awake, shouts of pain and fear. This one started low, rose swiftly into a register that sounded as though the screamer's throat were being torn apart from the inside, and then shut off abruptly. There was a crash and more screams, lots at once, layering on each other. A series of crashes echoed, followed by a noise that sounded like ripping fabric and then a wet, thick, pattering sound.

More screams; a sound that might have been a laugh, made by something that hadn't gotten the mouth shape to laugh properly and that had only heard laughter described in words before attempting it, another crash, a shout, and then a voice.

"I smell you, Fool," it called, the words echoing, climbing through the air to lose themselves among the lanterns and ceiling beams. "I smell you!"

The Genevieves in the room with Fool began to scream, their voices joining the cacophony of crashes and screeches and occasional wet gurgles that came into the room from outside. Fool stood, nakedness forgotten, pain forgotten, bladder forgotten, and limped around the bed. There was a doorless cupboard on its far side and his clothes were folded in it. He crouched, throwing the uniform aside quickly, looking for anything else that might be there. Looking for his gun, hoping that someone had picked it up and brought it to him while he slept.

It was below the uniform. Someone had cleaned it inexpertly and streaks of mud and Summer's blood were still ingrained into the seams and thickly welded joints of metal, but it felt good and solid and heavy in his hand. Using the bed as a support, he raised himself to standing and turned to face the door. It was now impossible to tell which screams were coming from outside the room and which were from the Genevieves inside. Some of the young men had climbed out of their beds, were scrabbling for their clothes. One—Parry, he thought—had managed to push his bed toward the door and was shouting at the others to do the same. The lanterns above them were swinging back and forth, creating shifting black and orange shadows through which the pink and brown bodies of the ward's inhabitants flashed and jittered. More of them were dragging and pushing their beds, upturning them at the door, the frames and mattresses forming an untidy pile. It looked fragile and insubstantial.

Fool raised his gun and pointed it at the barrier and the door beyond, shouting. It took several moments, but eventually most of the Genevieves fell to quietness and he said, "Good. Stay quiet, get behind me. Those who can walk, help those who can't." He hoped that whatever it was beyond the door would lose the smell of him, be unable to find him, but he doubted it. As if to confirm his suspicion, the voice came again, like air being forced through mud. "I still smell you, Fool! I know your smell, I know where you are!"

Fool was halfway down the room now, naked, arm outstretched and gun shaking in his hand, some of the young men shuffling behind him. Others were still in their beds, left by the others, and all of them yammered and cried and screamed. Their noise felt like a physical thing, unsettling Fool's vision and balance with its sheer intensity.

There was another terrible scream from outside, ascending above the others, rising to a pitch that made it impossible to tell whether the screamer was male or female. It ended with a snapping and a sound like drinking and then more of that loose, rumbling laughter.

The door rattled, hard.

"Here we are," said the voice from outside, almost conversational, and the door crashed in the frame, banging open and then rebounding from the makeshift barrier. Something beyond the door howled in fury and the door crashed open again, this time torn loose from its hinges and driven into the bed frames and mattresses. The barrier shifted violently, tumbling apart in a rattle of metal, and then the speaker was in the room with them.

It had to fold itself through the door, and it tore away more of the frame as it entered, the wood dragged loose from the walls by its broad shoulders. Its torso was huge, barrel-like, the head on it shaggy with tufts of hair and two curling, vicious horns, its eyes glowing furnace red. It was covered in long, greasy hair that stood out from it and danced as it moved.

"Fool!" it cried and then sent an impossibly long limb snaking out to grasp one of the bed-bound patients, and Fool suddenly realized he had seen the thing before, that it had been the huge spiderlike demon in the crowd in Crow Heights. A clawed hand tightened on the boy's ankle and yanked, dragging him back toward the demon, swinging him so that he struck the metal bed frames before being drawn against the demon's body. The Genevieve hit the flesh of the torso and his screams suddenly became muffled. There was a terrible, brief sizzle and then he dissolved against the demon's flesh, the hair wrapping around him and piercing his flesh, drawing on it, some of him crumbling away to nothing and the rest falling to the floor in a thick, splattering stream. The demon roared with laughter and lashed out again, this time taking a Genevieve from the other side of the room.

"Fool," it cried again as the second Genevieve hit it and sizzled away to nothing, "I'm here for you!" Fool had a moment's awful clarity, seeing the thing's body bloated with the dissolved remains of people from the Iomante and wondering whether Drow was in there, and then he fired.

The shot went high, blowing a chunk out from the thin wall behind the demon. It dropped to a crouch and scuttled forward like some huge spider, scattering bed frames and mattresses, and then rose up in front of Fool as his next bullet formed and he fired a second time. This time, the bullet tore into the demon's belly, releasing a foul odor and a spray of dark, thick liquid that steamed where it hit the floor. The demon lurched sideways, dropped back down into a crouch, and sprang toward Fool. He had a nightmare glimpse of it, limbs outstretched and hair rippling as it arced through the air toward him, its face distorted by pain, and then he dropped and it went over him. He tried to roll but was clumsy with stiffness, instead doing little more than crashing over. Splinters dug into his skin as he twisted around, trying to see where the thing was.

It had landed in front of the knot of Genevieves at the back of the room and carried on toward them, encircling them with its scrawny arms and drawing them in. Fool fired again, not caring what he hit, and the tip of one of the demon's horns disintegrated into dust and fragments. It yowled, spinning about and down and scuttling again. It rushed toward Fool, its mouth wide in a grin that exposed teeth the size and color of human skulls. Fool loosed another shot and one of the demon's eyes exploded, the red glow extinguished in a winking mess of flesh and pus. It screamed, shouting Fool's name as he threw himself sideways and it passed him, one limb missing him by inches.

The demon hit one of the beds, its occupant screaming once before being absorbed into its skin and hair with a noise like fat hissing on a griddle. It thrashed around, tangling itself in a swathe of muslin and the blankets from the bed, coming to an unsteady halt. Its limbs were shorter now, pulled in and trembling, facing Fool. The bullet hadn't formed in his gun yet. Fool was defenseless, scrambling backward in the hope of buying himself another second. Someone was screaming; it might have been him, he couldn't tell.

"You come to our home without invite and demand we tell you things," hissed the demon, "and expect us to simply allow this? You kill our brothers? Challenge the Bar-Igura in their own boardinghouse? You are human, Fool, less than nothing." It opened its mouth wider. Drool spilled from it, landing on the floor and beginning to smoke.

"Rhakshasas isn't here to protect you now, human," it said. "I'm going to enjoy this."

It sprang.

Fool fired, not at the demon but above it. His bullet tore through the lantern hanging from the ceiling, shattering its glass walls and tearing open the reservoir of oil. Liquid fire rained down onto the demon, soaking into the muslin and thin woolen blankets wrapped around it. The fabric caught the flames and sucked at them hungrily, and by the time the demon hit the floor it was burning brightly, writhing. Fool pulled the trigger again but nothing happened. The demon screeched, jerking spastically across the floor, leaving a trail of guttering flames behind it. Fool managed to stand, fired again, and this time the gun boomed, shooting into the blazing, writhing mass.

"Get out," he shouted, waving at the young men. They began to run, still screaming; Fool grabbed Parry as he passed and said, "Help the ones in the beds. Now!" Turning back to the demon, he fired again.

Its original shape was gone into the heart of fire now, an uneven black mass at the conflagration's center. A limb emerged, groped blindly across the floor toward Fool, dug into the wood, and then pulled, dragging the burning demon toward him. Despite the fire, it managed to speak, the voice even more distorted, spitting the words out on balls of flame. "You will die, tiny shit," it said, "tiny human nothing."

Fool felt the heat from the burning demon, could still hear screaming from throughout the Iomante, and raised his gun. He pointed it at the demon's head, now a ball of bright yellow flames out of which a single red eye still gleamed.

"All the demons of Hell will see you dead," the burning thing said. Its eye swelled and ruptured, its contents immediately becoming steam and evaporating.

"Fuck them," said Fool and pulled the trigger.

22

At some point, Fool had lost track of time. He had assumed that it was daytime, late afternoon or early evening, but the middle of the night was a receding memory when he emerged from the burning Iomante, and it had started raining.

Hell's storms were frequent and vicious, torrential downpours that soaked the streets and created cold tributaries that ran between the buildings and slithered against the bases of walls. It turned the streets to slicks of mud and stones, the water flooding down them. People were swept away by Hell's storms, caught up by water that carried so much mud and dirt that it was rumored to be like being struck by liquid stone. "Rumors," he said aloud, not caring who heard him distractedly. "Always rumors."

The rain fell in huge drops, hitting the ground hard enough to fragment and jump up against the downpour, and Fool's visibility was reduced to mere feet, breaking down the movement around him to little more than the shift of gray shapes without distinct form. The water caught the light from the fire and held it, a dull orange glimmer; despite the rain's heaviness, the Iomante burned fiercely. Clouds of steam rose over it as the rain hit the fire, billowing and sizzling up into the night sky and creating ghostlike, featureless faces that peered down on Fool.

He was still naked, sitting on the rough stone curb that marked the edge between the footpath and the roadway, arms wrapped around his legs and head tilted back. Somewhere in the chaos, he had dropped his gun and lost the bandages that had been wrapped around his chest, and the dark bruises and scabs stood out in stark contrast to his pale skin.

One of them had cracked and strings of blood ran down over his ribs. Fool's cheek was sore, stinging when the rain hit it.

Getting out of the Iomante had been a journey of scrambling and heat, dragging terrified Genevieves through thick black smoke that was alive with sparks and licking tongues of fire. As he went, the trail of men and then women following him grew larger as they picked up more and more desperate, terrified patients. Some carried others, some limped, some cried, some screamed, and some were grimly silent.

The demon had caused other fires through the building, knocked other lanterns over in its search for Fool, and the various conflagrations searched for each other as he had searched for an exit. Some doors he opened led into more wards, filled with smoke or fire and cowering people; some opened to flames and heat. Some were so hot when he placed his hand against the wood that he left them shut.

How many had died in the building, he didn't know; lots, probably. In one of the rooms he had seen a blackened tangle of bodies, still feeding the fires, the smoke pouring off them stinking of roasting meat and burned hair. Screams came from all around them, but which were human and which were the sounds of air expanding through rupturing and burning wood, he didn't know. His journey had been mostly random, since he had no idea where the exits or entrances were, and he had been reduced to simply guessing. At least once, he had ended up in a dead-end corridor and had then struggled to turn his group of terrified followers around, to get them to go back. His memories were jumbled, fragmentary, and contradictory. Had he found a room filled with glass jars, the contents of which were boiling, sending the stoppers exploding out of splintering necks in clouds of spraying liquid and steam? Had he stepped over the corpse of a Mary that was already being feasted on by two tiny things, demons that were already burning but ignoring the flames in the scavenging? He didn't know. He knew only that the Iomante was burning and that if he stopped moving, he would burn, too.

Finding the exit had been luck more than judgment. A descent down a narrow, smoke-filled staircase had brought Fool to a wide foyer, its entrance doors smashed across the floor. With black air escaping from the stairway's throat behind them, Fool had fallen into the air outside, gasping, and had vomited violently, spewing out smoke and not much else. People milled around him, some banging into him, as he thought about fire and demons and vomited again. His ribs hurt; his whole body hurt.

Something in the Iomante exploded and sent a clenched fist of fire into the air. The hospital's roof collapsed inward with a roar, the beams holding for a moment longer, outlined against the fires like a skeleton before they, too, buckled and crumbled. What was left of the building was mostly a framework of walls barely containing the flames within; the windows were ragged squares of orange and red and yellow and the doorway that Fool had emerged from was now filling with fire. Most of the Genevieves and Marys who had escaped the Iomante had run; those who remained had gathered into a crowd and were watching the building burn. More people joined them, coming down from the Houska, which was only a few hundred feet away. They reminded Fool of the Sorrowful, gathered watching and waiting and hoping, although for what, he had no idea.

"This is the second uniform you've lost, Fool," said a voice from his side. "You need to be more careful."

"Hello, Elderflower," said Fool without looking around. Fool had expected Elderflower to arrive; the little bureaucrat seemed to have the ability to turn up anywhere, walking out of the darkness or the light with equally delicate footsteps.

"What a few days you're having, Thomas," said Elderflower. "Chasing murderers, being attacked, quelling riots, and then rescuing a group of scared humans from a burning building. And you appear to have killed another demon, Thomas, not some street-dweller, no, an old one! There hasn't been a human who's done that in a generation, Thomas, in two generations or ten or more, so I'm told. Possibly it has never been done before!"

"Should I be frightened?" asked Fool. "Should I be worrying about my safety, about more of them coming for me to take their revenge for my sheer fucking disobedience? I'm not. I don't have the energy. Tell them that, tell them from me to send who they want, I'll kill them or they'll kill me. Either way, fuck them."

"You order me? Thomas, you forget your place, I think."

"I don't care," said Fool again. "I'm too tired to care, too hurt. If you have to punish me, then so be it, you can join the list of things that appear to not like me."

Elderflower laughed, a little indrawn giggle of breath, and dropped something onto Fool's tented knees: a new uniform.

"Dress yourself, Thomas. It does no good for Hell's Information Man to be naked." Fool opened his mouth to remind Elderflower that he wasn't *the* Information Man, he was *an* Information Man, but then he remembered: Summer was dead. Gordie was dead. He was all that was left.

He was Hell's Information Man.

There was underwear folded into the uniform, he saw, and pulled it on. He tried to do it while seated but couldn't, so he stood, dressing wearily as Elderflower looked on. It took Fool a long time, and every movement hurt. There were no boots or socks in the small pile.

"Here," said Elderflower and took something else from the bag over his shoulder, holding it out to Fool. "A further gift from the archdeacons of Hell, a token of how much they value you."

It was a gun, a new one. The barrel gleamed blackly, reflections of the fires oily and thick along its length. Elderflower handed him a holster and Fool strapped it on, dropping the weapon into it and securing it. The weight of it was both horrifying and reassuring.

"Don't lose this uniform, or this gun, Thomas. If you heed any of my advice, heed that. Listen, Thomas, as well as look, and do not lose a third uniform. Rhakshasas and the others are pleased with you, despite the seemingly endless provocations you present them with, but their pleasure may not continue if you're careless enough to lose another of their gifts."

"Fine," said Fool. Hell was pleased with him. *Which parts of Hell?* he wondered. Not the inhabitants of Crow Heights, one of which had tried to kill him. Not the demon that had killed the Genevieves and Summer, or the Man's killer, presumably the same, which had also tried to kill him. *Who*, he wondered, *or what could possibly be pleased with him?* "Who is watching me, watching us all? Just Rhakshasas and the other archdeacons? All of the Bureaucracy? And why me, and not anyone else?" he asked Elderflower, thinking, *Perhaps I amuse them. Perhaps they like seeing this story unfold, like reading its progress in the bruises and wounds I carry. Perhaps I make them smile, little stupid pointless Fool that I am.*

"Why, Thomas, the whole of Hell is watching, and it is fascinated with you." And with that, Elderflower turned and walked away.

He looked down. One of the leaflets drifted past his bare foot, carried by the water running along the gutter, and a version of his own face peered up at him from the sodden paper. The humans thought he was fighting for them, something within Hell was pleased with him, all of Hell was watching even as its buildings burned, he had just practically interrogated Elderflower, and Summer and Gordie were dead.

And something else had burned.

It came to him suddenly that the feather had been in his jacket, hadn't it? And his jacket had been burned when he was first brought to the Iomante. The feather had burned. He tried to think back; he had been holding it in the empty building before the demon attacked him. He hadn't seen it in the locker when he went for his now-lost gun. Had it burned? Or was it still there, in the building where Summer had been strung up between two pillars and had her intestines torn from her belly? He hoped so, and hated that he hoped.

He didn't take the uniform off when he walked into the water, mindful of Elderflower's advice. It made little difference anyway; it was made of some heavy material that became rapidly heavier as it got wet, was so soaked by the rain that wearing it into the muddy water could do it no more damage than had already been done. Fool held the new gun out ahead of him and tried to ignore the crowd at his back.

He had picked them up, unwillingly, as he went through the Houska back to the demon quarter, an arrowhead of Genevieves and Marys that had formed behind him, individuals emerging from the bars and alleyways to trail after him making loud catcalls and cheering as they walked but stopping each time he turned around. He wanted them to go away but they didn't, and he didn't know how to tell them to. He didn't know why they were following him.

He assumed that they wouldn't follow him into the quarter, but he was wrong. They did, quieter, though, more wary; they were in the Pipe, the home of demons, and although none appeared, the atmosphere grew tenser. This time Fool hadn't been cautious but had walked up the center of the street, and again he had the sense that he, they, were being watched from behind the boarded-up windows, and he couldn't understand why nothing came out to challenge them. This was a direct affront, humans walking up the street in a demon quarter, in the Pipe, not because they were being herded for work or taken for sport, but because they had chosen to. Because they wanted to, as though they were free creatures and not the chattel that most demons considered them to be.

When Fool reached the place where the water-filled alley split left and right, he took a last look back at the crowd. None had followed him into the water, but it didn't look like any had left either. They were grouped around the alley's narrow entrance peering after him and they reminded him of something, although he didn't realize at first what it was. It was only as he lifted himself through the still-open window into the building's interior, muscles complaining, that it came to him: they looked like the phalanx of demons that Elderflower had presented to him in the middle of the riot, looking at him expectantly. They looked like troops. The realization made him uncomfortable.

Walking silently through the building was impossible; he sounded like minor rainfall, water dripping from his uniform and striking the dusty floor in a constant *pockpockpock.* If anything else was here, it would know he was coming. His new gun felt odd in his hand, its weight and balance subtly different from his earlier weapon, and he wished that he hadn't dropped the gun he had become used to. *Picky Fool,* he thought and smiled to himself, and then he was at the place where Summer had been killed.

Her blood was still there. It had dried to a thick black crust, the pool of it huge, stretching between the two pillars and out toward the far wall. In the dusty, gray light the floor looked like a frozen shell of swirls and streaks. Fool went to the wall and found the symbols of his earlier presence, gouges through the patterns here, there a handprint and boot print.

Beyond them was the feather.

It was lying in a rough circle of clear floor, the blood around it thick and rippled as though it had been pushed back and then dried. There were little dead things crumpled around the feather, curled upon themselves like flies. Fool stepped gingerly across to it, uncomfortably aware that his wet bare feet were stepping on Summer's remains, and lifted the feather. It glowed at his touch, gentle blue light falling from it and making Summer's blood shimmer. Carefully, he placed it into his pocket, feeling a heat spread across his skin under it. Steam rose from his jacket around the feather as the material dried.

Later, back in his room, Fool sat on his bed and looked at the feather and the gun, one in either hand. He had arrived back at the office without incident, still being followed by the crowd, and was tired and thirsty. In the little kitchen, he drew himself a glass of water but it was lukewarm and didn't so much quell his thirst as shift it, dropping it from his mouth to lower in his throat. *Maybe I'll never be able to get rid of it,* he thought, looking at the glass of water. The glass was from the Flame Garden, was murky and warped, and the water it contained was a pale brown color. *Maybe I'll always be thirsty. Maybe the fire has dried me out so much I'll be permanently like this, a little dried-up Fool.*

The feather and the gun, one in one hand, one in the other. There were hundreds of unopened canisters in his office, but he had ignored them. It didn't seem important, not really. He placed the feather and gun on the bookcase, took another mouthful of water, put the glass on the bookcase alongside the shelf's other occupants, and lay back.

A feather and a gun and a glass of brown water. There was a logic there, a connection he was missing, he thought, but whatever it was could wait until the next day.

Fool slept.

PART THREE
ELEVATIONS

23

The rain had stopped when Fool arrived at the Assemblies House the next morning. His uniform had dried into wrinkles overnight and smelled musty, but he had put it on anyway. He hadn't wanted to initially, concerned that the uniform would separate him yet further from Hell's other humans, make him more noticeable, but as he sat looking at it, it occurred to him that the uniform was *his*, in a strange way the only thing apart from the feather and the gun that actually belonged to him, that had been gifted to him. Wearing it was important because it belonged to him, and in some way he liked it and what it represented. Wearing it would be a symbol of something that he could not understand, could not make out the edges of but that he knew was there, too big to fully comprehend and too important to ignore. So he dressed in his uniform, put the feather in his inside pocket, and strapped his gun and holster to his leg.

He was Hell's Information Man, the only one there was, and he would not hide.

Next to the angels, he still felt lumpen and imperfect.

Elderflower and Adam were at the head of the procession, Balthazar and Fool were at the rear, and in between them were the first seven people due for Elevation. They had been rounded up that morning and were still in their sleep or work attire; one was naked, and all were ecstatic but trying not to show it. Behind Fool and Balthazar was a huge crowd of the Sorrowful, those not picked, following them up to the Mount. Ahead of them, the wall came into view; the entrance to the tunnel was already gleaming and blue. This was where delegations arrived in Hell and where the Sorrowful left it, where Fool's back was set against Hell if he stood one way and turned against the walls to Limbo if he turned another, where lost and damned things crept in the shadows and called out in voices that were distorted and sly.

This was the edge, the place where everything changed.

Some of the Sorrowful were holding banners, but they held them down, were subdued and quiet. Elevation was Hell's hardest time for those not being Elevated, when misery overrode jealousy and everyone's thoughts, Fool assumed, were similar: *It could have been me, it should have been me, why them and not me? Why not me? Why not?*

Why?

The light falling from the entrance to the tunnel grew brighter as they grew closer, a gleaming blue that fell across the angels and those to be Elevated, casting their shadows back across Elderflower and the Sorrowful. When Adam reached it, he stopped; he would not enter the tunnel, Fool knew, but would usher the first of the humans into it. Even now, the naked man was pushing his way forward through the group, scrambling to get to the front. Adam's smile was beatific as he held a hand out and calmed the man.

"This is the time when your souls go free," he said, "when you are called to the greater glories of God and released from the terrors of Hell. Go with our blessing."

Stepping out of the way, Adam let the naked man pass. As he stepped into the light, there was an incredible blue flash that rippled in the air above them. Fool blinked and the Sorrowful made a noise, a collective sigh that was part misery and part awe. At the heart of the light, the man's silhouette was visible for a moment, a black shape burning free of its sin and cares, and then it was gone.

"Next," said Balthazar. He sounded bored.

It took only a few minutes for the seven to be Elevated, to be gone from Hell. With each flash, the Sorrowful made their noise, that little tired exhalation, and the black shape at the center of the light disintegrated into pieces that tore to the edges of the tunnel but vanished before they reached the walls. Fool had never really watched before, never seen the things in the middle of the glare. He didn't like it.

"You're beginning to see more clearly, Thomas," said Elderflower. "Your eyes are improving beyond even my expectations."

"Are they dying?"

"No," said Elderflower. "They are being reborn."

"Into Heaven?"

"Of course. Isn't that what was promised?"

"Tell me what Heaven is like," Fool said, wondering how joyous it could be if you could get there only by having your body burned away in a cleansing fire.

"How should I know, Thomas? I'm a simple clerk."

Fool looked at Elderflower, who was watching the last of the Elevations. "A simple clerk? No. I don't know what you are, suspicious Fool that I am, but you aren't that."

"No? Well, it matters not, Thomas. We're finished," said Elderflower as the last of the flashes scoured its way across the sky beyond their heads, fading as it hit the clouds above them. "Come. There are more discussions to be had." He turned and began to walk back down the hill; the crowd of the Sorrowful parted around him and left the path open for Adam and the Fool and Balthazar, the sound of the mass a low mutter as they passed. Fool couldn't hear words, just a low rumble of voices, and he unclipped his holster so that his gun was easier to reach.

The dead thing was lying at the side of the path.

It was sprawled in the tangled and wretched bushes perhaps twenty feet to their side, and Fool saw it only because he was at the front of the crowd with Elderflower and there was nobody blocking his view. In a place ordinarily thick with darkness that conquered even the daylight but lit today by the crowd's torches and the glow still drifting from the angels, Fool saw a clawed hand pointing to the sky. At first he thought it was simply another demon, one of the lurkers by the wall, something without even the intelligence to exist within Hell's ordinary society, watching the procession, but it didn't move as they came close to it. It was gray, the arm below the hand, and its fingers were curled down, the claws on their ends black. It rose from amid a thick knot of thorned branches that Fool thought were black but realized as he came nearer were actually bloodstained. The area *smelled*.

Stepping off the path and onto the softer earth, Fool went toward the arm. He drew his gun as he walked, felt the angels and Elderflower and the crowd at his back stop and watch him. *Little fool with an audience,* he thought briefly, *little watched Fool.*

"Thomas," called Elderflower, "we have work to do."

"Yes," called Fool over his shoulder. "I'm doing it."

It was a demon, and it had been torn to pieces. The arm Fool had seen was still attached to a shredded nub of shoulder, gray bone sticking out from ravaged flesh, and its torso was lying several feet away in a patch of trampled grass and foliage. Its head was lying on its side by the torso, and although Fool couldn't see any legs, there were several long things like tentacles in the ripped clearing. The stench was terrible and made Fool's eyes water and his belly roll.

"Thomas," called Elderflower again, his voice harder.

"In a minute," called Fool. There was something about the dead thing's face, its head, that bothered Fool. Its mouth was open and black blood stained its lips. Despite the smell, lifting the edge of his jacket to cover his mouth and holding his breath, Fool approached the head. The open mouth was a dark cave, hundreds of needle teeth visible behind the lips. Its jaw was distorted, pushed out by the amount of teeth, but it wasn't that; there was something else, something behind those teeth. Holstering his gun, Fool crouched. The head was as big as his own chest, the mouth wider than his clenched fist. The demon's eyes were open but had started to rot, their surface furred with green mold; insects skittered away from the body. This thing had been dead for a while, he thought, several days at least. All around him was the sound of movement in the undergrowth, Hell's tiny scavengers resenting his intrusion on their meal.

Fool reached out very slowly. His finger came to the edge of the mouth, paused without him consciously wanting them to, and then carried on. Rumors, always rumors: that some demons could live in pieces for months, even as they decayed, still full of bile and sour hate. At any moment, he expected the mouth to snap closed on his questing hand, to sever his fingers.

"Fool!" called Elderflower, the first time Fool could remember him not calling him "Thomas."

"In a *minute*," Fool called. He had hold of it, the thing in the demon's mouth. It was dry, scaly, hard. He tugged at it. The head shifted in the dirt but the thing didn't come free. Fool pulled again, and this time it came loose, starting to emerge from the mouth. It caught on the teeth, which were curved back inward, and he had to pull again to get it free.

It was a tongue.

It was forked at the end, and barbed, and it had been torn out at its roots. Thick cables of muscle and tendon dangled from the torn section, dried and curling.

"Information Man," called Balthazar. "Do you need help? Is the dead demon exciting?"

"No," said Fool, dropping the tongue. It meant something, was another way station on the trail, but a trail to where? Was it even the right trail? It was so confusing, trying to know what mattered and what didn't. Something had killed this demon, a feral thing that even the more violent inhabitants of the Pipe might have been wary of. Its tongue had been torn out and then crammed back into its mouth along with . . . along with dirt, Fool saw. Thick dirt also filled the demon's mouth.

"Thomas," said Elderflower, and this time his voice was dangerously quiet.

"Yes," said Fool and stood. His legs ached, his head ached. At his feet, the demon's head rolled back and stared sightless into the sky.

The discussions took hours, and were difficult. Fool and Balthazar took their places by the windows and waited as Adam and Elderflower argued back and forth across the low table, not as they usually did about a range of people but about one person. It often got like this, toward the end of the delegation's time in Hell, the final sifting through minutiae, decisions based on tiny things that Fool couldn't hope to understand.

There was no crowd outside the windows when they started, but by the time Elderflower and Adam were deep into their conversation, the Sorrowful were gathering. The first set of Elevations had subdued them, but as though reacting against their earlier behavior they were now restive. Currents of people moved through the rapidly growing mass, streaming in curling paths back and forth. Banners rose and then dropped again, only to reappear moments later somewhere else. Someone threw a batch of the leaflets up into the air and they fell like drifting snow.

"We will take one," said Adam.

"Three," replied Elderflower. They had finished the discussion about the sticking-point individual and were back to numbers again.

"One," repeated Adam, and so it went on. Fool watched the Sorrowful warily, not liking the way they moved. There was an edge to the shifting, the weave becoming a stutter. Scuffles broke out, visible as churning knots through the grimy panes.

"We need three," said Elderflower from behind him.

"One."

Fool saw it in reflection in the glass, a blurred and pale shape that rose behind him, and by the time he had turned, Adam's wings were open and extended, emerging from the back of his black robes like scythe blades. The angel rose, his voice echoing in the room as he said "One" again. Fool's hand dropped to his gun, but he felt the heat of Balthazar's flame at his throat as he grasped its butt.

"Do you think you could draw before I remove your head? Do you think that it would harm us even if you could draw and fire?" said the angel at Fool's side, his voice calm.

"No," said Fool. *I only ever seem to speak in single words*, he thought, *little wordless, stupid Fool.*

"No," repeated Balthazar. "Then let your hand drop from your weapon, Information Man."

"No," said Fool and then the things at the corner of his eye moved.

The shadows at the edges of the room thickened, streaming together and lurching forward. They weren't demons, Fool didn't think, not entirely. They were things of only partial substance, darkness coagulating into solidity for a few moments, part of Hell's defenses. They lurched as they moved, their bodies irregular and uneven but fast despite that, forming a closing circle about the figures at the center of the room. They drew what little light there was with them so that thick shades pooled themselves around Fool and Balthazar.

"Adam, please sit down," said Elderflower. "There's no need for tension. We need you to take three; we have need of the space."

"And we wish to take a single additional soul to those already agreed." The angel's wings stretched, if anything, even farther, their tips almost brushing against the shadow creatures. Fool's hand flexed around his gun and Balthazar's heat brushed more firmly under his chin. It stung, a thin line of pain against his skin. It pressed more firmly, the pain deepening, scoring itself against the underside of Fool's jaw, and then vanished.

"Leave them, little Information Man," said Balthazar. "This is part of the game, I think, and not for us to be concerned about." The column of his fire had gone and his hands were crossed over his smooth groin again.

Adam shook his wings, knocking one or two of the shadowed figures aside, and then pulled them back in. In response, the figures melted back to the edges of the room, unknitting around the windows and releasing the dirty illumination that had made them. The room grew lighter again.

"Excellent," said Elderflower, who had not moved during the incident. "So, we're back to where we were, yes? All is calm?"

"Yes," said Adam. "I apologize."

"No matter, Adam, no matter," said Elderflower, and that was when the rock crashed through the window.

It wasn't a rock, Fool saw, but the remains of a statue, a weathered head of some guardian stonework from one of the buildings that lined the square. It reminded him of the tongueless demon's head as it rolled across the threadbare carpet. In the time that he and Balthazar had been focused on Elderflower and Adam, the crowd had become more agitated, reached a flash point, and ignited. More missiles rose from the mass, began to bang against the walls of the building or fall short and land in the courtyard. Some bounced and sent sparks leaping when they landed; others skittered like insects. The crowd pressed forward against the fence, some beginning to climb, clambering up toward the rusting tips of the metal posts.

"Thomas," said Elderflower, "please deal with that distraction."

"Distraction?" asked Fool and then realized that Elderflower meant the crowd. "How?"

"You have troops, Thomas; they merely await your orders."

Troops? Fool looked and saw that it was true; ranks of demons were gathering in the courtyard, standing imperviously as rocks landed around them.

"Quickly, please, Thomas," said Elderflower. "We have work to complete. Take Balthazar with you."

"A fine idea," said Adam. Another missile crashed through one of the high panes, showering glass down onto the floor. Neither Adam nor Elderflower responded, although the sudden noise made Fool jump. The sound of the crowd followed the rock into the room, voices calling and screaming. Still unsure of what he was supposed to do, Fool left the room and Balthazar followed.

24

The sound had weight when Fool left the building and entered the courtyard, a physical presence that crashed and roared around him. There were no voices in the melee, unless the crowd itself had become a single voice that gave vent to all the fears and anger of the individuals within it. Rocks hit the ground and walls, the sound of them a staccato wave, bouncing around him. One caught him on the elbow as it went past, sending a bolt of pain along his arm, followed by a shiver of numbness. The rows of demons looked at him.

His troops looked at him.

Members of the crowd had reached the top of the rails now, were trying to clamber over; those lower down were, Fool saw, being crushed by the mass of people pushing forward. Faces were being forced into the spaces between the bars, mouths open, eyes squeezed shut or bulging, blood flowing. Here and there in the air above them blue sparks jumped, and he suddenly understood it was fragments of their souls tearing loose and wondered whether he should simply allow it to happen, allow them to die and be released.

No.

There was no point in drawing his gun; there were more people than he could ever hope to shoot even if he wanted to, and they would never hear the sound of the shot if he fired above them. The Sorrowful were like a single living entity, huge and mindless and furious, and he needed something big enough for it to see, for it to understand. He needed to get its attention, to pull its eyes up and give it something to be in awe of, something bigger than itself. "Balthazar," he said, "how much fire can you make?"

The column was huge, a pillar of flame stretching up into the sky, towering above the shifting crowds and throwing its light down upon them. Masonry arced through the air toward it, entered it, and did not emerge, and the heat of it was a rippling, scouring thing. Arm aloft, Balthazar sent his fires upward as Fool sent the demons to knock people from the fence.

"No killing," he said, unsure whether he was talking to the demons or to Balthazar, whose face held an expression of fierce, violent joy. The first row of demons began to knock people from the fence, dropping them onto the backs and heads of those below them, poking through the railings to detach feet and hands and sending people falling.

"Get them away from the fence," said Fool, and the rest of the demons immediately began to climb the railings. Seeing them approach and driven back by the heat of Balthazar's flames, the crowd began to shift, to change direction and move away. Screams rose, this time of pain, as streams of people began to move faster and faster away. Some of those who had been pressed against the base of the fence were unconscious or worse and fell away, blood frothing from their mouths and noses, their faces shiny with sweat, imprinted with the shape of the bars. In the fleeing crowd, lit by Balthazar's fire, people fell and were lost to view.

"Pull them out," shouted Fool, "pull them out now!"

Demons, his troops, waded into the crowds, dragging fallen humans loose and, in some cases at least, literally throwing them free. The screaming rose, the crowd's voice terrible, and the roaring of demons joined it. The air was growing hotter, the sweat running down Fool's face and across his body under his uniform, the rough material rasping at his neck. He couldn't see what was happening farther back in the mob and he looked around for something to stand on. There was nothing, so he went to the fence and climbed, holding his gun in one hand and clambering awkwardly.

The entrances to the square were small and huge clusters of people had formed around each, knotting tighter and tighter, pressing against the walls and buildings around the gaps. The air was hazy above the people, ripples of pale blue light fluttering here and there. As the demons made their way farther into the crowd, the Sorrowful tried to flee and the crushes became worse. The screams and roaring had blended, a morass of noise and pain, and Balthazar's fire burned high and fierce and painted the crowd red. *They're dying,* thought Fool. *I've panicked them and they're crushing each other and dying. This is my fault, little stupid* idiotic *Fool.*

Fires were burning in the square, although Fool had no idea how they had started. *Could the demons' own heat have escaped,* he wondered, *growing within them and stoked by the agonies they were surrounded by?* Hadn't Gordie said something to him about that once, that demons could sweat fire when they became excited or gorged? That it was why the wounds on the Genevieves and Marys rarely bled, because they were cauterized by the demon's heat, by the excitement they felt as they fucked or fought or killed? Embers of burning leaflets rose into the air, dancing here and there. Banners lay on the ground, tangled and flaming; the fires caught at the pushing, terrified people, took hold of their thin clothing, and breathed itself larger. The thought *Demons and fire and humans and pain and suffering, this must be what Hell used to be like* flickered briefly across Fool's mind and he heard closer screaming and realized that it was him.

"Balthazar," he was shouting, "do something!"

"What is there to do, Information Man?" said Balthazar, his voice audible even over the screaming. He came to the fence, the column of his fire dwindling to nothing, his entire body gleaming, throwing light out, his wings open and flapping. With each flap, air barreled past Fool, shaking him, and Balthazar rose several inches off the ground and then drifted back down.

"I control my own flames, not those of others," the angel said, and then a vast blue glow leaped up from the crowd.

It crashed across the square rapidly, expanding out from the tight presses of the Sorrowful at the exits, turning the fires into capering, shifting formless blue pools, turning the demons into cold nightmares and the Sorrowful into bleached, featureless things. It came at Fool fast, a wall exploding across the square, and hit him hard, tearing him from the fence. It sounded like a hurricane, like all the screams Fool had ever heard meshed into one stretched and ringing thunderclap, accompanying him along his brief journey to the ground, and as the jolt of impact slammed into him it shrieked louder. It burned his eyes, was visible even when he clenched them shut, raging into him. Images filled his mind, disconnected and multiplying, of Hell seen from above, from *outside,* of a wall that was the only wall, of countless souls pressed together in the oceans of Limbo with no breath and no self and no hope but that they might gain flesh and be Elevated, and Fool screamed and screamed and screamed.

The light lasted only a moment; it was the worst moment Fool had ever had.

When it was gone, when his eyes no longer burned and the pressure within his skull had dropped to something like normal, Fool stopped screaming. His throat was raw and he spat, seeing pink streaks of blood in his spittle, another injury to add to his list. He rolled over onto his back and then sat up. Balthazar was standing next to him, his head tilted back and his mouth open as though tasting the air.

"Did you feel them, Information Man Fool?" asked Balthazar. "All those souls? All flying free together, all released?"

"Was that what it was?" asked Fool.

"Of course," said Balthazar. "God was here, for just a moment, Information Man, traveling with the souls on their release." Fool, remembering the images within the light, said nothing. Instead, he stood and looked across the square.

Fires still burned, had spread into some of the buildings that lined the square and gave it its edges. Corpses littered the ground, some smoking, others alight. Not everyone was dead, though, and the silence that had followed the souls' freeing was rupturing with screams and moans. Fool walked back to the fence, his body and head weary, and took hold of the railings; they were warm. On the ground near him, a charred banner read WE DESERVE BETTER. *Yes,* he thought, *we do, but this is Hell, so we won't get it.* Looking up, he saw Elderflower at one of the windows. The little man nodded at Fool and then turned away and was gone, and the pane filled with silent shadows.

25

Clearing the square took the rest of the morning and part of the afternoon. Fool detailed some of his troops to help in the job, getting them to drag the mounds of burned and mangled flesh away from the exits. The corpses against the walls came loose with a terrible tearing sound, were bent in ways that humans should not be, their bones shattered by the weight of the crowd behind them. Some had suffocated and looked as though they were asleep when they were laid on the ground; others were only just recognizable as human, blackened and blistered, curled into tight balls by the heat. Those humans who were still alive and not too badly injured were pulled in to assist as well, stacking the bodies to make their collection and transport easier; even Balthazar helped, carrying corpses and piling them like cordwood.

Porters ran carts, directed by Fool, taking pile after pile of bodies to the Flame Garden, ferrying them on wooden carts and carrying them in hammocks of gray canvas. The air was thick with the smell of charred flesh and burned hair and burning wood. Clouds of steam spat from the buildings aflame around them as demons sprayed them with water, streams of warmed liquid spilling across the square and washing the dead flesh it contained.

When the square was finally empty of the dead, the ground covered in sodden ash and torn paper and clothing and banners and pools of blood and urine and dirt and water, Fool went and sat with his back against the fence. His uniform was filthy, but at least, he thought, he still had it. He had listened to Elderflower and obeyed, obedient Fool that he was, and this was the result; bodies ferried to the Flame Garden all day, souls torn loose by fear and pain, sent back to Limbo. Was he any better than the demon that killed the Genevieves? Or the one that had come to the Iomante to kill him and had slaughtered its way along the wards to find him? He looked at his gun, turning it in his hands. The barrel's mouth stared solemnly at him, black and open and waiting to breathe. Was he any different? Any better?

Was he a demon? After all, he ordered demons about now—some, anyway—and they obeyed his instructions without complaint. What was he? He was an Information Man, the only one in Hell, a powerless thing that suddenly, apparently, had power.

Power. He looked at his gun again and then holstered it. Was he powerful? Really?

No; he was simply a fool, he told himself, was *Fool,* a man like any other in Hell, and he was tired. He was as powerless as the dead, as helpless as the Genevieves and Marys who lined the Houska's streets and filled its brothels, but even as he told himself that, he knew he was wrong. He might not understand it, might want to back away from it, but he did have power, some power anyway.

The question was, if he had power, what could he do with it?

Later, in his rooms, Fool tried to work out where they had been and where he had come to. He had described what he was doing to Elder-flower as "following a trail," but what trail? It started with a body floating in Solomon Water and then traveled along past a body in the Orphan-age, another in the farmhouse and a pit of dead Aruhlians. There were branches off the path, all stemming from its single root: a feather that glowed and wouldn't hold blood, angels and Elevations and riots, the deaths of Gordie and Summer and the Man. Somewhere in this trail and its curling branches, there had to be hints as to the next steps, didn't there?

Didn't there?

Fool wrote notes to himself, questions and answers and more ques-tions, and spread them out on the table in the offices' small kitchen. Starting at the beginning, he tried to think through again each step he had taken so far, but there were so many, not all of them ones he had chosen. Right from the little demon at the lake, he had been as much moved as the one doing the moving; more, really.

The demon at the lake.

Fool looked at his notes about the first body. The demon had attacked them and tried to claim the body for itself, had battened onto it like a leech and then stopped. It had tasted its emptiness, hated it, but it had said something, hadn't it? What had it said?

It had said, "What did he do?"

"He," not "it."

He.

There was something there, something Fool had missed all along but could see now, something that might be important. It had said "he," not "it." Did that mean it had seen who killed the first Genevieve? Could it tell Fool what the murderer looked like? He rose, suddenly awake and not tired, trembling.

It was as he stood that he remembered; there was another witness, maybe two. Morgan had them, had Summer and the body from the alley, and Summer's flesh at least still housed her soul. Summer might have talked.

26

They were traveling through the industrial district, on their way to the Questioning House, and they were in a transport. The vehicle had been waiting outside his rooms as he left, idling on the street. There was a demon behind its wheel and Elderflower was sitting in its rear, holding the door open for Fool.

"This is quicker than the trains," said Elderflower, "and the Bureaucracy wishes you to be fast on this, Thomas. This has gone on long enough now; it is upsetting the balances. Hell has not seen riots for years, still less humans attacking demons. Death on the scale that occurred today is almost unprecedented and the oceans of Limbo cannot afford to be flooded with that many released souls. They are already awash, and there is a risk of flooding."

"A flood of souls?"

"A flood of souls, Thomas, is something you do not wish to ever experience."

"I don't?"

"No, Thomas, you do not. Trust me on this."

Trust Elderflower? Did he trust him? "Why?"

"Because, Thomas, I am all you have to trust." And in this, Fool thought sadly, Elderflower was right.

The journey took Fool through a Hell he had not seen before. The riots had spread, fires burning almost unchecked, some guttering behind the heavy stone walls and some raging, forcing their tongues out through broken windows and doorways in flickering leers. Humans no longer walked with their heads down, scurrying by themselves or in twos and threes; instead, great crowds of them patrolled the streets, blocking the transport's passage on several occasions. Even when they parted, they did so slowly, hemming the vehicle in as it passed, peering in through the windows at Fool and Elderflower and their demon chauffeur. The Houska seemed emptier but the streets linking it and the boarding-houses fuller. They passed a train moving slowly toward the Houska; it was on fire, its rear two carriages burning brightly.

"What's happening?" asked Fool.

"Hell is changing," said Elderflower. "Being changed. Something has emerged, something of such power that it's warping the things around it simply by being here. Slaughter isn't unusual in Hell, Thomas, you know that, but these are not usual times. These deaths, these murders, have become noticeable, Thomas. Things are being *seen,* rising above the normal tide of pain and suffering, and so we shall be seen to do something. I am to give you what assistance I can to put this situation, and by extension all those things happening as a result of it, to rest. Hell will have its control, Thomas. It will have charge of the things that occur within its boundaries."

The transport brought them to the House. "There are more Elevations planned," said Elderflower as they exited the vehicle. "We have collected the lucky few and they will be shown the way upward tonight. There will be yet more tomorrow, as well as the last of our discussions. You have permission to miss tonight's risings but will, of course, be there for the rest of our proceedings."

"Of course," said Fool.

"Go, Thomas," said Elderflower. "Go and look, Thomas, and listen, and solve this mystery."

"It's not a mystery, though, is it?" said Fool. "You know who's doing these things, you know what they are, where they are—you must."

"Must I? I have told you before, Thomas. Your job is to investigate just as mine is to aid you where I can. We are tiny parts of the biggest picture, it is true, and we might see the fragment we inhabit and understand what it means or not. What I may see and know I cannot say; those are the rules that I have been given. Now, there is a body awaiting you, Thomas, as there are Elevations awaiting me. You must attend to them, as I must attend to Adam and Balthazar."

The little bureaucrat turned and walked away into the night. Fool's last glimpse of him was of his coat flapping behind him and his hair, bobbing like dry grass, and then the darkness closed around him. *He walks through the darkness and light equally*, thought Fool, and still had no idea what he really was.

Despite the hour's lateness, the nearby industrial area was still noisy, the air full of smoke and grit, and his swallows were grimy and rough. Everything was rough, everything scratched, everything about him ached, but this was Hell and what else should he expect? This path he was on, supposedly on, following a demon whose appearance he didn't even know, how could he hope to follow it when each turn seemed to be a dead end, an end filled with the dead, where each new trail looped back on itself? Did he really think that Summer would speak, could tell him anything? That the little thing in Solomon Water might have seen something? That it might tell him the something it had seen?

Yes, because otherwise he might as well lie in the mud at the lake's edge and allow his lungs to fill with Hell's earth, allow himself to be trodden away to nothing. *That's my tiny fragment of hope, I suppose*, he thought, *little hopeful Fool, wanting to catch a demon so powerful it can eat souls and that can slip between the spaces of Hell without apparently being seen.* He thought of the demon that had come for him in the Iomante, about his escape. If he kept on, he'd end up back at the Heights, he supposed, and its inhabitants would notice him again, would move against him. Had they already sent something else after him? Or were they waiting, watching for his next move?

Could he stop? Simply climb back into the transport and tell it to drive him away? Return to the offices and pretend that the blue ribbons were no more important than any other crime, stamp them *DNI* or *Unknown,* and then sit in his rooms and wait for Summer's and Gordie's replacements? Stay quiet, stay low, stay out of notice? He had come so far, but achieved so little other than the death of the people around him he cared about, other than the battery of his own body to the point where all movement hurt.

Could he stop? Could he?

He looked at the Questioning House; it was time to decide. Fool put his hand on the butt of his gun, felt its shape and solidity and how small it was compared to the terrors that Hell held, and looked down at his hand, scabbed and pale like some injured spider. He looked back at the house, with its thick covering of vines, and thought of the Man lying dead with holes torn in his back, his musculature exposed and manipulated. *The demon could have killed me, but it didn't,* he thought. *It sent me to Crow Heights so that others would kill me. It was playing with me, making me dance for its entertainment. Elderflower, the demon, the Man, Rhakshasas, and the rest of the Bureaucracy that find me so interesting to watch, they're* all *playing with me, watching as I do what they want, dancing as they whistle.* He glanced down at his uniform, wrinkled and grimy already, and remembered the taste of Summer's blood in his mouth, the scent of Gordie burning and the sound of him screaming, the sound of the demon in the Iomante. *I wonder if they found that interesting? If any of it bothered them? If they watched me as Gordie died, not murdered but still killed by that demon, whatever the fuck it looks like?*

Fine, now they can watch me catch the bastard.

Even from the end of the path, Fool could see that the front door to the Questioning House had been torn off its hinges and was lying inside the wide hallway in a haze of splinters and wood. He drew his gun, looking at the jamb; the wards and runes that should have protected the Questioning House were still there. He ran his finger along one of them, a series of black shapes traced into a piece of thin paper pinned to the wood, feeling the tingle of them in his fingertips. They still had power, these spells against Hell's more violent denizens, yet something had waded through them and torn its way inside. *How powerful was this demon?* he wondered. How strong, to be able to smash through the protections that the Bureaucracy gave the Questioners?

Fool went cautiously into the building. The broken door wavered under his feet as he stepped over it, splinters digging into his soles. It was bright in the building, the lamps still burning merrily in their sconces, making the shadows thin and weak. Apart from the shattered door, there was no sign of disturbance; the signs on the wall reading FLESH and ADMINISTRATION gleaming, the polished floor reflecting a blurred image of Fool as he moved carefully forward, the long desk where the corpses were signed in empty and neat.

Steps led off the main foyer up to the Questioners' private rooms, the top of the staircase lost in gloom. Fool moved to the foot of the stairs and then stopped, knowing instinctively that upward wasn't where he needed to go; it would lead only along another branch, a smaller one. The main trail, he felt sure, would lie in the Questioning Rooms, which were at the back of the House. He went to move away but a querulous voice came from above him.

"Has it gone?" Tidyman, emerging from the darkness. His white hair was haloed around his head and his hands were clasped in front of him.

"Did you see it?"

"Tidyman was too busy running," said Hand, appearing from behind his colleague.

"Did *you* see it, then?" asked Fool.

"No, because I was running as well. We were in the foyer, Tidyman and I, discussing a new technique for questioning the dead when they are in pieces, when the front door was hit. Whatever it was sounded very determined, so we ran as the doors were hit again and came off their hinges. I didn't look back."

"Where's Morgan?"

"I don't know."

"Did you try to help him? Find him?"

"No."

"It's not our fault," said Tidyman as Fool looked up at them. "What could we do?"

"You could have tried," Fool said.

"We could have died," said Hand, looking at Fool as though he were an idiot. "Why should we put ourselves at risk for Morgan? Would he do it for us? Would you?"

"No," said Fool. "I'd do what you did, I'd run and hide and not look and hope that I survived." He was telling the truth, he thought, or at least, the truth that had governed his life until very recently. He turned from the men in disgust, unsure of where his disgust was aimed, and went back into the foyer.

He found the only other sign of disorder, a chair lying on its back, just inside the corridor toward the building's rear. He went past it and continued down the hallway toward the doors that lined its far end, all of them closed.

The House was silent.

Call or not, Fool wondered, *silence or noise?* And then, *If it's here, it'll know I'm here already. Call.* "Hello?"

His voice echoed along the corridor. "Hello?" he called again, but no one replied, and nothing moved. He took another step, listening; silence. Another, so that he was almost at the first door, reaching out, still listening, still hearing only his own breathing and the Questioning House's silence around him. "Hello?" he tried a third time, his hand closing around the door handle. It was warm, slippery.

The door opened easily, revealing an empty room. The table in the middle was bare, its metal surface and surrounding benches of instruments and bottles and scales covered in a thin layer of dust. Fool let out a long breath that he hadn't realized he was holding. The room opposite was the same, the table set up for a Questioning but clean and unused.

That left two doors. The first was locked but the second was not and opened a little when Fool pushed it. It grated as it moved, wood rubbing against wood. Closer, he saw that its upper panel was marked, two impact points set into its paint at about head height. He pushed at it a little harder, felt slight movement and then resistance, and pushed again. Something behind the door shifted, bumped against it, and then fell into the growing opening. Fool jumped back, reflexes singing, as Morgan's upper body appeared, the stump of his neck winking redly at him. A part of Fool, a part inside, screamed, but most of him was dispassionate, remained calm and silent.

Morgan hit the floor with a thick, glutinous noise, another dead body, another sack of ruptured and abused flesh like Gordie and Summer, and its interest to Fool was primarily in the story it could tell him and only distantly that it had once been someone Fool had liked. *What am I becoming?* he wondered, and the answer came on the thought's heels almost instantly: *An agent of Hell.* He pushed the door open and entered the room, stepping over Morgan's corpse to do so.

The room had been torn apart. The counter that ran the room's length along the far wall had been ripped from its moorings and the tools of Morgan's trade scattered across the floor. The air was filled with competing scents, of thick oils and rich blood and sharp chemicals and something else, something bitter and rank. A huge pool of blood had formed around the fallen counter, jagged sprays of it climbing the walls above the worktop like the silhouettes of distant trees. Morgan's head was in the center of the pool, resting on its side and facing back into the room so that its open eyes peered at Fool owlishly.

There were footsteps across the floor, etched in blood. Some were the imprints of Morgan's feet, smooth-edged, the blood still a rich cherry. Others were less distinct, the blood burned to a thick black crust, the prints uneven, some large, others smaller, distorted, looking not like feet but like clawed hooves. *The heat of it must have been furious,* Fool thought, looking at the burned smears of blood. Could he track the movements in this room, follow Morgan's last steps by following the stains? Step into the demon's tracks and chase Morgan's ghost? What would he see if he did? Fear? Pain? Anger?

"Can we help?" said a voice from the doorway. Tidyman and Hand, both in the corridor and peering in from around the edge of the frame, were half hidden from the room and its contents.

"Yes," said Fool. "Go away. Go back to your rooms and stay out of my way. I'm working." He turned away from them, ignoring them, and went to Morgan's slumped corpse.

"I'm sorry, old friend," he said and rolled him over. Blood had soaked into the man's clothes; there was little of the gray material left clean on his top half, and his thighs were spattered with thick, whorled stains. When Fool lifted Morgan's arms and examined them, not liking the way his flesh was still warm, he found several deep marks across his palms. Fool had a sudden image, a flash of Morgan backing away, holding his hands up and the demon lashing out, knocking the hands aside, tearing into them and then grasping Morgan's head and twisting, sucking on the soul as it emerged, slurping at it greedily.

Sighing, he let Morgan's hands drop and rose, looking around the rest of the room.

The Questioner's table, usually positioned at the room's center, had been tipped over and had skittered up to the far wall, its legs buckled around as though something had swept into them and torn the table from its fixings in the floor. A hand was just visible at the top edge of the table, the skin blanched and the fingers curled toward Fool as though in greeting. It was small and the edge of the wrist was marked by striations of red and black where it had been bound. *Tied between two pillars,* Fool thought. *Summer.*

When Fool pulled the table away from the wall, he found that her hand was the only part of Summer that hadn't been burned. The rest of her flesh was blackened and peeling, the surface of the table around her buckled. Her skin was split into a series of fire-torn grins, her head made bald and blistered by some intense heat. There was no soot, no marks more than a few inches from her body, no scars on the walls, no evidence that these had been human flames. Summer had been taken by the heat that lived in the demon flesh to stop her soul talking, to provide it with yet more food.

Fool glanced around the rest of the room, hoping that Morgan had conversed with Summer before the demon arrived, that he had made notes. How lovely it would be to find a note that stated simply the demon's name and where he could find it, all in Morgan's neat hand, but there was nothing. *Hope,* thought Fool, and grinned humorlessly. *I'm so helpless against it, I know it's pointless but I keep hoping anyway. Little hopeful Fool.* He realized he was crying and wiped his eyes, hoping to wipe away the pain and anger he felt along with the tears. Where did this leave him? Summer had been prevented from talking, his ally in the Questioning House killed and, he supposed, also prevented from talking; one look at the torn and wrenched flesh of the neck left Fool in no doubt that the violence of the death would have released his soul for the demon to eat. There would be a blue-ribboned canister with his details printed waiting for him back at his rooms, he knew, with orders to investigate. "I am," he said aloud and angry, "I am."

With Morgan dead, the only Questioner Fool trusted had gone, and his chance of finding answers was slimmer than ever. He had a Questioning House full of equipment and not the first idea of how to use it. He had *nothing.*

No, Fool suddenly remembered, *not nothing. I still have a little nameless demon in a lake.*

27

The bag swung against Fool's leg as he climbed out of the transport. It was heavy, made his arms ache, and he swapped it from hand to hand to try to even out the effort. *At least it's stopped dripping,* he thought, the puddle of blood on the seat beside him cracking and flaking as he lifted the bag. It left a stain on the coarse upholstery; he wondered what Elderflower would say about it and found that he didn't care. He tried not to think what was in the bag, what was banging against his leg.

About what he was going to do.

Fool had returned briefly to the office after leaving the Questioning House. He found what he was looking for in one of the supply cupboards; a coil of rope, dusty and tangled, that he wrapped around one arm, lifting it from its place on the shelf next to spare sheets and notebooks and a box of cheap, thin pencils. Afterward, he went into his own room, but there was nothing there; everything of value to him, everything he owned, he carried. The feather was still in his pocket, his gun was snug in its holster, and he had his uniform. The *Information Man's Guide to the Rules and Offices of Hell* he debated leaving but then decided against it, placing it into a pocket. They were his rules, after all, the rules of Hell as they had been given to him. This thing, this *investigation,* felt like it was moving now, but the movement was headlong, dragging him without control behind it. He had, somehow, to get ahead of it, to slow it down somehow, to take control. And then what? Fool had a grim sense that this might be the last time he would see this room, although where the sense came from he didn't quite know.

Actually, he did know, if he was honest; he could see the real possibility of his own death, not in the fearful way everyone in Hell feared their own death, but because of something concrete, something specific. He was changing, he realized, had already changed, had become something different. The old Fool was gone, burned away in the glare of attention and anger and a determination to solve this, to find the demon and make it pay. It was setting the trail for him to follow, he thought, and then trying to prevent him following even as he chased it, creating a mess of confusion in which new doors were opening and old, lost ideas were unfurling. It had killed Summer because she had gotten close to it, had managed to get within touching distance of it, but Fool had been close as well and had prevented it from taking her soul. It had made a mistake there, he understood, but it had not left it, had stepped ahead of Fool to finish the job and unmake the mistake. *Poor Summer,* he thought, *destroyed not once but twice. And me? It could have killed me when it killed the Man and I was in his room, but it didn't. Why? Because it wanted to see how far I could go? Because I amuse it the way I amused the Man? Because it didn't think I'd survive the traps it set me and it wanted to see me suffer? But I did survive, and I'm maybe not so amusing now. Next time, it won't hesitate.*

It'll kill me.

Following this demon wasn't simply taking Fool to new geographies, it was forcing him into new shapes. He had shot demons, killed them, ordered them to do his bidding and been obeyed. He had seen spaces within Hell that he had never known existed, had walked further and further from the Fool he thought he was, and had further to go yet. He turned to leave, knowing that even if he came back, he would be changed even more, and wondering whether he would recognize himself at all by the time this was finished.

Summer's room was neat, almost sterile, the only sign she had ever been there the spare clothes hanging on the rail and the folded pants and bras stacked on the shelves of the bookcase. Next to them was a small pile of paper weighted down with a pencil. Fool picked up the sheets and leafed through them; they were sketches, he found, lots of them on each piece of paper. Some were of places or people he recognized; in several, he saw Gordie, and in others, he saw himself. In the sketches, Fool looked serious and Gordie was always smiling. The last picture in the pile was of the three of them, three faces, roughly penciled but still recognizable; Summer and Gordie and Fool, Hell's Information Men, and now two were dead and the third was someone new. He folded the paper and put it in his pocket by his *Guide.*

Gordie's room was a mess. The walls were still covered with their paper adornments, stuck there with pins and tacks and, in one case, a fork. He read some more of them, intrigued despite himself, finding more cryptic ideas and thoughts ("Alrunes scream when endangered and predict the future," "There are secret trades and secret trade routes"), odd snippets of geography, tiny, poorly drawn sketches of items and demons and buildings. Some of the pieces of paper that were linked by lengths of twine, Fool saw, listed some of the crimes they had not investigated or had investigated and failed to solve. *Had Gordie started down this road before him,* he wondered, *down this recognition of trails and clues and possibilities and solutions?* Probably; that was what Gordie had been like, always wondering and looking and trying to place things into some kind of order. The room was heavy with his ghost and Fool left it, shutting the door quietly behind him.

The office itself was already growing a layer of dust like a new skin. In its corner, the pneumatic pipe descended from the ceiling, the floor below covered in containers, one blue-ribboned one in among the melee. Fool opened one or two, but not the blue one that he assumed was Morgan's, and found they contained the usual mix of murder and rape and beatings, of bitterness and misery and pain. One of the metal canisters was wrapped in a white ribbon and he picked it up. Before he opened it, he took Summer's picture from his pocket and smoothed it open on his desk. The three of them, caught as Summer practiced her drawing skills. The note inside the canister simply said, "MORE OFFICERS WILL ARRIVE SOON."

I have troops, and soon more officers, thought Fool. *A new Summer and a new Gordie. More than that, maybe?* He didn't know, didn't care. Soon, they'd take new souls from outside the wall and give them flesh and send them here. The last vestiges of Summer and Gordie would be removed, the bras and pants taken away, the pieces of paper torn down, and Fool would have new Information Men to train, to get to know. He looked down at his uniform, at the way the buttons gleamed, and stood. He put the picture back in his pocket, left the note on his desk and the catalog of crimes scattered across the floor in their separate containers, and left the office.

The bag was thin cotton, its handles badly stitched, and Fool hoped they wouldn't tear as he clinched the rope around them.

The journey to Solomon Water hadn't taken long. The transport, driven by its silent demon, had threaded its way through mostly quiet streets, although here and there groups of humans gathered, watching them in silence as they passed. The riots seemed to have retreated, as though Hell were pausing for breath, although once Fool was sure he saw a scuffle taking place far down an alley, but he couldn't make out who was involved and they were past it too fast for him to see much. The ground was littered with the leaflets and they swirled up as the transport drove through them, setting the papers capering in the air. Some of them were larger, Fool saw, folded over so that they formed little booklets; they were covered in writing. He wondered about getting the driver to stop so that he could pick one up and read it, but didn't. They were near the end, although what the end would be he didn't know, and he wanted to get there and get it done.

Once the rope was tied as tightly as he could make it, Fool began to swing the bag, initially back and forth and then higher and higher so that it was performing full circles around him, faster and faster. Finally he let it go, sending it arcing out over the water's black surface, letting the rope run through his hand but not letting it escape.

The bag hit the water, sending up a corona of spray, and even from this distance Fool saw the water soaking into the drying blood and freeing it, teasing it out from the bag and setting it loose into Solomon Water. Morgan's face was recognizable for a moment as the wet bag's side clung to the head it contained, and then it rolled and sank.

It took only a moment. The rope in Fool's hand jerked, first one way and then another and then forward, yanked several feet more out into the water. Fool clenched his hands around it and began to pull it in, feeling resistance but pulling anyway. The rope jerked again, tearing skin from his palms but he held on, wincing, and pulled. Wakes formed at the end of the rope, a larger central one moving back toward the shore as he hauled, surrounded by smaller ones darting in and out. Under the surface, a frenzy was forming about Morgan's head, lots of Hell's littlest things nipping and biting.

Fool needed to get Morgan's head to shore before the bag split; it was the only bait he had, and if the things in the water actually managed to chew into the flesh, they would realize that no soul remained in it for them to feast on. He didn't know whether they were like their counterparts out of the water, but Fool had to assume that the majority of their sustenance was pain and fear and sour memories, the stuff of the soul, and that flesh was merely the carrier for this. The moment they tasted that the head was nothing but flesh, they would leave, and he needed them to stay. He needed them to gather, and in gathering to bring the larger things to them.

As it came closer to the shore and the water became shallower, Morgan's head began to drag on the bottom. The bag broke the surface, went under again, and then reemerged, the rope taut between it and Fool. He pulled on, the water around the bag rippling and splashing as things flashed in and out again, their backs breaching the surface for brief moments before disappearing again. There were already tears in the bag, its sides and handles fraying where the swimming things had bitten it. Fool pulled and the bag came on.

When it was close enough, he reached out and lifted the bag from the water. He was just in time; a long rip had opened up along the bottom of the material and the stump of Morgan's neck was already pushing its way out, dripping. Fool held the top of the bag and shook it, letting the weight of the head open the tear farther until it was long enough and wide enough, and then it was out and bouncing across the ground. Fool used his feet to prevent the head from rolling back into the water, positioning it instead by the place where land and water met. Morgan's face peered into the sky, his features already looking less like his living self. Death and immersion had softened him, making his lips sag back and his hair trail from his scalp. Liquid spilled off the head and out of the mouth, trickling into Solomon Water, carrying, Fool hoped, the scent of death and of something that had once been in the lake but was now removed.

Mist curled around Fool's legs in pale tongues. What time was it? He didn't know, had lost accurate track of the hour. The middle of the night, he thought; it had been early in the evening when he left to go to the Questioning House, had spent time there, and then returned to the offices before finally arriving here. Was it late the same day? Early the next day? He felt detached from it, somehow, as though time were something that happened to other people. Was there an Elevation today? Yes, he thought, later on, in the morning. Was he supposed to be there? Yes. It was the last full day of the delegation's presence in Hell; he would be expected to attend to them and then the following morning he would have to escort them back to the tunnel when they left.

Fool sat, the chill water seeping through the material of his uniform and soaking his legs and buttocks. He was cold, and beginning to think this was a bad idea. Even if a demon came, how could he be sure it would be the same one? Gordie had said it was a breed of demon that had been gifted the waters, not a single one. Were they a family? Or individuals? Did they work as a group or were they territorial and solitary? He didn't know. There was so *much* he didn't know, had never known, how could he ever hope to grasp it, to understand? It was overwhelming.

"It is ours," said a voice from by Fool's ear. He started, scrambling away from the source of the sound, one hand going for his gun. *Should've had it drawn,* he thought fleetingly, and then he was facing one of Solomon Water's demons again.

It wasn't the same one, he could tell immediately; it was shorter and squatter, its limbs less spindly and more solid. Its skinless flesh was dry, the shifting musculature cracked and flaking at points. It looked old, was crouched up the slope from Fool, its head tilted as it looked at him. It glanced at the head and its tongue emerged, flickering at the air, and then vanished. "It is ours," it said again.

"It's yours," said Fool, saying a silent apology to Morgan, "in trade for something."

"No trade," said the demon and scuttled a little closer. "It is ours. Things from the water belong to us."

Something splashed behind Fool, a sound thick with cautious movement. Very deliberately, he pointed his gun down at the head, which was wedged between his feet, and spoke loudly and clearly. "If you or yours touch me, I destroy it."

"No! Ours!" the demon hissed.

"Trade," said Fool. The demon didn't reply. Behind it, almost hidden among the trees, dark shapes moved. Fool glanced over his shoulder and saw several more of the demons emerging from the water, stealthy, painted in the night's light and staring at him. When he looked back around, the one in front of him had darted closer, still crouched, its clawed hands digging into the mud a few feet from the head. Its eyes glowed redly as Fool shifted, his aim never wavering. "You're their leader?"

It nodded, tongue flickering in and out, tasting the mist.

"You know me? What I am?"

It nodded again.

"Good. I need to talk to the demon that attacked me the other day," Fool said. "Then you can have it."

"No, give it. It is ours," said the older demon. Fool turned, lifted his gun, and pointed it at the demon closest to him in the water and fired.

The sound of the shot boomed across Solomon Water's surface, the flash seeming to connect Fool and the demon for a moment, and then it screeched and leaped back, spinning in the air. It hit the water awkwardly, sending up a spray of thick, foamy liquid, still screeching. Fool moved quickly, yanking the gun back around and pointing it at Morgan's head. He had to finish this, and soon; they'd realize before long that if they all attacked together, he couldn't fight them off. He had to keep them confused, nervous; humans never bargained, never attacked, never had authority. He must seem to them as demons did to humans, armed and angry and demanding.

"Trade, now," he snapped, "or I destroy it. Last chance."

"Wait, wait," said the demon on the shoreline. "It is from the water, it is ours by right."

"It is *mine*," said Fool, "to trade. Want it? Trade."

The demon made a sound that was somewhere between a wail of pain and a groan of acceptance and retreated, never turning its back on Fool. It made it all the way into the trees and then stopped. Fool moved, keeping his gun trained on the head at his feet and trying to look everywhere at once. The demons in the water had backed away from the shore. The one he had shot was standing but bleeding from a torn wound in its shoulder, thick ropes of dark liquid spilling from the exposed flesh and spattering down. When they hit the water, tiny curls of gray steam rose, darker than the mist. The demon hissed at Fool but wouldn't look at him, its head lowered. More fear, another demon that would hate him not simply because he was human, but because he was a human who had dared to cause injury. *I must be the most noticed human in Hell,* he thought as he waited. *Little visible Fool.*

Good.

More shapes emerged from the lake, not coming close to shore but present nonetheless, visible mainly as ripples and shifts in the water forming around submerged heads and half-seen limbs. Turning farther, Fool watched as the shapes between the trees continued moving, slipping from trunk to trunk, gathering at the edge of the copse. Experimentally, he twitched his gun. The movement stopped, and when it started again, it was slower and at least some of it was away from him as the figures melted back into the shadows. They were, if not frightened of him, then at least cautious, the rumors they had heard about him thickened into a truth by his shooting of their companion and by the head he refused to give up. Good. *Good.*

The mist thickened, looping curls of it all around him. Visibility was dropping, and no matter how frightened or cautious they were of him, if he couldn't keep them in sight then the demons would kill him.

"Now!" he said, resisting the urge to shout. He jabbed at the head, forcing it down into the mud.

"One," he said, letting his voice drop lower. "Two."

"Here to talk," said a new voice. It came from inside a hank of mist, from a thick gray blur that resolved itself into the demon that had challenged him for the first body a few days and a whole lifetime ago. Its exposed muscles glistened wetly, its curved teeth uncovered and its eyes like glimmering coals. "Talk and then trade, yes?"

"Yes," said Fool. "You remember me? From the other day, when you tried to eat the body?"

"Yes. Stupid humans with empty body."

"Empty, yes. After you found it was empty, you said something. You said, 'What did he do?'"

"Yes," said the demon, its eyes darting between Fool and the head at his feet.

"Who did you mean?"

"The two in the trees, the boy and the other," said the demon and took several steps forward. It was within touching distance now, its hands flexing open and closed. Fool didn't look away, didn't look down. *How different I am,* he thought.

"What did you mean?"

"Meant nothing. Meant he took the taste away."

"Who?"

"The other one."

"What did he look like? Tell me."

"Pale," said the demon, "pale and white."

"I don't understand," said Fool. "It was pale?"

"Pale," agreed the demon and snatched at Morgan's head, now smeared in filth and diluted blood.

"No," said Fool, rolling it out of the demon's reach. "I still don't understand. Tell me more."

"What more?" it said. "He was pale. White."

"What shape was it? What kind of demon?"

"Not a demon, a man. Pale man, hitting the other one, hitting and hitting. Other man soon dead, pale man kept hitting then blue flash. Just a pale man," said the thing and then fell on the head as Fool stepped away with the world pitching beneath his feet.

28

The demon's screech rose into the air behind Fool as it discovered what he already suspected, that Morgan's soul had been torn free from his flesh and all that was left was the tasteless remnants. Fool trudged up the slope away from the water, ignoring the noise, his gun hanging loosely by his side. When he reached the trees, the shapes scattered about him, carving him a path to continue unmolested.

A man. A pale man. Could it be possible? It was one of the rules of Hell that humans couldn't kill each other; not a rule written down but a Law, the same as breathing to live and the sky being above the ground and only the chalkis flying in Hell and the Information Men having guns were Laws, things built into the fabric of Hell itself. Humans were born out of the Limbo outside, the knowledge of their sins removed from them except at the most basic level, and they lived at the whim not of each other, but of demons and their desires. There was no escape, no salvation except through the random process of Elevation, and what happiness there was tended to be fleeting and delicate.

A man. No, it couldn't be, men could not kill men. Was it one of the orphans, maybe, human from a distance but a demon closer? No, demonkind knew each other, knew human from demon, because that was how even the smallest and weakest of them knew whom to abuse and whom to avoid. If the demon said it had been a man, unless it was lying it had been a man. A pale, murderous man.

Under the trees it was darker, the light fragmented by the branches overhead and the thickening mist. It smelled musty and rotten, as though it never dried out, as though the dampness in the air was a permanent, sour presence. The bloodstained mud had been near here, with its uneven necklace of teeth with their clinging worms of gum.

Had a man learned the art of murder? Of violence? Humans had attacked demons during the riots, Fool remembered, the flames of that night fanned by his own actions and what people believed he had done at the lakeside. He had changed as well, he realized, was becoming something new; perhaps he was not the only one. *Could it be?* he wondered. A man who had changed, learned to somehow break the rules, was killing other men and releasing souls by their violence? Was there something about a human killing a human that freed the souls of the dead?

Could it be?

Something behind Fool crashed and then he heard the sound of footsteps, dull impacts as something ran across the damp ground, getting louder as it neared him. He turned and the demon from the lakeside was charging toward him, weaving between the trees, Morgan's head swinging in one clawed hand. It came within a few feet of Fool and pulled up, hurling the head at him. He ducked and Morgan's face curved through the air above him, a pale streak against the darkness, before hitting a tree trunk with a noise like a foot pulling loose from wet earth. It left a dark stain on the trunk as it bounced away, strands of the man's gray hair caught on the gnarled bark.

"It is empty," hissed the demon. "Foul!"

"I didn't say it wasn't," said Fool. He tightened his grip on the gun but did not lift it, was aware of movement around him, of shadows merging and flowing in a whirlpool whose center he had become. "You didn't ask."

As if in response, the demon bent over and vomited out a thin stream of slime that stank, strings of bile that were a pale ivory in color spraying from its mouth. It raised its head, peering at Fool; its eyes were cloudy, covered in a thin film, and the flesh around its mouth was dark, cracking. *Soulless flesh must taste really fucking horrible,* thought Fool and couldn't help but smile.

"Empty," the thing said again and hunched over, stretching its arms out and spreading its fingers wide. Its nails were curved into vicious claws and its fingers were webbed, and Fool understood in a disconnected way that the thin planes of skin would help it swim. He imagined it pulling itself through the dark underside of Solomon Water and wondered whether things appeared there in its depths the way they did in the Flame Garden's burning flanks. Solomon Water was rumored to be deeper than the sky was high, home to a whole other Hell of demons like the one that had come ashore the other year. This little thing, with its webbed hands and stinking vomit, wouldn't stand a chance against the water's other inhabitants if that was the case, he thought, and he felt a fleeting pang of sorrow for it.

"What did the man look like?" he asked, raising his gun.

"Pale, white," said the demon again and then something stepped out behind it and spoke.

"Do you consort with demons now, Information Man?"

"Hello, Adam," said Fool. "Do you need me?"

"God's mercy," said Balthazar, stepping out from behind Adam, and reached out. His hand glowed briefly and the demon between them simply dropped, its body suddenly limp. As it slumped to the earth, a tiny blue spark circled out of its mouth and rose into the tree branches. Its glow hovered over them for a moment and then it winked out. Something howled in the trees, was cut off abruptly with a noise like fat falling into fire.

Adam nodded at Fool. "You're needed," he said.

One of the water demons peered out from behind a tree; Balthazar's flame leaped to it, slicing it neatly in two across its torso. It fell to the ground, each part of it tumbling in different directions, and one of the others screamed and then they all appeared, the shadows gathering weight and momentum as they charged.

Heat was suddenly all about Fool, the air filled with the sound of sundering flesh and the stink of steaming blood. Adam came and stood by Fool as the demons fell before the other angel, Balthazar's glow painting the trees in tones of sullen red. One of the demons rolled up to Fool, pulling itself against his legs and shrieking, "Stop! Stop!" It was the old one, which Fool had assumed was the leader of this . . . what? Family? Group? Tribe? As it clung to him, its claws tearing into the legs of his uniform trousers, its skinless face was tilted back to him. "Please," it said, and then Balthazar reached out from the other side of the clearing and sliced its head off.

"Stop," said Fool. The glow was raging about him now, casting shadows in long, distorted angles, a burning fury with Balthazar at its heart. The flame was a living thing, not a column but a writhing cord that wrapped about the demons as they went from attacking to fleeing.

Trying to flee. The ground was scattered with bodies and parts of bodies, split neatly, severed edges smoking.

"Stop," said Fool again and turned his gun so that it was pointing at Balthazar.

"Thomas?" said Adam from beside him, the first time he had used his name. "You threaten an angel?"

"No," said Fool. "I'm not threatening him, I'm instructing him."

"Instructing him?" The cord of fire, thickening and brighter, curled around a tree. A spurt of steam and liquid appeared, followed a moment later by the dismembered body of a demon.

"As Hell's Information Man, I'm ordering him to stop," said Fool.

"Ordering me?" asked Balthazar. "You should be thanking me; I saved you. Again." The red line snapped upward and something fell from the tree above them. It was small, curled into a ball, and its head rolled away from it as it landed.

"From that?" asked Fool. "From them?" He nodded at the demons currently scattering down the slope and back toward the water.

"From being late," said Adam. He reached up and placed his hand gently on the barrel of Fool's gun, pushing it down. "We have business."

The air seemed to breathe in, the red glow sucking back into Balthazar, the vast tendril of fire contracting, dancing its way back between the trees and disappearing into the angel's hands. His wings, which Fool hadn't noticed were open, beat once and then folded back in, closing and merging into his back and around his ankles. His chest and belly, muscles perfectly defined through his skin, hitched once and then Balthazar was back to normal, or at least, as normal as an angel ever became.

"You threatened me," said Balthazar. His voice was soft, conversational.

"No," said Fool, equally softly, "I instructed you."

"You forget yourself, human," said Balthazar. He stepped toward Fool, who didn't move.

"There's nothing to forget," said Fool. "I'm an Information Man, and I have jurisdiction and there are rules."

"Indeed," said Adam. "Rules, and Elevations."

As ever, more people were Elevated this time than previously, the numbers growing each time until the last, the biggest raising of souls. Despite the deaths that had happened the last time they had gathered, the crowd of the Sorrowful was larger than ever, forming a huge parade leading out of Hell toward the wall and the gateway on the Mount, a solid mass of people waking together. Adam and Elderflower were at its head, followed by a group of about thirteen people to be Elevated, trailed by Fool and Balthazar and then the crowds. The Sorrowful were mostly silent, the odd shout emerging but never gaining company; some of the Sorrowful sang, not loud enough for Fool to hear the words, merely a tune in Hell's afternoon. They had never done that before.

The rhythm of walking was useful, Fool found, in helping him think through where he had been, where he was, where these last few steps along the trail had brought him. It was a trail that he had followed thinking that he was closing in on some grand old demon, but now it turned out that it was a man. It cast a new shadow on what had gone before. The Man's death, for example; how had that been accomplished? The *why*, in some senses, made more sense now: to send Fool to the one place he was almost guaranteed to meet with aggression and hopefully death. Somehow this unknown murderer had torn his way through the parts of the Man that lived in the garden, broken open the wall behind the Man, and then excavated two columns into his back, taken hold of his vinelike flesh, and operated him like a puppet, but how? It must have been fast or surely the Man would have defended himself.

And what about the slaughter of the Aruhlians? How had a single man accomplished that? Maybe there was more than one? A gang? But how could there be more than one?

How could there be even one?

The trails were turning back on themselves, taking him around in circles. Not a demon but not a single man, a group of men working together to do this, which seemed impossible, an impossible thing in a place of impossible things.

The entrance to the tunnel was already glowing, hungry for its new souls. As ever, there was no ceremony, Adam and Elderflower simply standing on either side of the portal and ushering the Elevated in one by one.

The first one stepped into the blue light and took several steps, and with each step pieces of his flesh tore loose, fragmenting away to the edges of the tunnel, strings of shadow like a moving spiderweb forming. Finally, there was a violent blue flash that reminded Fool of the rolling blue light rising from the pandemonium outside Assemblies House. He flinched as the memory caught him and saw Balthazar smile at him.

"Would you really have shot me?" the angel asked.

"Yes, if you hadn't stopped," said Fool.

"But they were demons, Information Man. Demons, not humans, foul things abhorrent in the sight of God. They deserve worse than they received from me."

"They are citizens of Hell and have the same right to protection as anyone else here," said Fool, and was surprised to find that he meant it. "We had traded and they had not attacked me when you killed them. They were innocent."

"Innocent?" asked Balthazar. "Demons are never innocent. By their very nature, they cannot be."

"At that point, they had done nothing wrong," said Fool, wondering why he was being so stubborn and arguing this with Balthazar. It wasn't the act, exactly; Fool had no love for the demons, for any demons, so what then? And then he understood.

"You interfered with my investigation. I was still talking to them."

"They lie," said Balthazar dismissively. "Whatever information you received would have been tainted, corrupted. Only angels are creatures of truth, Fool, angels and that which made them, the God above us." Balthazar glanced skyward, Heavenward, and then back at Fool. Around them the crowd shuffled, gazing at the pulsating light coming from the wall.

Another person was Elevated, then another, flensed apart by the light, their souls expanding, soaking into the stone. As each vanished, the Sorrowful made their cumulative, lingering *aaaaah,* the sound falling somewhere between awe and misery.

"Do you still hope to solve these killings?" asked Balthazar.

"Yes," replied Fool.

"Hell does not lend itself to solutions," said Balthazar. "I'm sure Adam could explain it better than I, but ultimately this is Hell, Fool, and it should be a place of no solutions, of misery and fear and pain and uncertainty. That being the case, why should you be able to accomplish this?"

"Maybe God will help me?" asked Fool and then found his neck burning. Balthazar had moved too fast to be seen, was pressed against him, and his flames were wrapped around Fool's throat, not touching but close enough to be painful. He smelled charring material and wondered whether the collar of his uniform was burning or merely smoldering.

"God works here through us alone, human," said Balthazar in a vicious hiss. "Through Adam and through me and the scribe and the archive. You are one of the cursed, and in years gone you'd have been one of the burning men, chained to a rock or swimming through a lake of fire until your sin was scorched from you and we decided that you were set free. All these meetings and deals and names traded? They aren't Heaven and Hell, little man, not nearly." There was a noise like a whip snapping and the heat was jerked away from Fool's neck. He lifted one hand and felt the line of small blisters, felt the heat of them through his fingertips.

"You, and the demons and the souls of everything and everyone here, they belong to Heaven, Information Man, and don't ever forget that. These deliberations happen because we allow them, and for no other reason. Don't start to believe you have power, or choice, because you do not."

"No," said Fool, and then, "but if I have no choice, then who's in control of me?" Balthazar didn't reply, and the crowd made their low noise as another person was Elevated from Hell up to Heaven.

29

And after the Elevation, life, such as it was, went on.

Fool returned to his rooms almost with a sense of anticlimax, of dislocation and things unsaid and energies unused, and spent hours opening the metal tubes, stamping the enclosed papers *DNI* without reading them, sealing them and inserting them back up into the pneumatic pipe. In among them, he found the blue ribbons for Morgan's and Summer's deaths. Because he had no stamp for it, he wrote *Investigation ongoing* by hand on both and sent them up the pipe after their companions, each throaty swallow feeling like the end of something. He had no idea where the canisters would end up. With Elderflower? Passed on to Rhakshasas, or some other member of the Bureaucracy? Or did they end up deep in Crow Heights being read by Satan himself, surrounded by flames as black as terror?

Not to the floor above, though; that wasn't where the canisters went, despite the fact that the pipe went up through the ceiling. Fool had once gone up to the floor above him but had found simply an abandoned suite of rooms, the pneumatic tube sticking into the still air, finishing halfway up a wall. The end of the tube had been rusted and buckled, too narrow for a canister to pass through, yet there was no sign of the thousands of canisters he had sent up in his time as an Information Man. He had wanted to ask Elderflower about it but hadn't, thinking at the time that his question might get him noticed; ironic, given what had happened since.

In the time he had been absent, Summer's and Gordie's rooms had been cleared out, the bras and pants taken from the shelf, Gordie's spare shirts and pieces of paper and pencils and notes all removed. There was nothing left of the life Fool had known for these last months, of the life he had understood since he was born into Hell years back. Even he was different, a new thing constantly shifting and evolving. *Hell's changing,* he thought, *rippling and buckling around me, around us all.* Men, a man, a pale man murdering other humans, demons frightened of him, uniforms, troops, fucking *demon* troops taking orders from a human.

And a feather.

He was holding it now, feeling the shimmer of heat and light emerging from it against his fingers. It had been with him since the beginning of this whole sorry, strange situation, since that night collecting the delegation. It had survived being taken by the Man, the riot in the Houska, the deaths in the square, being dropped in Summer's blood and left overnight, and it was unmarked, unaffected. What had the Man said? That it was a thing of beauty and truth, a grace note in Hell's music? Not that exactly, perhaps, but something like that. It had come from Balthazar, from the wing of an angel, from something that looked like a human but that was more, a thing of beauty and awe and terror.

Something, there was something dancing just beyond the tip of his tongue, waiting for him to speak it into existence. Something about the first bodies, about the wounds; their severity, he remembered. They weren't injuries caused by a human, they were demon in origin, were too extensive to be caused by a man. Hadn't Morgan said so? He couldn't remember, but he remembered how they had looked, torn and puckered and terrible. Not human injuries, demon-caused, but the thing from the lake had seen a man. A man, or a demon that looked like a man. But there were no demons that looked human; to look at a demon was to look at a warped and distorted reflection of a human, and besides, demons knew demons. So, if the thing from the lake had not seen a man or a demon, what had it seen? Something that looked human, looked like a man, was pale, that had the strength to tear the soul from the flesh and send it skittering into the sky. What had the demon said? Not just that it was pale, but that it was white. Pale and white.

"Those souls weren't consumed," Fool said aloud, giving the truth shape with his words. "If they were eaten, there would have been no sign of them, but there was, there was a flash rising into the sky. The souls were rising up, flying away, free. Whatever it was, it didn't eat the souls."

A pale, white man.

White.

"Oh, you idiot, you *fool*," Fool breathed, suddenly knowing. There were no white demons, no white humans. Only one thing in Hell was white.

Only angels were white.

30

If the thought that it was a man doing the killing had sent the world pitching under Fool's feet, then the thought that it was an angel was like having the floor drop away to nothing. He managed to stand and back away from the table and then felt his legs give way, and he sat down on the floor with a heavy thump. His chair skittered away and ended up on its side against the wall, legs pointing at him.

An angel, not a man or a demon.

An angel.

Fool felt sick, leaned sideways, and opened his mouth to vomit, but nothing emerged except a strangled choking sound. His throat constricted and then released, constricted and released, his belly clenching.

An angel.

Fool wanted it to be wrong but knew, *knew* he wasn't. The only white men in Hell weren't men, they were the angels, and they were supposed to be perfect, uncorrupted and incorruptible. It made a kind of twisted sense, he thought; Balthazar's perfection and his disgust and rage at the things he had seen here spilling out, uncontrolled and uncontained. Fool remembered the angel's anger at Hell, about its lack of perceived punishment, and thought that maybe Balthazar had taken it upon himself to inflict the kind of damage that he thought Hell ought to be delivering. He had become the Hell he believed should exist, had become retribution and torture, a thing of flame and pain and violence.

Balthazar was his killer, the warrior angel with his savage weapons.

How could Fool stop him? Bring him to account? Balthazar was brutal in his power, and worse, he was Hell's guest, more distant than even the eldest of the demonkind from Fool's touch. How could he accuse him? Arrest him? Did Fool's jurisdiction even stretch that far? No, no, surely not, it couldn't.

Yes, it could.

Fool finally sat up and then pulled himself to his feet, using the table for support. He reached into his pocket and pulled out the *Information Man's Guide to the Rules and Offices of Hell,* flicking through its pages until he found the passage he was looking for. He had read all of it before, of course, but it had never meant anything previously because he had never tried before, never followed trails or clues or thought about making arrests, but there it was in black, slightly uneven print: "If it walks or flies or swims in Hell, it is cast over by the net of law and by the authority of the Information Man, whose feet may tread where they will and whose word is all-informing." Which meant he could go anywhere in the pursuit of his aims, didn't it?

Didn't it? Could he try to arrest an angel? Track Balthazar and require him to submit? He thought of that great curve of near-invisible fire dancing in the clearing, stretching from Balthazar's hand up into the sky, thought of the lake demons falling in severed pieces to the ground in billows of steam and scalding scents, and tried to imagine Balthazar simply allowing himself to be taken, complying meekly. It wasn't an image that would come to him.

Where would he take him? There wasn't a place in Hell that could hold an angel, Fool didn't think. It was a fool's errand.

He had to try.

What choice did he have? This was where the trail had led him, and he had followed it this far, leaving the bodies of Summer and Gordie and so many others as the markers on his path, detritus in his wake, and if he had had it wrong about some things, about one thing he knew he was right: he had to solve this and bring it to an end.

Checking that his gun was still strapped to his leg, Fool pulled on his uniform jacket and left the office. This time, he didn't look around before he left; he had no time left for questions, and no hope of success. Alone, Fool went to arrest an angel.

———

His transport was gone. Fool stood in the street and looked toward the distant stain of Crow Heights, black against the thin night sky. It peered down on Hell, the highest point except for the surrounding wall, and the eyes behind its barricades were assumed to see everything. He thought about the black transports, the missing people, the rumors, and the sense that everything old and powerful and destructive lived in the Heights, and knew that Hell's inhabitants were wrong. It was deep in the bureaucratic district, in the Assemblies House where the angels had their rooms, that the most terrifying thing lived. Fool touched his gun again and started walking.

The train beetled along the wide road that ran out from the Houska. It was ahead of Fool and he ran to catch it; it wasn't hard as it was moving only at the speed of a fast walk. At this time of the evening it was quiet, the night's revelries not yet having swung into high gear. The train would take him to within a few hundred yards of the road to Assemblies House, but it would take a while, so Fool found a small carriage that was almost empty and sat. After a moment, though, he rose, unable to remain seated. Energy crackled in his arms and legs and his head was stuffy with thoughts, clustered together like sodden cotton wadding. Balthazar, with his flames and his anger, murdering Diamond and the others. He imagined him descending on the pit of the Aruhlians, his wings spread wide against the sky and his teeth huge in a face torn back into an expression of terrible joy, of him dragging the Genevieve down to the flooded cellar, his red gleam turning the water to a pool of blood, and Fool was frightened. He began to pace, swinging along the carriage and back again, using the straps dangling from the ceiling for support.

"Are you him?" One of the two other people in the carriage. It was a woman, younger than Summer, with dirt ground into her skin. She had come from one of the factories, he presumed, was making her way back to her billet. If she was lucky, it would be a room with her and only four or five other women in it; if she was unlucky, she'd be forced to share with up to twenty or thirty. "Are you him?" she asked again.

"No," said Fool and kept on pacing. To the end and turn, and as he came back along the carriage, still thinking about Balthazar, unable to shift the angel from inside his head, where the thought of him had pushed everything else to the side, the person sitting next to the woman, a man, spoke.

"You are."

"No," said Fool again. "I'm not. I'm no one," and it was true, he was no one, just a man in Hell, an Information Man, but no one special. He was no one, was happy being no one.

"You are," said the man and held out a sheaf of paper. "You're him. You're Fool. We recognize you."

Fool took the paper. Papers, really; there were several sheets, their corners folded together to keep them in a bundle. Each page was covered in tight black print and pictures, all hand-drawn. On the first page, under a thick heading that read THIS MAN CONTROLS DEMONS, was a picture he thought might be of him. It was badly drawn and Summer's image of him was better, but it was still him. The text below the picture was a list of things Fool had done, some true but most nonsense. All the sheets were variations on the theme, he saw as he leafed through them; details of his investigation, of deeds he had supposedly done, and of tasks he had apparently accomplished. All were at best exaggerations, at worst complete fabrications. On the final page, under the words MANY LIVES SAVED, there was another picture of him, or someone supposed to be him, outlined in flames drawn as heavy black lines and pointing as two caricatured demons slunk away, heads down. Underneath this image was the comment *He Conquers Hell.*

"What is this?" Fool asked.

"They're everywhere," said the woman. "No one knows who's making them, but they're in all the factories and streets. Demons keep clearing them up, but more appear. They're everywhere."

Everywhere. That meant that people had read them, demons had seen them, were reading them. Were reading about *him.* He wondered what Rhakshasas thought about this and didn't imagine he'd be pleased. He wondered who was making the sheets, whether he could stop them somehow, or get them to print something else, but knew that it was probably too late. Even if he did, another version of Fool had already been born in the paper, one that held little resemblance to the actual Fool. *And even he's not the same, because I don't really recognize him anymore,* he thought, and gave the paper back to the couple. He noticed that they were holding hands, their fingers tightly intertwined. He knew they wouldn't have dared to do that a few days ago.

Fool paced. When he reached one end of the carriage he turned and went back, along and along, and at each end faces peered through the quartered glass in the doors at him. At first he thought they were people who wanted to come in but then realized that they were simply watching him. He wanted to tell them to stop, to scream at them to stop staring at him, but he didn't. *Little noticed Fool,* he thought, *everyone's watching you now.* The train rattled and jolted, making its slow way onward.

The square in front of Assemblies House was quiet. Fool walked to its center, wanting to be away from the alleys and shadowed doorways that lined it. If attack came, he wanted some notice and a chance to escape or defend himself. He drew his gun, felt strange carrying it out like that, and put it away again. The windows around him were dark; this was a district used mainly in the daylight business of Hell. The ground was stained with blood dried to the color of old mud and burned patches, and there were still torn and trampled banners lying around. Shredded and mulched paper had been trodden into the dirt, stained red and black and brown. Fool pulled himself straight, standing as tall as he could, and went to the gates. They were unlocked and he went through, going to the main doors and knocking.

"What?" said a voice from inside.

"I need to see the angels," he replied.

"Shit to that," said the voice. "Who do you think you are?"

"I am Thomas Fool," said Fool. "I'm an Information Man of Hell and I have the right to enter and speak to anyone or any fucking thing I want. Let me in."

"Shit to that," said the voice again. Fool dropped his hand to his gun, starting to flick off the straps, when there was a dull thud from beyond the door. Someone, possibly the owner of the voice, said "Sir" weakly, and then there was the sound of locks slipping and opening.

"Hello, Thomas," said Elderflower once the door was open. "I wondered when you might arrive."

"You knew I was coming?"

"Of course. Rhakshasas informed me by tube of your imminent arrival a few moments ago."

Fool stepped into the hallway of Assemblies House, stepping over the prostrate figure of a man. He was shuddering, his arms tucked under his body and his hands cupping a face that was pointed to the floor. He was sobbing. Fool looked down at him and said, "What happened?"

"I merely showed him the folly of standing in the way of an Information Man doing his duty. You are Hell's man, Fool, and none should obstruct you in your path."

"I need to see Balthazar."

"Yes," said Elderflower. "You think he has something to do with all this?"

"Does he?"

"How would I know?"

"You know things about Hell," said Fool, halfway between a question and a statement.

"Do I? No, I think not, not I. And remember, Thomas, the angels aren't of Hell. They are from above and beyond and without. Shall we go?"

The corridors of Assemblies House were long and low once they were out of what Fool thought of as the "public" area. In his time in Hell, and always with Elderflower, Fool had been in several of the smaller meeting rooms and offices and the large ballroom but never behind them, into the Bureaucracy's area. The ceilings were lower, causing Fool to duck his head slightly, although Elderflower was fine. The light was dank and guttering, inefficient gas lamps burning yellow and orange in brackets on the walls. The air was claustrophobic with the smell of flame and gas and things dead and dying.

"These are their rooms," said Elderflower as they came to a set of arched double doors. Symbols were carved in the lintel above the door and in the frames down the side of the doors. They seemed to move in the shifting shadows and light, writing and rewriting themselves.

"A word, Thomas," said Elderflower. "Beyond the doors is not, strictly, Hell but is an offshoot of Heaven, a little bubble of perfection in our sordid world. Whatever you plan to do, you have no jurisdiction or power beyond this threshold. Your gun will not work, and I cannot help or protect you. Bring the angels out and they leave Heaven and enter Hell again, and your power is restored. Do you understand?"

"No," said Fool truthfully. How could rooms in Hell belong to Heaven? He supposed it didn't matter, not really. What mattered was all the dead flesh staring at him from inside his head, Summer dangling between two columns and Gordie lost under a burning, spastic mass of figures that were neither wholly demon nor wholly human, the Man slumping forward with holes torn in his back. What mattered were the dead.

Fool took a deep breath, drew his gun, and, using its butt, hammered on the doors. After a moment, they swung open. A wash of clean, blue light fell out from between them, framing the small figure of the scribe. Or maybe it was the archive, Fool wasn't sure.

"I need to speak to Balthazar," Fool said.

"It is customary to say 'please,' " said a voice behind the smaller angel. Balthazar stepped into the light, the shimmer of it across his flawless skin almost too beautiful to look at. "What do you want, Information Man? Come to give me instructions again?"

"Yes," said Fool and made a conscious effort to lower his gun. "We need to discuss one last piece of business. I need you to come to the ballroom." Was this the way to do it? Fool didn't know, had never had to do anything like this before. Was there a right way? A wrong? The trail had led him this far, but now that he was at its end, or near its end maybe, he had even less of an idea than normal how to act.

"What business?"

"Hell's business," said Elderflower, stepping forward.

"It is not on our schedule," said Adam, also stepping into the light. It was getting crowded in the doorway, thought Fool; the scribe or archive, maybe thinking the same, slipped back between Adam and Balthazar and out of sight.

"No," said Elderflower, "but it is important nonetheless. I must insist, Adam, that this be dealt with before you leave tomorrow."

"Very well," said Adam. "Balthazar, bring the others. We have business."

31

"What's this about, Elderflower?" asked Adam.

They were in the ballroom, Adam and Elderflower seated in the usual places, Fool and Balthazar standing behind them rather than over by the windows. The room was cold and dark, the only light the few lamps that Elderflower had ordered lit. If Elderflower's servants were in the corners of the room, they were hidden by shadows.

"Something has come to light," said Elderflower.

"And it will still be unclear and untrue," said Balthazar, "as is everything in this place."

"You still don't understand, do you, even after your time here?" said Fool, trying to keep his tone conversational. "Everything in Hell is true, even the lies, because they are believed. People see it all around them, see unjust, merciless punishment, and know that it is just because what they cannot remember, what they do not have, is the knowledge of their sins. The place is a curse made solid, a place where the truth is just as harsh and bitter as the lies are, and you should not underestimate the power of that."

"The business," said Adam, steepling his hands and leaning back, crossing his legs.

"Thomas?" said Elderflower. Fool tried to speak, found his throat had dried from speaking, swallowed a breath that was like sand, and tried again.

"Balthazar, why did you kill them?"

The angel did not reply, simply stared at Fool for a second, and then the sound of his laughter filled the ballroom, a dry rattle clattering up against the ceiling and swooping around the molded cornices.

"It's funny?" asked Fool, not raising his voice, feeling the anger build inside him and letting it. "The deaths, the murders, they're funny?"

Balthazar's laughter trailed away. "You're serious?" he asked. "You think I committed these murders that you've been investigating? Fool, I'm an angel."

"Yes," said Fool, thinking of the demons by the lake falling into pieces and the chalkis dropping from the sky in smoking segments, "you are, and all the way along you have destroyed my evidence and killed my witnesses. You destroyed the bodies of the Aruhlians in case they talked and—"

"I destroyed them to give them dignity," Balthazar interrupted.

"You killed the demon at the lake before it could describe you to me, you killed the Man of Plants and Flowers so that you could use him to send me off in the wrong directions. So, I ask again. Why?"

"Fool, I did not kill them," said Balthazar, formal now, making a statement. "My weapon has been used only in the tasks of protecting you. Why in the name of God would you think that I killed those poor souls?"

It was the question Fool had been avoiding in his head, the *why* of it all. Why would Balthazar kill the Genevieves, the Aruhlians, all the others? They disgusted him, yes, weak as they were, failing sinners that they were, but surely that wasn't enough? Was it? Yes.

No. No, because suddenly it was there, clear and shimmering in his head and in the air in front of him and he opened his mouth so that his tongue could chase it.

"Because of the souls," said Fool, speaking without pause, allowing the words to lead the thoughts. "Because what you did freed their souls and punished them at the same time. They weren't sent back outside the wall when you killed them; they were *released*. That's why the murders were so violent: they had to be to ensure that the dead weren't simply sent back to Limbo, the violence absolving the dead of their sins and freeing them. The blue flashes—they were souls escaping from Hell and rising up, gaining entry to Heaven."

"Very good, Thomas," said Elderflower, and then Balthazar's flame was dripping from his hand and beginning to rise.

"I did not kill them," he said again, and his wings were unfurling, curling out from his back in black arcs, smaller shadows around his feet opening, his arms coming up in front of the larger wings, his body taking on the color of flame and ash.

"I have a witness," said Fool. *Had a witness,* he thought, remembering the demon's head collapsing to the mulchy ground, killed by the angel he would have pointed his accusation at. He drew his gun, trained it on Balthazar, watching the whip of flame curling down from the angel's hands, growing longer and thicker, curling and flickering like a reptile's tongue. The light was draining from the room, the shadows at its corners thickening as Balthazar pulled the illumination in, became the burning center of the room.

"A witness," said the angel, "who saw what?"

"A bright man," said Fool, hearing as he said it how thin it sounded.

"Do I look bright?" asked Balthazar, who was churning with a dull, fiery redness now, convection patterns of heat boiling away from his skin and filling the air around him with mazy shades. "Do I, little Information Man, little Fool? Do I look bright?"

The flame curled up, dancing around Fool, encircling his wrist but not tightening. He felt its heat, saw the hairs across the back of his hand begin to shrivel and char and tried to stay still; one twitch and he had no doubt his hand and the gun it held would fall.

"I say again, I did not kill them," said Balthazar.

"No?"

"I'm not lying, Fool. I can't lie. Don't *you* understand? I'm an angel, Fool, one of God's holy things, and the truth is woven through me as surely as blood is woven through humans and evil through demons. You have my feather, a part of me. Haven't you noticed that people tell the truth when they hold it? That you tell yourself the truth when you have it near you, when you carry it or hold it?"

"Tell myself the truth?" asked Fool, but suddenly understood. All Hell's fog had burned away from him not because of anything he had done or anything inside him but because he had had the feather, had been carrying something beautiful and pure and clear. He had seen the trail, understood the marks on the path, the clues, because, once gifted, the feather had sharpened his vision. All the time it had been with him, it had been drawing him taut, sharpening him, bringing him into focus, bringing him *here,* and he felt betrayed and hollow. Sick.

"The feather only made you a better version of what was already there," said Balthazar, with something like tenderness in his voice. The curl of flame widened, tip lashing slowly, and then fell away from Fool's out-stretched hand. He flexed it carefully, feeling the tightness of the skin where he had been scorched.

"I am capable of killing," said Balthazar, "but I did not kill anyone or anything in Hell that did not deserve it, Fool. My work here is to service the delegation and nothing more."

"So if it wasn't you, and it wasn't a man or demon, then who killed them?" Fool asked, speaking out loud because his mouth was still run-ning ahead of the rest of him. He needed answers, something concrete to grip and understand. If it wasn't Balthazar—and it wasn't, couldn't be, because the angel was right, he wasn't bright but was a rippling, fleshy gleam that seemed to sweat shadows into the air around him—if it wasn't him, then who? "Who was it?" Fool asked again. "Who killed them? Who killed all those people?"

"I did," said Adam and then the room was full of the brightest light Fool had ever seen.

It was beyond light, somehow, had weight and mass and volume, pushed Fool backward and sent him stumbling. Somewhere, lost in it, he heard Balthazar shout and then the angel's red glow was extinguished by the glare. Fool squeezed his eyes shut and tried to swing his gun around to where he thought Adam was, but the weight pressing against him made it feel like he was moving through mud or heavy, oily water, clinging and pushing against him. Oddly, it wasn't painful; the opposite, if anything, and he felt the skin on his wrist soften and calm, the aches to his face and body flare briefly and then begin to fade. It was healing him, and even through his closed eyelids, the light was inexorable and he had to turn away from it. *The white man,* he thought. *White, and bright.*

"I gave them freedom," said Adam. "They thanked me."

"You murdered them," said Fool, and the light moved across his flesh and he could feel it, faster and faster, a whirlwind, and he wondered whether this was what it had been like for them, the center of something too big and too fast and too bright to understand but knowing that it was coming, terrible and painful and inexorable.

"It is not murder," said Adam, his voice a calm note in the maelstrom of light. "They are dead already. I merely did what Hell has stopped doing, and gave their souls release. This is Hell, and I had to be cruel to perform the greatest kindness, to unanchor their souls, but it was God's work I performed with those poor things."

"And so it begins," said Elderflower from somewhere in the room. He sounded as though he were moving, but when Fool tried to open his eyes he found he still could not.

"We aren't dead," said Fool.

"No?" said Adam. "Are you sure?"

"Oh, Adam, everyone here is alive," said Elderflower, his voice still moving, seeming to fade closer and then farther away. "Flesh with a resident soul is living flesh, you know that."

"Then you're a murderer," said Fool, feeling forward with his free hand. He found the wall and used it to stand, pulling himself upright. He held his gun forward, fighting against the weight of the light, heard something swish past him, felt heat cut through the light and pass over his skin. There was another noise, like chains going taut and snapping, and then the weight of the light was gone and the glare had faded from his eyes. He risked opening them, squinted through tears that came unbidden and turned the room into a blurred mess, and saw Adam standing in front of the windows.

Balthazar's fires were crawling over Adam, fingers of it wrapping around the angel's face and head and slithering down beneath his black robe. Adam ignored the flame and looked at Fool. "Will you arrest me, Information Man? Arrest God's representative in Hell on the word of a demon?"

"Yes," said Fool.

"Hell is God's domain, Fool, and the freeing of souls is God's work. Is it a crime, to carry out God's work?"

"Yes," said Fool. "In Hell, the rules bind even God's children. You had no permission to murder flesh nor steal souls. You went outside the remit of the delegation. Criminality is criminality, whether carried out by human, demon, or angel, and under the rules of Hell you have sinned."

"God will protect me," said Adam, reaching up and taking hold of

Balthazar's flame. He tugged and Balthazar was jerked forward. As he came within his companion's reach, Adam swung his other arm. It became a silver blur as it moved, sweeping up and chopping Balthazar across his stomach, lifting him and throwing him back across the room. His other arm swung after it, glowing silver and shining and growing until it stretched across the room and battered into Balthazar. The red angel groaned as he was thrust farther, his body crashing into the wall. Something cracked as he hit, although whether in the wall or within Balthazar Fool could not tell. Adam pulled his arm back and prepared for another strike.

Fool fired, his hand trembling, and a ragged line opened along the side of Adam's face. Light poured from it, splashing down the angel's shoulder like liquid, coating the side of his face. His arms snapped back, reducing, becoming simply arms again.

"Do you think you can harm me?" he said, and as he spoke his robes lifted, spread, fanned out behind him, and Fool realized that they were not robes, that they never had been. They were his wings, *its* wings, because Adam was no longer even an approximation of a human, had become something made of light and rigidity and gleam, humanoid but not human in the least. Its eyes were burning silver, its skin a flawless alabaster that gleamed as though lit from within, and its wings were huge, colors shifting across them like oil glinting on the surface of water, and when it spoke, its voice echoed in the room, shivering dust from the joints and beams above them.

"I am angelic, Fool, one of the host of Heaven. Your gun cannot touch me." Its wings curved, blocking the windows behind him, their tips brushing the walls with a sound like nails dragging across glass.

"In point of fact, you aren't," said Elderflower as he walked in between Adam and Fool. The little figure blurred, its edges lost in the angel's glare, reduced to a black smudge at its heart. "An angel, I mean. You're a criminal, nothing more. You murdered the citizens of Hell, attacked your companion. Scribe has it written, I believe?"

"Yes," said a voice, dull and toneless. *They* can *speak*, thought Fool, *they can!*

"Elderflower," said Adam, "what nonsense is this?"

"You're a criminal," said Elderflower, "and there are thousands like you in Hell, you're no different from any other thing here. Just a criminal. Whatever you were, that's all you are now. Thomas, if you'd be so kind?"

"Certainly," said Fool, and shot Adam again.

Adam, no longer an angel, now a pale and bright thing, exploded.

32

For the second time, the room filled with light. This time it was blue, dark and clinging, and it buffeted Fool. It wasn't bright, exactly, but it filled the space and it was thick, distorting the shapes of Elderflower and Adam into ragged things that appeared to be floating. Adam was shouting, screaming, and then everything in the room shifted as though it had tilted on its side. Fool was pulled, his feet leaving the floor, tumbling sideways, falling through the air and crashing into Elderflower and then onward into the thick, quartered windows. A moment later, Balthazar hit the glass next to them, and Fool just had time to realize that he was several feet off the floor and then the furniture was hitting the glass around him.

Fool was flat against the panes, his face pressed against one square of glass. A chair hit the pane next to him, cracking it, its dusty stuffing spraying loose as the material of the old cushion ripped. The air swilled blue around him, light eddying and coagulating in front of him. He heard an impact followed by someone grunting, and then Balthazar said, "Adam."

Adam screamed.

It was a wretched sound. It whooped, hoarse, agony and loss and fear all impacting and scratching, louder and louder until Fool's ears hurt. The light had a taste and scent, of old copper and spent saliva and long-dead flames, filling his mouth and nose. He couldn't breathe, felt it clog his throat, press his tongue down. He tried to spit but couldn't, and the screaming came again and was, if anything, worse.

"Adam!" Balthazar said again, and there was another high snapping sound by Fool's ear. The weight around him increased, pressing him harder against the glass, and he felt a crack snake its way along his cheek. The edges of the glass parted slightly, cutting into his skin, thin lines of pain slicing into his cheek, new pain to replace the injuries that Adam's angelic light had washed away. There was another crack, this one from somewhere farther down his body. His arm was pinned under him, the gun trapped and pressing into his belly. He tried to wriggle, tried to breathe, couldn't.

There was another crack. The blue deepened, and the rest of the room was lost to Fool completely. There was a third scream, half-formed words bubbling through it, and then the windows under Fool splintered farther. The wooden struts began to bow out, the weight against him increasing. He tried to speak, drew in a thick breath that got no farther than the back of his mouth, choked, and then he was falling in a mess of fragmented glass and wood and swirling, dancing blue.

It was dizzying. Fool fell out of the room and then shifted direction, still falling now not out but down, everything arcing along with him except the blue, which curved in the other direction, climbing. He saw Elderflower, coat flaring behind him like a cape, and Balthazar, wings beating. The scribe dropped past him, the archive following. *How many floors up is the ballroom?* he wondered. He couldn't remember. Glass fell like stars around him and the weight was removed from him, he had no weight at all and the smell was gone and he could breathe and he was looking out at Hell and then the ground was leaping toward him.

There was no mud; the square had been scraped after the riot and deaths and Fool hit the flagged ground feetfirst. His legs buckled up, his knees driving hard into his chest and then knocking him back, the breath driven from him in an explosive gasp. Glass crunched under him as he rolled, more falling around him, and he brought his arms up and wrapped them around his exposed head. The back of his head hit the stone hard, protected by his hand, and Fool heard the thin snapping of his fingers breaking moments before the pain hit.

It wasn't his gun hand; even as his roll came to a sprawled end and he curled around, nursing his hand, he was thankful for that. He had lost his gun in the fall, but when he found it he would still be able to hold it.

"Give me your hand." Balthazar, standing in front of Fool. His wings were folded up above his head, protecting them from the still-falling detritus. Fool held his hand out. Two of the fingers were twisted, bent at a strange angle.

"Look away," said Balthazar. Fool looked around; Elderflower was standing not far from him, the scribe and archive behind him, and then Fool saw the rising light.

It was streaming out of the ballroom and rising into the sky, piercing the clouds. It had formed itself into a thick column, was pulsing, and reminded Fool of one of the Man's twisting fronds, and then Balthazar pulled his fingers and the pain grew brighter than anything else. When the corona of white had faded from his eyes, the blue stream was fading and guttering. Several seconds later, it had petered to nothing.

"You'll need to strap the fingers," Balthazar said, letting go of Fool's hand.

"Thank you."

"He's been taken back," said the angel, looking into the sky toward Heaven. Fool grunted, not trusting himself to speak. Pain and anger surged in him, throbbing and raw. Adam had escaped, managed to avoid facing any kind of justice. Fuck. *Fuck!*

"No," said Elderflower, "he's not."

"Then where is he?" asked Fool.

"Falling," said Elderflower. Above them, the clouds boiled and bucked and then vomited out a mass of dirty blue light.

Everything's about light, thought Fool as a tendril of cold fire fell from the sky. *All this, from the very beginning, it's all been about light. Light that comes in, light that gets released. Light that means something. Adam and Balthazar are things of light, hot light and cold light.*

Falling light.

All of Hell was lit up by the pulsing coming down from the clouds, strands of filthy blue spilling down. They looked like sodden paper, threaded through with shit and grime, spattering earthward. Fool sat back on his haunches watching the light; as it hit the ground, there was a soundless explosion that sent sprays bouncing back upward, only to arc out and fall back to earth again. Finally, there was a brighter flash and an egg of blue flame belched down, wrapped in the dank tendrils, and crashed to earth.

There was a last, violent pulse of light, lurching into the air and rippling down in waves. Between the group in the courtyard and the murky lifting and falling light, some fragment of Hell's brutalist architecture was black and stolid. It looked like broken teeth in a mouth with no gums, jagged and irregular.

"What's that?" asked Balthazar.

"It's glorious," whispered Elderflower.

"A wall," said Fool. He recognized the top, saw in the stark shapes something that he knew. "It's a wall."

"The oldest wall in Hell, Thomas," said Elderflower, "around the oldest part of Hell."

"He's in the Heights?"

"Of course. Where else would Adam fall? He is Hell's first Fallen in years, and he is, in his way, important. Vital, maybe. He is old and powerful and has a taste for blood, a Fallen thing to fear. He'll make a terrible demon, Thomas, cruel and full of bile and bitterness, and he has fallen into the center of Hell's most private place. But justice still needs to be served, does it not?"

It took Fool a moment to realize what Elderflower was saying. The pyrotechnic display was coming to an end now, the light fainter, the writhing tendrils less pronounced. The Falling was almost complete. "I can't," he said.

"Do you have a choice?" asked Elderflower. "He's admitted his crimes, attacked a member of the delegation, killed humans and demons. He is Hell's, Thomas, just as you are. You have your role to play, and Hell requires it be played."

"He's in Crow Heights," said Fool, thinking of a demon aflame, screaming and spitting and sent to kill him, thinking of revenge and anger.

"A place deeper and larger than it seems from the outside, Thomas. You had best hurry or Adam may lose himself in its heart and emerge only after you are long gone, and who will stop him then?"

"I can't," said Fool again.

"You can," said a voice behind him. Hands slipped under his armpits and he was lifted gently, set onto his feet. Balthazar let Fool go and came around in front of him. Balthazar's wings were open, huge, and his arms wreathed in curling flames but his head was bowed.

"I am yours," he said. "I owe you an apology. Adam was my companion and I saw none of this, and in my blindness I have allowed a betrayal of both Heaven and Hell. He deserves capture, but I am only a soldier and cannot move against him without command."

"Marvelous!" said Elderflower, clapping his hands. "And don't forget, Thomas, you have other troops."

"No," said Fool immediately, wondering what would happen if he took his demons into Crow Heights, how strongly their allegiance would bind them to him when they came under the influence of the elders there. Some of the Heights' inhabitants were the first links in the chains of generations and breeding that eventually led to his troops, and he was, after all, only human.

I thought of them as "my demons," he thought suddenly. *What's happening to me?*

"Very well," said Elderflower. "Very well, you know best. This is your investigation, after all. The Bureaucracy simply requires you to take it to its end. So, you and Balthazar, Thomas, collect him, or make sure he does not remain a threat. There is a transport on its way."

There was a crowd around Crow Heights' gates, a mass of the Sorrowful milling together and scattered across the road. The transport, its demon driver as quiet as ever, had to slow as it approached, the mass of bodies becoming thicker and thicker around the car until Fool ordered it to stop. Through the windows he watched the Sorrowful; they were watching the walls and the gates, their expressions an uneasy mix of longing and fear and hope. They ignored the transport.

"They want to find the Fallen," Fool said, seeing the expression of confusion on Balthazar's face.

"Why?"

"They believe whoever first finds the Fallen receives Elevation."

"No," said Balthazar. "That can't be right. What if it is found by a demon? We would not Elevate a demon, or someone who hasn't yet repented or paid for their sins."

"Really?" said Fool. *Poor Balthazar,* he thought, *he wants so much to believe in the logic of all this, but there is no logic, not here in Hell. There's just each day and surviving it. Poor me, I'm feeling sorry for an angel. Little topsy-turvy Fool. Am I going to my death? With broken fingers and new bruises, sitting next to an angel who I'm realizing is as naive as I am out of my depth? I am.*

I am.

Balthazar was looking out of the transport's window at the Sorrowful. One or two of the humans were peering disinterestedly into the car and looking back at the wall. Some had started to move away, Fool saw, following the curved stone barrier around, and some would, he had no doubt, find the tumbled section he had stood on the other day. Would they enter? Climb those black and greasy blocks and venture inside the Heights? He wasn't sure. Unlike the crowds outside Assemblies House, these didn't seem angry enough to shoulder any kind of risk; not yet, anyway. Their presence might help him; he and Balthazar could try to mingle and lose themselves within the mass and slip through the gaps in the wall to enter secretly, he thought, and then, *No.*

No. They would enter by the gates, like the official visitors that they were. He would not be turned away, not now or ever again. Fuck the demons, fuck the guards. If he was to die chasing a Fallen angel, it wouldn't be skulking along the base of a wall like something verminous and shameful. "Come on," he said to Balthazar and opened the transport door.

Fool emerged from the transport into the cold air. Balthazar opened the door on the other side and climbed out, standing straight and flexing his muscled arms. His glow had simmered down to a faint pink gleam now, his skin shading back down to a ruddy, healthy skin tone, and Fool felt scrawny and ragged next to his beauty. The two of them went to the gates, Fool a step ahead of Balthazar, leading. The crowd parted before them, most turning to look at Fool and the angel but a few ignoring them, watching the wall. They had the same look on their faces as the Sorrowful wore when they stood outside the Elevation meetings, before the riots and the missiles and the banners, hopeful and desperate and guarded. From around them came whispers and mutterings as more and more of the Sorrowful watched. Fool raised one hand and, using the butt of his gun, hammered on the wooden gates.

"What?" said a voice. The same voice as his last visit? A different one?

It was impossible to tell. It was muffled by the inches of wood between them, and this time the speaker did not open the slot to see out. Crow Heights, it seemed, was closed.

"I'm coming in," Fool said. No choices, no offers, no requests. There was only forward and wherever it took him.

"You're not," said the voice. It reminded Fool of the last time he was here, and he had no time to waste now. *No more skulking,* he told himself again.

"I'm an Information Man and I have the right to enter," he said. "A last chance: will you open up?"

"Go piss yourself," said the voice.

"Balthazar?" asked Fool.

"Certainly," said Balthazar, and he tore the gates apart.

The wooden planks didn't splinter; they snapped like brittle metal as Balthazar punched through and yanked them outward. One snapped at its top hinge and swung drunkenly down; the other simply tore away from the jamb and fell into the mud at their side. The noise of it was huge, startling, the sound of orders being fractured and of something ancient shattering.

Beyond the broken gates, Crow Heights was bathed in fire.

Although the Falling had ended, remnants of its light were still scattered across the ground and slicked up the walls. As Fool walked into the Heights, the gates' guardian was nowhere to be seen, either having run or in hiding, and he was glad; he didn't want any more conflict. Around him, the fragments of light writhed sluggishly this way and then that across the ground. Where they touched against moss or the Heights' wretched shrubs, it flared and then guttered to nothing and the plants themselves crumbled to black, ashy remnants. Balthazar knelt and grasped part of the light and lifted it; he squeezed it and it curled around his biceps before fading to nothing, leaving faint blue striations on his skin.

"It's diseased," he said. "Rotten."

"Yes," said Fool and wanted to say, "That's Hell" but didn't. How long would it be before Balthazar changed, if he stayed here? How long before the things he saw became commonplace? How long before his righteous anger and disgust made him do the things Adam had done?

How long before he Fell, corrupted into something new?

Behind them, the Sorrowful were coming cautiously through the gateway, looking around and seeing the Heights for the first time. In front of them, buildings looked on, impassive. Nothing but the light moved.

"It's ahead of us," said Balthazar. Even without the angel, Fool would have known; the strands of light all led back in one direction, snaking back between the buildings, throwing glimmers of illumination up walls that were old and crooked and dark. From somewhere in the distance came a crash and then a long, inhuman scream. There was a rumble like something huge coughing violently, of falling stone, and then, from behind the buildings, a flash that lit up the sky and reflected down from the clouds.

Another scream, another flash, and then a howl of fury. It vibrated the air, louder and louder until it hurt, and then it cut off suddenly. There was a moment's silence and then another crash, and this time Fool saw movement to accompany the noise, a building tilting and then collapsing down in a rising mask of dust and splintering masonry.

"What's happening?" asked one of the Sorrowful, a man. He had picked up a long piece of wood from the ground, part of the broken gates, and was holding it out in front of him nervously.

"The Fallen thing is angry and is lashing out," said Balthazar. "It has lost the glories of Heaven." "It" again, not "him"; Adam no longer existed for Balthazar, Fool thought.

"What screamed? What is it?" asked the man.

"It? Possibly a demon, possibly something far, far worse," said Balthazar. He was grinning as he spoke, his teeth white.

"A murderer," said Fool.

"You have come to take it away?" This new voice came from one of the alleys ahead of them. Something was hunched far down in its depths, and although Fool could not see it, he had the clear impression of too many eyes and a shape that seemed to shift and ripple. "You are to remove it? It is tearing things apart. To pieces."

"You need my help?" asked Fool.

"Yes," said the thing in the alley. "It is like nothing we've encountered, not for years. For millennia."

"You tried to have me killed. You sent something to kill me, and now you need my help?"

"We apologize," said the thing easily. "You were an annoyance. Now this is worse, and you are here."

There was another crash, this one lower, somewhere underground, so that Fool felt it travel up from the soles of his feet as much as heard it.

"Fool, the longer we wait, the more chance there is of it escaping," said Balthazar.

"Where is it?" asked Fool. The thing in the alley raised something that might have been a tentacle but that ended in a pincer with three or four curved sections and said, "It fell into the house of the Bwg."

"Bwg?"

"Ghosts. It is in the house that isn't there, Information Man. Take your angel and go remove it."

"Yes," said Fool. He felt in his pocket and rubbed his fingers along the feather. This demon, all the demons here, would use him when they wanted and then kill him if they could, because it was what they did, and he wondered whether any of them really had choices. Right now, they needed his help to find Adam and because they were scared and would not risk facing the Fallen themselves, but then? They would hate him again, no doubt, because that was how they were created, what Hell required of them.

Was that the feather clarifying things for him? No, it was obvious; demons hated humans, used them, fed on their fear and unhappiness. *All the fear I feel now, I'd be a fucking feast for them,* he thought. *If they wait, I may be even tastier because I can't see this getting any less terrifying, only worse. Little scared Fool. Little terrified Fool.*

There was another crash, another howl. Adam was ahead of them, and there was only one way to go.

33

This part of Crow Heights didn't seem to have been built so much as grown. As Fool and Balthazar started down the alley, the walls twisted so that the buildings leaned in above them, blisters of stone and brick bulging from their sides, hollows curving back and creating pools of shadow. Holes in the brick might have been windows, glassless and their angles smooth and distorted, frames bent into swirls and irregularities, or they might have been mouths or eyes. Everything seemed coated with sweat, dripping in long, thick strings and making the air humid and sour. The demon, shape still muffled, slipped back into the darkness and disappeared. Behind them, there was a shout, a human shout, and a faint crash.

The alley opened out into a wider street similar to the one that Fool had been attacked in during his last visit to the Heights, lined on either side by houses of stone or wood. Their facades looked normal when Fool looked directly at them, but when he turned away they moved, swaying sinuously in the corner of his eyes. The empty windows made him think that someone or something had left the space only moments before, although he couldn't tell what it was that made him think that. It was Hell, he supposed, another of its tricks and terrors.

The writhing light, fainter now, was strung along the center of the road in thick limbs, shoots of it wriggling down the alleys and passages between the buildings. Steam rose from around the light, bringing with it the smell of baking earth and burning mud. When the steam hit Balthazar, it hissed and vanished; when it hit Fool, it clung to his uniform in wet, silvery streaks. Chalkis lined the roofs around them, watching them silently; wooden Alrunes were carved at the corners of some of the roofs, streaked in chalkis' shit, faces worn. They turned and watched as Fool and Balthazar went past, but stayed as silent as the flying things that were their companions.

There was another crash ahead of them and something spun up into the air, arcing toward them and then crashing to the earth at their feet. It was a lump of ragged flesh, not human. Balthazar prodded at it; after a moment, it rolled and sent out tendrils, began to crawl sluggishly toward the nearest house. Balthazar sliced it into smaller pieces and it stopped moving.

"It kills demons, Fool," said Balthazar. "Perhaps I should leave it be?"

"It killed humans," said Fool.

"And set their souls free."

"It broke the rules. It broke the law."

"Yes," said Balthazar after a moment's silence during which Fool heard another distant roar of voices. "Hell's law. This is a new situation, Fool, and I find myself unsure. I believe it has sinned, but surely everyone here has sinned? Isn't that the point?"

"Maybe," said Fool, and he was suddenly weary. "If I sinned, I don't know what it was that I did. I don't know what any of the dead did, except I know they died and I know that Adam killed them. Perhaps that was Hell's plan for them, perhaps not. Maybe this is all Hell's plan, my investigation and the trail I'm on, and if so, so be it. Adam came here and killed and I have to bring him to justice. Help me if you want or you can, or not; I'm going anyway."

"We don't have this in Heaven," said Balthazar.

"No," said Fool. "This isn't Heaven, it's Hell, Balthazar. The rules are different here."

"I'm not used to uncertainty, Fool," said Balthazar, and Fool wondered whether he was permitted to feel sorry for an angel; Balthazar sounded forlorn, lost. Even his gleam was low, his skin cast blue by Adam's Fallen light rather than his more usual red fires. "I am one of the angels of flame, belonging to Michael. Angels of the flame, of Michael, are always arms and guards, soldiers for the greater good. I need order, Fool."

"Hell has order of a sort," said Fool. "*We* have an order, a simple one. We have to stop Adam."

"Yes," said Balthazar. They had come to the place now, were standing in front of the house that wasn't always there, the house of the Bwg. "An order."

"Are you with me or not?" asked Fool. The house was fading and surging, one moment there, the next almost gone, only its outline visible against the surrounding structures. Dirty blue light spilled from its windows, strings of it dripping down the walls. The building next to the house had collapsed, dust still hanging in the air above it. As the house came back into view, its windows filled with faces, some human and some not, and all of them were openmouthed and screaming.

There was no sound, and as Fool watched, one of the windows filled with a dazzle of the blue light, submerging the faces; when the light vanished, they were gone. The house faded again, became something indistinct, the reflection of a shadow, and then drifted back into view.

"Yes," said Balthazar, "I'm with you. It needs stopping."

When Fool reached for the door handle, he expected his hand to pass through it, for it to feel insubstantial, but it did not; it was solid against his palm even as the house faded, and when he twisted it, the door opened without resistance. As the door swung back, the Alrunes on the buildings around them began to shriek and the chalkis took flight, circling up into the air and taking up the Alrunes' song, discordant and ragged.

"They sense danger," said Balthazar.

"So do I," said Fool. He went to draw his gun and realized that he was already holding it. He didn't remember picking it up after falling from the ballroom. He lifted it and used it to push the door open wider; it revealed an empty lobby with dirty wooden floors and a staircase lifting up from its far side.

"I'm scared," said Fool aloud.

"Don't be," said Balthazar. "God is with us."

This is Hell, thought Fool as they stepped into the house of the Bwg, *so somehow I doubt it.*

Inside, the house was solid and thick and did not fade and return. Its ghosts, however, did, flitting into existence around them and then shimmering away to nothing again almost as soon as they had appeared. Most were human, stunted men and women who darted past with their heads down, their limbs twisted and thin, but some were entirely demonic. Something that might have been an orphan scuttled past, almost running over Fool's feet, and a huge horned thing shaggy with matted hair was perched on the stairs. None of the ghosts paid them any attention; Fool wasn't sure whether they could, whether they were conscious in any way. Would Gordie have known? Maybe, maybe not; Bwg were rare outside Crow Heights, only appearing in some of the older structures. Most people thought they were rumors, that the dead of Hell never left ghosts, but Fool knew that they were one of the rare rumors that were also true, that there were occasional traces drifting along old corridors or screaming in the corners of rooms where terrible things had been done.

The stairs stretched up above them, rising to another floor; a stairwell fell away from the far wall, dropping down toward the house's foundations. There was another weak pulse of light, so pale as to be almost invisible, seeming to come from everywhere at once. Slivers of illumination rippled across the floor, leaving faint scorch marks, and then faded.

"We have to hurry," said Balthazar. "Whatever's happening is nearly complete. If it has an opportunity to get used to its new state, we'll have little chance against it."

Fool looked up. Adam had come in through the roof, would probably be on one of the upper floors. Ghosts filled his vision, were gone again. He wished they could speak, could tell him where to go, what to expect, but they were little more than pictures that moved. Upward?

He looked into the stairwell. Its bottom was lost to shadows, only ripples of shifting light escaping the dark's grip in a pattern Fool recognized.

"Balthazar, you said you were one of Michael's angels, a thing of fire. What was Adam?"

"He was one of Gabriel's, one of the water kind, but he is not Adam anymore. Whatever it is that's Fallen, it is not the same thing that ascended, and it's not made of the same flesh nor does it belong to that family now."

"I know that and you know that," said Fool, starting down the stairs, "but does it?"

The stairs led them down to a flooded cellar, dark water swirling over the last four risers, so that by the time Fool's feet were on the floor, he was standing in mud and the water was up to his waist. Balthazar stepped down next to him and waved one hand over the water, which began to recede, slopping back toward the distant walls to reveal an earth floor that had liquefied to thick, oleaginous slime.

The space about them was cluttered. Pillars were scattered haphazardly about, holding up the building above; old chests and tangles of rusted machinery and buckled and drawerless cabinets filled the shadowed corners. The water formed two high walls, reaching above their heads, and things floated in it: paper and torn material and other, less identifiable detritus. The exposed mud was uneven with half-submerged, unidentifiable shapes. Fool stepped forward, using Balthazar's glow to see by, his gun outstretched. His feet sank into the floor, made suckling noises as he pulled them free. Something glimmered ahead of him, something in the water that peered out at him. Fool took another few steps, approaching it slowly.

"Hello, Balthazar. Hello, Fool," said a quiet voice, and then the wall of water collapsed.

It hit Fool hard, spinning him and slamming him into the wave that came from behind him as the other wall came down. He caught a glimpse of Balthazar being buffeted sideways but not falling, and then Fool was underwater. It was foul, thick and stagnant in his nose. He hit something, or something hit him, and then he broke the surface and gasped for air. He was battered, objects crashing into him, and then a hand grasped him, yanked him upward, and held him. Balthazar gestured with his other hand, but the waters, swirling violently, did not part again.

"Did you think you were strong enough to stand against me?" said the quiet voice again. It sounded almost like Adam, like Adam speaking through a mouthful of cotton or dirt.

"Show yourself," said Balthazar. Fire curled down from his hand, looping around Fool but not coming close enough to burn him. Where it touched the water, it hissed and spat.

"Certainly," said the voice, and a pale arm reached out of the darkness and slapped Balthazar across his face and then was gone. A second later a fist at the end of a pale, stretching arm came from the darkness in a different part of the room and crashed into Balthazar's temple, knocking him sideways. The angel let go of Fool and he dropped. Currents in the water caught him, sent him staggering until he crashed into one of the pillars. Fool clung on, realized he was still holding his gun, and raised it, peering into the grimy air.

"Ah, little Fool," said Adam and a hand emerged from the darkness, reached for Fool's gun; it was slow, as though playing, and Fool avoided it easily, still holding on to the pillar. "You came to arrest me?"

"Yes," replied Fool. Something white shifted in the corner of the room and he fired at it. The bullet whined off far brickwork and sent a noisy splash up from the surface of the water. The white thing was gone.

"Do you think you can hurt me?"

"Yes," said Balthazar and sent a writhing twist of fire around the room. Fool ducked, dropping into the water, as it sliced through the air above his head, burning through the brickwork of the pillar and sending sparks and steam out around itself.

"Oh, Balthazar," said Adam, as audible under the water as above it, its voice almost pitying, and another pale fist crashed into Balthazar's head as Fool rose. Adam's arm seemed huge, an elongated streak in the darkness, but when Fool tried to work out where it came from, he could not; it was too fast. Balthazar stumbled and went to one knee and another attack came, this time from behind him, driving him into the water. The white thing moved again, streaking through the thick liquid, creating a bow wave that crashed against Fool's legs. He fired at it but the bullet splashed harmlessly where it had been and then it was on Balthazar and the water exploded as Adam rose out of it.

Falling had distorted the thing that had been an angel. Whereas before he had been a smooth, handsome male with a beard and salt-and-pepper hair, it was now entirely bald and his skin had chilled down to the color of frigid alabaster. His wings had lost their delicacy and become shredded, dark shapes that hooked away from his back like great, curved fangs. As it rose from the water, sending spray up around him and Balthazar, its wings thrashed, jerking open and cracking against the wall and one of the pillars.

Balthazar lashed out at Adam, fire leaping from his hands, but Adam knocked the flame aside and clasped Balthazar's head. Its hands swelled, the fingers gnarled and clawed, locking around Balthazar's skull and clenching tight. Balthazar grunted and opened his own wings wider, beating them. The pressure drove him forward and the two disappeared into the water with another splash.

For a moment, there was stillness, and then the water's surface roiled and ruptured as Balthazar broke through and carried on rising, held aloft by Adam and then flung against a pillar. The angel crashed off it and landed heavily on a huge wooden tallboy, splintering it. Fool fired at Adam and hit him, a black hole opening in the Fallen's shoulder. It swung toward Fool, the hole knitting closed as it turned. Its head had stretched and narrowed, becoming angular, and its eyes had become black orbs. They gleamed as he said, "In a moment, Fool. In a moment."

Fool fired again. Another hole opened, this time in Adam's neck, and then closed up. Adam spat, and a metallic lump arced into the water between them.

Balthazar came up behind Adam and wrapped the Fallen thing in fire, steam pouring from its flesh as the heat danced across it. It screeched and took hold of the flame, yanking it hard. Balthazar lurched and then Adam was spinning him, holding his flame and pulling him in a spraying, staggering circle. Balthazar screamed and tried to pull back, to stop the movement, but Adam yanked harder and the flames tore loose from Balthazar in a twitching, scorching ball. It flung them aside; they hit the water and hissed, writhing and fading as they sank.

Balthazar shrieked, holding his hands out before him, spinning and dropping to his knees. Adam took hold of Balthazar's wings, one hand enclosing both the wings close to Balthazar's back, and began to jerk them up and down. Balthazar shrieked again, and then the stems of both wings snapped. Fool heard the crack of them breaking, heard the wet snap, saw them bend to an unnatural angle, and then Balthazar's scream was beyond hearing and comprehension and Adam had cast him to one side and turned back toward Fool.

Adam's mouth opened, huge, its teeth curved and triangular, its lips lines of cracked gray that snaked across his cheeks and back toward his ears. Behind him, Balthazar floated facedown, shifting in the swirling water, wings loose and broken.

"It was so simple," it said, "so very, *very* simple. All those sinners needing absolution and I provided them with it, loosing the souls of the damned. How easy, to leave the rooms and venture into Hell when Balthazar believed me to be resting, to stalk through a riot, to kill a man made of little more than foliage and to use him against you. And you, Fool, little Thomas Fool blundering along, always behind, always late. I have been doing God's work, Fool, in the place where it is needed most, and if I have had to take on the mantle of sinner to do so, then so be it."

"God's work?" said Fool, unable to stop himself. "And yet here you are, Fallen. Maybe God didn't want his work done like this?"

Adam shrieked, its mouth opening wider, hands flexing out. Fool took in its claws and maw, imagined the teeth tearing into him, took a deep breath, and dove under the water.

He used the pillar to kick off, trying to drive himself in the direction of another pillar, his hands out in front of him. Things in the water banged against him, paper draping around him, more solid items striking him. The water felt thick, like liquid rock, and he struggled to move through it, kicking his feet. It was black, impossible to see anything except blurs as objects emerged to strike his face and outstretched hands. Finally, he hit something that didn't give and he pulled himself to it, breaking water, gasping and trying to get behind whatever it was in one clumsy move.

Without Balthazar's gleam or fire, the room was much darker. Flickers of blue came from all around him, fracturing and dancing over the water but doing little other than giving the shadows depth.

"Where are you, Fool? Do you think I won't find you?" said Adam. Something splashed in the water on the far side of the room and Fool took a cautious step along the shape he was behind; it was wooden, had handles. A cupboard? Not big, certainly. He crouched, submerging himself to his chin, and tried to spot Adam.

A pale shape flitted in the distance, there, then gone. There was another splash and then a wave broke over Fool's nose and he choked. Something gripped him under the water, lifted him, and threw him. For a moment he was airborne, out of the flood, and then he hit the surface, felt it beat against face and shoulders and he was under again.

He came up disoriented; where was the wall? The pillar? He lifted his gun, still gripped tight in his hand, and looked around, wiping the water from his eyes.

"Where am I, Fool?" said Adam, and for a second he was in front of Fool. As Fool fired, Adam dropped out of sight, disappearing under the water soundlessly. A moment later, something hit Fool in the small of the back and pushed him forward. He went to his knees, twisted, and fired. In the muzzle flash, he saw the bullet tear through Adam's terrible smile, saw the flaps of skin knit together, and then Adam was gone again.

"It's almost done, Fool," said Adam. "I am almost made again." Worms of light fell from the ceiling, writhing in through the gaps in the boards above them to land in the water, where they extinguished, glimmering.

"Time for you to die, I think. I may eat your soul, though, rather than let it go, and become the thing you believed me to be. I'm *hungry*." Adam rose from the water in front of Fool, ignoring the shot Fool placed into his belly, and grasped him around his head. The pressure was immense, waves of pain and sound crashing through Fool. Adam's hand stank of blood and shit and something older and fouler, and Fool's eyes felt like they were swelling, filling with blood. His vision swirled black, and at first he thought that the movement behind Adam was his own death coming, roaring across the room toward him, but it was not.

It was Balthazar.

The angel had managed to stand, his wings hanging bedraggled behind him. He limped toward Adam, and as he did so he reached behind himself and grasped one of his torn wings and yanked a handful of his feathers out. He raised them above his head and then plunged them down into Adam's back, groaning as he did so.

Adam howled and threw Fool aside, spinning where he stood, trying to reach around to pull the feathers free. Water scythed up in a silver curtain, spraying into the walls. He crashed into one of the pillars and the shafts of the feathers snapped off, leaving a part of themselves buried in his flesh. His questing fingers couldn't reach them, Fool saw as he pulled himself up from the water, using a wardrobe on its side for support. Balthazar had fallen and was floating away, this time on his back, his face a mask of agony. The water in the cellar churned as Adam thrashed, his clawed fingers finally reaching the broken feather barbs. He pulled one loose, dropping it into the water with a satisfied grunt. Black liquid spilled from the wound, trickling down his back and soaking into his own feathers. When he had pulled the others out, Fool knew, he would finish what had been interrupted and Fool would die.

Feathers. What had Balthazar said about his feathers? He reached into his pocket, found the feather that he now thought of as his own, and gripped it. Feathers. Balthazar had thrust his feathers into the Fallen's flesh. Why? Because it was the only weapon he had? A last desperate gesture?

No, no, there was something else, something more. Something about what the feathers did.

Adam pulled another shaft free and dropped it. Another. How many more were left? One or two, maybe? Certainly no more than three.

Another one went into the water and now Adam looked up, glaring at Fool. Its mouth twisted into a shape that might have been a grin, revealing those bleak triangular teeth again, and it said, "Are you ready, Fool?"

Another one fell. Adam flexed his hands and reached back over his shoulder, but he was already rolling his shoulders and flexing his torso; this had to be the last one. What was it? Fool gripped the feather tightly, hoped, and suddenly thought, *Truth*.

"How do I kill you?" he shouted.

"Wait until I'm open, Fool; that's your only chance."

"Open? I don't understand. What do you mean?" asked Fool, but it was too late. Adam pulled a last piece of Balthazar from his back and let out a long, satisfied sigh.

"Now, Fool," he said, "I'm growing hungry."

34

Fool was pressed back against a piece of broken furniture, the water swirling around his legs and feet, its sharp edges digging into his thighs. His head ached, the muscles of his legs were trembling, and his hand was cramping from keeping hold of his gun. He was cold, shivering, water dripping down from his hair, getting into his eyes and making them sting, and Adam was little more than a blurred ivory shape as it slipped down into the water and vanished.

Fool moved, keeping his back pressed to whatever it was behind him. Fragments of it dug at him, caught in his clothes, and held him, and he heard something tear. He was lost in the room, unsure where the stairs were. His only hope was to follow the wall around and try to find them. Was Balthazar alive, still floating on the water's surface, or had he died? Fool wondered about trying to find the angel and dismissed the idea; he had to get out.

Where was Adam?

There—a white shadow slipping through the water. Fool fired but the shape twitched away and the plume of water that rose from the bullet's impact was nowhere near it. It turned back on itself, zigzagging across the space, growing faster, the waves it made buffeting against the walls and echoing back into the center of the room in disrupted patterns. Fool fired again, the noise bouncing off the damp brickwork, and another plume of water leaped up. The shape didn't stop, didn't slow.

Sped up.

Adam's wings broke the surface of the water, dark triangles creating wakes behind them. It was still warping, its shape changing, now longer and thinner, less human. Was this a distortion of its true angelic shape, or something new? It veered again, was heading directly at Fool, and was rising up from the water. The surface broke around his now-conical head, its mouth open wide and wrenched into a wide grimace. It covered the distance between them incredibly quickly, finally exploding out in a froth of spray, silent. Fool tried to run, felt his jacket tear farther but couldn't get loose from the grasp of the furniture, and then Adam was on him.

Light was streaming from Adam's black eyes and out of his mouth, from the wounds in its back, the last of his angelic self untethering. It filled his nostrils and mouth, making the teeth vast against the swirling blue. Its arms came around, hands hooked, light bleeding from the fingertips and from the beds of his claws. Fool yanked up his gun, fired, and then Adam crashed into him and they both fell back into the water, crushing the piece of furniture under them. Fool could move again, tried to kick away, but Adam's arms had caged around him and its wings were curved, forming a hood over them. Its mouth stretched wider, a bolus of light forcing its way out from behind the teeth. The mouth opened wider still, the teeth gleaming, and its head descended. Farther and farther down it came, the mouth still stretched, lips pulling back from gums that had become pale and pitted and it was inches away and *He's open!* Fool thought wildly and jammed his gun into Adam's mouth and fired again.

For a brief instant, the muzzle flash and Adam's own light were in conflict in its mouth, and then it screamed and thrashed back. One wing came down and cracked into Fool's head, knocking him sideways and pressing him farther under the water. Liquid filled Fool's mouth and he breathed it in, his throat closing and then convulsing, ragged strings of air and vomit pushing out as he coughed. He dug upward with his hands, drew in another breath of water, and coughed again violently. His heart yammered, his lungs trying to suck as his mouth tried to close. Which way was up? Where was down? He rolled, still reaching, lost in bubbles and blackness, and then his hand was out, feeling air, flailing.

Fool vomited and coughed as he came into the air, emitting nothing but strings of bile, trying to suck in something other than water. He whooped inward, his lungs forcing his throat open, managed to draw one ragged breath, and then was coughing again. He caught hold of something, pulled himself into a crouched upright position, and then bent, hacking and breathing and spitting all at once.

Adam.

Fool turned, trying to see something, anything, but his eyes were filled with multicolored lines and sparks. He blinked, seeing nothing beyond them but hearing screaming. Water spattered against him, trying to unsettle him, and he gripped his handhold more tightly. Blinking again, he began to clear the lights, leaving him staring at a maelstrom in the center of the cellar.

Adam was spinning rapidly, its wings beating up and down against the water, screaming. Its head was wreathed in light, crawling webs of blue and white. The rear of its skull was a hole, large and ragged, the upper portion of his head missing, and it was not healing. Its hands beat at the light, covering the hole, then forced away by the emerging colors. The water was whirlpooling around it, battered to violent foam. *I've injured it,* thought Fool wonderingly. *It opened up to eat me, and I injured it. Good.*

Good.

He raised his gun and then realized that he no longer held it. He looked down, the water bucking around him, seeing nothing but bubbles and blackness. Experimentally, he moved a foot about, feeling for the gun. Nothing. Adam was slowing now, the flow of light from its ruptured head slowing to little more than a trickle. It stood lopsided, shoulders tilted, one arm hanging loose and one wing drooping, trailing in the water. It came to a sloppy halt, turned too far, and then came back around to peer at Fool.

Fool had never prayed; no one in Hell did, he suspected, because they knew that God was nowhere to be found, but he prayed now. Adam took a lurched step toward him, one leg dragging, thick ropes of tarry liquid now spilling down its shoulders from its head, and said, "I'm glad you're my first human meal, Fool." Its voice was slurred and broken.

"I'll eat you, and then I'll heal. I'm already healing, I can feel it," it said, its teeth clicking as it spoke. Fool didn't know how to pray, had no idea whom to pray to or whether he was doing it right, but he prayed anyway, *Help me, help me, helpme helpmehelpmehelphelphelphelp.* Adam took another step, stumbled, used its good wing to right itself, and carried on.

It was almost within touching distance; Fool tried to back away, but the thing behind him, a metal filing cabinet whose painted sides were thick with rust, refused to move. He pushed again as Adam made a noise that might have been slurred words but might have been simply a groan, and then his foot hit something.

He dropped to his knees and reached down *helpmehelpmehelpme-help* and his fingers closed around his gun. He held it up as Adam took another shambling step and reached out. He heard screaming, realized it was him, pointed the gun, and fired.

The bullet took Adam in its left eye, spun the Fallen, and sent it crashing back across the room. It was still open, still vulnerable, and Fool followed it, bearing down on the thing that was no longer an angel and firing as soon as his next bullet formed.

This one took Adam in the shoulder, above its drooping wing, and tore a piece of flesh and muscle out. The edges began to knit, Fool saw, but slowly, sluggish and inefficient. Scraps of skin formed and then broke apart, but it was healing. Fool fired again, and then again.

Adam managed to push out across the room, the muzzle flashes painting it in stark shadows across the walls, and then fell against the stairs. Turning toward Fool, it hissed and lashed out with its good wing; the other one was starting to move again, twitching, rising. The wing hit Fool, not hard but enough to knock him sideways. He went into the water yet again, emerged as fast as he could and firing but missing, a chunk of stone leaping free from the wall near Adam's head. In Adam's depthless black eyes, Fool saw something new, and he grinned and fired again.

Adam was scared.

This bullet tore through a wing that no longer had feathers but was simply a piece of thick, jointed flesh, and Adam howled. It scrambled up the steps, fast, leaving behind trails of water and thick blood behind it, and then was gone through the entrance at the top.

Fool went after it, firing at the empty doorway in frustration. He stumbled on the steps as he came out of the water, his legs weak, and had to use the wall for support. How much more of this could he take? Not much, he didn't think. There wasn't a part of him that didn't hurt, that wasn't throbbing or aching. He took another two steps up, his eyes coming level with the floor above, and that was when Adam reappeared and took hold of his head.

Fucking idiot Fool, he had time to think, and then he was yanked up and dragged through the entrance. Adam's grip was loose but not loose enough, and Fool couldn't shake it. He was dragged through the lobby of the house, brought his gun up but couldn't bring it around far enough to fire without being sure of missing himself, and then decided he was likely to die whatever happened and fired anyway.

He felt the bullet roar past his ear, its wind tearing at him. Adam let go of Fool and fell, crashing against the entrance doors. It hissed, wordless and savage, and then rolled back and tugged at the doors. Fool tried to raise his gun, but his arm was loose and weak and he could not bring it up off the floor. Ghosts came and went in his vision as Adam opened its cavernous mouth, the hiss turning into a shriek, and opened the doors.

The first rock hit it on the head, the second on the shoulder, and then Adam was lost in a hail of rocks and bricks. It was forced back into the house by the deluge and through the space it left came a vast flow of the Sorrowful. Some held poles and clubs of wood or metal and swung them at Adam, others had more rocks that they threw or held tight and struck out with. Adam was driven to its knees, turning and hunching its back to his assailants. One of the Sorrowful darted forward and hit the back of its head with a chunk of rock, leaving it embedded in the already gaping wound there. More of them came forward, striking.

Adam lashed out, snapping its jaws closed around the nearest neck, and there was a brief spray of blood. The Fallen shook its head back and forth, tearing the flesh, spitting it out after swallowing what fear it contained. Someone stabbed at it with a broken piece of wood and it grasped them, its mouth opening wide and clamping around the man's head. It lifted the man, slurping at his pain and terror, and then another Sorrowful hit it with a piece of brick.

Fool managed to sit up, the floor's covering of broken stones and brick biting at his hands. "Don't let him feed," he said, trying to shout, but his voice came out as little more than a harsh whisper.

"Don't let him feed," he called again. This time his voice was louder but was still lost under the shouts of the crowd. More and more people were piling into the house, all of them trying to get close to Adam, to hit it. Fool lifted his gun, let it drop; his grip wasn't secure enough to fire, and he couldn't get a clear shot. Adam's throat worked as it drank from the man, its wounds beginning to close as it took in sustenance.

"For fuck's sake, stop him feeding," Fool managed to shout and then slumped back. He was too tired, too damaged to do anything else.

The Sorrowful set about Adam again, hemming the thing that had been an angel in and preventing it from moving away. Someone within the mass swung a long, thick piece of wood, a section of the gate, and the blow shattered Adam's jaw, dislodging the human from his grip. *That's right,* thought Fool, *that's right.*

One of the Sorrowful—a farmhand, Fool supposed—had a machete, its blade nicked and worn but its edge sharp, and he clambered onto Adam's back, sawing and hacking at its wings. Adam reached behind, trying to spin, but its movements were slow and the man avoided the grasping fingers easily and carried on chopping. The mass of people was thickening now, kicking and punching, no longer throwing rocks but using them as hand weapons, using the edges to slash at Adam's flesh.

Its damaged wing came loose first, was cast back into the crowd to a great cheer, and was rapidly followed by the other. Adam screamed, tried to fall and roll, but the sheer weight and mass of the crowd kept it at least partially upright, kept it a target for their fury. It was simply too great, too violent, to be stopped.

The Sorrowful raged, forming a caul about Adam, and the Fallen was soon lost to Fool's view.

EPILOGUE

By the time the Sorrowful had finished, very little of Adam was left. It had been torn to pieces, the pieces carried out into Crow Heights' streets in a triumphant rally. Its head and wings were held at the head of the procession, their holders making swooping motions with them, nodding its head, and the crowd laughed.

Fool followed them, limping. He was tired, too tired to feel victorious even when members of the crowd came over to him and held him or shook his hand. He had caught the murderer, but at what cost? The Falling of one angel and the death of another? The death of his colleagues? Around him, the Sorrowful celebrated; they cheered and sang, but Fool had the impression things were gathering behind the Heights' windows, taking note. This behavior would surely be punished. Nothing in Hell went unnoticed.

Eventually, Fool made his way back to the main gates and sat by the wall, leaning against one of the stunted trees that grew there, watching. More and more of the Sorrowful flooded in through the damaged entrance. Some were carrying banners, some the leaflets; all were cheering. A constant stream of them came over to him, shaking his hand or touching his face or shoulders and thanking him, although he wasn't sure what for. One gave him a leaflet on which a barely recognizable version of himself was drawn over the words HELL NEEDS MORE OF HIM. He crumpled the paper after looking at it for a few seconds and put it in his pocket.

The crowd was spreading through Crow Heights. Fool heard distant shouts, the sounds of violence and things breaking, screams. *You may have killed the Fallen,* he thought, *but don't expect the rest of Hell not to fight.*

As if to prove him right, a group of the Sorrowful appeared, carrying an injured woman back through the streets and out of the Heights, her blood leaving a bright trail across the ground.

"It has been so wonderful," said a voice from behind him.

"No, it hasn't," said Fool without looking around. He was too tired to accept any more compliments, too tired and sick and sore and hurt.

"Oh, but it has, Fool," said the voice. It sounded dry and leathery, and when it laughed the noise was like two pieces of linen being ground together. This time, it came from above him.

Fool looked up; just branches and leaves. The tree had a vine curling through it, tiny orange flowers sprouting from it as he watched. No people, just plants.

Plants and flowers.

"That's right, Fool, that's so right!" said the Man, the leaves and flowers shaking as he forced his voice out through them. "Did Adam really think he could kill me? I live in the very smallest places, Fool, scattered throughout Hell's lands, and no mere angel can best me! But now Rhakshasas and those other old fools think I am gone, and I have you to thank. You got noticed, Fool, and how simple it was to point you in the right direction, to keep you noticed by human and demon alike so that they might use you against me, and that I might use the situation against them. I no longer exist, Fool, but I am *everywhere!*"

"Why?" asked Fool, too exhausted to be truly shocked, asking the *why* not just of the Man but of everything, hoping for answers even though he knew they would not be forthcoming.

"Why? Why not, Fool, why not? Now I am free, the most free thing in Hell, and intend to have fun!"

"Fun?"

There was no reply; he didn't expect one. Instead, the leaves shook above him one last time, as though in good-bye, and then the tree and the vine were still.

Fool sat for a long time, listening to the violence in the Heights, to screams and howls and roars and the sound of buildings falling and fires swelling, and eventually he thought he ought to move. He was just about to rise when he heard a second voice.

"You've done well, Thomas, very well," said Elderflower. He had appeared at Fool's side as silently as ever, as though he had stepped out of the air next to him.

"Have I?"

"Of course," said Elderflower, looking around at the running, shouting humans. He sniffed deeply. "Can you smell that?"

"No."

"It's smoke, Thomas. Wood smoke. Crow Heights is beginning to properly burn. It has been set alight by the crowds in their anger. By tonight, it will be ablaze. Down in the Houska everything's calm, but as word reaches the rest of Hell about today's work it, too, will ignite. Then the factories, and the farms perhaps. The boardinghouses, definitely. Everything will burn, Thomas."

Something was wrong. There was a new sound in the air, a rhythmic crashing, the roar of something mechanical. New sounds, like nothing Fool had heard before but somehow terribly familiar. Elderflower was right, Fool could smell it now: fires. Thick smoke was drifting toward them from somewhere in the Heights, black palls of it writhing and turning.

Elderflower was standing by Fool, his long coat flapping slightly, his hands clasped behind his back. He was facing into Crow Heights, watching the smoke, looking away from Fool. Fool lifted the feather from his pocket, looked at it and stroked it, marveling at its softness even after all it had been through, and then very carefully slipped it into Elderflower's cuff.

"What's going on, Elderflower?" he asked.

"Change, Thomas, change. Hell is changing."

"Why?"

"Why not, Thomas, why not? Hell was once a place of absolute burning and is now a place of uncertainty, and both are terrible but people can get used to anything given enough time. 'This is how it is,' they say. 'This is Hell. We will survive.' We cannot have that, Thomas, no indeed. This is Hell, Thomas, and Hell is not somewhere to be used to, to be complacent about. So we allow and encourage Hell to change."

"Change to what?"

"Can you hear it, Thomas?" said Elderflower, apparently ignoring Fool's question.

"Hear what?"

"You can, Thomas, I know you can. That sound, the sound of your new force."

"New force?"

"Demons, Thomas. Demons and humans all in uniforms as black as Hell's darkest night. Hundreds of them, thousands, imposing the law upon the rest of Hell's inhabitants. They're yours, Thomas, to order and lead."

"I don't understand," he said. His head hurt, his body hurt, but the worst was the feeling opening in his stomach as though it was hollowing out in increasingly large swathes.

"This is your reward, Thomas, because you played your role so beautifully."

"Role?" he asked. "I didn't play a role. I was investigating." Even as he spoke, he knew, though. Knew.

"Each step carefully designed, Thomas. Each one set for you to move along. All of it, Thomas, from Adam onward, all to get us to this point. Unstable Adam, ready to fall, exposed to the right sights, scared Rhakshasas, fearful of the Man and wanting answers, the Man himself thinking he was at the center of the web when he was really only another strand in the grandest design of all. And you, Thomas, scared and hurt but moving onward anyway, given the feather so that you might see clearly and grow in stature and become what I needed you to be. You're a hero, Thomas; people love you because you stood up to demons, because you issue orders and the demons obey, and they want more like you. More Information Men, more order, more control. And I will give it to them, Thomas, oh yes I will! And do you know the most wonderful thing? They'll welcome this change, hold their arms open and say how it's what they want, law and order and protection, and in a few months or years when the laws are suffocating them, and when the fear of being arrested and tortured and imprisoned on little more than the say-so of their neighbors is so huge they can hardly breathe, they'll remember that they invited this in and they'll hate themselves for it.

"And you, Thomas," said Elderflower, removing the feather from his cuff and turning to face Fool, "will be its head, and they will see a human, not a demon, responsible for their pain and they will hate even more."

Elderflower looked down at the feather and he suddenly seemed huge, his face filling the sky and his eyes gleaming, his hair twisting into great curled horns emerging from his temples. The feather bloomed to flame, burned briefly with a greasy smell, and then was gone apart from a smear of ash across Elderflower's fingers that he wiped away on his coat.

"I have grown tired of Hell the way it is," Elderflower said, "so I have changed it. *You* have changed it, Thomas, and for that you have my thanks. Great times are coming."

Then the first of the new Information Men arrived, ranks of them jogging in step with each other, their feet crashing down in unison and making that pounding, roaring noise. There were demons and humans, men and women, all in black uniforms with silver buttons. Large transports rolled in behind them, and when they stopped the rears opened and more Information Men emerged and began spreading out across the square. They formed into a phalanx in front of Fool and stopped.

"They're waiting, Thomas," said Elderflower. "The first orders of the new Hell need to be given."

Fool rose unsteadily to his feet, unable to speak. It was too big to hold in his head, too ungainly to fit his thoughts around. All of them, Balthazar and Adam and Diamond and the Man and Rhakshasas and Gordie and Summer and himself, all moving to the rhythms of Hell's beat. *Had he ever really been free?* he wondered. Ever had a choice? Were there places he could have acted differently, gone in a new direction?

No, he thought, and the voice in his head seemed to be his and Gordie's and Summer's all at once. This was Hell, and that was its purpose, and he was simply another speck grinding within its huge and grotesque wheels. Elderflower smiled at him, nodded, turned, and walked away, leaving cloven prints in the mud.

Around Fool, the smell of burning grew thicker.